HIDDEN WITHIN

Other Books by

RYAN D GEBHART

THE JEWEL OF LIFE

SPLENDOR OF DAWN

Hidden Within

PART TWO
OF
THE JEWEL OF LIFE

RYAN D GEBHART

Copyright © 2019 Ryan Gebhart

Library of Congress Control Number: TXu 2-141-958

Hardcover ISBN 978-1-7326355-3-1
Paperback ISBN 978-1-7326355-4-8

Distributed by Ingram Publisher Services
Printed in the United States of America
Cover design by Fiona Jayde Media

To Ashley,

always listening when my path changes.

Table of Contents

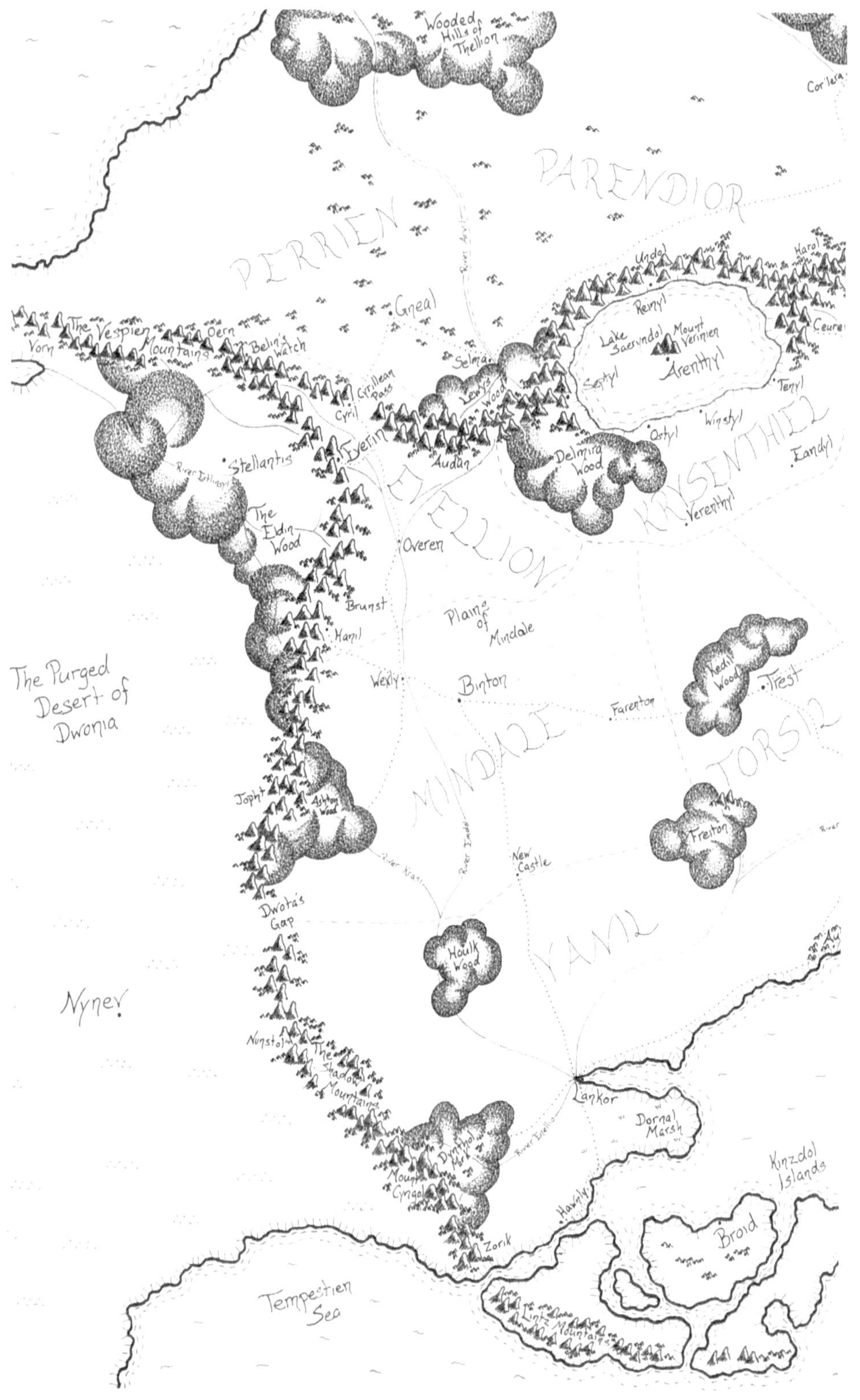

Wooded Hills of Thellion
PARENDIOR
PERRIEN
Corilera
Undol
Harol
Ceura
Renyl
The Vespien Mountains
Oern
Gneal
Lake Saervndol
Mount Verinien
Vorn
Belin's Watch
Selma
Arenthyl
Cirillean Pass
Septyl
Tenyl
Cyril
Lewys Wood
Winstyl
Everlin
Ostyl
Eandyl
Stellantis
Audon
Delmira Wood
KRYSENTHIEL
River Ethlosyl
Verenthyl
The Edin Wood
EVELLION
Overen
Brunst
Plains of Mindale
Hamil
Nedil Wood
Trest
The Purged Desert of Dwonia
Wexly
Binton
Farenton
MINDARE
TORSIR
Jopht
Ashton Wood
Freton
River Imdal
Nyner
Dwota's Gap
River Nian
New Castle
Houlk Wood
VANIL
The Shadow Mountains
Nunstol
River Endlio
Lankor
Dornal Marsh
Kinzdol Islands
Dynthol
Mount Cyngol
Hawnly
Broid
Zorik
Tempestien Sea
Linz Mountains

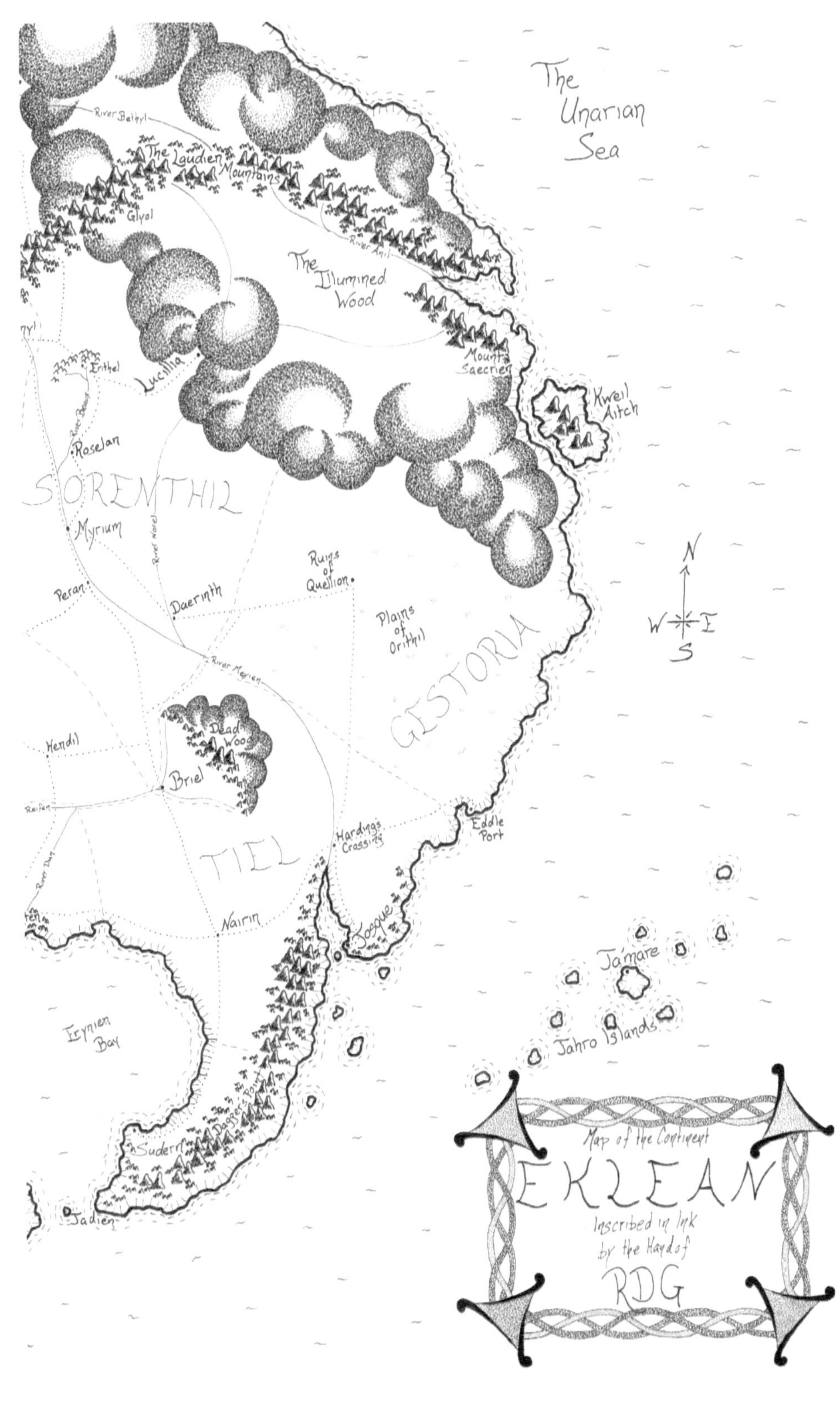

The Unarian Sea
River Bethyl
The Laudien Mountains
Glyol
The Illumined Wood
River Anil
Mount Saecner
Kweil Aitch
Enthel
Lucillia
River Brovil
Roselan
SORENTHIL
Myrium
River Norel
Peran
Daerinth
Ruins of Quellion
Plains of Orithil
GESTORIA
N
W E
S
River Marien
Dead Wood
Hendil
Briel
Reifen
River Dorg
TIEL
Nairin
Hardings Crossing
Eddle Port
Joegue
Irynien Bay
Daggers Point
Sudern
Jamare
Jahro Islands
Jadien
Map of the Continent
EKLEAN
Inscribed in Ink
by the Hand of
RDG

JEWEL OF THE RIVER

Karina, Queen of Sorenthil, stood on a private balcony and looked over the stone walls surrounding the city of Myrium, frowning at the normally gentle waters of the River Meyien below. The water rushed along either side of the island city, slapping against the city's foundation stones, uncharacteristically high and fast for this time of year, more usual during the snow and ice melt of early spring. This year, the winter had endured and the snows had maintained their icy hold over Sorenthil's mountains until Delenth, the last month of spring, part of the reason behind Karina's frown.

It was a yearly treat to see the waters at their current level, a phenomenon Karina and most Sorenth adored, for the added depths increased the beauty of their already stunning city. During the high-water season, travelers approaching Myrium were greeted by the mystical sight of the sun reflecting off the heightened river and onto the island city itself. The soft white stone of the buildings transformed, making the city seem alive with the rushing water. The citizens treated this time as something of a holiday, taking every available opportunity to spend many days outside Myrium's walls, enjoying the spectacle. However, this year, they had had no such luxury. Not only was the timing of the phenomenon off, but no one could enjoy it from beyond the walls where not one, but two armies had encamped nearly six months ago. Myrium had barred her gates and the Myrish Guard stood vigilant from her watch towers.

News of the events in Ceurenyl had quickly reached the queen, brought by a bird sent by her daughter, Myranda, with a second bird the following day from a secretary of the Seven Chairs of Septyl. Unfortunately, Myranda's note had provided little information and Karina's heart ached at not knowing how she fared. She had replied to Myranda's message immediately, but there had been no further correspondence, and six months had now passed.

Regardless of how many birds she had sent to Gwilnor, no reply had come until this morning. One of her own hawks had returned with a message in her daughter's flowing hand. Karina had read it several times, and swore she heard her daughter's voice speak through the ink and parchment.

Unlike Karina, Myranda could wield the erendinth. Nearly six years had passed since she had left to study with and join the Ei'ana of Septyl at Gwilnor Academy, Eklean's oldest school. Although the queen yearned to visit her only child, the opportunity had never arisen. Sorenthil required her constant attention. Every year, she told herself that she would visit Gwilnor and every year had ended with her writing an apology to her daughter.

Karina's thoughts of the letter lying on her writing desk turned back to the river and the vista beyond. In the crisp air, the music of the Meyien reverberated around her and through the city, amplified by the city itself. She could not fathom a time when Myrium did not rest on this island, cradled by the river.

The sight beyond the river soured her stomach. She had grown accustomed to the view in the past months, yet still felt ill in its presence. Tieli flags bearing the orange serpent flew above the grey tents pitched to the east. The queen had feared that her southern neighbors would eventually march into Sorenthil at the behest of their master yet had not expected it to happen so suddenly, without warning or indications that Erynor was again attempting to conquer all of Eklean. But what truly disgusted Karina were the Torsillian tents and flags displaying the grey wolf west of the Meyien. She and King Gordon of Torsil had maintained cordial terms over the entirety of their reigns, with many alliances grown and nurtured between their kingdoms. Gordon's recent treachery and cowardice sat uneasily in the pit of her stomach. How long had their friendship been duplicitous?

When she had first seen the Torsillian banners and flags appear on the horizon, she had thought that they had come to assist the Sorenth against the Tieli invaders. Sorely mistaken, she had watched from her balcony in growing horror as Torsillian soldiers slaughtered her messengers. Honorable knights, indeed.

The force camped near the city was not a substantial one, but it was intended to prevent Karina from sending support to Evellion, their truest ally. The invading armies gave no indication as to how long they would merely camp outside her city before beginning a true siege. So far, they had not bothered the villages in the area, nor had they intercepted any ill-advised traveler with the misfortune of having to cross the invading armies, allowing the travelers to pass through their ranks without interference to enter the city physically if not emotionally unscathed. The invaders did prevent everyone from leaving the city, however, forcing the travelers back into the city before they went very far.

When the invading armies had arrived, Karina had made it a priority to be seen in public, proud and resilient. Since her husband's untimely death several years ago, she had met great criticism among her court when she had refused to immediately remarry. Both Dorian and Karina had many supporters and were greatly loved, but by denying another marriage, she had caused many of her nobles to withdraw their favor. She knew that those who remained in Myrium would now take advantage of the siege and offer kind words and soothing advice, with the subtle suggestion that by taking a husband from their own House, she would then have the needed brawn to bolster and better defend Sorenthil.

She had already received several offers, weak as they were, and the greater Houses among her court would soon follow suit. However, Karina had no time to concern herself over courters. *Do they not realize we are at war? There is no time for festivities associated with a royal marriage.* It wasn't that she opposed giving the Sorenth a new king, but she simply could not bring herself to take the time. Her kingdom needed her to rule and protect, not marry.

A loud knock sounded at the door to her royal apartment, despite her explicit instructions that no one, other than her ladies-in-waiting, was to intrude while she was in her private chambers. Muffled voices came from the entry, indicating that one of the ladies had answered the door. Half-tempted to discover which bold noble had dared to go against her wishes, she also gave thought to which lord or lady would have put in the effort to climb the many stairs through the palace to reach the royal apartments.

Still gazing over Myrium, she marveled at the blue light shimmering off the river. The voices quieted, and she heard the door close. Relieved that the intruder had been sent on his or her way, Karina allowed herself to relax slightly.

"It is a beautiful sight, my queen, but do not allow the view beyond to tarnish this jewel," said a man's voice. Karina almost jumped from her skin. Perhaps, at a younger age, she would have, but moments of shock no longer had quite the same effect.

Irritation at her ladies-in-waiting arose. "And what sweet whispers did you provide to ensure that they not even announce your presence," the queen replied, disregarding his comment as she considered appropriate censure for her attendants.

Without turning toward him, Karina knew that the foolish man smiled. He always smiled when she was annoyed with him.

"No need to brood over what I might have whispered into their ears, for it is your ears I seek to softly whisper into. My desire to hear your own soft whispers is even greater," said Ferinn.

One of her oldest friends, Ferinn and she had met at court when she had been just a girl, a lady of House Roseraie visiting Myrium for the first time. They had formed a fast friendship and had shared many secrets, and through those years his love for her had never diminished. If she ever entertained the thought of marriage again, she might concede to him. But those thoughts were passing ones and she had pushed them aside as more pressing concerns demanded her attention.

"I have merely come to your forbidden chambers to retrieve you, with hopes of escorting my queen to her audience."

At last, Karina turned from the balustrade to look at Ferinn. His blue eyes danced, framed by wavy light brown hair, much longer than what was currently fashionable for Myrish men. He also dressed differently than the lords of her court; while it was not uncommon for a man to wear a robe, Ferinn wore nothing but and only of varying shades of blue.

At first, she had presumed that he wore blue to show his support for Sorenthil, whose sigil carried many blues around the Sorenth dolphin. However, the closer she and Ferinn had grown, the more secrets passed between them. One night, when they both had had more wine than they should have, they told each other many private things. The next day, Karina had felt embarrassed since she had revealed far more than any decent and recently married princess should to another man. Yet the secrets Ferinn had shared were much greater than her own, for that night, he had revealed that he had not been born in Myrium nor even in Sorenthil.

Eager to learn the truth of his homeland, she had asked which Eklean kingdom he came from. None, he had responded and went on to tell her what she initially took to be a lie. Offended, thinking he was taking her for a fool, she had asked him to leave the palace. Several weeks had passed before she had sought him out again. To this day, Karina still recalled how foolish she had felt for asking Ferinn's forgiveness. He had readily accepted her apology but had also forbidden her from sharing his secret with anyone. In that moment, she had understood that he had spoken truthfully, that he had trusted her beyond anyone else and had shared something remarkable with her, something which belonged in the stories her nanny had told her as a child.

Ferinn had not been born on any land of Eklean, nor any land, but in the sea where his people had dwelt as long as humans had lived on land.

Her friend was no human. Rather, Ferinn was a merperson from an ocean not drawn on any map she knew. She could not imagine how that was possible, since his legs were no different than any man's.

One dark moonless night, he had asked her to keep another secret and had taken her to a place hidden beneath the city, a private grotto built into the bedrock, just above the Meyien. He had discarded his robe, and had laughed at her for averting her gaze, telling her that it never ceased to amaze him how awkward humans were about their naked bodies. The closer he had drawn to the water, the bluer his hair had appeared. At first, she had thought it was just the water's reflection, but as she had looked more carefully, his light brown hair had actually held a hint of blue. He had stepped into the grotto's water, and it had begun to shine a remarkable blue, reflecting an incredible array of color and light against the grotto's walls. His legs had faded beneath the water and merged to form a single tail of a magnificent blue-green color that shimmered beneath the glassy surface.

After all those years, she could still picture it perfectly, and even now chided herself for having looked at his bare skin longer than any married woman should. Ferinn must have known her mind had wandered there for he said as he smiled, "You're not still imagining that time when I dropped my robe in front of you, are you?"

Karina swatted Ferinn then turned to stare indignantly toward the invading armies, refusing to respond, arms crossed tightly over her chest.

"Humans and their unease with nudity. If you tried living beneath the water, you would find that clothing would pull you to the sea bottom where a monster much larger than yourself would swallow you whole."

"Stop being juvenile, Ferinn, there's no time for that."

"Forgive me, my queen, but you never make time for pleasantries these days. The currents of time will rush past without you realizing it, and time will find you old and grey, restricted to a lonely bed. Luckily, I remain beyond all doubt that no matter how grey and old you might become, no woman will match your beauty."

Karina blushed at the compliment; it drove her crazy how easily Ferinn could flatter her, and even more so that his flirtation obviously appealed. "Come, I must attend my audience. It's important that my people see their queen." She fervently wished to change the topic.

Ferinn's disgruntlement at her response reminded Karina of a scolded puppy. His interior struggle was evident and Karina wished she could feel saddened for being its cause but too many things required her attention. Her people depended on her to ensure their safety.

"My queen, my dearest Karina," Ferinn began unexpectedly, then dropped to a single knee, "not a day has passed since we first met that

I have not loved you. Your lords and ladies will not cease pestering you until you wed another. I admired Dorian greatly and was jubilant when you married. But I cannot bear to see you wed anyone else. I offer you my hand, Karina. The love I bear for you reaches further than the deepest of oceans. Not even the Bowl of Theniel could measure against it. Name me your consort. Nothing more. I would hold no claim to your throne, only your heart."

Ferinn remained on his knee, his blue eyes holding her own. The strength and love in his made Karina want to fall into his arms as tears swelled in hers. She wanted to say no, that her duty to Sorenthil was above her own desires. After she had passed to an acceptance of Dorian's passing several years ago, the fantasy of marrying Ferinn had danced about. Gently, she lifted his hands and he followed until he stood just before her, their bodies nearly touching, his eyes steady, looking down at her tenderly as he waited. She wished he would say something, something to break the lock his eyes held over her own. Then, still gazing back at him, Karina heard a simple "yes" escape her mouth and saw Ferinn's blue eyes widen at the word she herself barely heard.

Immediately regretting speaking her heart's desire after successfully silencing it for so many years, Karina considered retracting her acceptance. Ferinn was right though, her nobles would not cease pestering her until she took a husband, especially now with Myrium under siege. She imagined what her life might become with Ferinn at her side as her husband. She doubted her nobles would be pleased. Granted, if she did choose among them, only one House would ultimately be satisfied. But Ferinn held no lands or titles in Sorenthil. He was a common sight at court and everyone addressed him as Lord Ferinn, but no one knew from whence he came nor where his nobility lay; only Karina knew.

She stared into Ferinn's eyes as the thoughts whirled, then a soft "Your Majesty" came from behind her. Suddenly cognizant of the hour, she remembered that she was still expected in court. With Ferinn's help, she donned her heavy golden crown, its intricate design giving a misleading appearance of lightness as it forced a controlled bearing of her body. Karina and Ferinn walked through the palace corridors together, trailed by her honor guard of Sorenth knights. Once in the throne room, she saw that the many nobles who had had to remain in the city after the invading armies had arrived had already gathered. She felt grateful that most of the nobles who ruled over their own cities were not present but were seeing to the protection of their lands and people.

As she moved about, greeting them, Lady Marianne approached, closely followed by a handsome young man, likely her grandson. Lady Marianne was without a doubt the oldest noble in Karina's entire court, and still head of House Lilaen in northern Sorenthil. She offered a slight curtsy, and the young lord gave a regal bow, his right arm flourishing before him, which Karina returned with a simple bow of her head.

"Your Majesty, I would introduce you to my grandson, Lord Jacques," offered Lady Marianne, her gloved hand gesturing at the man. He was certainly attractive with broad shoulders and clever blue eyes. However, when Karina looked into his eyes, she compared them to Ferinn's much brighter blue ones. "My grandson has never married, Your Majesty, and would make a fine and caring husband. You won't find a more compassionate and tender lord among the Sorenth."

"Thank you, Lady Marianne, your words are truly appreciated, and I have no doubt that Lord Jacques would make a fine husband. I must confess though, that as of this very hour, my hand is no longer available."

Karina turned toward Ferinn, who had stayed by the entrance just inside the throne room. He had never enjoyed interacting with the Sorenth nobility; he had once told Karina that there was too much pomp and feigned courtesy and he preferred to hover around the perimeter of the gathered nobles.

"Lord Ferinn has requested my hand in marriage." She smiled at Ferinn, a silly smile that she had not shown since she had fallen in love with Prince Dorian. Lady Marianne frowned but Lord Jacques did not seem disturbed by the lost opportunity to court the queen.

A murmur arose, the other lords and ladies present clearly eavesdropping on her conversation with Lady Marianne. The news of her betrothal would spread throughout the court and the entire palace, reaching even the servants in moments, and would have spread throughout the city by the end of the day. Rumors and gossip would follow before she could make a public proclamation about her betrothal the following day.

ALONE

Devlyn's stomach groaned, protesting his self-inflicted fast. He tried to quiet it by chewing on a piece of discarded bark. It felt gritty against his teeth, but it was better than the tiny, sparse, and hardly substantial berries he had found dangling from some of the easily reached trees and bushes. He had resorted to eating leaves and bark he found on the ground, desperate to fill his deprived stomach.

Before he had passed from Lucillia and into the Illumined Wood, Queen Vernal Roendryn, Aryl of Lucillia, had told him that under no circumstance was he to harm any animal for nourishment. He had found it odd at the time but was still reluctant to go against what the queen had said despite his constant hunger. In lieu of hunting game, Vernal had instructed Devlyn to allow the forest to provide for him, a concept that he thought ridiculous since it had left him famished shortly after leaving Lucillia.

His hunger had finally gotten the better of him. No longer capable of clear thought, Devlyn no longer cared to follow the Lucillian queen's edict. It was a ridiculous law anyway. He wondered whether the queen would prosecute him for poaching in the Illumined Wood. *Could she do that? Did Lucillia have jurisdiction over this forest? And how would she know?* Instead of trying to gather a handful of berries to supplement the bark, he threw what was left of it away.

From beneath a carpet of dense ivy, Devlyn retrieved an elongated stick that he had tucked away there the night before. When he had first found the stick, Devlyn had lied to himself, trying to convince himself that he could use it for a walking stick. But the lie wouldn't stick; he'd known it was going to become a spear the moment he picked it up.

Sitting on the ivy carpet, Devlyn pulled the rough-cut stone he had wielded from the ground shortly after finding the stick and continued his task of sharpening one end to a point. He didn't think about it, he just focused on whittling. Testing it, Devlyn poked his fingertip against the roughly honed wood. Satisfied, he then located the trail he had discovered the previous day, a trail he thought had been made by a doe he had seen once or twice before.

He followed the trail, tracking the doe for several hours before eventually coming across her standing contentedly under a tree, chewing something. Muscles quivering from weakness and head swimming from hunger, he tried to sneak up closer just as his stomach moaned again. The doe looked up at the sound and stared, ignoring his makeshift spear. Then, she turned back to the tree, one he'd not seen before, with leaves and flowers the color of rain-soaked silver, thick with moisture, and took a bite from a curious-looking, purplish-hued fruit. Most impressive was its size, twice the size of an ordinary apple! His stomach lurched again, the memory of tiny bitter berries and gritty bark nagging at his insides.

Dropping his spear, he approached the doe and the tree. Picking a single fruit, Devlyn sunk his teeth into it and was rewarded with incredible flavor, sweeter than anything he'd ever tasted before. He expected that juice would drip from the fruit and down his chin and was surprised when it did not. When only the core remained, Devlyn was amazed that his stomach felt full. Rather than wanting to rest after eating his fill, he felt energized as though he could walk a league before needing to rest again.

After that he found and ate one of the amazing fruit every morning. The trees bearing them were abundant in the Illumined Wood, leaving Devlyn to wonder how he had not come across them sooner. He never had to pick more than one fruit at a time, gathering only what he needed for each meal. He wished that when Queen Vernal had told him that the forest would provide for him, she had also mentioned the purple fruit.

He had no idea what the purple fruit was called but if not for his discovery of it, he would have killed and roasted that doe for a proper meal instead of thanking her for leading him to it.

Devlyn had no idea how long he had been wandering through the Illumined Wood, nor where he now stood in its vastness. There were no bells here to toll the hour of the day, and the urgency to know the time and day had washed away after he had been walking beneath the trees for seven days, searching for berries and bark. Well, Devlyn *thought* it had been only a week back what surely must be months ago, when it still seemed important to know what day of the week and what specific hour it was. He didn't even care whether it was Thenaen or Saraen.

The only time Devlyn was sure about now was that it was night, and given the absence of moonlight, a new month had either just started or would soon begin. Between the new moon and lack of stars visible through the thick foliage rustling overhead, this night felt uncommonly dark.

Direct sunlight rarely touched the forest floor. Instead, refracted light gleamed through the emerald leaves, diffusing softly through the always shaded forest. The leafy canopy had a mysterious quality, ancient and eerie as it loomed above, untouchable, but not quite forbidding.

Devlyn's first thirteen years had been spent living in Cor'lera along the edge of this forest, but then, he had never taken a single step into the forest itself. Cor'lerans told their children stories about the horrors that supposedly happened in the Illumined Wood, implanting fear of going into the leafy depths, supposedly for their own safety. Ever since he could remember, the ei'ceuril of the abbey school had said that anyone foolish enough to enter the forest had never returned. He'd even heard a rumor of his own grandfather entering the wood before Devlyn's birth. He had never learned whether that was true, and he didn't even know his grandfather's name.

After living for a few months—well, probably months, not just a few weeks—in the Illumined Wood, Devlyn still did not understand exactly what supported the notion that no one ever returned, despite the fact that he was undeniably lost in a forest larger than most kingdoms. *What happened to those who never returned? Why didn't they return?*

Devlyn gazed up into the canopy, a canopy that was apparently no different than any other forest he'd been in, yet during the day, he would swear that from the corner of his eye, he could see traces of silver and gold lining the leaves. But, no matter how fast he turned, or how hard he looked into the leafy canopy, he never did see anything more than the mysterious green, no hint of silver or gold ever visible. Devlyn had grown accustomed to the peculiar effect in the green of the foliage and didn't expect to see anything different this time. *It's only the light playing tricks on my eyes*, he had convinced himself repeatedly, seeing only green, no silver or gold.

An eastern wind brought his attention back to himself as it brushed across him, carrying a single leaf from some high place.

"Like a leaf upon the wind..." Brother Bernard's face bloomed in Devlyn's mind and he could almost hear the old ei'ceuril recite his favorite prayer in Cor'lera's abbey school. *What a foolish prayer!*

Devlyn felt the wind pass, light and free. Although curious about where it came from, he was more interested in its destination. He wished that the wind could carry him along on its western journey and return him to where he should still be: Ceurenyl and its uncertain conditions.

Before going to Lucillia and the Illumined Wood, Yelaris, a blue dragon, had flown Devlyn away from Ceurenyl, home to both ei'ana at Gwilnor Academy and ei'ceuril at the Temple of Ceur. He had been taken to the wood in haste, so that he could begin his novitiate as an ei'ceuril, a decision made on the frightful night when Emperor Erynor Meriden, believed to have perished over fourteen hundred years ago, had attacked Ceurenyl, thereby revealing himself to Eklean. Ceurenyl had been the only city to withstand Erynor's previous reign. This time, however, the city had not been able to provide much resistance against the Erynien Empire after her city gates—set in Ceurenyl's massive stone walls—had exploded in a single assault. That should *not* have been possible.

On that horrendous night, not only had Erynor unleashed his shadow elves to wreak havoc and destruction on the city, but he had also taken the lives of hundreds of knights who had vowed to protect the city and her people. Devlyn had left on Yelaris, narrowly escaping the besieged city when they had been attacked just as they left without knowing how the battle had ended. That uncertainty clawed at his conscience.

Even now, months later, the heinous screeches of the shadow elves still woke him in a fright. The tormenting thought of those abominations still lingering in Ceurenyl, patrolling the cobbled streets as dictators and executioners, terrified Devlyn. His eyes remained opened most nights as he lay sleepless, fearing the worst for his friends. His imagination had built upon his ignorance and intensified the potential of devious deeds done there.

It wasn't just Devlyn's concern for his friends in Ceurenyl that kept him awake. A frustrating prophecy also tormented his restless nights; most interpretations had fate all but demanding that Devlyn become an ei'ceuril, or he and the rest of Eklean were doomed. He still thought the decision he had made a hasty one under the circumstances, considering he had agreed to join the ancient order in the midst of the attack on Ceurenyl.

There was no logical reason for the prophecy demanding that he become an ei'ceuril. What good was hiding in a temple that prevented anyone from wielding? And how would that help at all in the dawning war against a reforged Erynien Empire?

He had figured that the least he could do was to obey the prophecy and become an ei'ceuril. It certainly couldn't hurt the war effort. What benefit could a fourteen-year-old boy have in a battle against the Erynien Emperor, let alone against a single shadow elf? And that thought brought another to mind. He *thought* he had turned fourteen. His birthday on the first of Marenth had to have passed. He had no way of knowing exactly how long he had dwelt in the forest, but it was surely at least four months.

After he had solved the problem of finding adequate food, he had spent a good part of each day practicing wielding the erendinth, without noticing any improvement. The incredible strength behind the wields that Erynor had thrown at him, and at Yelaris, as they had fled from the battle was beyond anything Devlyn could imagine. Even if the prophecy's interpretation accurately named Devlyn, he doubted that he could ever rival Erynor. It didn't matter whether he was an elya, mastered the ways of the Phaedryn, and became an ei'ceuril. The Erynien Emperor would still destroy him just as easily as he had obliterated Ceurenyl's gate, not to mention the thousands of Phaedryn that Erynor had murdered during the Ceurendol War more than fourteen hundred years ago.

Brushing those thoughts aside yet again on this starless night, Devlyn watched as the leaf parted ways with the wind and fell near his feet.

"Is that supposed to be a sign? That I'm right where I need to be?" he asked the unresponsive leaf.

Frustrated, Devlyn bent to inspect the seemingly ordinary leaf. He gave it a gentle tug and was surprised when it resisted. He brushed the sides of the leaf until his fingers reached the stem where freshly sprung roots burrowed into the dirt. While this was not the first fallen leaf he had seen grow roots into the forest floor, the speed of the phenomenon still startled him. Unlike most leaves that shriveled and died after falling from trees, those in the Illumined Wood immediately sprouted roots and continued to thrive in a new manner of existence, creating an ivy-like carpet.

As the night drifted on, exhaustion finally caught up with Devlyn. He gave some thought to where he might rest. A nice warm bed sprang to mind and he longed for his bedroom in Gwilnor's North Tower, its luxury of privacy and protection all but a distant memory. Not that he needed either in this forest, but they were a dearly missed small comfort.

During his time in the forest, Devlyn never stayed long in any location. He had grown flexible, adjusting regularly and quickly to new shelters. More often than not, he had resorted to resting in a hollow created by the roots of one of the exceptionally tall trees. He did not mind sleeping among thick moss-covered roots, but he did find them to be a poor substitute for a bed.

The roots of the tall trees were larger than most tree trunks, nearly double the girth. Here, they supported the largest trees Devlyn knew to exist, weaving across the forest floor before delving into the dirt. He doubted that even the fabled stellendi trees in the Eldin Wood could compare to these. The thick twisting roots offered sizable hollows creating dwellings for people or animals. Luckily, he had not yet intruded on an already occupied dwelling.

And while he had yet to encounter a threatening beast, he remained vigilant nonetheless. He had never seen or heard of wild animals acting in the peculiar fashion he'd encountered here. Whenever he came across them, which occurred fairly frequently, they would draw near to inspect the visitor. They never showed signs of fear or skittishness and never fled from him.

Somewhere in the branches above, a single owl called to the night sky. His pointed ears perked toward the hooting sound and he scanned the now still leaves for any movement. The call brought the phoenix to his troubled mind once again. Devlyn longed to hear the phoenix sing, and the owl's hooting from above was not the phoenix's melodious sound. He hadn't seen the phoenix since he had stood on one of Gwilnor Academy's tallest towers, long before fleeing Ceurenyl. It was yet another point of tension in the pit of his stomach. *Did something happen to our bond?*

Whenever he tried to open his consciousness to search for the phoenix, the attempt always ended in failure. He worried that their bond had somehow broken. He wondered if he should have stayed in Ceurenyl to fight Erynor and thought that perhaps the phoenix did not want to bond with someone who ran away from battles. Ashamed of what he considered a cowardly act, Devlyn tried to console himself that he had had little choice in the matter. Ceurtriarch Ealyndol Roendryn, High Archsteward and Arbiter of the Light, had insisted that he begin his novitiate, and Yelaris' impatience with his reluctant acceptance for the necessity of his immediate departure had pushed him to leave the city.

Thinking back to the last time he and the phoenix had been together, the height of Gwilnor's Dragon Tower came to mind. What had he done to call the phoenix to him? Had he even done anything? Was height an important factor? Devlyn's eyes craned toward where he thought the owl's hoot had come. The sound had not repeated but he didn't like the idea of climbing any of these trees.

In the stillness of the forest, he yearned for companionship as his loneliness and fear intensified every day. He knew he should retrieve the violet jewel from his coin purse. Tucked into the purse after leaving Lucillia and kept stowed in a secret pocket inside his robes, the lucilliae was twice the size of Cor'lera's blue ice grapes. It had a peculiar tendency to disperse whatever fear loomed; however, the power the jewel held over fear had no impact on loneliness. *I wonder if there's a jewel that cures that?*

Emptiness had claimed his heart and he didn't know how to ease its ache. In the months that had passed—maybe a year for all he knew—the silence had become a heavy burden, his loneliness intensifying daily.

Desperate, Devlyn cried out that loneliness, yelling with all his being, both his mind and his voice shouting through the Illumined Wood. Leaves fell from their branches and slumbering birds flew from their roosts at the unexpected sound reverberating through the still, dark night. Falling to his knees in despair, Devlyn felt the solitude smothering his mind.

With no other option, Devlyn submitted to it, accepted it.

The quiet and stillness were all about him, thrumming against his consciousness while in the quiet of his heart, a familiar tune softly vibrated. In that stillness, Devlyn saw a clearing on a moonless night, a clearing he had not yet come across in the Illumined Wood and was shocked at the possibility that it existed anywhere in this dense forest.

After directionless months of solitude, his being was flooded with purpose and, more importantly, a destination. There *was* a clearing where he might get a glimpse of the moonless sky when the stars glimmered brightest! Then he remembered that the moon was young that night and the nights when the stars were brightest had just passed. Undeterred, hope rising, he vowed he would find it.

Devlyn trod carefully on uneven terrain, pressing himself into aquaeys, seeking a body of water—*any* body of water. He knew his best chance of finding a clearing lay near a lake where trees were limited to the shoreline. With his senses heightened to aquaeys, he trusted his wielding to guide him through the wood.

He had always been able to see further than others could, but here, his eyes had adjusted to the dark nights and the days without direct sunlight, and the roots of the trees were difficult to detect, since many lay hidden beneath blankets of ivy. Still, he pushed forward, drawing nearer to the water he felt through wielding the erendinth.

The moon had grown old and offered no light, leaving the stars to twinkle softly. Devlyn had grown appreciative of nights like these. Over a year had passed since that first night he had joined with the phoenix on his thirteenth birthday, a night very similar to this one. He was still in awe at the magnificent light he had seen through the phoenix's eyes that first time in Cor'lera's abbey school.

More time had passed as he sought the clearing he now could see in his heart every day since crying out in desperation, needing to look on the night sky, and perhaps once again see the phoenix. A longing he could not explain filled his heart, and he simply could not understand why the phoenix remained hidden. If asked, he could not say how he knew of the phoenix's presence, but he *knew*. The phoenix was within his heart and while Devlyn longed to bond once again, he'd be happy to just see the phoenix, and continued his search for the clearing. He knew it lay nearby—he could feel it.

Finally, the trees began to thin and through his wielding, Devlyn sensed a body of water. Excitement coursed through him when the trees finally opened onto a bank along a moderately sized lake. He had never before seen water so clear and he found it impossible to resist, plunging his hands in to cup a handful to taste and savor the pure and refreshing water.

Thousands of stars twinkled above, dancing to an eternal tune that Devlyn could not hear. Less anxious and desperate, Devlyn's eyes grew heavy as the hour grew late.

He lost track of time as he sat on a small stone on the bank of the lake but dared not take his drooping eyes from the sky above. His neck ached from craning it upward, but he wouldn't lie down lest he fall asleep. Once again, Devlyn's thoughts drifted to his friends as he waited. They had been able to stay together while Devlyn had to be alone during his novitiate. Although he had dealt reasonably well with his solitude, he longed for companionship. Permeating through his mind and heart was a single thought.

He sat on that single stone, alone, no one near to share word or meal. His eyelids grew heavier still and he repeatedly blinked and rubbed the sleep from them. Finally, just as he opened his eyes yet again after prolonged rubbing, a star high above danced oddly. *Shooting stars don't move like that.* Devlyn concentrated on the star, his heart pounding in growing excitement as he remembered another night, when he had stared out his dormitory window on the top floor in the squat tower of the abbey school and had that same thought.

Dancing as it descended through the night, the star that wasn't a star soon flew across the surface of the small lake, talons dipping occasionally beneath the water and breaking the smooth glassy surface. From the lighted bird flowed the familiar wondrous song stirring the entire forest in response. From their disturbed slumbers, all sorts and sizes of animals drew near the bank.

Devlyn paid little mind to them, preferring to watch the phoenix soar about the lake. Warm, comforting light emanated from the bird, like fire trailing behind it, but a fire that did not burn. The phoenix circled the perimeter of the modest lake, passing closely to the trees along its shores, lighting the gathered animals and causing soft flowers of silver and gold to unfurl from what, just moments ago, had been green leaves. Petals of the same hue fell from the branches as the trees responded in abundant floral joy to the phoenix's presence.

A euphonious tone escaped from the phoenix, answered by a low pitch drumming, humming from somewhere nearby. The hum began slowly, quickening the longer it went on, seeming to come from beneath Devlyn. Listening attentively, the drum-hum reminded him of trees as though the tree roots, digging far into the soil, were stirring. Cracks and groans soon joined the humming, and Devlyn's jaw gaped when he saw the trees sway back and forth in acknowledgement of the phoenix.

The trees themselves lauded this bird of light! The curious sounds they made reminded Devlyn of one stirring from a long and restful sleep, one overspent in slumber. The animals joined in the hymn of the trees; they belonged to the forest just as much as the trees.

Before long, the tranquil forest transformed, became wrapped in the ode, rising and falling with every breath, reverberating in a triumphant song. Barely audible at first, it intensified and soon washed through his entire being, growing to such a volume that Devlyn could not tell whether he was hearing it with his ears or whether it came from within.

Soon, he too joined the trees and the beasts in the hymn of the forest, words of praise flying from his tongue, words he didn't recognize, words that did not belong to the Common Tongue. It was an older language, more ancient than any other and the words came not from him, but from the phoenix, and Devlyn realized that he was now bound with the phoenix. The song of the forest had so preoccupied his attention that he had not noticed connecting with the phoenix. Or had the phoenix connected with him?

Devlyn gazed from the perspective of the phoenix and was awed to see every animal glowing, pulsing from its core, the sounds coming from them melding in an incredible, almost visible, wave. Devlyn watched as the trees' silvery bark bent back and forth, silver and gold flowers swaying gently above. Light pulsed and vibrated from the trees. Forms materialized from the undefined shimmer. They looked oddly akin to people, perhaps elves, but with a distinct form that Devlyn had never seen before. A genus of their own, a race unknown to him?

His gaze moved upward, to the bright sky above. The brilliance of the stars would have blinded the average pair of eyes. The moon, previously hidden from sight because of its youth, now outshone the sun on the brightest of days. The amount of light throughout the forest and sky belonged in a way more profound and truer than the surest of realities.

The creatures by the lake had doubled since Devlyn last took notice, and newcomers continued to arrive. The ethereal forms originating from the trees grew more distinct, their faces jubilant. They swayed much like the trees from which they materialized; no, they didn't sway, they danced!

Then, amidst the joy of the phoenix's return to the forest, a shadow fell over Devlyn's heart, a shadow that came from without. An image of the phoenix soaring through the branches of the trees burst forth, and suddenly the thick foliage transformed into charred branches and smoldering remains. The vision appeared as a memory, but with it came a sense of terrible urgency.

WORDS UNSPOKEN

Devlyn took another mouthful of the purple fruit he never seemed to tire of and watched the phoenix return from the canopy above. Only a week had passed since they had reunited and it felt as though they had never parted.

With his consciousness now endlessly open to the phoenix, the two relished each other's presence, each exploring the other's inner being. Devlyn remembered hearing stories at Gwilnor of those who had bonded with the phoenix so long ago. It was said that when the two became a complete Phaedryn, they would be nearly one being—elf indistinguishable from the phoenix. The further he explored the phoenix's mind, the more he felt his own change.

Already preferring the phoenix's vision of their world to his own, Devlyn adjusted his own actions and leanings to those the phoenix favored. One notable circumstance was his recent aversion to eating meat. While the opportunity to do so never arose here in the Illumined Wood, Devlyn didn't know whether it related to the purple fruit or whether it was tied to the phoenix's aversion to eating flesh. The thought of avoiding meat once he was out of the Illumined Wood continuously crossed his mind. Would he be able to refuse such a meal if offered?

Deciding not to worry himself over things that had yet to happen, he took the last bite of the purple fruit. Refreshed and revived, Devlyn opened his consciousness and embraced the ever-constant presence of the phoenix. Their thoughts melded, his heavily troubled mind blending with the phoenix's calm and whimsical consciousness.

When Devlyn thought about it, their different minds appeared at odds, yet astoundingly, when bound, they did not polarize. While Devlyn thought he could probably spread his anxiety across the entirety of the Illumined Wood and still have some to spare, the phoenix was otherworldly and emanated peace. That disparity made Devlyn fear that his being would repulse the phoenix, leaving him abandoned once again. He was rather hesitant to delve further into the bird of Light, for it was an exchange: the more Devlyn learned about the phoenix, the more the phoenix knew about him.

Devlyn wondered whether his unwillingness to completely interchange was the cause of the phoenix's long absence. Even as he pondered freely and openly within their melding, sensations of urgency coming from the phoenix swam about. Devlyn didn't understand how their form of communication worked, but he didn't doubt that it worked. The phoenix was relaying a sense of urgency about something happening to the south of their current location, some sort of strife in the Illumined Wood requiring their immediate attention. Images of a tree larger than any he had ever seen or thought possible flashed through his mind, a tree with a trunk larger than most houses in Cor'lera.

As impressive as the tree was, the image or memory expressed by the phoenix did not represent it as merely a tree, but rather as a dignified creature, a friend even.

Is this tree like the forms we saw at the lake? Devlyn still relied mostly on converting his thoughts to images, the way he had communicated with Yelaris, but words always came easier for him. And something about the phoenix made him think that dragons and phoenix communicated differently, but he hadn't quite figured out the right way to communicate with the phoenix.

An image of an ethereal form standing before the vast tree appeared in his mind, and as the form grew distinct, the face of a woman took shape. Fine winkles etched the corners of her eyes where tears flowed freely. Her face was strained with what appeared to be unsurmountable pain and the wrinkles on her face multiplied, the woman aging by the second. Her lips were tightly pursed as she silently cried for help.

The image faded and Devlyn's worry grew for the woman, one of the miervae. He had no idea what the miervae were, but he *knew* that this was one of them. While Devlyn had been experiencing the image, fixated on it, the phoenix had come to perch in front of Devlyn. Brilliant golden eyes brimming with light stared intently into his own. When had he landed? A sense of movement filled Devlyn, not words or images, but the simple understanding of swift movement.

Without questioning how or why, Devlyn stood and began jogging at a quick pace south through the trees. There was no need to gather any belongings, for he had none, just the itchy white ei'ceuril robe he wore and a small pack with a few belongings inside. The two lumols and the curious violet jewel were safe in the pocket against his chest.

Even as he moved, he knew that the chances of seeing this same place again were slim. The phoenix flew at his side, no longer needing to guide Devlyn who could not say where they were going, only knowing how to reach it.

Devlyn's strength waned as hours passed at the pace he'd set. He sorely wanted to rest for just a moment but the stronger sense of urgency remained, although he doubted he could maintain his current pace much longer. He eased his strides, not by much, but enough to tempt him to stop altogether, and as he did, a hollow in the roots of a tree came into view, the sort that he preferred to sleep in. Thoughts of stopping increased; he longed for just a quick nap.

It would only be for a bit, that way I can travel further after, Devlyn thought, convincing himself to stop. His legs ached, and he yearned to ease their burden. He slowed even as he pushed forward toward the hollow. *Just a few more steps and I can rest.*

Even as the thought formed, the phoenix was there in his consciousness. The earlier urgency that had since faded in significance as he had raced south now returned tenfold. Even as the sense filled him, Devlyn felt his weariness diminish. His legs no longer ached, his lungs refreshed, and the sharpness of his mind returned as a surge of energy rushed through his veins.

Devlyn took a final glance at the tree when he ran past it, no longer tempted to rest beneath her hospitably swaying leaves. Rather, he felt the strength of his leg muscles tense and relax rhythmically, smoothly moving him forward over the soft ground beneath his feet.

The phoenix remained bound with him and just as he could feel his own muscles, he was also aware of the phoenix's, separate, but also *within*. The phoenix's wings were incredibly powerful, astounding Devlyn as they beat without the slightest effort. While Devlyn had to pace himself to endure the entire day, he knew that the journey would not faze the phoenix in the slightest. When the incredible wings flapped, Devlyn felt the phoenix's entire body involved in the process, beginning from the muscles of his chest and extending outward in a fluid motion.

As the air flowed across the phoenix's body, almost caressing and guiding him, Devlyn felt the similarity to wielding aerys. Whenever he did, he felt a heightened sense of the element and was able to manipulate it however he wished, serving his needs, just as the phoenix did as he flew. Even the way the air touched the phoenix resembled how aerys felt to Devlyn when he interacted with it. It was certainly similar to how the air felt when it brushed against his body as a breeze, but a distinct, yet subtle difference remained. At Gwilnor Academy, Devlyn had learned that the actual elements were the physical manifestations of the elemental erendinth; the erendinth itself was the essence of the elements.

To Devlyn's surprise, the sun began to sink in what was surely only a matter of minutes since he had passed the tree with the enticing hollow. The candescent light cascading through the leaves had already faded without him realizing it, and the leaves far above his head showed only a dim green darkening with dusk.

It was full dark when Devlyn and the phoenix finally did rest. *You could probably continue for the rest of the night, couldn't you?* thought Devlyn, trying to translate what he thought into images for the phoenix, and receiving a thought of the phoenix resting with him for the night. No notion of the phoenix's ability crossed over, only that they would rest together.

The following morning was like the many that had come before during Devlyn's time in the Illumined Wood. The sun had not yet risen, yet the surroundings had begun to glisten. The phoenix nestled nearby, perched with his head close to his breast.

Are you awake? Devlyn thought, still trying to translate his thoughts into images.

The phoenix's golden eyes sprang open, no drowsiness in them, and they stared directly into his waking own. An image came to his mind and it seemed to say, *we do not sleep, we rest.*

Devlyn could not say how he understood the image turned into a phrase. No voice was present, and even the image did not seem definite. It was as if an idea or a concept came into his mind and he immediately knew its entire meaning.

Clearly, the phoenix understood what Devlyn was beginning to unravel about their communication, for a sense of amusement passed between them. *Was that a laugh?* Concentrating, Devlyn thought without words, just concepts and meanings swirling through his mind. He organized them in structures and used the concepts as he would use words and images, expressing one concept after another to the phoenix. First a concept of location came to him, followed by an understanding of himself and the phoenix. Amusement again flowed from the phoenix.

Growing frustrated with his inability to properly communicate, he felt like a toddler trying to pronounce a new word. Or worse, trying to pronounce an Aelish word. An assuring presence fell over him, encouraging him to continue. Concepts of language and communication flowed in, revealing the source of his difficulty.

It was not that he was unable to communicate in this distinctive way but that he was complicating something simple.

A healthy pride flowed from the phoenix, letting him know he was on the right path.

Simple. That's all I have to do. Make it simple, Devlyn thought, knowing the phoenix understood. Usually, before speaking, he would think of how to form a sentence, but before that, there was always something present waiting to be said, even when he did not think before speaking. Something that came from within. Something primitive, before words or images.

That's what he needed to communicate with the phoenix.

Trying again, Devlyn held what he wanted to say, looking at it from within. The words necessary were on the tip of his tongue, yet the words could not convey the deeper meaning. There was an emotional context laced throughout, but it was more; it was an interior awareness going beyond description. It was unrecognizable to Devlyn, yet perfectly understandable.

He saw how he could easily translate it into words or images; sounds or descriptions; art or music. It was communication on a level he had never known existed but that was the very source of language itself. It gave meaning to what flowed from people's mouths and brushes and quills. There was no complex set of concepts describing this from that, only a simple understanding of what he wanted to express.

Quieting his mind, Devlyn focused on his heart and without forming words or images managed to convey in a single breath, *where are we?* Knowing precisely what he communicated, he felt at ease and knew that what he wished to express was indeed conveyed.

However, there was something perhaps more difficult than conveying ideas, words, or thoughts to the phoenix, and that was receiving what the phoenix wanted to communicate to him. It took a deeper sense of awareness of one's self. It also required the awareness of another. Devlyn doubted that he would have been able to receive this understanding if he had not first been able to tap his interior awareness. For it was there—in that stillness within—that the phoenix communicated.

We are in the Illumined Wood, far to south. There were no words from the phoenix, only silence, stillness, touched by whimsy and warmth. But in that silence was understanding; comprehension more profound than Devlyn had ever known. He knew exactly where they were and he could point to their precise location on a map without error.

Devlyn now understood readily, unlike the messages he'd received from the phoenix before his recent clarity about awareness and concentration. Now, neither images nor words came, just the simple essence, but as complete as any words or images could ever be, and with far less effort to prepare and send. Devlyn just *understood*. Receiving the response from the phoenix required the same awareness and concentration required to communicate himself. This was unlike any other communication he had received from the phoenix in the past. Before, they all came across as images which he translated into words, but now, neither images nor words were present. Devlyn knew the message from its very essence.

Joy passed from him to the phoenix. Even the word joy now paled in comparison, as if there ought to be a word which better described how he felt. A heartfelt smile was the only means he could externally express that interior elation.

Do you have a name? Devlyn wanted to learn more about the phoenix. He still didn't know who the phoenix was and he longed to discover more now that this veil was lifted.

My name is within you.

Does that mean I name you? Devlyn conveyed. *How else could his name be in me?* Devlyn thought, forgetting that his thoughts were present to the phoenix.

My name was given by Another. It is not for me to tell you who I am. You will discover it, and many other things, within yourself. Devlyn felt the understanding permeate him.

Where are we going?

A miervae, one of the Great Trees, dies at the hands of another. We must gentle her soul, lest she turn into a wraith, consumed by hatred and despair as happened to those of the Briel Wood.

A forest of wailing creatures burning in menacing flames flashed across Devlyn's mind. Agony filled his heart as he witnessed a brief glimpse of events that had transpired during Erynor's previous reign. Creatures of all sorts had been prevented from fleeing the Briel Wood, doomed to perish alongside the miervae and nymphs of that forest. In their despair, they had turned from what they were, corrupted from their nature into wraiths. Their appearance grew cloudy, their serene facial features distorted by scowls of anger. Before long, a fog had covered them, and their former beauty was hidden from all. The forest itself was now known as the Dead Wood.

Based on his impressions of the few nymphs that Devlyn had met, he could not believe that they could transform so awfully, their green tree-ish appearance no longer present, replaced by disease and death.

As Devlyn experienced the past, the phoenix rose from his perch and took wing. Even as Devlyn followed, knowing they needed to move on, he had questions.

Can you tell me if I'm meant to become an ei'ceuril? Devlyn hoped the phoenix would have more insight than himself on the matter. So far, every passing hour led to an accumulation of questions needing explanations. Ever since he'd come into the Illumined Wood, he had pondered these questions, and the more he figured out, the more confused and uncertain of the future he became.

The clear response which Devlyn longed for never came; rather, a tingling sensation grew in a portion of his heart. He didn't understand the meaning of the sensation but he knew that the phoenix was trying to guide him toward the answer.

But what about the prophecy?

Rather than respond, the phoenix began to sing his familiar hymn to the forest and its creatures as he flew onward. Again, gold and silver flowers sprung forth at the song and invisible calls throughout the Illumined Wood responded, being, beast, and bird alike.

Despite wanting to better decipher the prophecy, Devlyn knew that even if he focused all his energy on it, he would discover nothing more today on the matter. He listened as the phoenix and the forest joined in song. Not even the great courts, he imagined, possessed melodies as grand as this one.

As they moved on through the forest, Devlyn quieted his mind to focus on that tingling part of his heart. Since his time at Gwilnor, whenever he practiced such exercises, he was always astounded by the number of levels in his heart. It was something far greater than a physical organ; the further he delved, the larger it grew, as if opening one box inside another. However, unlike with physical boxes, the inner boxes grew impossibly larger; the depth of his heart only grew with each passing revelation and he had yet to reach the final box, if indeed there was one.

How does something bigger fit in something smaller?

The phoenix found his thoughts entertaining, and Devlyn felt that mirth pass between them. He doubted he'd get an answer from the phoenix—at least not today.

It would be easier to get a straight answer out of Therril! The old ei'ceuril magister of theoreticals sprung into his mind.

Continuing to focus on his heart, Devlyn brushed against an odd sensation he had not felt since fleeing Ceurenyl. Lightness filled his heart, and a goofy smile lit his face. He recognized the feeling and was surprised that it arose from simply probing his heart. The sensation brought to mind silvery gold hair, and vibrant green eyes encased in brilliant silver. A soft voice followed, an elegant and gentle voice, capable of calming a tempest while inspiring an army. Nothing else mattered in that moment; his concerns diminished, leaving him to relish the feeling as they raced along.

LIFE AMIDST DEATH

Devlyn trod carefully through a ghastly frigid mist swirling about his feet and calves, threatening to creep above his knees. The vibrancy of the forest had faded to corruption, plainly visible on the bark and leaves of the surrounding trees. The incredible green he had grown so accustomed to in the past months was now laced with sickly veins.

The phoenix's concern was evident. The two were still connected and Devlyn felt his worry over the miervae deepen in this area of the forest. *I thought we had more time*, conveyed the phoenix.

Devlyn didn't know what was happening. He assumed the miervae had died and was now plaguing this portion of the Illumined Wood as a wraith, just as those in the Briel Wood had done. The phoenix shared Devlyn's fear without actively communicating it to Devlyn.

With the disease abundant around them, no animals were to be seen or heard, as if they all had fled from the area surrounding the miervae. Devlyn took another step without paying attention, and was startled when a crunch came from beneath his foot. Appalled, knowing what he had stepped on, he hesitated to move his foot to confirm, deeply aware of Queen Vernal's strict instructions to not harm any of the animals inhabiting the Illumined Wood.

Knowing he could not put off confirming his fear, he slowly lifted his foot and looked to the forest floor wreathed in a grey fog. Waving his hands around to clear away some of the mist, he managed to see a smashed rabbit, wrapped in the diseased ivy and clearly dead for quite some time. In a near panic, he batted at the fog just above the ground in a widening circle and noted dozens of other animals littered about. Stomach churning with fear, he saw birds, squirrels, and even deer, all with eyes staring into nothing. While Devlyn had never felt discomfort over the death of animals, the sight of the arbitrary death sickened him.

Devlyn felt sadness flowing from the phoenix. It was different from his own emotions, as if the phoenix had a deeper connection to the creatures sprawled across the ground.

They continued their trek through the unexplained sickness. Devlyn could not imagine how such a thing was possible. As he pondered his surroundings, the temperature dropped, and the visibility diminished severely. The bond between the phoenix and himself intensified, highlighting the phoenix's concern. The fog now rose well over his head and he felt it brush across his face. When he breathed, some of the mist managed to infiltrate through his nose and into his lungs. Unable to restrain himself, and with increasing fear, he coughed brusquely to purge his lungs of the poisonous mist; it explained the death of the animals.

It's not yet strong enough to harm you; the mist, that is. The phoenix tried to settle Devlyn's nerves. Even with that assurance, he took care to breathe out hard to expel as much as possible whenever he exhaled.

Directly in his line of sight rose a vast form with a girth wider than most houses. The further upward it extended, the wider it grew. It was easily recognizable as a tree, and by the looks of it, a once proud one. The leaves on its branches now lay dead, listlessly rustling in the dank air.

This was one of the Great Trees, a miervae. To hear her name spoken by a breeze among her leaves was truly a blessing for any fortunate enough to hear. Now, her only means of communicating her name withers before us.

Is it possible to speak her name even though she has passed? Devlyn craned his neck, following the trunk into the bare branches above.

Only a gentle breeze among her leaves can reveal her identity. The phoenix's mind stilled and Devlyn sensed the phoenix preparing for the worst. The closer they drew to the once Great Tree, the more depressing the air became. Hope had departed, taking with it all that was once beautiful. The tree was nothing more than a husk now, the corpse of what had been an incredible and ancient being.

Unable to sense any other living creature in the area, Devlyn approached the dead trunk and placed his hand against it. It was brittle to the touch, and dust or ash fell from beneath his hand. The sadness he had felt before touching the tree intensified, pushing into him, nearly consuming him. Despair and dread filled him as thoughts of his lost family surfaced, followed by fear for family and friends incapable of protecting themselves from shadow elves, who might be losing their souls to the evil beings who could be feasting on them to extend their own wretched lives, all because he had fled Ceurenyl when Erynor attacked.

Losing himself in his own misery, Devlyn also lost touch with his own surroundings and forgot where he stood. *Do not give in, Child of Luminare.* The phoenix's presence grew in Devlyn, filling him like the flickering light of a candle in a dark room. The utter despair lifted, and he became aware of his surroundings again, not surprised that tears of sadness and loss rolled down his cheeks.

He wiped his cheeks and was further eased at the sight of the phoenix flying around the dying miervae in great swooping arcs, singing his melodious song. Devlyn wondered if the beautiful tune had enhanced the phoenix's communication to break through his despair.

Then a harsh wind reeled through the grove and Devlyn thought he could hear anguished words carried on it. The plaintive sound mixed with the phoenix's song and the two seemed more at odds than anything Devlyn had ever heard.

"It is too late," came the sound on the foul wind. "All those who called me mother are dead or dying of my disease. Leave this place before you too are lost."

The melodious call of the phoenix grew louder, and Devlyn understood what the phoenix was conveying to the lost soul speaking through the wind. *There's another way, dear friend. I implore you, tell me who brought this disease to you?*

"The one presumed dead," howled the voice on the screeching wind. It grew louder, and the tone shifted from despair to anger and a powerful sense of betrayal. "He said his Master sent him to corrupt this forest, to prove that not even this sacred Wood is protected from his reach."

The wind became a torrent, twigs and leaves lashing across Devlyn's face and body, forming a cyclone around the dying miervae. Bracing himself, he wondered whether he could physically resist the intensifying conditions as debris lashed his exposed skin, his neck and arms laced by tiny cuts.

"I thought Erynor couldn't enter the Illumined Wood," Devlyn yelled over the howling wind. "I thought he was nearly destroyed the last time he tried."

The voice on the wind grew to a berating screech, contempt lacing every word. "Fool! Erynor Meriden has no power in this Wood! I speak of Aren Lorenthien! That ancient Luminari aryl who led your people from the Skyland of Luminare to the lands below. How he was beloved—lauded for his supposed heart of gold and for sacrificing himself to rescue as many Aldinari as possible from their doomed Skyland. Pah! Your ancestors thought his act of salvation so noble that they named their new dwelling, Arenthyl, in his forsaken memory!" Her screeching and howling intensified as her words derided elven historical events. None of this made any sense to Devlyn who had of course heard of Arenthyl but had never been told who it was named for. "He has destroyed who I once was with tenebrys—corrupted my very essence. I can feel myself becoming a wraith. My corruption will spread through this sacred forest and poison all! Now leave or meet the same fate as the trees and animals here."

Devlyn really did want to go, even though he felt that if he moved away from the corrupted miervae, he would very likely be swept into the cyclone. Still pressed against the trunk, he wondered if the tree was still at all connected to the despairing spirit. Worried, fearing it would soon change to a wraith, an urge to submit himself to something greater came over him —something external. As the feeling deepened, he began to sense the erendinth pressing against him; he also sensed the phoenix encouraging him. The erendinth animys, the essence of spirit, consumed him, and as it did, he searched deep into the tree's husk for a sign, any sign, of the presence he sought.

Pressing deeper into the empty husk, Devlyn felt the pain of its attack, a sensation he had never experienced before. The residue of the attack, the corruption, reminded him of umbrys, but darker and more terrible than the shadowy erendinth could ever be; pure darkness. *Tenebrys.* Deep within the immensity of the once Great Tree, Devlyn sensed a faint, benevolent presence, and further within was a vague, nearly imperceptible glimmer of hope; a voice, a mere whisper in the howling tempest, teased at his hearing. Calming his mind, he continued to wield animys, interlacing it with aerys so that he entered the cyclone even as he continued to delve further into the corpse of the miervae.

The winds swarmed and the erendinth Devlyn wielded streamed along. He drove his power into the winds of the miervae, seeking to calm the gales. The winds rebelled and fought against his influence, growing even more powerful. Still bound to the phoenix, Devlyn's ability to wield strengthened, and he applied more force to the calming effort. Deeply aware of the phoenix's presence, awe filled him as another force supported his wielding, a force that grew larger with every passing moment. It was foreign but not malicious, something he'd never felt before, vaster than anything he could imagine, dwarfing the immensity of the miervae. Following his instincts, Devlyn focused not only on the torrential wind, but included the poisonous mist infecting the forest. With the added strength, Devlyn soon had control over both.

Now an image of forcing the mist and wind into the corpse of the Great Tree came to the forefront of his mind. It was not from the phoenix; it felt different. Trusting the guidance of the new presence, Devlyn wielded animys, aerys, and aquaeys, the three erendinth swirling about to encompass all the elements infecting the forest. He felt the strength of the winds and the sickening death in the mist pushing to spread and understood that it was only with the extra help from the growing and still unknown force that he could manage to constrain the monstrous wind and disease to the dead miervae and away from the rest of the forest. The more he forced his hold on them, the more they intensified, immense, *evil.*

Barely able to contain the thrashing winds, he exerted all his strength with a final push and forced them into the tree's husk. Immediately, an image of fire entered his mind. Understanding precisely the intention of the message, Devlyn immediately pressed himself into ignys and ignited the dried husk.

The trunk was so dry and brittle that the inferno grew within seconds, engulfing its entirety, voracious flames licking up the trunk and stretching toward the bare branches above. The heat rose to such a temperature that Devlyn had to back away. Holding onto his control of ignys, he struggled to prevent it from spreading to nearby trees.

Soon, the flames and heat diminished as the inferno had nothing more to consume. Before long, Devlyn released his control over the erendinth and the fire went out. All that remained of the once miervae was a pile of ash. As he gazed on the ash, Devlyn wondered whether her deep roots could have survived the inferno. The howling wind was gone, and an eerie stillness filled the empty clearing. The miervae was gone too, her soul now in the place where the souls of all the living went in death.

The incredible presence that Devlyn had felt had gone too. He turned away from the pile of ashes to see if its source was about, but to his shock, hundreds of animals filled the grove. There was no single creature of incredible strength, simply a raft of assorted animals from large beasts to smaller critters. Devlyn startled when a panther brushed against his thigh, his heart skipping a beat at the fierceness of the beast. The animals present seemed to be mourning for the miervae. Devlyn was further surprised to see the ethereal forms that had appeared when he first rejoined with the phoenix. However, unlike before, the nymphs did not dance with joy, but swayed sadly as they mourned their loss, their mother.

Strangely, Devlyn knew that that was what the miervae was to those present; a mother. He too mourned her passing, aware of a dark emptiness in his heart.

A desire arose, pushing away his burgeoning sadness as he held onto the erendinth. Still bound to the phoenix, and without knowing the cause of the desire, he opened to it and from within, an incredible light bloomed and spread throughout his entire being. Incapable of holding in the magnificent light, he let it explode from his interior to soak the area in a light that eclipsed the moon and stars that had been visible above.

Bound more intimately than ever before, Devlyn saw the phoenix for who he was and was awed by his miraculous nature. The phoenix's past flashed before his eyes; millennia spent in a crystalline egg waiting to hatch at the birth of another; leaving a fortress in an unknown land high in the mountains to grow in the Illumined Wood once strong enough to fly; and ever watching the growth and maturing of a young boy maliciously ripped from his family. Part of Devlyn's awe was at the understanding that flowed through his mind and the joy that filled his being.

His newfound joy yearned for expression, and he found himself speaking a name.

"Aliel."

They basked in each other's presence as the light flowing around them intensified. Knowing Aliel's name brought a sense of identity and great understanding to Devlyn. He was acutely aware that the phoenix was different from himself and any other anacordel; there was something distinctive about this bird of Light.

United with Aliel, Devlyn felt the immense Light surrounding them; following the phoenix's lead, their spirits mixed with the Light and soared about the grove, caressing the erendinth he continued to wield before the incredible Light plunged deep into the ground where the miervae once proudly stood. The depth the Light delved far surpassed what Devlyn thought possible as it stretched deeper than the tallest trees. A calling forth was on Devlyn's heart; he knew not what or who he called forth, but the Light he had no control over beckoned another to the forest above.

Exhaustion consumed Devlyn as he withdrew from the depths. Without clear intention, he and Aliel disconnected and the world returned to its former dimness although the animals and nymphs remained in great numbers, and all were looking reverently at the miervae's ashes. Devlyn looked about, searching for whatever he and Aliel had called forth. Nothing seemed to have changed.

Then, something translucent jutting from the center of the miervae's ashes caught his eye. *A twig?* Devlyn looked curiously about and confirmed that it was the twig sprouting from the pile of ashes that held their solemn attention. Dumbfounded, Devlyn looked at the crystalline twig again.

"And a shoot of the Tree of Life shall rise from the ground to grace the land anew," said an unexpected voice. Devlyn jolted in shocked response—he had not noticed anyone draw near. And when he looked toward the speaker, Devlyn was even more astonished; the newcomer had the torso of a person, yet from the waist down, Devlyn saw the body of a horse.

TREE WARDENS

Devlyn tried not to stare at the oddly formed creature as it—no, not it, *he*—approached, all four of his chestnut fur-covered legs moving. The fur faded to a lighter brown above his navel before becoming coarse skin on his upper body. The hair on his head matched that on the lower body, but as Devlyn stared and blinked, he recognized moss in the chestnut locks.

"Many centuries have washed away since one of your kind has last walked across our threshold," said the creature.

"I'm sorry?" Devlyn asked, curious about the unusual creature, but also puzzled by his words. He hesitated, held back by the creature's stern, unblinking gaze.

"Your eyes betray that which is hidden beyond."

Devlyn guessed that meant that his thoughts were plainly shown in his eyes.

"We are anacordel, as is your elven kind," the creature went on. "My people have followed the stars above for countless nights since a link existed between our two races. At the time of the Great Blessing, our people lived among the trees with the miervae and narils—you met some of them and might better know them as nymphs. We cared for them, as did the fauns, and could not part with them when the time came for a decision on our future. Such was the outcome of the Great Blessing; our people were graced with great endurance, better to traverse many leagues in order to uphold our duty to the ones we care for.

"My kin protected the miervae which stood here. Many other anacordel perished as a result of Aren's attack. My kin, the tree wardens, fought admirably, but ultimately failed against his power. Yes, we are tree wardens, shadows of the forest, star gazers. Those beyond our land call us centaurs," the creature said proudly, although he spoke somberly, distantly, seemingly without emotional attachment. "I am called Oreniel. I find it curious, how one who hardly knows his own identity should dare to ask another for theirs."

Offended by the last remark, Devlyn opened his mouth to rebuke the centaur, but Oreniel had turned away to walk around the newly sprouted tree. He studied the twig intently, as though he was reading a book or examining a piece of art. Devlyn trailed behind, quickening his step to keep pace. Oreniel sporadically halted to examine the sprout from a new perspective.

How fascinating can one find a tree? thought Devlyn.

The centaur turned his gaze sharply on him, his green eyes piercing Devlyn to his core.

"Have your people grown so young that you have forgotten what stands before us!" Oreniel's anger flared. *Can he hear my thoughts?* Devlyn wondered. Oreniel scoffed and turned away again to continue his inspection. Confused, Devlyn followed along, like a child tailing an adult, yearning to gain some of the elder's knowledge. Oreniel ignored him.

Exhausted from his interaction with the now vanquished miervae, Devlyn sat on the ground nearby at the edge of the clearing and watched the centaur examine the tree. Nearly an hour passed and most of the other creatures had gone, each paying reverence to the centaur before disappearing into the thick foliage past the clearing. Even Aliel had flown off to a higher branch to rest, although Devlyn had noticed that Aliel was the only creature who hadn't shown reverence to the centaur.

During his pondering, Devlyn had realized that here was a creature from whom he might learn much about the past, the Illumined Wood and the mysterious crystalline twig, and about the curious but daunting centaur. When only the two of them and Aliel remained in the clearing, Devlyn got up and approached the unmoving centaur.

"Yes?" Oreniel asked, without turning toward Devlyn.

"I have a question for you," he said humbly before his courage ebbed, shoulders hunched, and gaze on the ground.

A moment passed and when Devlyn looked up, he found the centaur staring intently into his eyes. "That, young one, is evident. Even though you are curious about the nature of this tree, it is not in the forefront of your mind. My ability to seemingly know your thoughts frightens you, and you desire to understand how such a phenomenon is possible; you thought it was only possible between yourself and the phoenix. But I do not intrude on your thoughts. Be at ease, even though your troubled mind screams what you try to conceal; your eyes betray what lies beyond."

Unconsciously blinking rapidly, Devlyn took a few steps back as the centaur spoke. A gentle wind blew through the clearing. The centaur turned without saying a word, but Devlyn understood that he was to follow. The two left the grove and traveled a short distance away from the lingering sickness. The disease brought on by the corrupted miervae was gone, but the grove would take time to heal, even with the translucent twig. Oreniel walked in silence before stopping at the base of a towering tree, surrounded by healthy fauna once more.

"You must rest. What you accomplished this night was no small task. We will speak further when the sun falls tomorrow. Unlike those who live beyond the Illumined Wood, my kind sleeps during the warmth of the day."

Before Devlyn could manage a farewell, the centaur disappeared in a hastened gallop. Devlyn lay down and closed his eyes, falling deeply asleep amidst the nightly sounds of the forest.

Somewhere high above, larks sang their morning song. Devlyn recognized the cheerful tune, but his body refused to respond. He wasn't sore or achy, but he did feel as if every ounce of his energy had drained away. His limbs felt weighed down and his eyelids refused to part. Something dug into his lower back, something rough that didn't belong on his bed, even if his was the most uncomfortable bed in Cor'lera's abbey school.

With effort he put one hand under his body to find a gnarled root pressing against his back. *How'd that get into my bed?* Trying to ignore it, he swept a hand to one side to find his blanket and pull it over himself to doze off again. In his drowsy state, he finally managed to clutch something that was not quite as soft as his blanket, and which resisted his tug.

Is that ivy? His eyes opened at last and he was mildly surprised that the first streaks of sunlight were not gleaming through the east-facing tower window. The soft reflective light surrounding him showed that he had not slept in his bed at the abbey school last night. *Oh right*, he thought, *the Illumined Wood.*

The previous day returned in a rush. He didn't know exactly where in the forest he was, since he'd just followed the centaur and Devlyn had no idea in which direction they'd gone. The dead miervae and the crystal twig lay south of where he had first entered the Illumined Wood, but aside from that, he had no idea. He supposed that the centaur would be back—Oreniel had said they would speak again at the end of today—but he didn't know what time of day it was either, and he didn't know why the centaur was coming back. Wasn't the novitiate a solitary venture?

But Devlyn did want answers and the answers he had received yesterday had only resulted in more questions. *What is so special about that twig?* he mused. The only remarkable thing about it besides its translucence was that it had appeared from the ashes. *Is that what makes it special? Its translucence? Did it come from being called forth by his connection with Aliel? Or did the incredible Light play a bigger role?* Surely, he had only been able to call it forth because of his connection with Aliel, elya or not!

The more he thought about the Light and the crystalline tree, the more his thoughts fell on Aliel. Without knowing exactly how much time had passed since their first meeting, it had been quite some time, maybe even a year, before he eventually learned Aliel's name. And knowing that somehow deepened their relationship, as if something had been missing before. Oddly enough, knowing the phoenix's name had also revealed part of himself, without Devlyn being able to say exactly what that was. His self-awareness had grown, much as it did each time he and the phoenix were bound, only somehow, the knowing of Aliel's name had brought even more self-knowledge. Or, was it the opposite? Had his deepened awareness revealed the phoenix's name?

What Devlyn still could not fathom was that Aliel was not an ana-cordel, at least not in the same manner as himself. When they had wielded that wondrous Light together, the phoenix's true nature had revealed itself, astonishing Devlyn. Aliel was an anadel, pure spirit, a creature with no physical body. The more he thought on it, the less sense it made. After all, he could see the phoenix's body, and he felt it when they were joined together; it's what made Aliel a phoenix.

Tired of attempting to riddle the answer himself, he quieted his thoughts and opened his heart. *How is this possible?*

My kind is similar to the tree nymphs from the clearing and the other narils you have not met—but we came to Teraeniel much later than they did.

But how do you have a body if you're a naril? Anadel are pure spirit.

Be at peace.

Devlyn had expected—wanted—a full explanation. Frustrated by the continued lack of details, he decided to wander around a bit. Even though he sensed that he had woken late into the day, with most of it still to pass before the centaur's return, Devlyn knew he should spend some of it in meditation, something he had been neglecting lately.

It always surprised him that meditating could gentle his troubled heart. While he desperately wanted answers to events and things beyond his understanding, Devlyn knew that there was nothing he could do to bring about such knowledge any sooner. Perhaps he could manage to un-ravel one mystery though, through quieting his mind, through meditation. He looked about for a comfortable place to sit and saw a majestic tree stretching high into the forest canopy just to his right. The tree's bark was soft to the touch and thick with moisture. Its large roots provided a com-fortable nook to rest.

Even after closing his eyes and opening his mind, Devlyn had diffi-culty getting himself beyond his physical body. His mind wandered aim-lessly as he sat with his legs crossed, aware of just how one leg felt crossed over the other. Always, before he could truly meditate, he had to deal with the thoughts at the forefront of his mind. Lately, those thoughts had typ-ically revolved around the prophecy. Opening his eyes, he squinted at the robe he wore, the itchy white robe that marked him as an ei'ceuril novice.

It felt wrong.

Were his feelings for Ellendren reason enough to prevent him from pursuing the ei'ceuril? In spite of his tender feelings for the Lucillian princess, she was betrothed to Trethien. It didn't matter if he was a descendent of Feolyn and technically an elven lord—an actual ei'ethil. He didn't grow up in a manor house like Trethien and he certainly didn't know anything about becoming an aryl. All that Devlyn knew was that some prophecy dictated that he become an ei'ceuril. Irritation niggled at him as Trethien's face floated before him and he banished it in favor of the prophecy itself.

The explanations he'd been given about its meaning had been that he had three choices: become an ei'ceuril, die, or doom all of Teraeniel. *Not the best of choices, huh?*

Aliel conveyed reassurance in response.

Pushing aside his thoughts on both the prophecy and Ellendren with Trethien, he quieted his thoughts yet again, this time successfully reaching beyond his physical body. He searched for something without knowing exactly what it was. He didn't necessarily want to channel the mysterious force from the events in the clearing, but he did want to discover what it was. Remembering the feeling of its vastness, knowing what the force felt like, Devlyn searched for a trace. Whenever he recognized something akin to it and mentally reached out to connect, it quickly vanished. *It would be easier to hold water*, he thought as he imagined whatever he was seeking slipping through his fingertips.

One benefit of seeking that power was the myriad lives he could feel throughout the forest, a variety that left him in awe as he sensed creatures of every sort moving from one to another. The Illumined Wood thrived; he felt its vitality within his own being, invigorating him.

"You should eat," came a voice that tickled at his ears, barely audible, but breaking his focus.

Opening his eyes, Devlyn could not believe how much time had passed. The forest had darkened completely, and the first stars shone through the infrequent openings of the canopy above. Confused, Devlyn looked at Oreniel towering above him with a purple fruit in his hand, just as his stomach rumbled. Devlyn gladly reached for the fruit, and bit into it, that first bite revealing just how hungry he was. He had meant to find one of the fruits earlier in the day but had lost track of time while meditating, not expecting that the entire day would pass. Typically, the meditation would make him drowsy after only a quarter of an hour.

"Connecting with the Life of the Wood is an arduous task. Only those who have devoted their entire lives in preparation have managed to do so. Among your kind, it is called the Mystery of the Wood, and it encompasses all that lives here. It is not a single being. In times of great need, we join our essences to serve the forest or other creatures. Only in great need, such as the death of one of the miervae and the need to contain that corruption, was it possible to lend the strength of that force to you," Oreniel explained as Devlyn devoured the tasty fruit. "It is also the power which now protects Lucillia."

Still confused, Devlyn wasn't sure how to phrase a question, let alone exactly what needed clarification. The more he learned about the Illumined Wood, the more he realized how little he knew.

"There is someone I wish to take you to meet but first, we must talk about what occurred last night," said Oreniel.

Devlyn quickly rose, eager for details, even if he was still eating.

"Do you understand what you managed to do?" Oreniel asked.

Thinking back, Devlyn remembered the incredible power he had wielded, how he and Aliel had called forth the twig. "It felt like I summoned that twig out of the ground, yet I had no power over it. It didn't remind me of the miervae that stood there before; it was different. I can't say what though. At first, I thought it was a new sprout from the previous miervae." Devlyn recalled.

The centaur said nothing at first, his gaze focused on the ground as he considered Devlyn's words, arms folded across his chest. "I am not sure how you managed it, but what sprang from the ground was no mere tree; even a miervae pales in comparison. My kind remembers when the Phaedryn of old would call forth such marvels, but we thought the art lost following their demise at the hands of Erynor. Apparently, it is an innate ability, common to even an untrained Phaedryn, not fully realized."

"But what is it?" interrupted Devlyn, eager to know what that twig was.

Oreniel gave Devlyn a stern look before continuing, clearly disapproving the interruption. "It is known as a verathel, a sprout of Verakryl, the Tree of Life. Erynor and his shadow elves destroyed all the verathel and crafted weapons of significant power from them. It is said that the roots of Verakryl lie throughout every land, connecting and giving life to all of Teraeniel and everything that lives on her."

"I thought the Tree of Life was just a story for children."

"For no reason other than that only children have the ears to listen to such tales," responded Oreniel, which didn't tell Devlyn whether the story was actually true. "Now come, we must leave this place. Finish your vaer so we can leave."

"Vaer? Is that what it's called?" Devlyn took another bite of the purple fruit, taking care to wait until after he'd asked the question, not wanting to speak with a full mouth. Oreniel nodded in response and waited for Devlyn to finish eating.

With Devlyn's final bite of the vaer, Oreniel turned and walked away, not slowing his pace so that Devlyn had to run to catch up.

"Where are we going?" Devlyn asked, gasping for breath, hoping but not really expecting an answer, and so not surprised at Oreniel's lack of response. In fact, he was growing accustomed to being ignored by the centaur.

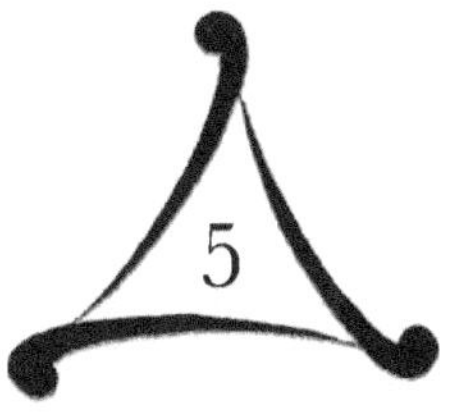

5

THE GIRL

Oreniel walked several paces ahead of Devlyn who was quite relieved to finally walk on his own two feet. Earlier in their journey, the centaur had insisted that Devlyn ride on his back, arguing they would never reach their destination if they had to keep to Devlyn's slower two legged pace. While there was merit to that, it had been an ordeal. Devlyn had felt incredibly uncomfortable with his arms wrapped around Oreniel's chest to stay seated as the centaur galloped swiftly through the forest. When they had eventually stopped to rest, Oreniel had told him that they were very near their destination and would arrive the following day. Delighted that he would not have to climb onto the centaur's back again, Devlyn now followed Oreniel obediently through the forest.

Without the distraction of trying to stay seated on Oreniel's constantly moving body, Devlyn opened his awareness to the phoenix. Aliel soared through the canopy above, diving in and out through the leaves, his amusement at seeing Devlyn ride a centaur coming through clearly.

It's not that funny. Devlyn was discomfited.

You need a better sense of humor then. Aliel's song wove through the branches above, sending dozens of birds to flight.

With his mind opened to the phoenix, Devlyn sensed another presence nearby. Instinctively, he crouched low and scanned the area for movement yet couldn't see anyone.

Apparently unconcerned, Oreniel continued walking, but his steps had a hint of reverence, his hooves falling more gingerly to the ground.

Remaining alert, Devlyn caught up with Oreniel, who now strode through a shallow pool surrounding the base of a miervae, its roots twisted and intertwined above and below the pool's surface. Unlike the miervae that had died, this one rose proudly through the little clearing caused by the pool, her strong vibrant branches lifting ever upward so that she towered over the other trees. Fruits of every sort grew from her branches, adding a sweet fragrance to the moist air. Curiously, vaer hung among the branches next to fruit Devlyn had never seen before. *How could a tree have two different kinds of fruit?* he thought.

Inclining his head while extending his palm, Oreniel placed a hand on the miervae's massive roots. A soft breeze followed, brushing lightly against Devlyn as it swept by.

Wanting to show his respect, Devlyn also approached the miervae. Just before his hand connected to one of her roots, he sensed movement in the area although he didn't hear anything to indicate that someone else was nearby. He pressed into the erendinth to wield kien and turned from the miervae to scan the clearing.

The moment he turned, his eyes locked with a pair of brilliant deep blue eyes gazing back, no white surrounding the iris and no black pupil encased in the blue.

"Stop hiding. I see you." Devlyn strove to keep his voice steady as he looked into the unnerving pair of eyes.

"How dare you speak to her like that!" came another voice. Devlyn had not sensed a second presence. Before he could investigate, a sharp lash of air whipped him across the back. Still pressed into the erendinth, Devlyn delved into aerys to locate the other wielder and was shocked to discover a male elf.

Terrified at the thought of an untrained kien wielder, Devlyn not only pressed himself into aerys, but also the other elemental erendinth. He wanted to catch the kien wielder unprepared and subdue him before he could retaliate.

Before wielding the erendinth at the elf, he heard him say, "My apologies, I did not know he was your brother," and felt the stranger's wield withdraw.

Surprised, he too withdrew from the erendinth. No words came to mind, only disbelief.

"Ei'lythel." Oreniel inclined his head in respect toward the blue-eyed girl. "We had hoped to arrive at your grove on the morrow."

The girl did not respond to Oreniel but rose from her crouch and walked barefoot into the clearing without making a sound, holding a slender wooden staff. Devlyn's eyes widened. The same hair as his own fell around her shoulders, the same traces of blond, red, and black in the light brown tresses. A young man followed her. He looked older than the girl and had an uncanny resemblance to Ellendren.

"Open yourself if you wish your sister to communicate with you," Oreniel said under his breath. Puzzled, Devlyn looked at the centaur.

"It's like meditating. I trust your kind hasn't forgotten that too."

Devlyn quieted his mind and instantly felt the girl's presence. "Leilyn? Is it…is it really you?" Devlyn managed, his annoyance with the centaur ebbed.

Brother. Devlyn heard the word clearly in his mind, as if it were his own thoughts, except with his sister's voice. *I feared the worst for you but was comforted by my lorendil that you were safe, all those years ago. I have longed to see you again.*

"What's happened to you? Your eyes…" Devlyn's voice cracked.

I will tell you the entire tale if you wish, but first, there is another you must make acquaintance with. Leilyn turned to walk through the foliage.

The stranger extended his hand in greeting to Devlyn. "Prince Aaron Roendryn of Lucillia, although really it is Ei'ceuril Aaron now. My sincerest apologies for attacking you prior to a formal introduction; passions are not the easiest to tame, even after living in the Illumined Wood as long as I have. I imagine the ei'ceuril have grown concerned over my prolonged absence."

"What do you mean by your prolonged absence? And, how long *have* you been here?" The more he looked at Aaron, the more he saw Ellendren.

"Three years now, if I'm not mistaken. This is actually my second visit to the Illumined Wood. The first was during my novitiate with the ei'ceuril, and, looking at your robe, I'd say that's what you're doing now. When it concluded, I returned to Ceurenyl and eventually professed the vows. When I finished my studies, I was sent yet again to the Illumined Wood, for the Return, the conclusion of initiation for ei'ceuril who are to become stewards. It is only intended to last a month, perhaps a little longer, like an extended retreat. However, halfway through my Return, I happened across your sister. She was under the impression that she could safely instruct me to wield. Learning to communicate with her through our minds was even more difficult.

"I am ashamed to say that, I thought she was either insane or a servant of Shadow. It took some convincing, but she eventually told me that she was an elya and that it was quite safe. While I am capable of controlling my wielding, I am far from mastering the erendinth, unlike you. I see that you have become quite capable." Aaron spoke sincerely, with a kind tone that helped Devlyn forget that Aaron had attacked him.

Leilyn, waiting for them a little further into the forest, motioned for them to join her. Devlyn followed Aaron to walk beside her along the bank of the shallow pond around the miervae. Oreniel remained in the pond with the miervae.

As he trailed slightly behind them, Devlyn wondered whether there was anything intimate between the two. It was evident that Aaron cared deeply for her.

Perhaps that means it is possible for ei'ceuril to be with someone? Devlyn hoped for enlightenment, but Aliel didn't respond.

"Is it true that you've bonded with a phoenix?" Aaron asked with a hint of excitement. "We knew it had hatched but could only hypothesize as to who it had chosen. I think Ellendren was disappointed that it never came to her."

Devlyn expected that the legends of Phaedryn were common knowledge to a Lucillian prince. Rather than answer his question, Devlyn invited Aliel to introduce himself to the others. In great splendor, he soared from the canopy high above and hovered before Leilyn and Aaron. Warmth flowed from the phoenix into Devlyn, Aliel's familiar touch a source of great comfort.

You know who desecrated the miervae. Leilyn's thoughts filled his mind.

Devlyn nodded, then realizing that he was behind Leilyn and Aaron, said "Yes."

Aren is also a Phaedryn. I would tell you more about him, but I know little. However, there is another who could tell much and more of Aren Lorenthien. It was she who granted me Sight from the River she watches over.

Devlyn didn't know who the mysterious other was, but followed Leilyn along the shallow bank, marveling at the sinuous roots flowing in and out of the silvery water, yet another aspect of the forest revealing itself.

A young girl sat on one of the large exposed roots above the pond, swishing her ankles in the water. She looked no older than nine and wore a flowery garment like Velaria's. Devlyn thought she might be the daughter of whomever Leilyn wanted him to meet.

The girl looked directly at him. "Welcome Devlyn, Child of Luminare." She spoke with the wisdom of great age, her voice reminiscent of a gentle, flowing river. The girl's eyes sparkled, a deep pond of blue.

"Who are you?" he asked.

Turning her head toward the glistening water, the girl smiled, her not-quite blond hair spilling over her shoulder, making Devlyn think of a waterfall. "If you listen closely, the water will sometimes speak my name. She speaks another name more frequently, but sometimes she says mine."

Although the girl made no sense to Devlyn, he decided not to ask the same question twice. "Leilyn says you can you tell me about Aren."

"My brother knew him better. They had many conversations before he left to save those still living on the Skyland of Aldinare; he was a marvelous elf."

Devlyn could swear that he had heard the girl correctly. "I'm sorry, but how's that possible? That would make you ancient; there aren't any elves that old any more, and you're just a child."

The girl smiled again. "You are quite mistaken. There are some who still live here in the Illumined Wood, many more in the Eldin Wood, and some still locked within the walls of Arenthyl with my brother. But my brother and I came before any of them. And yes, we are Children."

Devlyn turned to his sister for validation.

You speak with one of the Children. Before the Great Blessing and creation of the separate races, all peoples were as she and her brother still are.

"Your sister is quite right, but we are the only two left. All the others aged with the time they so desperately wanted. Only those who became known as elves remained in the valley with us, and while they aged, Anaweh preserved their immortality after the Great Blessing and the different races were solidified. My brother was given watch over the Tree, while I was to watch over the River which flowed from it."

Turning again to his sister, Devlyn saw Leilyn nod in agreement. But it seemed to be new to Aaron as well, for he looked as shocked as Devlyn felt. Except Aaron probably knew more of the history this girl described, given his better educated background.

Questions rapidly piled into his head, questions especially about the elves, but before he could voice any of them, the girl spoke again. "You will learn more of them later. Our time together is short, and we must speak of Aren Lorenthien. He was a magnanimous elven aryl who shepherded his people from Luminare to the land beneath, so that they might not meet the Shadow which eventually consumed their homeland. That was believed to be the work of the Evil One, despite anyone understanding how it could be possible, since he was secured in his prison far below Lake Saeryndol.

"When Aren learned that the Aldinari had not abandoned their Skyland, he took forty other Phaedryn with him to convince the aldarchs to flee their home and bring their people to this land. Unfortunately, when they arrived, they found the situation in Aldinare much worse than it had been in Luminare. Dark clouds encompassed the entire Skyland and lightning without light forked through the sky, striking everything that tried to fly from the Skyland, scarring the sky with dark voids. Wielding with all their might, the Phaedryn broke through that sinister storm, led by their aryl. They could not reach any of the aldarchs in their sanctums and could only reach a single city near the Skyland's edge.

"All forty companions escaped that doomed Skyland, managing to rescue four Aldinari each. However, to help them escape, Aren remained behind to direct the black lightning away from his companions. After the last Phaedryn escaped, Aren was never heard from again and he was presumed dead."

Devlyn waited for the girl to say more but it seemed that was all she could say about Aren. "That is not much to go on if I have to fight him."

"I cannot say what might help you further, only that Aren's attack on a miervae is very unlike the Aren Eklean remembers." The girl looked into the pond longingly. "I should be leaving; enjoy your time with your sister while you dwell in the Wood. If you see my brother, tell him I miss him." Before Devlyn could respond, the girl dove into the water, disappearing well below the surface.

Devlyn and Aaron shared a look of bemusement, but Leilyn seemed to think the girl's action completely natural, a normal occurrence. *I would like to say that I understand her despair over not seeing her brother, but they were cut off from one another when Krysenthiel fell, over fourteen hundred years ago. Whatever that Shroud surrounding the Lake is, it blocks their communication.*

"I can't imagine not seeing my sisters for so long; granted it's been several years now, but still. I hope they're safe. Ellendren had only just begun her studies at Gwilnor when I returned to the Wood." Aaron looked over his shoulder, as if he expected to see them.

"I was with Ellendren in Ceurenyl, and your parents in Lucillia before the Protection of the Wood was raised," said Devlyn.

Aaron turned anxiously to Devlyn. "They raised it? Do you know which one of them raised it?" he pleaded.

Devlyn was confused by Aaron's dismay. The Protection of the Wood would protect Lucillia from Erynor. What was upsetting about that?

They never told you how the Protection of the Wood works. For the shield to be raised, a monarch must give of themselves to save their people, Leilyn shared as she placed a comforting hand on Aaron's back. *The faith of one to save many.*

"It had to be my mother; she is a direct descendent of Roendryn. Have things grown so desperate?" Aaron managed, wiping away tears. Then his demeanor hardened, and determination covered his grief. "I have to help them. The Enemy has far more wielders than we do. It's no secret that they train kien wielders without taking any regard for their own safety or anyone else's." Aaron paused, making Devlyn think that Leilyn was speaking to Aaron privately, and when he went on, his frustration was evident. "I must help my people. I can't hide behind the temple walls while all of Teraeniel is threatened by the growing Shadow!" Aaron sounded like he was trying to convince himself more than convince Leilyn.

Another moment of quiet passed. Leilyn's eyes remained gentle and calm, reminding Devlyn of the image of their mother that Lex had taken from him. Even though they were no longer the same color, they still had the same form and outline, and held the same affection.

"I can leave the ei'ceuril, and we can be together." Aaron spoke desperately, sharing a desire he had held in secret. A few moments passed as he seemed to listen and the desperation faded to sorrow at Leilyn's response.

Devlyn felt sad on Aaron's behalf, but it was not his place to interject. While he was curious about what Leilyn might have said to Aaron, he did not disagree with anything the prince had said. This was a time of war, and people of strength and vigor were needed, especially those who could wield safely.

Aaron turned and walked away toward the miervae, leaving Devlyn alone with his sister.

LEILYN

Leilyn sat on a large root that popped above ground before diving into the stream. She patted a section beside her, indicating to Devlyn that he join her there. *He is terribly conflicted and requires the quiet to enter his heart for peace to blossom,* she said. *Come, it has been too long since we have seen each other.*

While Devlyn appreciated Leilyn's defense of Aaron, he had more questions than he could count swirling in his head and was more anxious to get some answers than worried about whether Aaron would find inner peace. His sister's disappearance that awful night when Lex had slain their father, Dolan, and forced their mother's family into Gneal's prison had left every Cor'leran curious about her survival. Many assumed Leilyn had perished after she'd disappeared into the Illumined Wood. Cor'lerans firmly believed that it was not possible for a little girl to survive on her own in that forest, especially one who had been rendered blind and mute.

"I just don't understand how you managed to survive," Devlyn said, scratching his head. "It's just, well, anyone from Cor'lera who went into the Illumined Wood was never heard from again. The villagers claim it's an act of suicide to come in here. I know that's not the case, well, I know that now, but, well, you were only six years old. How…?"

Amused with Devlyn stumbling over his words, Leilyn chuckled, and an odd sense of relief washed over him at the sound. Although she couldn't speak, she was still able to laugh.

There was a lot of confusion that night, and right after mother submitted, after the shadow elf caused me to lose both my voice and my sight, my guardian anadel, one of the lorendil, appeared, invisible to everyone but me, and perhaps our mother, although

I cannot say for certain. Yes, I saw the anadel, even though I could not see anything else, and she guided me away from the wreckage at the inn and away from Cor'lera. Two soldiers chased me all the way to the edge of the forest, but my lorendil led me in, and I kept running even though I couldn't see anything. She prevented me from tripping or running into trees. I don't know how long I ran; I was too scared to stop or look back, in spite of being out of breath and exhausted. But I eventually understood that I was not being chased and had not been since I had gone into the Illumined Wood.

So, I lay on the ground and fell asleep. I can't say it was a particularly untroubled sleep, but I did rest. When I woke the following day, I heard someone greet me. I was very afraid, because I could hear him, but not see him. He told me that he was a Saecrien monk, which did not explain anything to me, but it oddly comforted me. He led me by the hand to the Monastery of Kyrendal on the southern slopes of Mount Saecrien where I lived among the monks for a decade. They knew that, like you, I was born an elya, and capable of wielding, so they taught me. Through wielding, I was able to sense the world, but I was still frustrated as it was not the same, and I could only sense a dim shadow.

"Hold on." Devlyn shifted his weight on the root. He thought he had heard his sister correctly, but that wasn't possible. "How is it that you were taught to wield? You make it sound like there are only kien wielders at this monastery."

Her amused smile returned. *I didn't know who or what they were at first, but after living among them, I discovered that they are the same as us; most of them are Luminari. However, unlike us, they have lived in this wood for five thousand years. Before Lucillia gave birth, before the fall of Krysenthiel, even before the Jewel of Life came into being. They took a vow of nonviolence and left the world to live in solitude. By entering the monastery to begin this way of life, they were no longer what they once had been. Their fates were not connected to Ceurendol, and so, they maintained their immortality and the Balance was not broken for them.*

"That's incredible!" Devlyn couldn't believe that there were still Luminari from before the fall of Arenthyl. "They can tip the scales in this war! They can return and teach wielders how to properly wield again!"

They will not.

The swift refusal caught him off guard. Devlyn wanted to argue. Perhaps, if he could only talk to them, he could reason with them and convince them to help. But even as he thought it, he knew it wasn't possible. If they had remained faithful to their vow of nonviolence through the fall of Krysenthiel, through the death and enslavement of their people, he doubted they would change their stance and intervene now.

As if she had not been interrupted, Leilyn continued. *While living in the monastery, I spoke with another girl who sounded close to my age. I did not discover her true identity until much later, but shortly after we first spoke, she gave me a gift. She brought me to a river deep within the mountain. Though I could not see it, I could feel the purity emanating from it, thick in the air. She took my hand and guided me into the freezing water. In spite of the cold, I didn't shiver but I was afraid that I would slip along the slick ground and get washed away with the current. The girl gently submerged me and at that very instant something remarkable happened.*

Devlyn listened intently, fascinated. "What happened?" he urged when she paused.

Leilyn turned her gaze from the stream to Devlyn; he looked back into the blue pools of her eyes. *I was gifted with Sight. Not as I once had; rather, I see the seven erendinth within their physical embodiments. The girl told me that I see the world as the anadel do, that by having my eyes purified by the Tears of Anaweh, I would be unable to view the world as I once did.*

Devlyn wondered whether her vision was anything like Aliel's lighted vision. "When the phoenix and I connect, I see the world differently. On the darkest of nights, when I look through Aliel's eyes, it's as if it were the brightest of days. Is it anything like that? That light?" Devlyn paused before continuing, trying to figure out how to describe the phoenix's vision. "Am I seeing through the seven erendinth?"

From what I've learned of Phaedryn at the Monastery of Kyrendal, it's different. I see only the invisible realities, not their physical representations. The Phaedryn see both through lumenys. After receiving Sight, I was able to venture from the monastery and travel across the Illumined Wood. I've even left the Illumined Wood on several occasions. I desperately wanted to visit you but Kyrendal told me my interventions would not end well. On one occasion, I traveled just north of Cor'lera and did manage to catch a glimpse of you in the distance. You were traveling along the farmers' way in a small group, but rather than trying to approach you, my lorendil urged me to continue west toward the Wooded Hills of Thellion. It was there that I came across the ruins of that once great kingdom, where the castle still stands among the city's ruins, untouched by time.

Before I could draw near, I was greeted by an elf named Aewen. I later learned that she was originally from the Skyland of Aldinare and had married one of Thellion's kings. I stayed with Aewen for a whole moon cycle before she brought me to a hidden grove deep in the forest. The trees stirred as we walked past, recognizing who walked among them. Aewen told me that they were ilithae trees from the Skyland of Aldinare, planted by the Aldinari after Thellion fell into ruin, as a memorial.

There was a chill in the air, yet when we drew close to the grove, the air warmed. We waited briefly and then a herd of the fabled alicorns came to greet us. Their coats and the horns on their foreheads shimmered like silver. Unlike the unicorns which originated on this land, these had feathered wings sprouting from their bodies as naturally as a bird's wings. Aewen told me that she was a favored follower of Aldarch Endruil, and had spent millennia in his sanctum, Kir'enon, and when she left her Skyland to marry the human king, Endruil permitted her to bring a small herd of the alicorns. Aewen told me that she could see the Aldinari in me. Part of my heart possessed the virtues prized among the Aldinari. And the same is true of yours and all of Roendryn's and Feolyn's descendants.

Astonished by these details, Devlyn recalled a bridge of the same name as the elf that Leilyn spoke of, a bridge he, Alex, and Velaria had crossed from Parendior and into Perrien.

Before the words on the tip of his tongue spilled out, Devlyn heard shuffling nearby. Assuming that Aaron was returning, Devlyn turned and was about to call out his name but his jaw dropped when he saw a brilliant creature, its shimmering silver coat blindingly bright. An alicorn!

"Leilyn…" he trailed off, staring at the creature in awe.

Leilyn was silent as the creature drew nearer the stream. Aliel flew from the canopy above and swooped before the alicorn, hovering just before its head, communicating with the beautiful creature.

"How did you come by her?" he asked Leilyn.

How is it that Aliel came to you? Did he not approach you first? While I was in the Wooded Hills of Thellion, one of the alicorns approached me. She allowed me to brush her coat. Aewen told me that Maiya had chosen me, and that the two of us would leave the forest together and that we would care for one another to the end of both our days.

Still rather shocked at the sight of the creature that had stepped out of legend before his eyes, Devlyn didn't know what to say. He wanted to approach the creature but was too awestruck to move, and even as he considered it, Aliel sprang into the leafy canopy, followed by the alicorn who quickened her pace to a gallop before stretching her wings to follow Aliel.

"She's marvelous, Leilyn." Devlyn watched Maiya soar into the air, her powerful wings bringing her next to Aliel in a soaring flight.

She truly is. Leilyn's completely blue eyes followed the alicorn into the leafy canopy above.

While Aliel and Maiya flew together somewhere above, Devlyn talked to Leilyn about his past. Nothing he told her about Cor'lera surprised her, in fact, she anticipated it, commenting here and there as he talked. She found the news of Ceurenyl discouraging. She was frightened at the thought that the great temple city had been so easily besieged, not so much for it now lying vulnerable, but more so that so much of the knowledge the ei'ceuril had once possessed was now forgotten.

"Out of curiosity, do you remember an elf with bright red hair named Velaria?" Did his sister remember?

At the mention of Velaria, Leilyn's expression lightened. *A truly remarkable woman. I remember when she and Arlyn visited us; she was a few years older than Liam. I trust she's become an ei'ana?*

"Oh, yes, she's actually the Chair of Azurelle now. She's also bonded with a blue dragon who is named Yelaris. I flew on Yelaris to get to the Illumined Wood," Devlyn told Leilyn, then went on to talk more about his past, most of it about the events after Velaria had come to Cor'lera and taken Alex and Devlyn away to Gwilnor. He talked about his classes, and the varied things he had learned at the school, eventually trailing off when he noticed a troubled tone in his voice.

You're leaving something unspoken. Leilyn's tone was calm even though his thoughts were not.

"It's just that…I don't know." Devlyn had hoped that she wouldn't pick up on it because there was one last detail that he had intentionally left unsaid, not because he wanted to hide it from his sister, but because of how conflicted he was about it himself. "They want me to become an ei'ceuril. They say that Lucillia's prophecy, the one she spoke just before she gave birth and died, claims that if I don't give of myself completely, we're either doomed, or I die."

Shaking his head, Devlyn tried to think of a better way to explain it. What he had just said sounded too simple; the reality was much more complicated. Before he could figure out what more to add, Leilyn's thoughts filled his mind again.

Don't feel discouraged, and don't let it bother you so. Prophesying is a funny fluid thing. It doesn't dictate the actions of the future; it only speaks of what might come. There are some who believe that a prophecy is to be taken as a guide, intended to aid difficult decisions, especially when it deals with the actions of we anacordel. Devlyn tried to find peace with his sister's words but remained troubled.

Come, let's return to the miervae. Oreniel and Aaron are waiting for us. Leilyn hopped off the oversized root and led the way back. Aaron sat on the ground, legs crossed, a stricken expression on his face, while Oreniel stood near one of the miervae's roots.

"I apologize for my outburst," Aaron said, standing at their approach. He neither looked at nor acknowledged Devlyn, focusing intently on Leilyn instead. "I cannot say that I am not disturbed, but I am more at peace, at least for now."

A moment passed without words, and Devlyn knew that Leilyn spoke with Aaron. Hearing only half of the conversation was odd, yet the results of the exchange were evident as Aaron's face hardened in response, then softened when Leilyn embraced him in an extended hug. It was not the sort of hug people exchanged when they would see each other soon. This hug was a long one, and had a parting quality written all over it. Tears touched the corners of Aaron's eyes when they finally separated.

Unable to speak, Aaron walked away from Leilyn toward the edge of the clearing.

He will leave the Illumined Wood with you, Leilyn told Devlyn. *Teach him what you can of wielding. His path lies hidden from him.* Even in her evident distress, her communication was a soothing presence. *I do not know when, but we will meet again beneath these boughs before this war ends. Be at peace, brother.*

Realizing that Leilyn's words meant they too were parting now, Devlyn asked, "Can't we spend more time together? We've only just been reunited." He didn't want to leave his sister—not yet, not again.

Leilyn's smile was calm. *Learn to enter the Dream. You do not know it yet, but you are a Dreamer. There are those who can help you.*

Devlyn thought that his sister had lived in seclusion for too long since she sounded like Abbie Wintyr. She smiled again, aware of his thoughts. "Are you saying she's not crazy?" Devlyn recalled Abbie's agitated disposition before Ceurenyl was attacked.

The druids of Kweil Aitch are among the first to have ever entered Somnaeniel: the World-in-Between.

Devlyn was now completely lost. He had never heard of a somnaeniel before. A world between what? Leilyn spoke before he could ask another question, moving toward him for a hug.

Our time together has come to an end for now; you must leave and return to the world.

Devlyn embraced his sister. The care and love her hug conveyed made Devlyn want to cry. Leilyn released the hug, turned, and leapt high to land elegantly on a branch above and then another and was soon out of sight in the canopy above.

Turning to find Aaron, Devlyn was mildly surprised to find him right beside him and gave him a pat on the back.

"She's gone, isn't she?" asked Aaron, obviously attempting to mask his emotions.

"She is."

"Well, we'd better be on our way then. It's impossible to tell how close one is to the edge of the Illumined Wood." They turned to a patiently waiting Oreniel to say their goodbyes, Devlyn adding his thanks for the centaur taking him to meet Leilyn. Devlyn wondered whether he would see Oreniel again; it was difficult to say why, but he hoped he would.

Devlyn quieted his mind and opened himself to Aliel who appeared suddenly to hover just before Devlyn and Aaron for a moment before flying off. Once again, Devlyn marveled at Aliel's speed—how had Aliel known just when to appear? And how did he know which direction they needed to take? Devlyn assumed that the phoenix was leading them west.

DISAPPEARING

Broad rays of light touched the ground ahead through thinning trees. As Aaron and Devlyn neared the border of the forest, the near-solid overhead canopy of leaves now had patches of open space where bright light fell through, adding to Devlyn's growing sense of excitement. He half expected to find himself skipping past the last trees and onto the grassy plains beyond. Devlyn had looked forward to leaving ever since he had first stepped into the Illumined Wood, a feeling he was sure was not shared by his companion. Aaron had spent longer than he had originally planned in the forest, although it seemed that Aaron had done so quite willingly. For Devlyn, the time spent in the forest to complete his ei'ceuril novitiate had seemed very long, and even if he wasn't sure exactly how long it had been, he was quite sure that it was at least a year, since he was finally leaving the Illumined Wood, and Ceurtriarch Ealyndol had told him before he had left Ceurenyl that his novitiate would last an entire year. An entire year that could have been spent studying and learning the finer points of wielding, perfecting his ability. He worried that it might have been better if he hadn't come at all, especially since he now doubted his vocation with the ei'ceuril more than ever.

As Devlyn took that first step past the last tree and into the open area beyond—somewhat relieved that he didn't actually skip past—he had to shield his eyes from the sun. Not having been in its fullness during the time he'd been in the shaded depths of the dense forest, his eyes had become very sensitive to the piercing brightness. Aaron shared the difficulty, using both hands to shield his eyes which he held to mere slits as he waited beside Devlyn.

I should have never left Gwilnor. I could've studied with the ei'ana and ei'ceuril, Devlyn complained to Aliel, bouncing from one foot to the other as he waited for his eyes to adapt.

If you had not come to the Illumined Wood, you would not have learned to communicate with me. The miervae would have turned into a wraith, a verathel would not have been brought forth, and you would not have met one of the Children nor your sister. Aliel perched on a branch just above Devlyn, scanning the landscape.

What of Ceurenyl? What if it's fallen into Erynor's control? Shadow elves could be marching through the streets and hundreds of innocent people might be dead. Who knows how many are held in chains. Devlyn's excitement faded as his anxiety overcame him. He should have never left, despite the many wondrous things that had come to pass.

Aliel did not respond, choosing to convey comfort through their bond instead.

Finally, Devlyn's eyes adjusted and he was able to scan the area, hoping to get a sense of where they had come out of the Illumined Wood. Mountains lined the northern horizon and flat plains rolled west and south.

"Which way do we go?" Aaron asked, following Devlyn a few steps further into the sunlight to get a better grasp of the land. The obvious answer was west, but Ceurenyl would require weeks of walking to reach. Devlyn knew that a road eventually led to the temple city, but no one had ever told him where that road started.

"Psst." A hushed and worried voice called from behind them. Startled, Devlyn and Aaron turned toward the sound.

"Who's there?" Aaron demanded. "Show yourself!"

"Quiet! These Woods are watched. Now come quickly…" A shrill horn sounded, cutting off the squeaky voice, which then exclaimed exasperatedly, "Oh, now you've done it!"

The ground rumbled with the sound of galloping horses. A breath later, they came into view—Perrien grey coursers mounted by armed soldiers, at least twenty of them.

"I guess their allegiance is no longer a secret," Aaron commented as the soldiers galloped toward them.

"Was it ever doubted?" returned Devlyn, remembering his brief time in Perrien's capital city of Gneal. His mother's entire family had died in Gneal's dungeons, while her whereabouts were still unknown.

From the shrubbery at the edge of the forest a minum waved wildly, beckoning the two. "No time, hurry, come now!" just as a bolt of lightning, darker than death, shot to the ground, exploding it around them.

Ears ringing, Devlyn grabbed Aaron, relieved to see that they were unharmed beyond a few scratches from flying rocks and dirt. Devlyn could sense another bolt of the deadly wield forming, and quickly pressed himself into the erendinth, hoping to redirect the attack, but he couldn't influence the sinister tenebrys wield. Whoever was wielding it was incredibly powerful. Adjusting, Devlyn pressed into the ground beneath his feet, found a massive stone, and hurled it in the lightning's path. Rubble showered them as the stone exploded above.

"There's no time for that!" The minum waved his hands and a sphere appeared between his palms, showing a dark space beyond. "Through the seguian, hurry!"

Devlyn hesitated, torn between escape and doing something about the winged figure shrouded in Shadow that hung in the air. The figure resembled an elf but the colorless skin, dark grey wings, and complete lack of hair were like no elf Devlyn had ever seen. His eyes were emotionless amidst the foul shadow oozing from his body.

Aaron stood frozen before the malevolent apparition. Devlyn tightened his grasp on Aaron's arm, and plunged through the seguian taking Aaron with him into a small windowless room with stone walls and the musty scent of a cellar. The minum appeared next followed by Aliel and the seguian sealed right behind the phoenix. The light he gave off brought an unparalleled brightness to the small room.

They stood there in a breathless pause before the minum spoke, craning his neck up to look at the much taller prince.

"Well, this is most unexpected. You were thought to have abandoned the world for the Illumined Wood, Prince Aaron."

"I almost did, and might have, if not for the news of the world reaching my ears. But I would speak with the Ceurtriarch, to inform him of my return. Please, tell us where we are."

"My apologies, Ei'ceuril, but I cannot say, not even to you. No one may know where Devlyn is hidden; the entire city knows of Erynor's threat, and it is unsafe. I can open another seguian to bring you into the Temple of Ceur. But know this, once you leave here, you will not be returning." The minum bowed his head.

Aaron paused to consider the minim's words, nodded, turned to Devlyn and extended his hand. "I expect we will meet again. Until then, I will return to the temple, learn what I can, and hopefully, I will be permitted to continue my studies in wielding. The ei'ceuril and ei'ana will most likely be resistant, but they may yet yield, especially in our current predicament."

The minum opened another seguian, this one gleaming, the stone walls of the space beyond producing their own light. "That's as close to the Chamber of Light as I can get you. No one is to know that you came with Devlyn. As far as you, or anyone else is concerned, you two have never met."

Aaron nodded and passed through, the seguian closing immediately behind him.

"Has Ceurenyl fallen?" Devlyn's question embodied his great fear, and to his relief, the minum shook his head before responding.

"No, but we are certain that shadow elves and servants of Shadow are hidden throughout the entire city. The temple is secure; thankfully, malicious wielders cannot enter such a holy site. The instant they enter the Chamber of Light, their wickedness collapses them to the floor. But you cannot stay there—not yet. They have informants everywhere! Within moments of your arrival in the temple, they would know. And while shadow elves can't reach you, a knife-bearing servant of Shadow most certainly could. Certain precautions are needed before you return to the temple."

A sense of relief washed over Devlyn at the news that the city remained free of Erynor's grasp, but his worry was not entirely dispelled. Just how safe could it be if he had to hide? "May *I* know where we are?"

The minum tilted his head a bit, a look of intense thought creasing his forehead. "I suppose there's no harm in telling you. I was only told that no one was to know where you are hidden, or even that you are in Ceurenyl. It is unfortunate that the Lucillian prince knows. I doubt the Keeper would deem it worthwhile to correct that."

"What do you mean by correct?"

"Oh nothing. At any rate, we are in the western part of Ceurenyl, in the cellar of an inn. The *Broken Lantern* if you must know. They presumed that you might be with the phoenix, and feared that if you were above ground, the uncommon light emitted by the phoenix might give you away." The minum looked toward the bird of Light, a slightly awed expression revealing his amazement at being in the fabled being's presence, his beautiful light emanating around him.

Aliel perched on the back of a chair, his head nestled between his breast and wing.

"How long am I to remain in this tiny room?" Devlyn didn't like the idea of being restricted to a windowless cellar. If he had to stay here, perhaps being in the Illumined Wood was not such a terrible thing, despite it not being anywhere near where Devlyn felt he needed to be.

"Well, I can't say precisely, but you're perfectly free to stroll about the city if you feel the need for some fresh air and daylight. But do stay clear of the temple and Gwilnor. The closer you get to them, the more likely someone will recognize you. This isn't the most well-to-do neighborhood, but it's certainly the least likely place someone will recognize you. I, after all, thought it a preposterous place to bring you, but at least none of your acquaintances at Gwilnor are likely to encounter you here."

Relieved that he wasn't restricted to the tiny room, Devlyn looked down at his ei'ceuril robe. It had lost its initial white cleanliness after the year spent in the Wood, in spite of his regular attempts at washing it when possible.

"Oh, that will never do." The minum said as he looked at the once-white robe as well. "You'll find clothing that should fit you quite nicely in the wardrobe. Can't have you sticking out as an ei'ceuril novice! Now, I must be off. There's much to be done."

"Before you go, please, perhaps you can answer one more question?" There was one thing he desperately did want to know. "How long was I in the Illumined Wood?" He had already shared his question with Aliel, but the phoenix didn't seem to have a sense of time—it simply did not matter to him.

The minum paused with his hands partially raised to open another seguian and thought.

"Well, let's see. You went to the Illumined Wood just after Ceurenyl was attacked; last Vespenth, yes?" The minum didn't wait for Devlyn's response. "Just over a year; a year and a day, to be exact. It's the second of Vespenth 7887 of the third era, or 1209 of the fourth age, if you prefer."

Shocked, unable to conceive that a whole year had indeed passed, Devlyn could only wonder how that could be possible. He had expected it, but hearing it confirmed was still something of a shock. Aware of Devlyn's dismay, the minum softly added, "Time flows very differently in the Illumined Wood. It probably only felt like several months, if even that long, but in reality, an entire year and a day has come and gone. Now, I really must be off."

"Goodbye, and thank you," Devlyn managed to say before the seguian appeared and disappeared, taking the minum with it.

Taking a deep breath, Devlyn went to the wardrobe and found a pair of trousers and a simple linen tunic with a hood. As he removed the robe, he struggled with accepting that that much time had passed by. Not only had he missed his fourteenth birthday, but he was more than halfway to his fifteenth—now just five months away. When he had met Oreniel, he had been under the impression that his novitiate was only halfway completed.

The reality was impossible to comprehend. It felt as though he had slept an entire year without any awareness of its passing. Lost in his thoughts, it was only when a shiver ran over him that Devlyn realized that he was sitting on the edge of the bed in just his small clothes. Standing, he momentarily shook off his dismay with the relief of finally wearing trousers and pulled them on. While the robes were comfortable enough, he always felt odd not wearing the more familiar trousers. Robes had been the usual garb of both his time at Gwilnor and over the past year in the Illumined Wood. He pulled the tunic over his head, and immediately felt both warmer and more comfortable.

Devlyn retrieved his robe from the floor to fish out his overstuffed coin purse then emptied its contents onto the bed. The lucilliae's violet light competed with Aliel's brilliance in the room. The two lumols made the silver jents, copper lewts, and iron angots seem like cheap and unrefined currency. Devlyn returned the lumols and the lucilliae to the purse. On the nearby desk, next to a metal key, another coin purse lay, presumably left for him by whoever had organized his accommodations. Devlyn scooped up the remaining coins and put them into the new purse, startled to discover that it contained not just one, but three golden crowns! He tucked both purses into his trouser pockets, keeping his own in the left side pocket where he'd be less likely to mistakenly pull it out and reveal its special contents. The lucilliae's violet light would spill out for anyone to see. Or worse, ask questions.

Fully dressed, Devlyn was desperate to discover the state of Ceurenyl. While the minum's description of the city was soothing, it hadn't eased his anxiety entirely. Any number of awful events might have occurred over the past year and a day. He really wanted to check out the city. *I'm going to see for myself.*

Aliel understood and conveyed both reassurances and willingness to stay behind.

And to think, no curfew! In spite of his disquiet, Devlyn had to express a little excitement at not being required to return to Gwilnor castle by a specific time, something that didn't seem to register with the phoenix.

Devlyn opened the room's door and looked down a dark and narrow corridor with a stair at the far end. Light poured down the stairwell and sounds of laughter and the clanking of dishes indicated that the room above held many folk. Stepping fully out of the room, Devlyn closed and locked the door behind him, and took the stairs, noting that there were several stories above the cellar as he went up the first flight.

Dozens of people crammed the common room. He'd always known that Ceurenyl was a large city but he had never expected to see so many people crowded into a single inn. Pushing his way through and toward the exit, overheard conversations as he passed told him that many of the people at the inn were Sorenth refugees. They talked freely to their neighbors of things that had happened where they came from, leaving Devlyn shocked at how many people had felt the need to abandon their homes. How desperate had they been to risk going to a city which itself had failed to hold off an attack? *Was all Sorenthil being invaded?*

Giving the door a good push, Devlyn found himself shielding his eyes from the bright sun again. It felt like autumn and even in the middle of a city, the scent of dried leaves and plants filled the air. *It smelled like this when I left. I really have been gone for a whole year!*

The streets were just as crowded as the inn and Devlyn accidentally bumped into several people. In spite of the sameness of the smell of autumn, there was something different about the city. It had not been as crowded as it was now, and there had not been any Sorenth refugees a year ago.

It was difficult to hear one conversation over another, but he gathered that the people who crowded the streets around him were also refugees. All of Ceurenyl's inns were bursting at the seams and some people, Devlyn discovered, had to sleep in the stables with the horses.

Wandering aimlessly through the streets, but not venturing too much away from the western side of the city, he soon found himself near the city's bell tower in a large curved plaza framed by intricately carved stone buildings and the ruined city gate. Much of the stone was still charred from fire and the gate remained in a massive pile of rubble. Each ruined stone block was the size of a wagon. Devlyn's spirit sank as he imagined the force required to cause destruction of this magnitude. Even after a year, the ruined gate remained untouched—the rubble was piled halfway up the height of the surviving walls. A wooden ramp spanned the rubble, and a young family followed the crisscrossing construction over the ruins of the gate.

Fixated on the young family now carefully walking along the ramp to this side, Devlyn leapt in his skin as the bells began to toll, deep, sonorous tones echoing off the surrounding tall buildings. *Twelve. Won't be long 'til dusk*, he thought, counting off the bells. Turning away from the rubble to look up at the twining stone tower, Devlyn remembered how he had set the bells softly pinging that night long ago when he'd wielded aerys and flew through the sleeping city. Since, then, he had badly wanted to investigate the bells firsthand, but had never had the opportunity.

He circled the tower in search of an entrance and with his head tilted up to the soaring walls, he bumped into a man clothed in dirty rags resting against the side of the intricate structure. The man grasped a tin cup.

"Sorry, sir, I didn't see you there."

"Oh, not to worry, dear boy, I've suffered far worse." The man patted at his brown and grey rags then scratched his patchy beard. "Looking for a way inside, are you?"

"Well, yeah, but I don't see an entrance."

"That's because there isn't one."

"Well then, how do people reach the bells to ring them?"

"Wielding, of course. Not that anyone has to do anything to make them toll; one of the Lorenthien aryls of old shaped these bells, and not once have they failed to toll the hour since their making. No tuning or anything of the sort required with these beauties." The old man stood, setting something clanging in the tin cup. "These are Arenthylean Bells, said to symbolize the four types of elves. Four different materials were used in their crafting: gold, bronze, silver, and glass substances. No one remembers exactly what the materials are anymore, but I can tell you that the regal gold bells symbolize the Luminari. They ring the morning hours. The bold bronze bells symbolize the Cyndinari and toll loudest during the day. The proud silver ones represent the Aldinari and we hear them at dusk. And lastly, the glass Eldinari bells chime quietly at night. There are four bells that are purely of one material, while the others are melded. The bell for high noon, the sixth hour, is pure bronze, and the loudest of them all, while every bell after is mixed ever more with silver until the pure silver bell rings at dusk at the twelfth hour. And just so, the silver begins to mix with glass until we have a pure glass bell that tolls softly at the eighteenth hour, and then the glass mixes with gold before we have the pure gold bell announcing the new day in a wondrous melody at dawn, and the gold bells mix with bronze until we have the pure bronze bell again."

Impressed by the beggar's knowledge of the bells and their attributes, Devlyn thanked him and placed a coin in his tin cup. As his hand went out toward the cup, the beggar tipped it slightly toward Devlyn, giving him a glimpse of the other coin at the bottom. It was a lumol, just like the one he had found at the Cor Inn on his thirteenth birthday!

The beggar smiled, noticing Devlyn's surprise and recognition of the beautiful coin. "Ever will we be at your service, Ei'ethil," he said with a small smile.

Taken aback by the beggar addressing him as an elven lord, Devlyn took a few steps away before turning away and hurried back to the inn. Walking quickly, he put a hand into his left side pocket where his fingers brushed the coin purse with the lightweight lumols and violet jewel. Even if he wanted to check whether both his lumols were still in the purse, he didn't dare open it in public, not with the lucilliae and its violet light.

Devlyn's stomach growled as he walked back to the noisy inn, and he thought of the vaer. As happy as he was to have returned to Ceurenyl, he knew he would miss the tasty and filling purple fruit and wondered what the inn might have on their menu to appease his hunger. In the still crammed common room, no one paid him any mind as he stepped around the clusters of refugees. This late in the day when the sun had already set, no tables were available, but that was just as well, since Devlyn had no intention of eating in the common room. Far too many people.

An exhausted and irritated server, only a few years older than Devlyn, rushed between tables, carrying a tray with several bowls. Devlyn marveled at the server's ability to keep the bowls' contents from spilling over. It was impossible to smell what might be on the inn's menu—there were simply too many people to distinguish any scents from the kitchen.

Pushing his way through the crowded inn toward the beleaguered server, Devlyn grabbed his arm before he could rush away with the empty tray. The server glared, causing Devlyn to release the server's arm immediately, with an apologetic "sorry." Devlyn offered a smile as well, but the server's irate expression did not soften.

"What type of stew's on the menu?"

"It's stew, what more do you need to know? Go somewhere else if you don't want ours." The server looked toward another table eagerly awaiting his attention.

"Fine, I'll take a bowl." The server moved on and Devlyn wondered if he'd ever see the bowl of stew he'd ordered. The server swerved through the common room, eventually disappearing into the kitchen to return almost immediately with another trayful of bowls, delivering them here and there before finally returning to Devlyn with the last one on the tray.

"That'll be two lewts," he demanded, his hand firmly on the bowl of stew.

Devlyn wondered how untrustworthy he looked if the server insisted on payment before handing it over, tapping one foot impatiently as Devlyn fingered through the coin purse in his right pocket. The exchange concluded, the server disappeared into the crowd, and Devlyn carefully returned to his room in the cellar.

Aliel watched Devlyn eat the flavorless strew. It had little substance, pale vegetables floating unappealingly amidst some sort of grain in the opaque liquid. Devlyn was thankful that it had no meat, since he wasn't sure what he would have done about that. However, it certainly was not worth two lewts.

He decided that he would stay in his cellar room the following day, worried about leaving the safety of his hidden space, lest someone less kindly intended recognize him. He couldn't say for sure that the beggar had known exactly who he was, but he didn't dare take another chance so soon. Certain that someone who knew about his hideout would soon come to the inn and tell him what was going on, he remained where he was.

The next days went by with him eating his meals alone in the common room, rarely speaking to anyone. He occasionally left the inn to stretch his legs and breathe fresh air, air that grew colder with every passing day, but outings were rare once he noted the number of beggars on the streets in Ceurenyl, fearful that one of them might be more than a beggar and recognize him and then disclose his whereabouts in exchange for coin.

The only books in the cellar room were a few Holy Tomes, books revered by the ei'ceuril for their contents. Devlyn knew little about them. Cor'lera's abbey school possessed several volumes, but they were kept under lock and key, Abbot Entiel insisting that the books were too expensive for children to touch let alone read. Of course, Brother Bernard tended to forget to lock them up.

Bored by his seemingly unending stay and wishing someone had thought to provide other forms of entertainment, Devlyn flipped through some of the Theseryn's pages, opened the Fathoril only once, and left the Deneth Qir completely aside. He supposed he would have to start reading the Holy Tomes more regularly now that his novitiate had ended and he would soon begin his lessons at the Temple of Ceur.

Aliel remained perched peacefully on the chair he had claimed as his own that first day. Devlyn could not believe how much patience the phoenix had.

So, how much of these Holy Tomes do you think are real? Did these stories actually happen? Among other stories, the Theseryn told of Teraeniel's creation and the Great Blessing.

Aliel conveyed a sense of amusement.

It's not that funny.

A simple answer of yes or no will never satisfy your curiosity. The answers must be experienced.

And how am I expected to experience them when restricted to a small room with only these books to read? Devlyn asked, his irritation bubbling over at being stowed in the inn's cellar. He tossed the Theseryn on his bed, the pages undoubtedly wrinkling, and crossed the room to Aliel.

Devlyn wanted to touch his fingers to Aliel's feathers, and when he neared, he felt a small draft from the floor beneath the chair. Crouching low, he ran his fingers over a crack in the floorboards and felt cool air flowing weakly through. There also seemed to be a loose floorboard. Apologizing to Aliel, he moved the chair, and tugged on the loose board, shocked when several connected boards lifted to reveal a hidden tunnel beneath the inn.

New Passages

A narrow ladder attached to the bedrock allowed Devlyn to descend into the dark tunnel. Just as he prepared to wield a globe of light, Aliel flew down beside him. The phoenix's light flooded the small tunnel below and Devlyn thought to pull the trap door closed. No one from the inn had made a visit, but leaving the trap door open seemed unwise, so he climbed back up the ladder to shut it. When he stepped onto the rough stone floor of the hidden space again, Aliel's light showed a long and empty tunnel that reminded him of the tunnel connecting Gwilnor Academy to the Temple of Ceur, and he set off to explore, hoping that this one too ended at either Gwilnor or the temple. He grew a little discouraged as the tunnel seemed to go on forever. Finally, after he'd been walking for at least an hour, the tunnel walls widened.

Do you think we're close to wherever this ends up? Devlyn turned toward the phoenix hoping for an answer.

If I was not accompanying you, you would have already begun to see natural daylight spilling into the tunnel.

Are we really that close?

Close to what? Aliel pivoted his golden head.

The sudden change in Aliel's mental tone disturbed Devlyn. *Are we supposed to be going anywhere in particular?*

Instead of responding, Aliel flew ahead and disappeared. Following quickly, Devlyn entered a shallow cave with daylight coming from the cave's mouth to Devlyn's left. The cave's mouth couldn't be seen from the tunnel they'd come out of, and it was only because Devlyn had moved into the cave that he noticed it. If the two openings had been aligned, he probably would have felt a draft in his cellar room sooner and would have discovered the tunnel sooner too! Although perhaps not, since the tunnel was a very long one.

Pausing, Devlyn took a moment to listen carefully and look about. Servants of Shadow and shadow elves were known inhabitants of Ceurenyl now, and although there weren't any signs of habitation, this cave could very well be one of their hideouts.

Devlyn had been asked to stay hidden and thereby safe. He did not necessarily have to stay inside his room but strolling through a mysterious tunnel to a cave who-knew-where was likely pushing the limits of those instructions. For all Devlyn knew, this cave was outside of Ceurenyl's walls, and the little protection the city offered was now behind him.

While Devlyn could see the sunlight beyond the cave's mouth, little of it spilled into the cave itself. *There must be an overhang or boulder blocking the sun*, Devlyn conveyed to the phoenix. His connection with Aliel had made it difficult to judge the daylight from the tunnel, but now his eyes could see the different vibrancy beyond the cave's mouth.

Or it's facing north.

Then let's see where it goes. Aliel followed Devlyn out the cave's opening into a narrow valley between the mountains encompassing Ceurenyl, mountains towering far overhead, and a low rumble nearby told Devlyn that they were not too far from Ceurenyl. Aliel took flight to soar up high and fly along the mountain walls, his powerful wings beating to their full extent, a trail of golden light following him.

Looks like you're enjoying yourself. Aliel had not been able to fully stretch his wings for quite some time.

A cellar is no place for a phoenix.

Their transparent form of communication still baffled Devlyn. The meaning conveyed always surpassed what voiced words barely touched, and he was still getting used to it.

Just be careful, we don't want anyone to see you. Remember, we're not supposed to be here. Devlyn watched Aliel climb higher into the bright sunny sky, and then, unable to resist, he closed his eyes and reached for the phoenix's presence just outside his own consciousness. Easing in gently, Devlyn was, as always, overwhelmed by the experience. Aliel's essence was wholly other than his own; it washed over him, embodied him. He was part of the power and light that pulsed through the phoenix.

Now Devlyn saw as Aliel saw, light bursting from everything in sight. The mountains glowed with awesome, majestic splendor. Wanting to explore more of the hidden valley, they soared up, closer to the ridges for a better view from further into the sky.

From there, through Aliel's lighted vision, Devlyn saw himself standing just off from the cave opening they'd come through, and then he noticed a dark area in the rock—an opening to another cave—near to where he was standing. His curiosity piqued, he returned to his own body and walked the short distance to the new cave, relieved that he didn't have to scale any steep precipices. Once there, he peered into its dark recesses.

Wait for me—I don't want you going into any strange caves without me, conveyed Aliel, still enjoying the refreshing autumn sky.

Wielding a simple sphere of light would remove much of the cave's obscurity. But still, Devlyn waited for Aliel, taking the time to examine the cave's exterior location. Like the one they had come from, this one also faced north. Only during the height of summer would either cave receive a glint of a morning or evening sun ray.

Devlyn didn't have to wait long. Aliel soon flew past and into the darkened cave. Devlyn followed, and paused just beyond the entrance to look about. Aliel's additional light revealed a depression on the side wall. Not just an alcove, but another tunnel. Devlyn suspected that this one might lead to where he really wanted to be. Granted, he had thought that about the first one. Taking the tunnel, he again walked for what seemed to be about another hour. Looking at the rough stone walls, he thought of the smooth dwarven excavations that put these tunnels to shame. Devlyn imagined Oma poking her head through these tunnels, trying to discover what forgotten secrets these stones held. Odd how the old dwarf came to mind so readily. Devlyn hadn't seen her since he first came to Ceurenyl through a seguian from Everin.

Oma vanished from Devlyn's mind and his jaw dropped as he and Aliel stepped across an invisible portal and into an incredible apartment. Stunned, Devlyn turned to look behind him, and saw an extravagant, large mirror, with the fanciest molding he had ever seen on a mirror. Gazing about the room, he noted several doors lining the sitting room, one with large glass panes that let out onto a balcony. Luxurious furniture filled the room, treasures of a distant age were displayed on tables and shelves, and tapestries depicting ancient marvels hung on cloudy stone walls.

Devlyn blinked a few times, and then closed his mouth and straightened when he finally noticed someone in a white robe standing with his back to them, studying one of the tapestries. Devlyn's heart jolted as he realized that they must have trespassed into a private apartment in the Temple of Ceur. Whoever the man before them was, he was most likely an ei'ceuril and an important one, given the wealth of this apartment.

"This image depicts the Skyland of Luminare. Look how the light engulfs the entire landscape. Everything built or grown there was said to magnify the Light. The crystal streams sang with the anadel and the golden kryseniels unendingly blossomed. No other Skyland soared higher than Luminare. Not even Aldinare could compare with her exalted beauty. Our ancestors fled from that wondrous land as the encroaching Darkness spread," said a soft weak voice before Devlyn could apologize for their unannounced and unexpected entrance.

He knew that voice though. The old man turned to look at Devlyn, his eyes widening slightly when he saw Aliel. The phoenix flew past Devlyn to a golden perch near the balcony doors. *Why's there a perch in this room?* Devlyn thought.

"Ceurtriarch Ealyndol." Devlyn inclined his head to the wizened ei'ceuril, quite embarrassed at the circumstances of this meeting. Had they stumbled across a hidden entrance into the Ceurtriarch's private chambers?

"It is good to see you, my son. And this must be the phoenix I have heard so much about. What a magnificent creature." Ealyndol drew close to Aliel. "Have you noticed that the light he gives off is similar to the light in the Chamber of Light?"

"Yeah, I guess it is."

"I see you are not wearing your novice robes." While the Ceurtriarch said it without any note of censure, Devlyn still felt somewhat ashamed for not being appropriately dressed for his station, especially when addressing the Ceurtriarch.

"Forgive me, sir, it was to blend in." The old man's gentle smile at his response left Devlyn relieved by the Ceurtriarch's kindness.

"Not to worry, my son. The world has been interesting since you left us. I do hope you found illumination in the Wood." The last part of the Ceurtriarch's words held understanding, and he paused before going on. "There are matters that we must discuss. I would prefer to invite you to sit leisurely for a time, but unfortunately, that will have to wait."

Ealyndol's pause was much longer this time. He seemed to be waiting for something or someone. When Devlyn thought that perhaps he could talk about the things that had happened and the people he had met in the Illumined Wood during his novitiate, the Ceurtriarch seemed uninterested, just silently looking about, marveling at the space, as if seeing it for the first time. Devlyn just stood, still by the mirror to the tunnel, waiting for either someone to come in, or for Ealyndol to indicate what was going on.

"This apartment once belonged to another Phaedryn. That was long ago, mind you, but they were never altered after his death, partly because they've been uninhabited all these years. He was one of the few who chose to consecrate his life to Anaweh and live as both Phaedryn and ei'ceuril."

Ealyndol's mention of a Phaedryn being an ei'ceuril brought an odd reaction in Devlyn. It was more than confusion but doubt was not the right feeling either. Even as he opened his mouth to ask for details, Ealyndol quieted him yet again with a raised hand that seemed to say, "Patience."

A CONFERENCE

More minutes passed in silence while Devlyn tried not to shift from foot to foot wishing that he felt brave enough to take a seat before a knock came at one of the doors.

"Come in," Ealyndol said softly as the tapestry continued to hold his focus.

Doubting that whoever was beyond the door heard the aged Ceurtriarch, Devlyn turned to answer the door and was surprised when it opened, then closed just as quickly, bringing in two very welcome faces. Velaria's bright red hair and soft smile immediately caught his attention. Therril walked just behind her, his curious silver eyes highlighting his even more curious expression.

"Oh, is it good to see you again." Therril chuckled in his raspy manner as he pulled the younger elf into a hard hug. "I assume you've learned much and more while in the Illumined Wood. Hmm?" Therril hummed, then looked over at the phoenix resting on the ornate perch. Aliel looked back into Therril's eyes, and Devlyn felt that Therril's usual curious manner indicated that he once again knew more than he might tell.

"I guess I did learn something." Devlyn's thoughts were on Aliel.

You should introduce us. Aliel conveyed.

"Aliel, his name is Aliel. I learned it when we wielded lumenys together. At least, I think we wielded lumenys."

Exasperation passed between the other three at this news, then it seemed as if Therril was on the brink of congratulating Devlyn, but he stopped himself when he caught Velaria's concerned expression.

"Did something happen in the Illumined Wood that made it necessary for you to wield such an erendinth? I confess that I am surprised that you were able to," she said. "Arlyn, your uncle, is the only recorded person to have tapped that erendinth since the fall of Krysenthiel. And he's made it a point to not confide how he managed it.

Devlyn wanted to know more about his uncle, but had learned from experience that Velaria would not reveal more than she said, so he instead described the death of the miervae. "But the miervae's death wasn't what caused us to wield the erendinth, lumenys. After we purged the area of the sickness the miervae caused, there was a stirring in me, an urge, in both of us actually, something calling strongly, longing fiercely to be called from beneath the forest. Truthfully, I had no idea what we were doing, but something incredible happened. In the place where the miervae died, a translucent sprout shot from the ground."

"And a shoot of Verakryl shall rise to grace the land anew," Therril quoted, dazed. Velaria held one hand over her opened mouth, eyes darting from Therril to Ealyndol and back to Therril, almost as though she sought validation that it had been possible for Devlyn to achieve such a thing.

"Oreniel said the same thing. He's a centaur." Devlyn felt a need to assure the others that it had truly happened.

"My son. If there was any doubt before, there can be none going forth." Ealyndol was barely audible, and Devlyn strained to hear. "The prophecies have stated so. Events are in motion that might finally see old wrongs righted and life immortal returned once again to the elves, and, by extension, all anacordel."

"There are more prophecies? Do they never end?" Devlyn's face reddened when he realized that he'd unintentionally spoken out loud.

"Scribes and prophets have recorded our Holy Tomes since the second era. Theseryn covers prophecies revolving around Verakryl," Ealyndol nearly whispered.

"I believe we have stood long enough. Shall we continue our discussion in a more comfortable fashion?" Despite Velaria's phrasing as a question, it was not a suggestion.

"Of course, Mother Velaria," replied Ealyndol, choosing a straight-backed chair next to two sofas that faced one another. The others took seats on the sofas, and Aliel, who had not budged from the perch he had first settled on, tucked his head between his breast and wing and seemed to go to sleep.

"To start, I'm not comfortable with you wielding what you do not understand—what *we* do not understand. The result was remarkable, certainly, but it could have equally been catastrophic. And whether you truly wielded lumenys is another question. We'll speak of that later and I'll tell you what I've deduced from your uncle's experience." Velaria was clearly concerned. "Devlyn, we have agreed that it is in your best interests that Aliel remain a secret, for the time being at least. We know that there are shadow elves and servants of Shadow throughout the entire city. We fear that both are probably in Gwilnor as well, although we have no evidence to support that. And while shadow elves cannot enter the temple, they certainly have servants who can and who possibly have been here since before you were even born."

Ealyndol's expression saddened at the talk of servants of Shadow inside the temple walls. "It's true, my son. Not even the wise ones of both our orders should know about the phoenix. At least, not yet."

"We suspected that you might return with the phoenix once you achieved a more, well, we could say intimate relationship. Such being the case, we have taken precautions to prevent anyone else learning about the phoenix." Therril glanced toward Aliel.

"Why keep Aliel a secret?"

"Erynor knows that you two pose a threat, one that he likely views as more of a pinprick than a threat really." Therril returned his attention to Devlyn. "If he were to learn that your connection with the phoenix has progressed to such a degree that you now spend all your time together, he will devise a means of eliminating any further risk, before it can progress further."

"With the phoenix remaining a secret, you present less of a danger," Velaria finished.

"So Aliel is to remain tucked away somewhere whenever I walk around the temple or go into the city?"

Velaria, Therril, and Ealyndol exchanged glances. Clearly, they were keeping something from Devlyn.

"Well, to begin with, this apartment is where the two of you will stay. Once you begin your lessons with your fellow ei'ceuril novices, the news of your return will spread quickly throughout the city." Velaria spoke for all three. "Because of the uncertainty surrounding Ceurenyl, you must not leave the temple; it's far too dangerous. In fact, even leaving your quarters remains questionable."

Devlyn didn't like these restrictions. After spending just over a week hiding in a small room, he was now being confined to the temple, and even that might be limited to a single apartment. At least he had been able to walk through the city when he had been in that cellar room. Struggling with his new restrictions, he looked about the spacious apartment that now was his. The sitting room alone was large enough for Aliel to soar around without feeling overly constricted. And even the ceiling had orna-mentation beyond anything Devlyn was used to, with intricately carved vaulted beams above. This ornate room now belonged to him! Alex would be fuming once he found out. Still, that didn't change the fact that he was now restricted to the Temple of Ceur where wielding the erendinth was impossible. Devlyn did feel slightly relieved that the balcony offered access to the outdoors.

"How will I continue to practice wielding if I'm to remain locked up in the temple?"

"By going through the passage you followed into here and out to the valley. It is beyond the temple wards, and well hidden, so you can wield in secret. It's the principal reason for lodging you here and not in a typical novice's cell." Velaria glanced toward the tunnel's mirror entrance.

"It's pivotal that you master the ways of the Phaedryn; the path you must take lies within both of you, the phoenix and yourself." Ealyndol seemed uneasy, but continued, nonetheless. "It is of utmost importance that you learn the art of kien as well."

Devlyn accepted Ealyndol's words with difficulty. He had spent an entire year in the Illumined Wood and only a small part of that had been with the phoenix. Yes, they had learned to communicate and Devlyn had discovered Aliel's name, but they had yet to become a full Phaedryn, the kind that was spoken of in legends, where the two were one being, capable of power beyond reckoning, known to fly freely through the sky. Devlyn was not at all relieved.

"I don't mean to sound ungrateful, but I practiced wielding on my own for over a year, and I haven't noticed the slightest improvement. And Aliel and I still have much to learn before we become a full Phaedryn."

"He has a point." Therril rubbed his beardless chin. "And he's also fallen behind in his studies at Gwilnor."

"I wonder how beneficial it would be for the people in the city to see Devlyn and Aliel alive and well." Ealyndol seemed to study the floor. It was evident that the Ceurtriarch blamed himself for the city's destruction the previous year.

The three debated the idea while Devlyn tried not to chafe at how things were going. Velaria remained opposed to Devlyn revealing himself outside the safety of the temple, however, it was evident that she was the only one of that opinion. "Your safety is our utmost concern. Shadow elves walk our streets in disguise and any number of their servants with a concealed knife could be roaming the halls of the temple. Tenebrys isn't the only thing that can harm you."

"Perhaps we could devise a plan for Devlyn's safekeeping even while exposed to danger." Therril offered. That sounded promising.

"We can speak of it at a later time. I agree, he should not be restricted to his quarters or the temple, but at present, we have not the proper safeguards in place to keep him safe beyond its wards." Velaria spoke testily, showing signs of losing her composure. She looked to Therril and Ealyndol before proceeding. "Now, there are others not gathered here who also know of your return. There is Aaron of course, but two others in the temple know, as well as one person at Gwilnor." Velaria paused, then continued with a small smile. "Your cousin, Alexander, has been notified, and is quite eager to see you again. Also, Liam and Jaerol are aware. They have been training with the temple knights; both are capable of wielding, unsafely mind you, but under my instruction, we believe they, and a few others as well, can learn to control the erendinth properly."

"I was very much against it," said Ealyndol, "but that was before Aaron returned to us. He has indicated an interest in studying with the ei'ana so that he might continue to refine his wielding. If he manages it, he will be the first male of our order to safely wield in over fourteen hundred years, not including yourself, of course. Following the Seven Chairs' entrance test, he has since been welcomed by the ei'ana to take lessons at Gwilnor."

"His abilities are unrefined, and far less impressive than your own, but near the level achieved by many of our girls after wielding for only a year. He is past the stage where he can prove harmful to himself or others, thanks to your sister." Velaria smiled. "I'm delighted to learn of her well-being."

Therril sat quietly, observing Devlyn all the while. "If you wouldn't mind, since we have spoken about everything we needed to discuss, we would like to hear of your experiences in the Illumined Wood." Therril leaned forward, his interest clearly piqued.

Devlyn gladly described in detail all that he had come across, then spoke at greater length about Aliel's arrival, his meeting with the centaur and the tree nymphs, the death of the miervae, and the calling forth of the verathel. He spoke excitedly of meeting Leilyn and Aaron, and of his introduction to a Child through Leilyn. The others listened with great attention and interest, asking very few questions.

"There's one other thing." Devlyn paused and considered how he might speak of that other very important thing. "It's about the miervae. She claimed that she was attacked by Aren."

Everyone stared unblinking, not daring to be the first to speak, not quite disbelieving, but unsure how such a thing could even be possible. Velaria broke the silence. "Aren? *The* Aren Lorenthien? The elven lord who, with his wife, initiated the elven migration from the Skylands?"

"I also think it was he who attacked us right after we came out of the Illumined Wood. He had black wings and wielded some sort of black lighting at us, similar to when the shadow elves attacked, but much stronger."

"How can this be?" Ealyndol glanced at the tapestry depicting Luminare.

"As implausible as it sounds, I fear we cannot rule out this possibility. Undoubtedly the work of the Shadow, but I cannot say how. If what you say is true, he has power that Erynor himself would envy. A corrupted Phaedryn fighting for our enemy does not bode well." Therril looked at no one in particular.

They sat quietly for some time before Ealyndol rose from his straight-backed chair. "My attendance, or lack of, does not go unnoticed. I believe that unfriendly eyes follow my every move."

"Forgive me, but won't those unfriendly eyes grow suspicious about you coming to this room?" asked Devlyn, truly concerned.

The lines on the Ceurtriarch's face lightened, and his lips curved into a knowing smile. "There are still perks to being Ceurtriarch of the Temple of Ceur. Good day, my son." Then, he just faded away.

Devlyn gaped at the spot where Ealyndol had stood. Therril chuckled at Devlyn's shocked expression. "Crazy old bird! I wasn't aware that he'd discovered how to do that."

"Discover what? What just happened?" Devlyn looked back and forth between Velaria and Therril.

"The Ceurtriarch was never here. Well, he was, but he wasn't."

One of Velaria's eyebrows rose above the other as she too waited for an explanation.

"Past Ceurtriarchs, all capable of wielding mind you, had special privileges inside the temple. What Ealyndol just managed, appearing then vanishing, was considered a very minor accomplishment. Much and more impressive acts were performed by the Ceurtriarchs of old. After all, it was their knowledge about the Temple of Ceur that safeguarded this city during Erynor's previous reign." Therril's response managed to avoid answering the question asked while sparking more questions in return.

Still pondering the curious disappearance of the Ceurtriarch and what it indicated about his ability to wield inside the temple, Devlyn was distracted by bells sounding in the distance, signaling the ninth hour.

According to that beggar he'd met, these had to be an equal mixture of bronze and silver, or whatever material they were that resembled bronze and silver, for the ninth hour.

"I really must be going," Velaria said, standing at the sound of the bells. "While I don't believe I'm being followed yet, I doubt my own absence will remain unnoticed for much longer in the castle. I've rarely had any time to myself since I was raised to the Chair of Azurelle; nothing but meetings. And it's only gotten worse since Erynor attacked Ceurenyl last year." She moved over to the door, and Devlyn wondered if she too would one day learn how to disappear like the Ceurtriarch. Or was that ability restricted to the Ceurtriarch in the Temple of Ceur?

"So long, Velaria." Therril waved at her just as the door closed behind her, then looked at Devlyn. The two were still sitting across from each other on the sofas. "Now before I forget, there are some things you must know and adhere to while in the Temple of Ceur. Maintaining a low profile is pivotal. You're not being confined to these spacious rooms, at least not yet, but it's for the best that you eat your meals here, they'll be delivered of course, and spend most of your leisure time here as well. Also, no one is to know that Aliel is here with you. Meaning, that no one should find themselves visiting you here in your apartment—far too risky. Also, since you have returned to the temple, you are to don the ei'ceuril robes again. You are still a novice with us."

"I thought I had finished my novitiate."

"While the ei'ana novitiate consists of a single year in the Illumined Wood, the ei'ceuril novitiate includes one year or more in the Illumined Wood, and an additional year in the temple under our supervision."

Devlyn expected to hear more instructions about all sorts of other things, and was surprised to see Therril stand. "Go on now, get your robes on. Didn't I say you can't leave these apartments without them?"

"You didn't mention we were going anywhere."

"Huh, huh, huh. I suppose I didn't." Therril trailed off into his own thoughts. Devlyn left him to it and looked around the room for a door that might lead to the bedchamber. He opened nearly all of them before finding the right one.

In the surprisingly large bedchamber, two simple white robes hung from a hook in the wardrobe. They looked exactly the same as the one he had left in the cellar beneath the inn, although much cleaner. Hanging beside the ei'ceuril robes were four very different garments, made of a lighter fabric that he thought might be silk, and with ornate scrollwork in the weave of the fabric. Ignoring the ornate outfits, he removed his tunic and trousers and donned one of the ei'ceuril robes. Instantly, he began scratching various parts of his body. It had not taken him long to become accustomed to wearing normal clothing again, and he had forgotten about the itchiness of the robes. With a longing look toward the finely made garments, Devlyn closed the wardrobe door. Surely, those other silken garments would not be itchy. Maybe he could slip them on when he was here alone.

Devlyn emptied the trouser pockets. Despite the discomfort of the itchy white robes, there was one thing he did like about them. Stitched on the robes' interior side was a secret pocket, accessed by a slit on the left side of his chest. He had grown fond of that pocket during his time in the Illumined Wood. Because of that pocket, he never had a reason to worry over accidentally losing the two lumols and the lucilliae, and he happily put both coin purses into it.

Devlyn returned to the large sitting room and noted that Therril looked gleeful. Without explaining what had made him so happy, Therril led the way to the door and left the apartment.

He's probably having a chuckle about how itchy this thing is, Devlyn thought, following Therril through the door and was startled to find himself in a small bedchamber. Turning around, Devlyn was amazed to find not the door he had just closed, but himself reflected in a large slender mirror. Therril's gleeful expression had changed to a mischievous grin.

"You didn't think we would place you in a room where just anyone could find you, did you? The Phaedryn who last lived in that apartment cared little for visitors; he said they distracted him from his meditations. Said he would have remained in Arenthyl if he had known that he was going to be bothered as much! So, rather than make a sign requesting privacy, he converted the entry vestibule into a novice cell, making everyone think he was going to retire to his humble chamber. Now pull up your hood before we go into the corridor." Devlyn pulled the robe's large hood over his head and followed Therril out.

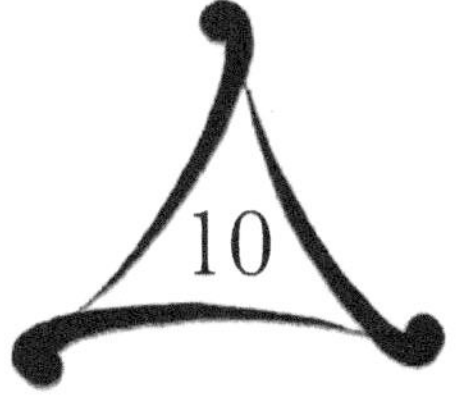

POSTURES

Devlyn's legs cramped from their crossed position—the proper manner for meditation in which the left rested over the right. Therril had made it seem like it didn't matter but Steward Lacus had a contrary opinion and had spent half an hour lecturing on the finer points of meditation posture. A full ten minutes had been devoted to which leg crossed the other. *Left over right.* Devlyn thought the lecture arbitrary, especially since his schedule listed this exercise as a silent meditation in the novice chapel—a simple, yet still elaborate space just off the Chamber of Light, one of the smaller chapels surrounding the voluminous chamber. All the smaller chapels had the same cloudy white, semi-opaque walls and columns that gave off a light of their own, but no more than fifty people would pray in this chapel, while some of the larger chapels held four hundred comfortably.

Twenty-three other novices sat in neat orderly rows of six, all with their left leg over their right. Devlyn had only just joined this novice class and had been startled by the number of novices enrolled with the order of Ei'ceuril, wondering how many could wield kien if given the opportunity. As far as he knew, only he and Aaron had permission to leave the temple to practice wielding kien. Most boys came to the temple the moment their capacity to wield had been discovered. Some of them came to the temple to devote their life to Anaweh, the Creating Light, others choosing to remain as lay votaries, a position created for kien wielders or anyone else who lived in the holy temple and did not become an ei'ceuril. The order of Ei'ceuril had decided long ago that simple laymen could not take up residence in the Temple of Ceur—everyone had to belong to a station worshipping Anaweh.

While there were currently twenty-four novices, at least double that number of kien wielders—or more—had come to the temple in the same year and had *chosen* the life as a lay votary. The lower levels of the temple overflowed with kien wielders forced to live their lives as lay votaries. They took no vows, and no one considered their lifestyle a pious one, but they did live comfortably with all their needs met, so that they had no reason to rebel against their confinement to the temple. After all, they outnumbered the ei'ceuril three to one. Fortunately, the temple knights were counted among the number of lay votaries, taking up residence in the levels that separated the ei'ceuril and the non-ei'ceuril residing in the lower levels.

Devlyn still had not had any reason to travel to those lower recesses of the temple. The closest he ever came was to Therril's office and the window that was not a window. Therril made certain that Devlyn stayed clear of that particular room, not wanting to tempt Devlyn into sneaking off to Gwilnor. At least not sneaking away yet. *Who else knew about that secret passage?*

Shouldn't you be meditating? inquired Aliel, comfortably ensconced in Devlyn's quarters. For Devlyn to maintain a low profile, Aliel definitely could not accompany him through the temple corridors. Fortunately, Devlyn had spent little time in the temple before Erynor's attack last year, which meant few people knew what the Phaedryn from Cor'lera looked like. Still, his simple white and scratchy hood rested on his head, concealing much of his face along with his unique golden-brown hair with strands of red, blond, and black.

You didn't have to listen to Lacus lecture about posture. Devlyn absentmindedly straightened, the movement causing an itch on his lower back that he reached around to scratch.

"Novices will maintain their posture at all times." Lacus hummed. "If you cannot overcome the temptations of an itchy robe, you will never succeed in overcoming the temptations of this world."

They purposefully make these things itchy! Devlyn glared at Lacus from the safety of his drawn hood, imagining he could see through the fabric.

That's not why they're itchy, chimed Aliel.

The white fabric of his hood hung only a handspan away from his eyes, blocking out most of his surroundings. *I can't believe these are crafted to be itchy*, thought Devlyn, knowing that Aliel heard it. Taking in a deep breath through his nose, Devlyn held it for a moment in his lungs, then audibly exhaled. He repeated it and felt his mind sway. *Not like a leaf on the wind*, he told himself.

Again, his breathing calmed his mind, his concerns loosened as forgetfulness washed over him, not willful negligence nor ignorance, but a soothing lapse as he floated in a timeless void. Devlyn continued the steady and intentional breathing exercise and found that the posture really did help.

A drawn-out bell finally tolled, the sonorous sound diminished by the shuffling of twenty-four novices standing to stretch. "Novices will maintain the proper decorum of silence in the temple." Devlyn's peaceful state of mind vanished with Lacus' voice.

"We're not allowed out of the temple," whispered the novice who had been sitting next to Devlyn. "When are we expected to not be in *decorum*? They won't even let us relax in the novice wing when nothing is scheduled."

Devlyn didn't know why, but there was something very likeable about this novice. Both of them had their oversized hoods covering their eyes and Devlyn lifted his to get a better look at the other novice. "Are they really that strict?" he asked.

"Lacus is the worst of the bunch and the most dedicated to our supervision. I'm Taen."

"Pleased to meet you." No one was to know Devlyn's identity; he was just another novice.

Taen lifted his own hood, his eyes widening in recognition. "No one announced your return…" Taen trailed off as another student slapped Taen on the back, drawing Lacus' glare.

On second glance though, Devlyn recognized Taen. Kevn had spoken with him briefly when he had given Devlyn a tour of the temple, long before the attack on Ceurenyl. Devlyn let his hood fall back over his eyes; he hoped that only Taen had recognized him.

"Who's your friend, Taen?" asked the grinning newcomer.

"Um, no one, Brother Kaeyth."

Devlyn's heartbeat quickened. He had never met this other novice, but he quickly understood that no one would ever consider subtlety and quiet as two of Kaeyth's attributes.

"Dear brother, why so formal?" Kaeyth smiled mischievously then glanced over his shoulder to a disapproving Lacus. "Don't pay him any mind. What are they going to do? Kick us out and force us to live a lowly life as lay votaries? You wouldn't believe the rumors I've heard about them. I have half a mind to move down there today!"

"And that's exactly where you'll end up if you continue spreading vulgarity," said Lacus.

"Let's get moving. I know of a little-used chapel to umm…pray in." Kaeyth tried to sound reverent, but clearly, he was done praying for the day. "Thank you, Steward Lacus, for your brilliant observations. I'll continue to practice my posture in my spare time."

Lacus' disposition brightened. "I'm here to serve you novices and be as influential as possible. The Ceurtriarch doesn't trust just any ei'ceuril in this pivotal role."

Once outside the novice chapel, Kaeyth led the way through the Chamber of Light and up the ornate stair hall. The novice quarters were in the opposite direction—down, not up. Still, Devlyn followed Taen and Kaeyth upward, leaving the stair hall at the landing just below the topmost one. Kaeyth continued to lead the way, this time down a narrow empty corridor, stopping at an unadorned door, grinning broadly. He pushed the door open to reveal a storage room.

"This is your chapel?" Devlyn's eyebrow rose at the cluttered space.

"We did organize it a bit and made a space for quiet prayer in the corner over there," offered Taen.

"You only put a prayer pillow there so you wouldn't feel guilty about lying to that prat, Lacus. Did you hear all that nonsense about ol' Ealyndol himself appointing him as a novice advisor? Not the director, mind you, an *advisor*! Trying to make us believe that Ealyndol personally delivered his appointment. I bet he hasn't even met the Ceurtriarch. Thinks he's Anaweh's gift to the temple, that one does."

Devlyn snorted; he'd never heard anyone speak about an ei'ceuril like that before, let alone another ei'ceuril.

"Well?"

"Well, what?" asked Devlyn. Had he offended Kaeyth by snorting?

"Don't 'well what' me. What's your name? I know Taen well enough to know when he wants to keep a secret. Not from me of course, he's a terrible liar, but from the other novices. Prefers to omit saying something rather than outright lie."

"You're just the worst." Taen stifled a laugh. "Kaeyth might be brash—and that's quite the understatement—but he won't mention who you are if you don't want anyone knowing. I still don't understand that bit."

Devlyn turned from Taen to Kaeyth and pushed his hood back. "I'm Devlyn."

Kaeyth's eyebrow rose questioningly. He clearly didn't recognize Devlyn and the name meant nothing to him. "So, Devlyn, what's with all the secrecy? Don't want anyone learning that you're not a holy novice like the rest of the lot?"

"Well, it was kind of a rushed decision. I didn't exactly dream about becoming an ei'ceuril as a child."

"Join the club. I think Taen here is the only exception. We aren't given much of an option when we're carted off to the temple; fortunately, they allowed me to remain conscious during the trip. I mentioned some rubbish about desiring to serve Anaweh since I was six years old. But honestly, if those ei'ana intended on locking me up in the temple the rest of my life, I wanted to at least see as much of the world as possible before, and that meant staying awake as we traveled from Lucillia to Ceurenyl!" Kaeyth had taken a seat on a crate turned chair, and stretched his legs out before him, quite relaxed as he spoke. "That's when Taen and I met. We grew up in the same city, but not once did Taen leave the confines of his lordly father's house to see the rest of Lucillia."

"I left my family's house plenty, just never went to the merchant quarter," Taen rubbed his eyes, clearly getting worked up by Kaeyth's remarks. "You really don't know who this is, do you? I told you about him. Remember? The kien wielder studying at Gwilnor because he's a Phaedryn."

"Well, why didn't you just say so?" The news didn't seem to bother Kaeyth at all. "So, I take it they decided you were too dangerous and ended up tossing you into the temple anyway?"

"Not exactly." Devlyn wondered whether he should introduce Aliel to his new friends, but Velaria's stern warnings won. "There's a prophecy that gave me little choice in the matter."

"You always have a choice. I could spend the rest of my days as a lay votary if I wanted, but I chose to become an ei'ceuril, even if that means putting up with that pretentious Lacus. Anaweh calls us all, although our response stinks worse than horse dung if it's not authentic," said Kaeyth.

"That was almost poetic," Taen commented.

"I'm well read, thank you very much. Have to do something while locked in this temple. Now, if I was truly smart, I would have stayed longer in the Illumined Wood! What a treat that was!" Kaeyth replied then looked pointedly at Devlyn. "You still haven't answered my question about the secrecy."

"I'm not sure how much I'm allowed to say."

"Well, say as much as you can, and Taen and I will let you know if you said too much."

Devlyn and Taen both laughed at the ridiculous proposal. "I don't think you understand what a secret means," Devlyn managed between laughs.

"Oh, I understand perfectly, but that doesn't mean I think keeping secrets applies to me. This place would run much smoother if everyone just told me all their deepest and darkest secrets. Light knows this place is brimming over with them!"

Still laughing, Devlyn decided that he liked Taen and Kaeyth. What harm was there in telling two people?

Those two people telling another two people. Aliel swam in his mind. *But, these two seem trustworthy. Besides, we can't hide forever.*

Devlyn grinned.

"What's so funny?" asked Taen.

"I'll tell you later."

"Great, more secrets!" exhaled Kaeyth.

"Well, I can tell you that Ealyndol, Velaria, and Therril don't want anyone to know that I've returned to Ceurenyl. Something about it not being entirely secure."

"Hold on, you met with the Ceurtriarch and the Chair of Azurelle? And you're on a first name basis with them?" Taen sat on the edge of his crate. "You actually spoke with Ceurtriarch Ealyndol? In person? Face to face?"

"Don't all novices speak to him when joining the order?" asked Devlyn.

"This isn't Gwilnor, Devlyn, the Ceurtriarch doesn't have time to meet with and admit those interested in becoming ei'ceuril. Only archstewards have personal meetings with the Ceurtriarch. Wise ones are sometimes invited to those meetings, but it's understood that that's an esteemed honor and privilege, and they're only invited so the Ceurtriarch can gauge whether or not they're worthy to become an archsteward one day." Taen had leapt from the crate he'd been using as a seat and brushed his hands through his hair. "They must have big plans for you if you're already meeting the Ceurtriarch."

"Taen here fashions himself as a candidate for archsteward."

"Don't be ridiculous, Kaeyth." Taen blushed. "But Devlyn has already met with Ceurtriarch Ealyndol Roendryn, Arbiter of the Light!"

"Yeah, he's already said that. Now, sit down, you're making me nervous, bobbing up and down like that."

Taen sat, but it looked like he was in the Chamber of Light, about to float off his crate and bump his head on the ceiling.

"Better?" Kaeyth held Taen in his eyes, as if that would keep the excitable novice seated. "Go back to the bit about the temple not being safe. What haven't the higher ups said? I've always said there was something off-kilter about this place."

"There's no proof, but there might be servants of Shadow in the temple. There'd be no way to tell them apart from anyone else, it's not like they're shadow elves, they're just normal-looking people who might have a dagger concealed in the folds of their robe."

"You mean a dagger like this?" Kaeyth flashed a shiny piece of metal, twirling it between his fingers. Devlyn hadn't noticed Kaeyth retrieve the dagger. Where had he hidden it?

Shocked, Taen fell back, toppling to the floor, his robes twisted around his legs as he kicked at his robe and tried to stand.

"Calm down, Taen." The dagger disappeared as fast as it had appeared. "I've told you how I feel about this temple."

"An ei'ceuril would never harm another anacordel!" Taen insisted, still struggling to get to his feet.

"What if they're not really an ei'ceuril? What if they're just disguised as one? Not to mention the temple servants and all the lay votaries in the lower levels—you know the latter don't hold the ei'ceuril or temple knights in high esteem. Servant of Shadow or not, I'll not be having anyone sneak up on me without a dagger to defend myself."

Devlyn stared bewilderedly. Perhaps he'd been unwise to trust Kaeyth after all.

Can't imagine a better person to watch your back. Nowhere near as proficient as I am, but he'll do if I'm to stay cooped up in your chambers, Aliel conveyed.

Bells chimed in the distance. Was that six?

"About time, I'm starving!" Kaeyth stood and walked out the door. "What tome are they reading from for lunch today, Taen?" Kaeyth asked over his shoulder. Taen finally scrambled to his feet, patted his robes down and glared. "Oh, don't be moody, Taen. If anything, you won't have to worry about any spooky servants of Shadow stabbing you in the back while around me."

"Fine, but don't let Lacus find out what you're concealing." Taen scratched his arm, joining Kaeyth in the corridor. "I think the reading is from the Deneth Qir. At least, that's where we left off this morning."

"Still? I thought we were finished with that one." Kaeyth groaned.

Devlyn hesitated, still in the storage room. Velaria wanted him to eat his meals in his quarters. How was he supposed to sneak off from these two and retire to his apartment? The entire novice class was supposed to eat together. Wouldn't the other novices think it suspicious that one of their classmates didn't eat his meals with them?

"Don't tell me you're skipping lunch? It's one of the few things we have to look forward to here." Kaeyth waited impatiently in the corridor.

"I'm supposed to keep a low profile."

"So, put your hood up and act like one of those annoying holy novices. Light knows they pretend at it!" Kaeyth and Taen started down the corridor.

Devlyn followed them to the novice's refectory, his hood pulled low over his face. He could only see the floor, and the lower part of Taen's robe and feet just ahead of him. He followed the others to a long wooden table on one side of the room, sitting between them. Another table mirrored this one on the opposite side, and a shorter table joined the two long tables at the head of the room, so that the three tables resembled a horseshoe, with everyone facing inward. Lacus sat at the head table with two other ei'ceuril, just to one side of the central seat. Steward Dorien, Devlyn's animys tutor, sat proudly in the center. Devlyn had never enjoyed the sessions with Dorien and was happy they hadn't resumed yet; Dorien was one of those who still didn't know Devlyn had returned. Dorien was a wise one though, one of the youngest in the temple, and he enjoyed a station well above Lacus.

"Who desires to read from the Holy Tome of Aboronian?" Dorien asked without much interest. Kaeyth hmphed under his breath, as if to draw attention to being right about the morning's reading having finished the Deneth Qir.

"Rather than wait for one of the novices to volunteer each time, I've arranged a schedule," Lacus announced. "Iren will read today. But we still have two more chapters from the Deneth Qir."

Taen now hmphed under his breath.

"Were you asked to make a schedule?" asked an annoyed Dorien.

"The novices benefit from our demonstration of orderly ways."

"Save it, Lacus," said the much older ei'ceuril on the other side of Dorien. Kaeyth snorted loudly, then pulled his hood up and over to hide his expression.

"Who snorted?" Lacus demanded, his chair scraping the stone floor as he stood. "I expect the guilty novice to reveal himself and his shameful conduct, and repent!"

"And I expect us to eat!" snarled the older ei'ceuril. "Iren, will you please start reading from the Aboronian?"

Amidst muffled laughter, Iren went to the podium in the middle of the room and switched the tome opened there with another on the podium's shelf. The laughter quieted only when servants carrying bowls of soup came in, waiting on the ei'ceuril at the head table first. Iren cleared his throat and began. "Leirol, son of Jouol, exclaimed to the wilderness…"

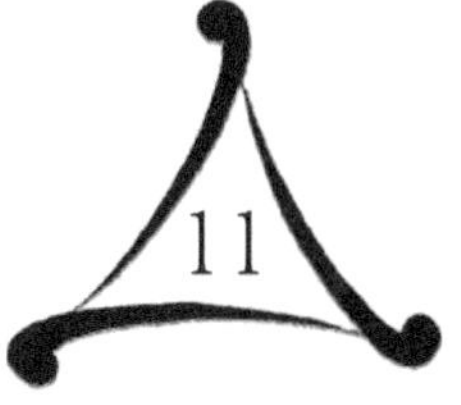

KIEN

The warmth of Devlyn's temple apartment flashed through his mind, as he stood in the valley with his cold feet covered in snow. He had watched the peaks of the mountains grow whiter over the past month as Estlenth ended and Orenth began. The powdery snow had eventually spread lower and lower until it had blanketed all Ceurenyl and the surrounding area. Of course, Devlyn was not permitted to explore the snow-covered city. Instead, he had to look out one of the temple's oversized windows to glimpse the city's slate roofs and see them disappear under the snow. The temple was too far away for him to see the people crowding the streets. Maybe it was for the best, given that hundreds, perhaps thousands, of refugees had to huddle together for warmth, reduced to living on the streets with Ceurenyl's inns filled to capacity.

Was anything being done to help house them? Devlyn felt a pang of annoyance. Gwilnor Academy had loads of empty rooms with empty beds. It's not like anyone was traveling to Ceurenyl for an education now. His cold feet served as a harsh reminder. However, unlike those left vulnerable in the city, his feet would warm by the fireplace in his apartment, where he would also enjoy a hot meal and a hotter beverage.

Those comforts would have to wait though. Instead of toasting next to a roaring fire, he had to deal with the fast approaching globe of fire about to strike him square in the chest. He pressed into ignys to overpower the other wielder and caused the fireball to explode. He welcomed the added warmth, the heat of the blast penetrating through his layers of clothing to warm his skin, but it had the unfortunate result of melting the snow covering his feet, which were now cold *and* wet.

He couldn't rejoice in his escape from a near-burn because another fireball was coming from behind. The wield for this latest attack was not as powerful as the previous one, but it was much more intricate, requiring Devlyn to spend precious moments trying to discover how to unravel the intricacies invisible to the naked eye before pressing himself further into it to defuse it.

The heat intensified as the fireball drew closer. *Almost there*, he thought with an exasperated breath, ignoring the bead of sweat that fell from his brow. Overcome by panic, he realized that the burst of fire was too close for him to deal with it by wielding. Instead of pressing further into the fiery wield, he dodged the blast and fell safely into the deeply piled snow surrounding him just as the fire exploded where he had been standing moments before.

"Strength in the erendinth will not guarantee survival, Devlyn," Velaria called from across the valley.

"That one was too finely wielded; there was no other way. How was I supposed to unravel that?" Devlyn responded through gasps, half buried in the snow that hadn't melted from the blast.

"Will you ask the same of a shadow elf?" asked Liam, making the others practicing with Devlyn in the valley laugh, but having the opposite effect on Devlyn as he cursed under his breath.

Velaria had kept her word and now Devlyn and Aaron were not the only kien wielders in the Temple of Ceur capable of controlling the erendinth. Liam and Jaerol readily agreed to participate in Velaria's practice sessions in the valley. The lessons were still too controversial to open the invitation to the entire temple, so she had started instructing men that she knew and trusted. Granted, Jaerol already had some training wielding kien, but controlling his wielding had never been a concern for him or the Erynien Empire, so he too needed direction on mastering the finer points of wielding.

The five of them had begun practicing in the valley shortly after Devlyn's return to the temple. Practicing daily had proven difficult, especially since they strived to maintain a sense of secrecy. The only way that Devlyn knew how to reach the valley from the temple was through his room. Luckily, no one had asked any questions about Devlyn's frequent visitors, probably because his apartment was in a little-used part of the temple. Still, Velaria insisted on irregular meetings.

She had designed the small gathering to have all of them press simultaneous or near-simultaneous attacks on Devlyn. Cold, and getting tired, he resignedly pushed himself to his feet, quieted his mind, and once again pressed himself partially into each of the different elemental erendinth, sensing the four elements around him. Holding his breath, he awaited the first attack. A lash of air, a strong gale, swirled through the valley, Aaron's style written all over the wield. Aaron had grown strong in aerys and more refined in his wielding since returning to Ceurenyl. Thanks to his time in the Illumined Wood, time spent learning and perfecting his control under Leilyn's tutelage, he was the first male ei'ceuril to be able to control his wielding after the fall of Krysenthiel. Since returning to Ceurenyl, he had focused on learning as much as he could from the ei'ana at Gwilnor and it showed during the practice sessions directed by Velaria.

Devlyn could easily overpower Aaron's wielding, but he had to remain focused on the others present as well, since they were waiting for the opportune moment to attack him. If he concentrated on overpowering Aaron, the others would have a golden opportunity to gang up on him.

Playing it safe, Devlyn entered a little more into aerys to form a slightly stronger gust of his own, redirecting Aaron's wield from himself just as he became aware of a splash of water swirling beneath his feet. Liam had recently passed the tests for control and had leave to wield, but with great caution. Since he was still new to it, he had to be careful to not press himself too far into the erendinth.

Devlyn, a more capable wielder, pressed into terys and hardened the ground beneath his feet with a mild sense of satisfaction. Terys always amazed him; the sheer enormity and strength of it was incredible, its entirety interconnected in some larger design. What could the dwarves teach of terys, those few among their kind who were outright wielders?

Before he could wield a counter against his brother, Velaria called for a pause. Perplexed, since the practice seemed to be going quite well, he withdrew from terys and the erendinth and instantly felt their absence.

"That was a fine warm up. But Devlyn, we do not need you to be a *mere* wielder." Velaria raised her voice so that everyone could hear. "You are a Phaedryn, and as a Phaedryn you must wield. Henceforth, you shall conduct all our exercises while bound to Aliel."

Liam and Aaron instantly groaned, not keen to wield against Devlyn while he was bound to the phoenix. Since Devlyn stood at the center of a broad circle formed by the other wielders, Liam and Aaron easily heard Velaria, but Jaerol stood furthest from her with Devlyn between them.

"What was that?" called Jaerol and Liam repeated Velaria's instruction to Devlyn.

"We won't have a chance," argued Aaron.

"That's not the purpose of these sessions, and you know it," Jaerol replied, disagreeing with the ei'ceuril.

"He's right, we're not practicing for the Erendinth Games here. Those games are for students, not for fighting shadow elves." said Velaria.

A smirk rose on Devlyn's face as he sought Aliel and welcomed the phoenix's warm presence and the whimsical tune that washed over his being.

It's about time we stopped wasting time. Aliel was delighted. *We would have reversed that wield from Velaria in no time had we been bound sooner.*

Devlyn found it amusing how competitive Aliel had grown during their practice sessions, always wishing for Devlyn to grow stronger in his wielding and to advance as a Phaedryn. *Shall we stick to the elementals?* It would be an unfair advantage if they surprised the others with an attack using a transcendental erendinth, which besides themselves, only Velaria was capable of wielding.

Aliel soared above the valley with Devlyn below, awaiting the first attack, once again pressed into the erendinth. With their bonding, Devlyn had no blind areas. He would discern the others' attempts before they could fully press into the erendinth and form a wield of their own.

The valley emptied of light, and a shadowy form pelted toward Devlyn. Several of the same forms swirled about him, none of them clearly discernible. Devlyn's confidence was momentarily shaken since he hadn't expected any of them to wield umbrys, and he was unsure about how to counter it. He knew that lumenys had an advantage over it, but Devlyn had never managed to wield lumenys through his ability alone, if at all. So, following his instincts and with Aliel's guidance, Devlyn pressed fully into animys, unsure about how it would act against the shadowy erendinth.

Every erendinth was invisible to the naked eye, but animys did not have a physical embodiment as did the elemental erendinth, nor did it hold the visible presence produced by shadow and light. Yet, while connected to Aliel, Devlyn could see a purplish presence around himself, a presence that grew larger and denser even as he crafted his wield.

Feeling the shadow closing in, Devlyn wielded spirit toward the first approaching form. Although he had never tried using animys as a weapon against umbrys, when Velaria's shadowy wield struck his spiritual nets, it thinned and completely dissolved.

That's a neat trick. Did you know it would do that? Devlyn asked Aliel.

You're the first person I've ever wielded with. I was inside an egg for millennia, remember? How much do you think I know?

The two shared a quick mental chuckle as they continued to wield animys against Velaria's attack. However, Velaria refused to give up quickly, and through the phoenix's eyes, Devlyn saw that she too was wielding spirit amidst shadow, intertwining the two. He caught a quick glimpse of her confident smile as she swirled her curious stick through the air.

Pressing further into animys, Devlyn wielded it against the transfused erendinth, and managed to prevent Velaria's attack from drawing too close, but he couldn't dissolve it as he had done with the other attack.

Changing tactics, Devlyn formed a shield of animys around himself and Aliel, now hovering just above his shoulder. It wasn't a permanent solution, but it did give him time to devise a counter-attack. Through the shield, he could feel the various forms of shadow and spirit, and he realized that the others were also wielding. There was fire roaring from Jaerol, air rushing from Aaron, and water flowing from Liam, none of them yet able to wield more than one erendinth at a time. Pressing himself further into the erendinth, Devlyn intertwined stone into his wield. He felt the vastness of the valley beneath his feet, the strength of the surrounding mountains, and even the city of Ceurenyl beyond them and more. Most importantly, he felt his opponents.

He felt their weight on the ground, two with a commanding stance, and two others moving. He felt the erendinth thrumming through them. By interweaving terys with animys, he gave the transcendental erendinth a physical embodiment. The stone and spirit pulsed together and with a quick burst of energy, Devlyn sent four separate waves across the ground toward his attackers. The ground loosened beneath their feet and shook violently, the snow mostly melted from the immediate area. Removing his focus from Jaerol, Liam, and Aaron, Devlyn now concentrated on Velaria. He felt her intricate melding of umbrys and animys once again and attempted to disengage them.

He pressed himself into both and felt the incredible control Velaria had over her wield. But bound to Aliel, Devlyn discerned the separate erendinth more clearly and pressed into both. She had a strong hold over them, but she was no match for Devlyn's added strength from the phoenix. Together, they soon gained control over both erendinth, stripping them from Velaria.

He now directed his newly won wields back to their originator, dividing them into a dozen lances. But before Devlyn could land his attack on Velaria, an enormous blast of water hurled him from his feet. His wields slipped from his grasp, leaving him doused in freezing water. He had forgotten to pay attention to the others! The air and fuzziness in his mind cleared amidst peals of laughter echoing in the valley.

Devlyn didn't find it at all funny. It wouldn't have been so bad if he had simply lost, but they had caught him by surprise, and he was embarrassed as he lay sprawled on the ground soaking wet and freezing in the crisp air.

Shivering from shame and the cold, he wielded a bit of air and fire to dry his clothing.

"Well done, Liam!" Velaria called from the other side of the valley. "He almost had me there. Unfortunate that he placed all his attention on me with three other wielders nearby."

"Yeah, yeah, yeah, rub it in. I'll get you next time." Devlyn's shivering stopped as his clothes dried.

"That's a mistake you won't make twice. Imagine if that had been a deadly wield intended to end your life. Remember, every wielder is a threat so long as they still breathe. And these shadow elves won't stop their attack until they can't." Velaria's intent was not to scold, but to instruct her student, and keep her friend safe. "Anyway, we should head back to the temple. It won't be light out for much longer and we've practiced long enough for today."

Everyone readily agreed, all of them exhausted from the day's session, and headed for the secret passageway. The hour-long journey through the tunnel was mostly quiet, everyone too tired to talk. Velaria excused herself to return to Gwilnor as soon as they arrived in Devlyn's quarters, but the others remained, pleased at the chance to exchange news of happenings at Gwilnor. Devlyn still did not have leave to resume his classes there, and the few notes he and Alex had exchanged had not provided much detail about Devlyn's other friends' doings.

"Have you found anything out about Ellendren yet?" Devlyn asked Aaron, trying not to sound overly interested.

"I finally found the ei'ana Velaria told me about. A Crimsyn, and near-impossible to find," replied Aaron. "Can't remember her name, but she told me everything I needed to hear. She had escorted Ellendren to the Illumined Wood for her novitiate."

"I thought she was going to Erithel, to practice healing at the hospital there." Devlyn tried to remember exactly where the Sorenth city lay on a map.

"Velaria had thought the same. Although I can't tell you how relieved I am that she isn't in Sorenthil. Doubt I'd be able to just sit and wait for news on her wellbeing if she was." Aaron looked nervously out the window.

"Have you had any updates on Myrium?" asked Jaerol.

"No, none. King Gordon is a right scoundrel though! All those years feigning his allegiance only to double cross us all! And to join Queen Alesei in the siege!" Aaron's voice rose in disgust.

"Gordon is the Torsillian king and Alesei is the Tieli queen. Both supposed allies," Jaerol summarized in response to Liam's question in the form of a raised eyebrow.

"Part of the Erynien Empire now?" Liam asked.

"Yeah, who's to say for how long though," replied Aaron.

"Their true loyalties might not have been known to the Aryl of Lucillia, but their emissaries were a constant sight in Broid," Jaerol added.

"Not surprising, especially Alesei." Aaron returned his gaze to the window. "Poor Myranda, she must be worried sick about her mother."

"Myranda's the Sorenth princess, right?" asked Liam.

"Yeah, we met her that day I was accepted into Gwilnor, remember? She was with Ellendren and some others," Devlyn replied. His attention was, as always, on Ellendren, and while the siege of Myrium certainly disturbed him, there was little he could do about it. "Do you think they'll have a minum keeping watch for her as they did with us?"

"I would imagine so, especially after we were openly attacked just one step out of the Illumined Wood." Aaron sounded concerned. Ellendren wasn't just his younger sister, she was also the future of his kingdom, the crowned princess and future Aryl of Lucillia.

The conversation shifted quickly when Liam jumped in with a question. "Do you think they'll let me become an ei'ana? I've been thinking about it for weeks now, ever since you came back and we started practicing to wield."

Surprised by the change in topic, Devlyn didn't know what to say. Ei'ana tried to stick to the age restrictions set by the order as best as possible and Liam was already twenty-nine. Most students started their studies at Gwilnor when they were ten. Then there was the aversion to kien wielders. It was one thing to help them learn to control the erendinth, but to have them also study at Gwilnor to become ei'ana was a risk the Chairs were not willing to take.

While Devlyn took time to consider his response, Jaerol began talking. "I'm sure they will. They need everyone they can get. I doubt they'd turn away a kien wielder capable of controlling the erendinth. In fact, we'll do it together. The Temple of Ceur has been good to us and all, but we're no ei'ceuril." Jaerol had a sly smile as he patted Liam on the back encouragingly. Jaerol was only two years younger than Liam.

Jaerol had changed a great deal while Devlyn had been in the Illumined Wood. The last time Devlyn had seen Jaerol, the elf had seemed cold and emotionless, but now he was quite friendly. It also pleased Devlyn that Jaerol and Liam had warmed up to each other. Devlyn would never have expected that Liam would forgive Jaerol for his involvement in the events in Gneal that had led to their family's murder by shadow elves in Gneal's dungeons.

"Would you?" Liam turned his head toward Jaerol, grinning.

The thought of his brother and Jaerol becoming ei'ana brought Devlyn's attention to the ei'ceuril. "Aaron, when will you be anointed to the Light as a steward? Did I say that right?"

A slight shiver ran through Aaron. "I asked the Ceurtriarch if I could wait for Elle to return. It would be nice to have at least one family member at the ceremony."

"Well, that shouldn't be too far off. She left shortly after Devlyn did." Liam gave Devlyn a funny look, one eyebrow raised as if to ask whether Aaron knew how Devlyn felt about his youngest sister. Devlyn ignored Liam and allowed himself to feel excited about Ellendren's return.

The room grew quiet. They just sat, each in his own thoughts, and all too tired to go on to other pursuits without a pressing reason to do so.

Almost half an hour later, a quiet knock came at the hidden door. Liam looked through the small peephole before unlatching and opening it to allow Therril through. They all stood to happily greet the old steward, although Devlyn's greeting was lackluster. He was still bitter about being restricted to the Temple of Ceur. Therril instantly noticed his less-than-happy tone.

"Well, I don't think that attitude is necessary, especially considering the news I bear." Therril's piercing silver eyes looked directly at Devlyn. "Ealyndol, Velaria, and I have devised a plan to keep you safe while allowing you increased freedom, specifically, going into the city and also resuming some of your classes at Gwilnor."

Therril now had Devlyn's full attention, eyes widened and mouth agape, prompting a quick hearty chortle from the old ei'ceuril.

"Firstly, you will be able to go out and about, since the entire world knows not only that you are here again, but that you're a Phaedryn, despite our attempts to prevent the news from spreading. And when there's a Phaedryn, there's a phoenix nearby. I suppose that it is so wondrous an event, after so many years, that it was inevitable that everyone would learn of it. It does mean that you and Aliel shall never be parted, especially when in public. It will do wonders for the city's morale and more importantly, keep you safe."

Devlyn felt joy pass between himself and Aliel. *I would have expected something more restrictive*, Devlyn conveyed.

"Secondly, both the temple and Septyl knights have graciously agreed to accommodate our request to accompany you whenever you are outside the temple and castle. I'm sorry, but it's a necessary precaution with shadow elves and servants of Shadow hiding throughout the city. Lastly, and unfortunately for you, you still may not be in the city after dusk. If you find yourself at the castle past curfew, you will just have to stay in your old room in the boy's dormitory there; no one's taken it."

Too eager at the chance of stepping outside the temple and into the city again, Devlyn quickly agreed and didn't even care that he once again had a curfew.

"Since your return is common knowledge, your lessons at Gwilnor will, of course, resume, including your private lessons with your tutors, all of them."

Pleased with the turn of events, Devlyn looked forward to seeing everyone again, especially Alex. Since Erynor's attack last year, Gwilnor's students were forbidden to leave the castle, so the two had not been able to meet, only exchange letters.

"There is one more precaution that won't be in effect yet." Therril paused, ensuring he had Devlyn's complete attention. "If something should happen that jeopardizes your safety, an additional guard will be with you at all times, including in the temple and the castle."

His stomach knotted, but his excitement kept him from dwelling on it. It was only if things turned bad. "Velaria was just with us; why didn't she tell me?"

"Well, aside from being the busiest elf I know, and that's saying a lot mind you, those ei'ana never allow themselves any time for leisure. How she manages it all, I'll never know. But that's beside the point. It wasn't finalized yet, since we only just finished polishing the details, after your practice ended." Therril nodded knowingly. "Well, I must be going. She's not the only busy elf in this city!"

"Wait." Jaerol leapt for the door. Intrigued, Therril paused and turned back to look at Jaerol. "Liam and I have a request."

Liam's face drained of all its color. He hadn't thought that Jaerol would ask so soon.

"Can you help us gain admittance into Gwilnor Academy, as student wielders?" Everyone waited with bated breath for Therril's response. "We thought, since you teach there, you might have some influence over Velaria and the other Chairs."

"Huh, huh, huh. It's about time you two asked!" Therril's broad grin returned the color to Liam's face. "It's possible that the Chairs might listen to a crazy old elf like me. Who's to say? I've heard that you can both wield with control now and since Aaron has already begun his lessons there, there is precedence. It might be possible. We can't continue to lock kien wielders away in the Temple of Ceur if they can control the erendinth. And the Ei'ana certainly need their numbers bolstered!"

"Our ages won't be an issue?" asked Liam.

Therril pointed to the many wrinkles on his face with a sheepish grin. "You might not be a child, but you both have more years ahead than behind you!" With that, Therril was out the hidden door and on his way.

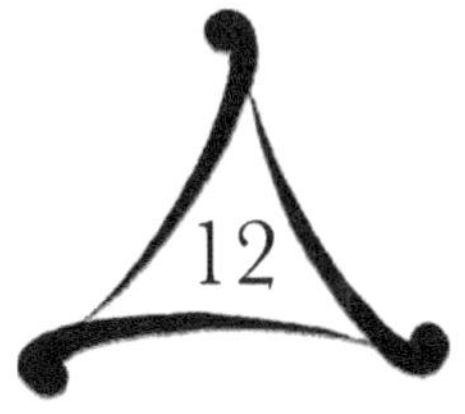

SOMNAENIEL

Devlyn blinked to melt the heavy snow flake that had somehow swept into his eye as he rushed through the crowded streets of Ceurenyl. Aliel soared above and two temple knights marched behind. The number of people crammed in the streets on such a cold and snowy day was unbelievable. Devlyn had expected that the heavy snowfall would slow the city down and keep everyone inside, at least, those who had no pressing need to go about outside. Instead, Devlyn had to push between one person and the next, everyone going about their busy lives despite the snow covering their cloaks.

In truth, no one missed seeing Devlyn and Aliel as they hurried along. Comments and happy calls, sometimes even cheers came from every side as he wound his way through Ceurenyl. He really didn't have to hurry to Gwilnor, but he found himself too excited to slow down, and a little embarrassed by all the attention. Even without Aliel, the sight of two temple knights keeping a close step behind made them highly noticeable. But Devlyn had missed his friends over the past year and was really looking forward to seeing them. He hoped Ellendren would be among them, because while he wouldn't admit it to anyone, she was the one he really wanted to see most. He hadn't heard that she was finally back but had hoped that by the time he could walk freely about, she would have returned.

As he turned another corner, the gentle curvature of Ceurenyl's streets opened, the buildings set further back from the street so that the castle was visible, rising in the distance. Seven towers pierced the sky in various heights and sizes, the Dragon Tower most prominent among them. A wave of relief washed over Devlyn. The castle was unscathed. He had never had any indication that the structure had ever been threatened or had been sabotaged, but he had imagined the worst during his novitiate.

A broad curved plaza opened beside the narrow stream that separated the castle from the rest of the city. Passing through the plaza, Devlyn reached the stone bridge and crossed the stream, leaving the cluster of Ceurenyl's buildings behind. Devlyn stopped at the bridge's height to stare at the magnificent castle, only then realizing just how much he had missed it. The snow made Gwilnor even more beautiful.

Her grey stone towers disappeared into low hanging clouds, slate roofs peeked between patches of heavy snow, and the plate glass windows were lit from the inside. The castle appeared alive as candles and magical lights flickered behind the glass. Her firm foundations dug deep into the mountain, hiding at least a third of the entire structure beneath the ground. Flying buttresses sprung from grey stone walls, allowing wondrous stained-glass windows to span the structure. The buttresses resembled incredible sculptures, wrought by master craftsmen, rather than a structural support system.

The castle's main entrance lay before him, but it had been barred since the murder of the Chair of Arantiulyn last year. Devlyn caught a glimpse of the intricate crystal columns rising to meet in pointed arches surrounding the main entry dais. It looked like they formed seven gateways or portals, shimmering in the sun.

The door at the center was the largest door he had ever seen, solid wood and rising taller than most houses, certainly taller than any house in Cor'lera. A rose window of seven different interlacing colors hung above the door, dwarfing the door in scale and beauty. The window contained smaller images depicting the sigils of the seven Schools of Septyl.

Descending the other side of the bridge to follow the path that led to a second, much longer, bridge spanning a deep chasm, Devlyn passed through a large archway, its heavy iron portcullis raised, into Gwilnor's largest courtyard. Also known as the quad, the paved courtyard's centrally located fountain splashed water and the sound reverberated off the surrounding walls. From here, Devlyn could only see two towers, the Dragon Tower bustling with activity and the South Tower in an abandoned wing of the castle. History had once seen the entire castle busting at her seams with every room occupied, but the broken Balance had left much of the castle uninhabited with whole wings sealed off.

Seven knights stood before the only unbarred entrance to the school. They each belonged to one of the seven Schools of Septyl, identified by the tabards they wore, each a distinct color that indicated which School they served. Devlyn wondered whether any of them worried that the person standing next to them might be a servant of Shadow. He couldn't imagine how difficult that might be for these men who had studied and trained together since their youth. Archers lined the parapets, and all took notice of newcomers entering the courtyard.

As Devlyn approached the entrance to Gwilnor's second largest hall, all seven knights bowed their heads.

Devyn noted three ei'ana standing in the recessed opening of the entrance hall, protected from the falling snow. *Since when do ei'ana have guard duty?* Devlyn conveyed to Aliel. While the Septyl knights were proven warriors, Devlyn doubted they would provide much resistance if a shadow elf decided to siege the castle, and he supposed the ei'ana had been added to bolster the defenses.

Presumably immediately after Erynor attacked the city. Aliel still hovered slightly above Devlyn's shoulder. Other than depictions on tapestries or in scrolls or books, he was the first of his kind to be seen by all those present.

Only the ei'ana with golden-brown hair greeted him, speaking on behalf of the other two. "Your return has gladdened the hearts of all in Ceurenyl. I trust you will be resuming your studies with us," she said. Devlyn could tell by her appearance that she was Luminari, and likely from Lucillia.

"Thank you for your welcome, Ei'ana," Devlyn replied, inclining his head courteously in return. "My studies have been postponed long enough."

"It's good that you've returned," blurted the youngest ei'ana, casting her eyes to Aliel, and the other two frowned in disapproval of her daring to speak.

"Thank you, but you will have to excuse me, my lessons are about to begin." Devlyn bowed once more and passed them to open the door. With a hopeful look over his shoulder, Devlyn let out a quiet sigh when his guard did not follow him into the castle. Instead, they turned to march back to the temple, as had been agreed—a pair of Septyl knights would escort him back to the temple before his curfew.

Devlyn made his way to his first history class in well over a year. The familiar corridors and wall hangings were a welcome sight; it felt as though he had finally returned home after being away longer than he'd wanted. The Temple of Ceur and the ei'ceuril had welcomed Devlyn as one of their own, but he still felt like he belonged to Gwilnor.

A mix of students filled the class, many familiar faces grinning at him when he opened the door and stopped just inside the classroom, while Aliel slipped in to hover just above his head. Despite his earlier rush to get to Gwilnor, he was a bit late and Magister Ethyl was mid-sentence. She stopped, and every student turned to see who had disturbed the lesson, many gasping at the sight of the phoenix. Immediately, Alex jumped up from his seat and pushed past the younger students to give Devlyn a strong embrace, squeezing the air from his lungs. The other students crowded in behind, waiting impatiently for Alex to step aside.

Finally breaking the embrace, Alex punched his cousin in the arm.

"It's nice to see you too." Devlyn massaged his tender upper arm, shocked to discover that he had missed his cousin's rough play.

"Do me a favor and tell me next time you intend on leaving for a year! Not a single person told me a thing of what happened to you. It took me a week to track Velaria down before I got a straight answer after the siege. None of us knew what happened. We heard Erynor booming his threats and the next thing we know, you've gone and disappeared!" Alex embraced Devlyn again, as though he didn't quite believe that Devlyn had returned whole, despite the notes they'd exchanged since Devlyn returned to the temple.

Magister Ethyl and the rest of the students greeted Devlyn in turn, then Ethyl led him to a seat and asked Devlyn to recount his adventures. It was very unlike the elderly magister to abandon her lesson plans. In her five decades of teaching, she had never before veered from her lecture. Either she was genuinely interested in what had happened, or more likely, she had correctly assumed that nothing else would be accomplished during this lesson. He *had* returned accompanied by a phoenix, after all—that had to count as historical. Devlyn's recounting of his past year was often interrupted by questions about Aliel, now perched at Devlyn's side, so the time went by fast, if confusingly.

When the bells rang to dismiss the students, Devlyn and Alex left together, some of the younger students trailing behind, and Alex talking non-stop. They did not make it through two corridors before they were approached by yet another familiar, but not so welcoming face. Abbie Wintyr stopped before them.

"Hi, Abbie, nice to see you again." Devlyn really was pleased to see her, no longer considering her crazy, but convinced that she was of a very sound mind, after Leilyn had told him that the druids of Kweil Aitch were Dreamers.

"You fool!" Abbie's abrasive tone had not changed since Devlyn had last seen her. The younger students suddenly lost interest in Devlyn and Aliel and found another corridor to scurry away into. "You complete and utter fool. Not once did you enter the Dream! An entire year in the Illumined Wood, and not once did you even try."

Devlyn opened his mouth to respond but before anything came out, Abbie pressed her fingers to his temple. The world shifted and Devlyn felt himself fall backward, without crashing to the ground. Quickly taking notice of his surroundings, he could tell that he was still in the castle, yet everything around him was different, almost vague. Alex was gone, but Aliel still hovered just above his left shoulder. In front of him, an oddly wispy Abbie stood with her arms crossed.

"Where did Alex go?"

"He hasn't gone anywhere; we have."

"What are you talking about? I haven't moved a foot."

"This is Somnaeniel, the World-in-Between. Also known as the Dream. It is between our physical world and Lumaeniel, the World-Beyond," said a voice behind Devlyn.

Devlyn spun to see a boy, slightly older than himself and with more freckles on his face than Devlyn had ever seen; not even Abbie had so many. Like Abbie, he had the same bright emerald green eyes and curly red hair, although not as long as Abbie's.

"Devlyn, this is Eagan Wintyr, my brother."

"How did you get into the castle?"

"We are not technically in the castle, Devlyn, Child of Luminare. But yes, you should be concerned about the castle's security. If I so chose, I could enter Gwilnor through the World-in-Between, and so could anyone else who knows how. Let me assure you, there are many." Eagan Wintyr reminded Devlyn very much of Abbie in the way he spoke, yet his manner was nowhere near as fiery as hers; he was soft spoken compared to Abbie, and his eyes seemed to look into the beyond.

"Child of Luminare?" Devlyn wondered what Eagan meant, he wasn't the first to call him that.

"Those who are able to Dream are capable of much, and know much, even that which is forgotten." Eagan seemed to look past Devlyn.

Great, more riddles.

Not a riddle, but the truth, came Eagan's voice in Devlyn's mind.

Frightened that his thoughts were not private, Devlyn almost spoke his fear before Eagan continued. "Thoughts are immaterial, just as this World-in-Between is immaterial. Thoughts and dreams belong to this world, just as words and bodies belong to the physical world."

Coming to terms with where he was, Devlyn asked Aliel, *How did you know Abbie was bringing me here? I mean, you were just there as soon as I was.*

Aliel's response conveyed his amusement. *I have gone nowhere.*

"Aliel is a phoenix, and like all anadel, belongs to the World-Beyond. They simultaneously appear and interact in all three realms if they so choose," explained Eagan.

It is so, Aliel affirmed.

"The druids of Kweil Aitch have long entered the World-in-Between and are aware of many of its mysteries. However, we are not the only ones with such knowledge, the aldarchs came before we could even fashion iron tools. We have always been aware of others entering accidentally, stumbling in as they dream unaware.

"There are those with knowledge of the World-in-Between, who enter with just as much ease as we druids do. If they wished, they could implant thoughts or harm others who cannot guard themselves within the Dream. Within you. For this reason, my people have asked us to instruct you in the ways of the Dream. You and I will only meet in the World-in-Between, and train here, while Abbie will train you in person, wherever you may be. If you do not learn the ways of the Dream, the Enemy will use it against you. Know that his prison grows weak, and soon he will have influence over this World-in-Between, his preferred dwelling."

While he still grappled to understand everything Eagan said, more questions surfaced without Devlyn being able to voice any. They all intertwined, creating only confusion. "So, what can one *do* in the World-in-Between?"

Both Eagan and Abbie smiled, and Abbie took Devlyn's hand in her own.

"Allow me," she said, and the stone walls of the castle faded to become a lush jungle with plants and trees that Devlyn had never seen before.

"Where are we?" Devlyn gawked at the unfamiliar surroundings. What happened to Gwilnor?

"How big do you think Eklean is? Would you believe that it is the smallest of Teraeniel's continents? If you don't, you should, because it is. We are currently in Ogren, in the Kingdom of Charren, a human kingdom constantly warring with its neighbors, who just so happen to be ogres, half human and half giant. Their southern neighbors aren't much better. They make the ogres seem almost civilized."

Shocked by the thought of not only instantly being in a different location, but also that other kingdoms existed beyond Eklean, and ogres and giants as well. Devlyn had looked at maps of Eklean often, and each time, he had wondered what lay north where the maps stopped in a snowy tundra and what lay west where the maps ended in a desert. Suddenly, Devlyn was eager to see more, to know more.

"What else can you show me?" he asked enthusiastically.

Abbie's eyes lit up and her smile grew brighter as she grabbed his hand again. This time, the area did not fade as before, but rather, they soared above the ground. "I'll give you a view your cartographers would kill for!" said Abbie as the two rushed into the sky, Aliel and Eagan soaring beside them.

As they flew upward, Devlyn didn't feel any wind against his face. It felt wrong, as if he should have to shield his eyes. He had to remember to ask her how it was possible at a later occasion; right now, too much adrenaline coursed through his body. Abbie stopped in midair.

"Look down," she said.

His eyes could not believe the sight below. Coastlines undulated, forming incredible land forms with intricate lines. Mountains rose, and valleys fell into rivers and lakes. Lush green forests and jungles gave way to encroaching deserts, and frozen lands lay to the north. Abbie moved on, traversing the sky and soon, Devlyn recognized Eklean below, her mountain ranges and rolling rivers slicing through her land. It was one thing to view landmarks on a map, but to see them in real life from the same perspective stole his breath.

Devlyn couldn't believe the extent of the Illumined Wood, barely able to view the entirety of it before the world curved out of sight. Following the forest south through vacant lands to the coast, Devlyn spotted a chain of islands he had never seen on a map. "How come those aren't drawn on any map?"

"Because the inhabitants do not want the people of Eklean to know of their island home. Those are the Jahro Islands, home to humans who first came from Ja'Horan, a land where the sun is brighter and stronger than anywhere else in the world. The natives claim that the sun has kissed their skin, allowing them to adapt to their continent. If ever you come across one of them, know they will make a strong and formidable ally of unshakable loyalty. However, you will not think of them as potential allies, for Eklean knows the Jahro seafarers as pirates."

Devlyn had heard of the pirates that braved the wild oceans but had never heard of Jahro.

"I don't understand."

"When Arenthyl fell and your ancestors were enslaved, the Jahronese withdrew their advanced ships from Eklean. They well knew the powers that Erynor held, powers that were first unleashed on their own land, sucking the life from their once vibrant and lush continent. When Erynor's reign fell to a pregnant woman and two infants, they remained on their islands and ventured to the shores of Eklean only sporadically. But when they did, they did not wish to form any relationships, in fear of Erynor's return one day. The southern kingdoms along the coast began calling those seafarers with their dark-brown, nearly black skin, pirates, after they tied up at their docks offering riches beyond measure for trade. According to the folk in those southern kingdoms, the trade goods had been pillaged from places unknown." Abbie explained and before Devlyn could ask another question, she took his hand and once again their surroundings faded.

When their surroundings reformed, Devlyn and Abbie were back in Gwilnor, yet it was a distinctly different Gwilnor. The walls were not stone, but appeared to be of a shadowy form creeping ever outward. Devlyn watched as several students passed by, heads weighed down to look toward the floor beneath their feet as though their shoulders slouched under an unseen burden.

Once again, their surroundings faded, and this time, Devlyn found himself being held up by Alex in the real, stone-walled Gwilnor. Embarrassed, Devlyn quickly stood on his own, and apologized, not at all certain how he had ended up in his cousin's arms. He quickly patted his chest, relieved to feel his secret coin purse concealed in an interior pocket of his robes.

"I don't know exactly what happened, but not to worry, I couldn't just let you crumble to the ground like a lump of coal. And you've put on weight since I saw you last. My arms are actually sore from holding you all that time." Alex chided in his playful manner. "What happened? You were talking to Abbie, and then you fainted, and she just sat down on the floor and waited while I held you up. And she's been ignoring me the entire time." At Alex's explanation, Devlyn glanced at Abbie, still sitting on the ground with her legs crossed, back straight, and eyes closed.

"Oh, er…I'll explain some other time. And I'll have to remember to do it like that next time. Just in case you're not there to catch me." The two cousins shared a quick laugh. "Did anyone else see me faint?"

"You missed Trethien walk by. You should've seen the look on his smug face."

"Great," said Devlyn, not happy that Trethien had seen him unconscious in Alex's arms.

"He had a quick quip about me holding you."

"Fantastic," Devlyn muttered, grateful for the first time that he didn't live in the castle and wouldn't have to overhear Trethien in a common room later that night.

"Don't worry about him," Alex dismissed. "He's nothing more than a privileged spoiled brat." They barely had time to exchange another laugh before Abbie sprung up and turned on Devlyn, pressing her finger to his chest.

"Have you seen that before?" she asked fiercely.

"What? No, of course not, it was quite exciting to see it all from above." Scratching his head, Devlyn doubted there was a right answer.

"I mean the vision of Gwilnor, all shadowy and everyone walking around looking depressed." Abbie's annoyance seemed to grow, even as she continued to poke him in the chest.

"Once or twice in a dream, maybe more. It's hard to say, you know how it is remembering dreams, especially whether they are recurring ones."

"You had better learn to remember!" said Abbie as she continued poking. Poke, poke, poke.

Despite his usual confusion with things Abbie said, he asked, "Why? It was just a dream; not like it means anything."

"Don't be a fool, it means a great deal." Finally, she stopped with the poking.

"Do *you* know what it means?" asked Devlyn, exasperated.

"Only the one who Dreams it can properly interpret it. I can guess, but it's impossible for me to know with certainty," explained Abbie.

"Sure, it was weird, but students walk around like that all the time," said Devlyn skeptically.

"Not as they did," scolded Abbie. "And besides, didn't you take notice of the walls? There was something wrong about them. You had best put some thought into it. Remember, the more frequently a Dream occurs, the closer it is to fulfillment."

"What are you two talking about? You speak as though Devlyn has seen the future," Alex interjected, not following the conversation.

"Prophesy has many different avenues, but the most common prophecies come through Dreams," said Abbie, not removing her gaze from Devlyn, who unintentionally groaned at the mention of another prophecy.

"Hold on," Alex interjected. "All those dreams you had—whenever you woke in a fright—you're telling me that they weren't just nightmares?"

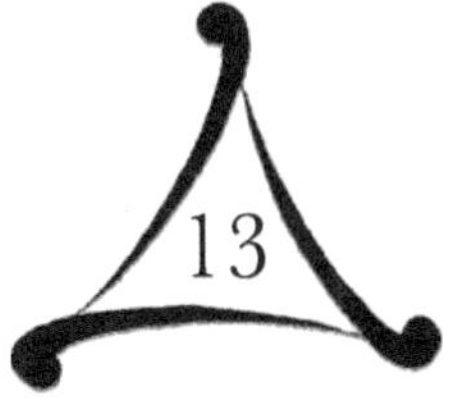

SECRETS

Wispy clouds washed across the crescent moon that hung low in the sky, its slight reflection visible on the sea below. A distant memory arose of a time when a young moon was much desired since it produced the darkest of nights. While the memory endured, why he had once longed for it didn't. He felt no emotional connection or enthusiasm as he looked off the balcony toward the fading moon.

Searching for the missing memory had the same results as staring into the vast depths of the ocean in hopes of locating a single ship. Pressing into its vastness, he felt the enormity of its depth and its secrets. When he would have delved deeper, someone called his name, summoning him.

"Aren!" A name he recognized, but only understood that it also belonged to him because others identified him with it. Lost in his empty thoughts, Aren lingered before hearing his name called out again, this time with a voice raised in anger.

The emotion bewildered him. He couldn't recall ever personally experiencing anger and wondered what caused it to surface in others. What caused any emotion to surface? While unaware of the reason behind the caller's anger, he had grown all too familiar with pain and knew that if he kept the Master's servant waiting, he would yet again experience pain. As he moved to respond to the summons, he reached into his mind, seeking a time when he did not experience pain as a matter of course. Oddly, that seemed more distant than anything, more unattainable than when he first began to suppress the pain inflicted by torture. When and how were beyond his grasp, but Aren distinctly recalled a moment where he had chosen to ignore pain. Unable to reach further into his past, Aren treasured it as his first memory.

When Aren entered the imperial throne room, huddled spectators moved away as he passed through them. Just ahead, he overheard the second half of a conversation. "…you know what we will do to Freiton if you disobey us." The creature he had captured earlier cowered before the speaker, the one who called himself emperor.

"Please," begged the minum, tears spilling down his face. "My people have done nothing against you."

Erynor lounged in his throne surrounded by elves scarcely dressed in thin silks, both men and women, little of their bodies left to the imagination. They were youthful elves with vibrant red hair and silver eyes. They looked far healthier than many of the others currently populating Broid, with their grey and ashy skin, and thin, fading, and lusterless hair. The loss of the silver of their eyes was most noticeable though; any trace of color they had once had was lost and the eyes swallowed any light. The emperor only chose the youthful and healthy-looking ones for the imperial throne room, at least, while they remained so. They would be demoted to a less prestigious role in the palace or tossed into the kitchens once their appearance deteriorated.

But among the elves present was one whose golden-brown hair had hints of silver, and eyes where the silver gave way to emerald encircling the pupil. Those eyes now stared into his own. They did not plead nor mourn, only stared. A memory of such a woman tickled at his mind, but the memory dissolved like smoke when he tried to grasp it. Aren only knew that she had come from a small village—Cor'lera?— and that Erynor wanted something from her.

"You are right." Erynor shifted on his throne, unconcerned. "If you or your people had done anything, we would not be in this predicament. I would not be threatening to scorch your home and people. Perhaps it would have been better if you minums had remained in chains; a more obedient slave never existed than when the minums served the greater races. You minums are proof that nothing is more abominable than the results of interbreeding races! Fortunate that such a joining produced exemplar slaves, else I would have every one of you exterminated. Even more deplorable is the order created for you by the Lorenthien aryl by restricting seguians to your race! Be consoled that that is the only reason I allow you to still draw breath."

The minum shivered uncontrollably; Aren knew that he was experiencing an extreme level of pain, recognizing the suffering all too well. A silent moment passed before a wail escaped the minum's mouth, reverberating off the walls. Instinctively, Aren wanted to cover his ears to block out the near-deafening screech.

"For such a small slave, you are loud." Erynor maintained his gaze on the minum. "Aren, before you bring another Time Warden to my court, be sure it is made aware of my sensitive ears. It might suffer less when in my presence."

"It shall be done." Aren inclined his head to Erynor.

"It shall be done, *your Imperial Majesty*." Erynor scowled at Aren.

"Our Master is not here. I serve him alone. If he desires that I address you so, I shall."

A small smirk came to Erynor's face followed by a menacing laugh, echoed by the surrounding elves. However, the elf with the golden-brown hair did not share in the amusement. Rather, a single tear fell and as it did, she spoke softly, barely audible.

"What have they done to you, Ei'denai?"

Her face immediately contorted in agony. Aren watched as Erynor wielded the pure darkness of tenebrys against the defenseless elf. The all-consuming erendinth ate at her essence. If Erynor desired, he could end her life instantly and take it for his own. "The line of Lucillia will fall into nothingness by my hand! Not a single child of that wench shall breathe beyond my chains. I will allow my shadow elves to feed off your lives as punishment for her crimes!"

A few more tears rolled down her cheeks, yet no sound escaped her mouth. Erynor gave no reason for punishing the elf and she did not ask why. Without understanding why it mattered, Aren wondered who she was. *What is her name? How had she fallen captive to Erynor? She must be an enemy of the Master,* thought Aren; *she will die, as do all his enemies.*

Even as he had these thoughts, he felt Erynor wield once again. Aren recognized the forms creating the lightning without light and knew where Erynor would direct it. It unleashed to explode against Aren's chest, sending him flying backward, halfway across the hall. The pain was excruciating and unbearable, nearly ripping him to pieces, tearing at his very being and separating him from his body. Focusing away from the pain, Aren emptied his mind and forced it to the corner of himself where he always held it. It did not disappear, but he could ignore it.

"You will bring the entirety of that line to me! Your failure to capture the two boys will not be forgotten."

Pushing himself to his feet and regaining his sight, he looked toward Erynor enshrouded in darkness, holding on to that incredible erendinth lest it slip from his grasp and dissolve. Erynor was forming the necessary patterns once again, creating another wield but before he could let it go, one of the elves at his side addressed his emperor. This particular elf was also enshrouded in darkness as though he was covered by a robe with a cowl, near-invisible to most, yet Aren's altered vision let him see past the shadow, awful to look at, resembling a corpse more than an elf.

"It is not yet time for him to die, father," said what was once a Cyndinari. It was now one of the Deurghol—a Deathless, neither living nor dead—and this one was one of Erynor's true offspring. His voice held a sick tone, one that said the incarnation should have parted from its body long ago, leaving it to decay and return to dust.

The forms of tenebrys faded as Erynor released his hold over them. "You are right, my son," he said, eerily calm. He did not look toward the Deurghol but kept his gaze locked on Aren, staring deep into his soul with hatred. There was a forgotten past between himself and Erynor; the emperor's eyes showed it, yet the memories of what that had been were no longer available to Aren, who looked back blankly.

Returning to his throne, Erynor sat with head bowed and eyes closed. Finally, he spoke.

"To the north rules a queen. She has grown quite vocal among her neighbors and is beginning to sway those already sworn to me. I intend you to deal with her." Erynor spoke calmly, periodically punctuating his words with waving hands. "She thinks she has the ability to take Torsil and Mindale from me; her ignorance is shameful. They have been mine for the last half century and will remain mine! I want an example made of that woman. I want her to grovel and beg for mercy before you destroy her. I want her killed in broad daylight for all her loyal subjects to witness."

Erynor looked to the right, and spoke to a proud, richly dressed man. "Does my intention cause you distress, Prince?"

"No, your Imperial Majesty. Daerinth is Sorenth no longer. As you know, our origins are Daer, not Sorenthil. And our loyalties are to the Erynien Empire." The prince bowed.

"What of her kingdom? Surely, they will rise unified, seeking revenge," said a shadow elf, an advisor to Erynor, but not entirely interested in Daerinth.

"No. They will cower and whimper once their queen is dead. Let them hide behind their river and city walls, but do not break the siege. If they raise their banners against me, they will join their queen in death, by the hundreds of thousands." Erynor's gaze was on the floor, not looking at anyone.

A moment passed where everyone in the imperial throne room remained silent, Aren standing among them, still as a statue, horrible to behold with his black wings folded on his back. Darkness seeped from his body.

"What are you waiting for? Destroy her and leave her corpse for her people to mourn over." Erynor raised his gaze to Aren.

Aren required no further instruction. He returned to the balcony overlooking the ocean. Just as he stood on the edge, preparing to leap off, the elf with the golden-brown hair came to his mind. *She knows me*, he thought, *how does she know me? Why did she name me ei'denai?*

Taking a deep breath of the salty sea air to fill his lungs and strengthen his wings, he extended them to their full width then leapt over the balcony railing, folding them as he dove down the side of the castle on a seaside cliff. Just before reaching the rocky bottom and the crashing waves,

Aren unfurled his wings, allowing the wind to catch them, carrying him safely above the rocks and sea. He rose above the castle and for a moment had a glimpse of the city of Broid, its buildings of aggressive yellow curving stone and red tiled roofs neatly laid out below, before he turned north toward Myrium.

What's an ei'denai?

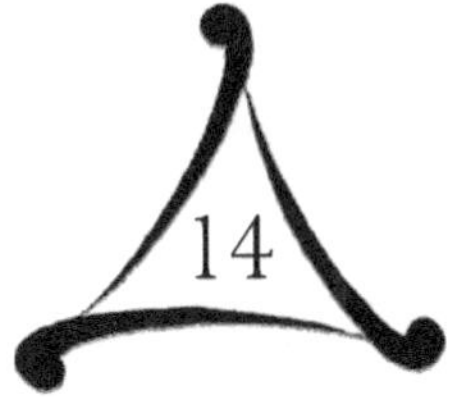

Too Long Apart

Devlyn sat on his bed with his legs crossed in the quiet and tried to still his mind for his morning meditation. His instructors often spoke of the importance of daily meditation and while Devlyn tried to incorporate it into his routine, an entire week had passed since he had last meditated. Following his meeting with Emdian yesterday, guilt had ridden in his stomach, and without that push, he probably would not be sitting alone in his bedchamber trying to meditate, not when Liam and Jaerol waited for him in his sitting room.

Eyes closed, Devlyn focused on breathing steadily, listening to each breath as it came in and left his lungs. Even though the room was quiet, listening helped diminish distractions. He inhaled deeply and felt his breath channel not just through his lungs, but through his being, as if his physical breath touched a spiritual energy that traveled throughout his body. It began in his mind as gentle rhythmic swirls that then flowed through him, reaching through his core to his fingertips and toes.

But after a single steady breath, Devlyn found it impossible to replicate the experience. His breathing remained controlled, but his mind was a whirlwind. Unable to slow the onslaught, he stood and paced. The Dream he had experienced with Abbie a few weeks ago now occurred more frequently, visiting him three out of seven nights each week.

Devlyn had learned that everyone occasionally did enter the World-in-Between while they slept but he still could not enter intentionally on his own. For now, every night, Eagan was there to pull Devlyn into the Dream.

After the first week of the nightly Dreaming, Devlyn protested that he needed to sleep so that his body and mind could rest. Eagan had laughed at him, assuring him that he was sleeping and that neither his mind nor body were without refreshment. Devlyn didn't believe Eagan since he woke each morning feeling exhausted.

Every night, Eagan insisted that Devlyn explain the vision he'd seen, and every night it was the same story. Devlyn could tell that something about the vision bothered Eagan, but Eagan wouldn't explain his feelings, insisting that it would jeopardize Devlyn's interpretation.

Before Abbie had pulled him into Somnaeniel that first time when he had just returned to Gwilnor, the Dream of Gwilnor had only occurred twice a month, if that often. That it now occurred more often bothered Abbie and Eagan more than him. For Devlyn, the dream was a nuisance. He had no idea what it meant or even what it might symbolize. Abbie's temperament reminded him of the last time she learned of his frequent dreams and that ended with Erynor attacking Ceurenyl and Devlyn beginning his novitiate in the Illumined Wood. He did get to meet his sister though. *Do you have any idea what this dream means?* Devlyn asked Aliel, stopping mid-pace.

We might be bound, but the Dream belongs to you and only you can interpret it.

Devlyn resumed his pacing. The recurrent dreams seemed less important than the letter Gwilnor had just received from Myrium, a short message, yet composed with all the flourish only a royal court could produce. Devlyn had not read the letter himself but could only imagine the flowing prose from the Sorenth court.

The letter had arrived two days ago from the Sorenth queen, requesting that her daughter, Princess Myranda return to Myrium in light of the extended siege. The letter did not provide any detail as to Myrium's state beyond saying that two separate armies sieged the city and that the prince of Daerinth had not only seceded but had also struck an alliance with the Erynien Empire. Since everyone knew about the siege of Myrium and feared Erynor's growing influence, rumors about the letter's arrival and its contents had spread rapidly through Gwilnor and even to the residents of the Temple of Ceur.

Velaria's reaction to the letter was to request an increase of Devlyn's personal guard to five knights at all times outside his chambers. Fortunate-ly, Therril had reminded Velaria that the danger described in the letter was in Myrium, not Ceurenyl, and the door to Devlyn's quarters remained guard-free and he still only required a guard of two, not five, when travel-ing between the temple and castle.

At least that's one thing I don't have to worry about, Devlyn conveyed to Aliel.

As if knights could protect you better than I can, Aliel remarked.

Well, she still wants to increase my guard to five while in the city.

An unnecessary precaution. But you can't blame her, she feels responsible for you.

Why? I'm with the Ei'ceuril now.

She led you and Alex from Cor'lera.

If she hadn't, Lex would have carted me off in chains to Gneal's dungeons to join the rest of my family.

That doesn't mean she doesn't still feel responsible for you.

Even if Aliel was right, increasing his guard to five seemed over-pro-tective.

Devlyn also thought the queen's request for her daughter's return odd. *Why take Myranda away from the safety Gwilnor provides?* Devlyn ques-tioned. He wasn't the only to wonder. Some rumors claimed that the queen was sick, others remarked on her unexpected and unusual marriage to someone outside the Sorenth court, insinuating that her ability to rule was lacking, while still others seemed to expect that Myranda's ability as a wielder would turn the tide in the siege. Devlyn didn't know what to think.

Perhaps the queen thinks the people need to see their crowned princess alive and well. Aliel suggested.

But in a war zone?

Imagine what the Sorenth would say if she stayed away during their darkest hour. They would never accept her as their next monarch if she cared more for her own safety than theirs.

Myranda's preparations for departure from Gwilnor had begun immediately after she had received the letter. Enemies threatened her kingdom and nothing else mattered. Myranda felt she needed to protect her people in some way, something she couldn't do from Ceurenyl, despite the hordes of Sorenth refugees filling the city. As a princess, Myranda had soldiers of her own and a few Sorenth knights in Ceurenyl, but under the circumstances, Septyl knights would also accompany her and the rest of her entourage until she arrived safely in Myrium.

Devlyn chafed at the restrictions that prevented him from leaving the temple to go to Gwilnor to wish her safe travels. He had agreed that he would only leave the temple to attend classes at Gwilnor. Mustering knights as an escort was no simple task on the weekend when Devlyn did not have classes and so would prove a challenge today.

News of Myranda's departure had brought Ellendren and her continuing absence to his mind. Nearly a month had passed since the day of her anticipated return, yet she still had not arrived. He knew others also worried, especially Aaron, who had pleaded with the Chairs to take measures toward locating his missing sister. For all anyone knew, she could be in life-threatening danger, or worse, dead.

Devlyn wished he had a way to locate her. Whenever he practiced wielding out in the valley, he would press into terys and exert his ability as far as possible in hopes of finding her. One very surprising discovery was that he was able to feel the entirety of the mountain Ceurenyl rested on in fine detail, including individual footsteps. Devlyn could almost count all the people in the city just through wielding terys; he could distinguish a faint sensation of each body standing or moving on the ground and their varying weights. While Devlyn could sense most of the city's inhabitants, he couldn't find Ellendren.

Devlyn glanced at his bedchamber door as he paced, Ellendren and her whereabouts at the forefront of his troubled mind. The simple thought of her outside the city's protection increased the cyclone of his thoughts. If he could only help search for her.

Abandoning his attempt at meditation as a complete failure, he opened the door and went into the sitting room. Liam and Jaerol lounged on one of the couches, their backs to Devlyn, but facing Aliel's empty perch.

"Finished with the meditation?" Liam didn't turn toward Devlyn, but Jaerol took a quick look over his shoulder.

"We should see Myranda off. I can't stay hiding in here without saying goodbye." Devlyn avoided Liam's question, and waited to hear that they agreed with him.

"I don't see why we shouldn't see her off. She's a nice girl. Although, you do intend on putting more clothes on, don't you? It might be a bit chilly walking into the city bare chested wearing nothing more than your small clothes." Jaerol chided then gave Liam a funny look.

Devlyn gave an uncomfortable "ha, ha," and went to get a robe from his wardrobe. Since his return, he had received an entire new wardrobe of fine clothing, in addition to two white ei'ceuril robes. Most peculiar to him were not the finely ornate clothing that he had yet to wear, but rather the small clothes. The material they were made of was much thinner than he was accustomed to and far more revealing than any clothing on that part of the body ought to be. He quickly covered himself in the simple white robe of the ei'ceuril, its fabric still odd against his skin, as if it did not belong, and not just because of the itch.

"Happy now?" Devlyn returned to the sitting room and extended his arms to show Liam and Jaerol that he was fully dressed.

"You didn't bother me any." Jaerol commented then laughed as he stood. "Would you like us to escort you to the castle? You'll have to ask nicely though."

"I thought you had already agreed?"

"Did we?" Liam inquired, turning to Jaerol.

"Just because we said it would be nice to see her off, doesn't mean we agreed to do so. And besides, you're only supposed to leave the temple for classes, not seeing princesses off." Jaerol smirked as he stretched his arms then lounged again on the couch, extending his legs across the cushions.

"You're exhausting." Devlyn went to the door as if to leave. "Are you coming?"

"Only if you ask nicely. This couch is far too comfortable to abandon," said Jaerol, eyes now closed.

"Fine. Will you *please* escort me to Gwilnor?"

"What do you think, Liam, was that sufficient?"

"Come on, we've tortured him enough." Liam pushed Jaerol's legs off the couch and stood himself.

Devlyn led the way out into the faux novice bedroom, Aliel following closely behind. Devlyn carefully cracked open the door to the corridor and peered through to make sure it was vacant before passing into the corridor and the rest of the temple with Aliel hovering above his shoulder and Liam and Jaerol only a few paces behind.

Just outside the temple, Aliel nudged Devlyn's consciousness, reminding him that the phoenix offered an additional protection. Devlyn bonded with the phoenix, his senses immediately heightened but he maintained his own vision so he didn't see the world with the phoenix's lighted sight. As an added precaution, he pressed into both terys and aerys, enhancing his perception. They descended the winding terraced path toward the city proper, where Devlyn had expected to find the city bustling with activity. Instead, empty streets snaked through Ceurenyl. Devlyn couldn't figure out where everyone was until they approached Gwilnor, where masses of people crowded the streets and plazas, drawn by all the activity before the open gates and in the school's courtyard.

As Devlyn, Liam, and Jaerol crossed the castle's long bridge and approached the raised portcullis, the people parted as Devlyn and his guard walked through. He wondered if they noticed that his eyes were golden since he was bound to Aliel.

Even though the citizens of Ceurenyl had shown a great deal of interest and excitement when Devlyn had returned with a phoenix making him a Phaedryn, they still distrusted all kien wielders, including Devlyn. It didn't matter that he had repeatedly shown that he had control over the erendinth. The attack by the shadow elves remained fresh in their minds, both because of the parts of the city that remained destroyed, and because they were aware that it was impossible to discern one shadow elf from another person if they concealed their true appearance. To the people of Ceurenyl, all kien wielders were only capable of destruction.

As they crossed the courtyard, through Aliel's vision, Devlyn saw a large number of knights and soldiers astride, their horses hard to control in the general anxiety to get going. Even the coachman of the carriage in the center of the long line was having difficulty keeping its team of four white horses from bolting. Behind them, the castle gate to the large courtyard was open and Devlyn could sense a great number of people gathered in the smaller entrance hall. He and his entourage moved with difficulty past the guards and knights on their horses who did not make room for them to pass until they were only a few paces away. The Sorenth knights were especially stern looking. Liam and Jaerol followed Devlyn and Aliel inside.

Princess Myranda Lariviere was easy to locate in the confusion that reigned in the hall. She was quite distinctive in a blue riding dress and matching cloak, surrounded by several ei'ana in their customary Crimsyn School red. It would seem that they were to accompany the princess to Myrium, to make sure she stayed safe on the trip. Myranda was still a student at Gwilnor, albeit one who had returned from her novitiate, participated in her Choosing ceremony, and joined the Crimsyns.

Myranda easily saw them—Aliel was rather distinctive—and waved them near. The ei'ana clustered around the princess were not as eager to give way as were the people in the streets, but nonetheless, Devlyn finally reached her, bowing slightly as she curtsied. "I'm sorry to hear that you must return home. My heart goes out to you and your people."

"Thank you, Devlyn." Myranda's blue eyes were determined. "Some of the ei'ana have agreed to accompany me to serve as my tutors, so that I may complete my studies and return to profess the Counsels in two and a half years."

"That's good to hear. Forgive me for asking, but how do you intend to reach Myrium? Isn't it under siege from both sides of the River Meyien?" asked Devlyn, truly concerned. "You and your company don't intend to cut through Erynor's forces, do you?"

"Not at the moment." Myranda's expression turned grim, and Devlyn understood that she was quite prepared to meet the invading armies in battle, despite the disparity in their forces.

"You might not be aware of my mother's origins," Myranda went on, "but she was not born into her crown. She married into it. Before she had any claim to the crown, she was known as Lady Karina of House Roseraie, the ruling house of Roselan. It just so happens that along the River Meyien near their city stands a castle, ruled by the same house. That particular castle has a port along the river and Roseraie ships anchor there—we'll sail from Roselan to Myrium. My grandfather, Lord Roseraie, will ensure my safety with his armada."

Devlyn recognized an elderly ei'ana, Mother Loretta Javie, Chair of Crimsyn, coming toward them from behind Myranda. The Chair smiled at them and addressed Myranda.

"Daughter, I had always hoped that your responsibilities to Sorenthil would not take you from us, let alone so soon. But never forget, you are also a Crimsyn. Should ever you require our assistance, know that it is yours."

Tears swelled in Myranda's blue eyes but did not fall when Mother Loretta and the princess shared a long embrace and bid each other farewell. Devlyn added his wishes for good luck and safe travels—he too had to say goodbye to his friend.

When Myranda turned toward the castle doors to take her place in the awaiting carriage, someone walked through the opened doors. The newcomer stood in the doorway and the light behind her made it almost impossible to see who it was, but Devlyn's heart lifted as if it was light as a feather, thrumming so loudly in his chest that he hoped no one could hear it.

Once Myranda realized who it was, she ran toward the door just as Ellendren ran toward Myranda.

"Don't look too excited," Liam whispered for only Devlyn to hear. It had not been a loud comment but still Devlyn quickly looked about to see if anyone had overheard.

Devlyn tried to slow his heart beat and control his enthusiasm. He didn't know why he allowed himself to grow so excited, since she wasn't free; Ellendren was betrothed to Trethien. Devlyn's scratchy white robes also reminded him that he was an ei'ceuril novice.

Ellendren and Myranda hugged, and laughed, tears now rolling down both their faces as they spoke quickly to one another. He wondered whether Ellendren had seen him; she must have—it might be one thing to miss him, but to miss Aliel was impossible. Both girls drew near Devlyn.

Don't stutter; don't stutter, Devlyn told himself.

A sense of amusement passed from Aliel, and Devlyn conveyed his own embarrassed annoyance in return.

Ellendren smiled. Her eyes were just as beautiful as he remembered, the elven silver encasing the emerald around the pupil. Her silvery blond hair, much longer than he remembered, framed her angular oval face.

"Oh Devlyn, it's so nice to see you. Your eyes are different." Ellendren looked into his eyes—his now golden eyes—and wrapped her arms around him in a warm hug. "I had hoped we would cross paths while we were in the Illumined Wood, but we must have never been near one another. It's quite large after all, but I did hope."

"It's great to see you too, Elle." Devlyn didn't want their embrace to end. The memory of his loneliness in the Illumined Wood returned. How he would have appreciated such a simple sign of affection! "I heard that you were expected to return over a month ago; what kept you?" *Stop sounding desperate.*

"I'll tell you those details later, but I do want to tell you that before I left the Illumined Wood, I was approached by a magnificent creature. I could not believe my eyes when I saw her!" Ellendren began to describe the creature, but Aliel recognized it before she could finish, which meant that so did Devlyn.

"An alicorn! How did you come by her?"

I thought there was only one in the Illumined Wood, Leilyn's, and the rest are with Aewen in the Wooded Hills of Thellion. Devlyn's mind turned to Aliel.

It seems there were two.

"You know of them? She's incredible, Devlyn, you and your phoenix must meet her."

I forgot to introduce you to her.

I am Aliel; it is a pleasure to finally meet you. Ellendren's smile faded and her brow furrowed in confusion when she heard the phoenix in her mind.

"It's how they communicate, phoenix that is." Devlyn not only heard Aliel communicate with Ellendren, he understood her confusion, and sought to reassure her. With the length of time they had been together, Devlyn knew precisely what Aliel had conveyed, but he doubted that Ellendren could capture it all. After all, it had taken him a year and half to fully understand.

"How did you know?" Ellendren trailed off and looked back into his golden eyes. "You're bound at this very moment, aren't you?"

Devlyn nodded and tried not to feel uncomfortable as she gazed into his eyes.

"Incredible."

"It really is. But let me introduce you. You remember Liam, of course," Devlyn reintroduced his brother to Ellendren, "and this is Jaerol; I don't think you've met."

"It's nice to see you again, Liam, and very nice to meet you, Jaerol." Ellendren noticed his bright red hair and pointed ears, clear indicators that he was a Cyndinari but did not comment. "Forgive me, I hope to speak with you again, but I must say goodbye to Myranda before she leaves." Ellendren turned to Myranda and the two made their way out the door, Myranda giving one last wave to those gathered in the small entrance hall and leaving the castle, her accompanying ei'ana close behind.

Now everyone left in the hall went about their business elsewhere, leaving Devlyn, Aliel, Liam, and Jaerol alone. Devlyn wanted desperately to catch up with Ellendren to hear the details of her time in the Illumined Wood. Since he did not have classes or private lessons on Saraen, they decided to return to the Temple of Ceur. As they came out of the castle, they watched Myranda and her escort's departure toward the city gate, still lying in ruins from Erynor's attack. Devlyn hoped that the makeshift ramp was sturdy enough to carry the royal entourage. Devlyn, Liam, and Jaerol moved toward the bridge over the shallow river to the temple but before they made it out of the quad, Ellendren approached Devlyn again. She gave him another long hug and whispered in his ear, "Don't read it yet."

He was about to ask what she was talking about when he felt her press a small piece of parchment into his palm. Her troubled expression was new to Devlyn.

"Aaron is here, in fact, he's with the ei'ceuril again. He would love to see you."

She smiled at the news, but walked away, turning her head only once to look back in their direction.

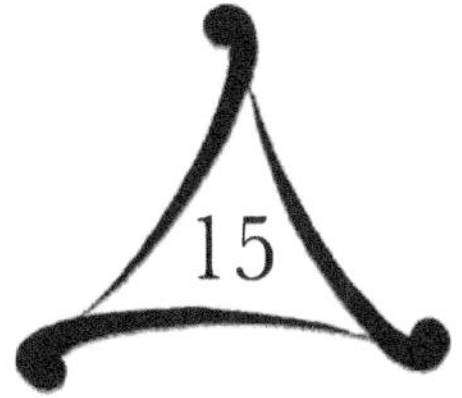

Encroaching Shadows

My dear, I understand that you had an incredible experience while in the Illumined Wood, as most novices do. But, when you left here, your intention was to join the Crimsyn School when you returned," said Cathleen, a youthful ei'ana Ellendren barely knew, but who was one of the wise ones of the Ei'ana in spite of appearing to be only a decade or so older than Ellendren. Only Chairs and wise ones were invited to the Choosing ceremony in the Chamber of the Seven Chairs, so clearly, Cathleen was rightfully in attendance, but Cathleen's tone leaned toward censure, and it was hard to take from someone so near her own age.

Don't let her bait you, Ellendren told herself. The Choosing ceremony was a public declaration of the young wielder's choice of School to pledge her further allegiance and area of specialization. Ellendren knew of other girls who had opted to join a School other than the one they had originally intended. It was a final decision though, and once she declared her choice at this ceremony, there was no switching Schools.

Cathleen's words struck Ellendren though, and she pushed away her irritation, distracting herself by wiping her hands down her robes as though to flatten them. Since her arrival at Gwilnor Academy as a ten-year-old, she'd had every intention to become a Crimsyn ei'ana, an intention she shared with one of her closest friends, Myranda. The two had planned to travel the world together and offer healing to anyone needing it.

But everything had changed after she had gone into the Illumined Wood.

Instinctually, she had been aware of the Protection of the Wood that had been raised around Lucillia and that it meant that one of her parents had sacrificed themselves to protect their people. That saddened her, and without knowing which one, she mourned both even as she contemplated her future. With the king or queen of Lucillia dead, the throne would pass to the next generation, and as the youngest child of the Aryl of Lucillia, the crowns would pass to her and her future husband on the day of their wedding. And the death of one of her parents made that decision ever more imminent. The thought of Trethien as her husband and reigning as king was troubling to say the least, since she had had little choice in the betrothal. Sure, he was a decent elf who came from the right House, but he was no king. He just didn't seem to be aware of much beyond his own small sphere and seemed to hold no interest in the welfare of others. Oddly, Devlyn infiltrated her mind. He was handsome, even though she had never seen an elf with his hair color before and she could not decide whether or not she found it attractive. He also seemed to care about the larger world, even if he was blind to politics and the current world order. She still felt embarrassed for him when she remembered that he had once said Lankor seemed like a nice place to visit. *Idiot.*

She had had time to consider her future while she was in the Wood, and the more she thought about being the Aryl of Lucillia, the more she reconsidered her choice to profess the Ei'ana Counsels in the Crimsyn School. Eklean was being torn asunder by war and while there was great need for healers, there was even greater need for justice. Near the end of her novitiate, she had decided that her duty to her home and kingdom pointed to a different direction, and she determined that, at the Choosing ceremony, she would join the Vyoletryn School.

"It's of course your right to select another School. This ritual is not named the Choosing without merit," another wise one spoke from the opposite side of the Chamber of the Seven Chairs.

Only the wise ones spoke at present, each offering commentary on the student's choice before the novice professed her choice of School. They stood behind their respective Chairs. The only Chair permitted to speak during a Choosing was the Chair of the School chosen by the student, and that was reserved for the closing of the ceremony.

Ellendren had grown tired of listening to the wise ones' arguments.

She had entered the seven-sided chamber an hour ago. At least, she thought an hour had passed. The castle's foundations muted the bells' sonorous tolls preventing the sound from reaching this chamber. She stood patiently, listening to each argument, both in support of and against her decision to change her School. No argument against her switch had swayed her; in her opinion, none had held merit.

Before anyone else could speak, Ellendren turned to the eldest woman in the room, the one with a purple shawl wrapped about her shoulders.

"I, Ellendren of House Roendryn, daughter of Vernal and Harnyl, Aryl of Lucillia, do declare that I will profess freely the Ei'ana Counsels as written in the Holy Tome of Minothyl at the instruction of Ceurtriarch Telerius by request of Roendryn, first Aryl of Lucillia. To these Counsels will I adhere in obedience as a sister and daughter of the Vyoletryn School, at the completion of my studies."

Her part was done. The Chair of Vyoletryn maintained every right to deny her request. That rarely occurred but not so infrequently that every young woman who stood before the Chairs held a measure of fear that she might be one of those very few who were denied. The last recorded occurrence had been eighty-three years ago.

Every ei'ana in the room took her seat, and Mother Paurel Roendryn, her great aunt on her mother's side, sister to her grandfather, the late king of Lucillia, stood proudly, her smile so wide it revealed her teeth. "Daughter Ellendren, I receive you into the School of Vigyl Vyoletryn. Henceforth, you are acknowledged as a student of Vyoletryn. Receive our emblem and bear it for all to see."

From below, Ellendren looked toward Paurel and the oversized Vyoletryn emblem on the wall behind, marveling at the golden emblem with the violet drapery behind that highlighted the emblem's details: a naked female and male elf standing in the face of injustice, each grasping a staff. Above them flew an eagle. On a table set in the center of the room next to where Ellendren stood were seven emblems representing each of the seven Schools. Glancing at the Crimsyn emblem, she picked up the Vyoletryn emblem and pinned it to her breast. The personal emblem bore the golden figures wrought within the circlet. Her clothing would supply the violet field.

She was not yet an ei'ana, but she was one step closer to professing the Counsels and becoming one.

The ceremony now officially over, the wise ones and Chairs moved toward the exit from their balcony behind a secret door when Ellendren spoke up. "Wait! There is something you must know."

Surprised, they turned to look at Ellendren since normally the ceremony concluded with a silent departure.

"The day, no, the night I left the Illumined Wood, the moon was incredibly bright, lighting much of the plains beyond the Wood. Just past the last few trees, I saw a minum waiting anxiously. I could tell that he was terrified, and before I could approach, a young woman with all blue eyes stopped me from behind. I didn't even notice that she was with an alicorn at first. From where I stood in the forest, I saw a winged person cloaked in shadow strike the minum with a foul wielding a moment later. Not even the shadows of the trees were as dark as what struck the minum. The creature hoisted the unconscious minum under his arm and flew south."

Everyone in the chamber stared at Ellendren, appalled at her words yet uncertain about what could be done about it.

"You are certain of this, Daughter?" Paurel's aged wrinkles amplified her concerned expression. Ellendren nodded, and Paurel turned to Velaria.

"Mother Velaria, is there any protection against a seguian?"

It took Ellendren a second to grasp the significance of Mother Paurel's question. *Could a minum be forced to open a seguian?* Ellendren's thoughts swirled at the possibility. If Erynor destroyed that minum's resistance, he could infiltrate Gwilnor or any other castle without warning. Not even the Temple of Ceur could prevent a seguian from opening.

"The only known safeguard today is the Protection of the Wood, currently shielding Lucillia, a tremendous power that we don't fully understand. Such power might lie within Devlyn and his phoenix since it was the Phaedryn who limited the use of seguians to the minums. Unfortunately, Devlyn is nowhere near unlocking the knowledge necessary to guard against a seguian opening into our strongholds." Velaria was just as alarmed as Paurel. "As for Aren, he has power only the Phaedryn of old would possess. If he decides to openly attack, there is little we can do to stop him. Our only option is for us all to reach our potential." She paused to take a breath but looked around at the women present so that they would know she was not finished speaking. "Our potential in the use of kiara and kien. We need kien wielders to control the erendinth which will help us to reach our potential strength as kiara wielders. Devlyn cannot do it alone."

Ellendren forgot her breach in protocol, her disruption of the ritualistic silent filing out of the chamber quickly overshadowed by what Velaria just suggested. The noise level on the seven balconies rose as every ei'ana began speaking at once, some in favor, others vehemently opposed to the radical idea of encouraging kien wielders to wield the erendinth freely. Still standing below, Ellendren listened as wise ones in the room argued, eventually noticing that only the Azurelle wise ones were unanimous in their support, while the Arantiulyn wise ones all opposed the suggestion, and the rest of them all varied in their opinions, loudly arguing across the chamber to one another. None of the Seven Chairs participated in the argument. Still on her feet, Mother Paurel raised her voice to a level Ellendren did not expect possible.

"Is this how wise ones discuss among themselves?"

The entire room slowly faded to silence and Paurel spoke again, this time at a normal level. "This matter will be discussed at length, but not in the presence of a student, and the decision belongs to the Seven Chairs alone. You will be summoned to a symposium to discuss the matter. I suggest everyone temper themselves before we reconvene. Ellendren, my daughter, we will hold a reception in your honor in the grand salon of the Vyoletryn Wing. I trust you know its location."

"You're not concentrating; try harder." Eagan Wintyr chided Devlyn who was trying to shift between places in Somnaeniel. He knew where he wanted to go, and he could vaguely visualize it: the short wooden wall surrounding the original village of Cor'lera, with wood and thatch buildings inside and outside its defenses. "Physical appearances are not enough.

Nearly every small village looks like Cor'lera; you have to concentrate on the place itself, its location in the world and why it's there and not somewhere else."

What makes Cor'lera different? Aliel was attuned to his thoughts as always but didn't provide any insight; Devlyn had to figure this out on his own, and he knew it.

The Illumined Wood lay just to the east of Cor'lera; that certainly made it unique, but that wasn't enough. *The grapes*, he thought with certainty, *they don't grow in any other location in the entire world!* Quickly focusing his attention on the light blue ice grapes which produced the popular Cor'leran Blue, Devlyn felt the world begin to change, but the grapes weren't enough either.

Disappointed and discouraged, he thought again about Cor'lera. An insignificant village on the fringes of Parendior, it meant more to Devlyn than any city he had visited. Terrible things had taken place there and the natives had suffered greatly at the hands of Perrien. Despite everything that happened to him there, it was still his birthplace. He once had a family there.

Now, Devlyn felt the world around him change, shifting with his will. The stone buildings and streets of Ceurenyl vanished, replaced by sights and landmarks Devlyn knew better than anywhere else in the world.

"Well done." Eagan looked around the village. "However, you do not have an emotional attachment to every place you will wish to shift to in the World-in-Between. If you limit yourself to places you care about for the trigger that causes the shift, you will limit the number of locations considerably."

"How am I supposed to shift to someplace if I've never been there? How am I to see it, if there is nothing for me to visualize?" Devlyn was frustrated. Eagan Wintyr asked the impossible. He had managed to shift to Cor'lera only because he had lived there for thirteen years. He couldn't shift to the place Abbie had taken him to on the other side of Teraeniel.

Eagan's emerald eyes smiled, just as Abbie's would. "I told you, it is not a matter of visualizing. You have to place yourself there; you have to will it."

Devlyn wanted to argue with him but knew that he still lacked the understanding that would make shifting readily possible for him.

"Let's try to shift someplace that you have never been. I want you to shift to Jadien."

"Jadien? Isn't that a small island filled with pirates?" Devlyn remembered seeing the small island between Dagger's Point and the Kinzdol Islands on a map. But what if he missed the tiny island and shifted into the Erynien Bay? Could he drown here?

"Remember, what you know of the place or think you know of the place does not matter. Get that through your head."

"All right." Devlyn thought aloud, not that thinking to himself did any good here. His thoughts were just as loud as his verbal words were. "Don't visualize it, just place myself there." He knew nothing of the pirate island of Jadien. He didn't know if the island had sand, jungles, or mountains. It could have low rolling hills for all Devlyn knew. But apparently, none of that mattered. How could none of that matter? How could the physical features of a place not define that place? Was there something deeper, something truer about a place than its physical expression?

Devlyn stopped thinking. His mind went blank as if a missing puzzle piece fell into place and cleared the picture. He looked at Eagan and his smiling eyes. "But what is it? What is truer about the land than the land itself?"

Eagan didn't respond, but Aliel provided a vision of a radiant light basking everything, not just the land but the creatures as well. The golden light did not come from the sun, nor a particular location; rather it simply emanated from everything completely, bringing forth the true natures of everything it lit or emanated from. Devlyn couldn't describe it. There were no words for it. It reminded him of looking through Aliel's eyes.

"Reality is much different than you perceive it, Devlyn." Eagan's quiet voice held a prophetic tone. "Few are gifted with such ability to view reality as it actually is in our world. The day will come when you will see it as nothing other than as it is. We see through a fogged mirror with beveled edges on a cloudy day; an image so imperfect that it hardly represents that which is beyond our sight. The world we live in is not ugly and gloomy as so many believe it to be, a place of only sin and death. It is not the world that must change, but rather how people view the world."

Closing his eyes, Devlyn recalled how connected the world felt while he wielded terys—not that he could wield in Somnaeniel—but he knew it was as connected as Teraeniel. It was not the stone that bound everything firmly together, but something else entirely. He didn't visualize where he wanted to go but willed himself to be there. He couldn't say how it happened; it simply did.

Jagged mountains covered the small island. They weren't the tallest mountains, but they were taller than he would have expected for an island the size of Jadien.

Wanting to see the city of the same name as the island, Devlyn shifted again, with more ease this time. It still didn't happen instantly, but it was faster than when he had tried to shift to Cor'lera. The city lacked a defensive wall and all the buildings shared the same yellow sandstone.

As they walked through the streets Devlyn saw a woman standing in the middle of the road. Her skin and hair were dark-brown, nearly black, as were her eyes. The woman didn't appear to hold any ill will toward them; she simply stood in the middle of the street, staring directly at them.

"Do you know her?" Devlyn whispered to Eagan so she might not overhear.

"Not her personally, but her people are not unknown to mine. I cannot tell whether she is here intentionally or if she simply dreamt herself here accidentally." Eagan's eyes stayed on her.

The woman began to speak in a language that Devlyn had never heard. She was trying to communicate with them, but no matter what she said, Devlyn simply could not understand her. Eagan did seem to understand and listened as she walked toward them speaking determinedly. Devlyn stepped back, unnerved by his lack of understanding.

"She means us no harm. She's warning us that it is not safe to enter the World-in-Between. She says that the Evil One is exerting his influence over it once again, and that his servants already Dream without hindrance."

The woman came closer still, only several paces from them now, not stopping. As she extended her hands toward Devlyn, he wanted to step back again, but remained planted where he stood. The woman placed one hand on each of his temples, and now, when she spoke, he understood her speech even when her hands dropped away. The words were not translated; he just understood them.

"My people have suffered enough by the Evil One's hand. There was a time when we walked this World-in-Between just as much and as often as the aldarchs and the druids and we still would, if not for the Evil One. The Dreamers among my people were driven mad when he last reigned here. We now call this place the Shadow Lands; land of the dead." The woman's black eyes pierced Devlyn's own.

"How, woman, do you remember when the Evil One last reigned in these lands? My people remember, but not even we could count the number of years. It was when Saeryndol was a valley lost to all and not a lake—before the Great Blessing itself." Eagan's words left Devlyn lost and confused.

"The Chronicle Stones do not forget the past as do our minds with each passing generation." The woman violently shook her hands. "The prison grows weak and Life shall pass into Death. You cannot save it, Phaedryn; it will die, and Light shall be consumed by Darkness."

"You speak the impossible." Concern grew in Eagan's voice.

"The weakened prison is not unknown to you, Druid. Prepare yourselves for the Darkness that will envelop all worlds!" The woman faded and disappeared.

Devlyn was confused. "Was she a Jadien pirate?" Devlyn thought it the simplest question, but Eagan Wintyr was very troubled.

"No. She does come from where those who you call pirates originally came from though, a continent far to the south and west of Eklean, with a great ocean in between, known as Ja'horan. And what she spoke of would be a living nightmare if it came to pass. Beneath Saeryndol Lake stretch the roots of Verakryl—the Tree of Life. They are neither solid nor liquid; no other substance is like those roots. The roots stretch across the entire world, beneath every land and sea, but only in Saeryndol Lake are they exposed. They cover a cavern on the bottom of the lake, a cavern that holds an ancient creature of incredible power. The creature was once counted among the greatest anadel before rising against Anaweh and subtly corrupting his Children while they still dwelt in the Valley of Saeryndol and even after they departed that sacred valley."

"I know this story; it's told to scare children, to make them behave and go to bed when they're told. I heard about this Evil One when I caused trouble as a little kid, just like everyone else. What's next? You're going to tell me that after people began to die, they tried to fight against the Evil One and after a battle of unimaginable proportion he was locked in his prison?"

Eagan was clearly frustrated with Devlyn's mockery. "Did you ever imagine that such tales are told to children because they are the only ones with ears to listen to such truth?"

Slightly taken aback by Eagan's seriousness, Devlyn looked to Aliel for confirmation of this farfetched story.

There is much that has been forgotten through time. Only two can recall from their own experience the events Eagan Wintyr speaks of, and you have spoken with one of them, Aliel replied. Hearing it from Aliel provided more surety than hearing it from Eagan. Not that Devlyn doubted Eagan, but he had the same tendency as his sister to say unimaginable things, making the listener question their mental soundness.

"If what she said is true, how do we stop it from coming to pass? Do the ei'ana and ei'ceuril know of it?" asked Devlyn, still not entirely concerned about this Evil One. Erynor was more than enough to occupy his mind; a real enemy causing real harm to Eklean.

Eagan stood motionless, his head slightly bowed and looking toward the ground. "The only way to know for sure that the prison is secure is to go to it."

"That's physically impossible; the Shroud prevents anyone from drawing close, and it covers the entirety of the lake and all Krysenthiel," said Devlyn just as Eagan grabbed his hand.

Jadien faded, replaced by an area mostly in obscurity. A single patch of sun shone through from above, while on every side was a dense, sickly mist. Devlyn knew this place, and he wished more than anything to be as far away as possible.

Eagan's emerald eyes stared intently into Devlyn's own, not with their usual smile. "Was this patch not created by you and Aliel?" Eagan walked to the edge of the narrow clearing to take a closer look at the Shroud that tried to press in and take back what it once possessed.

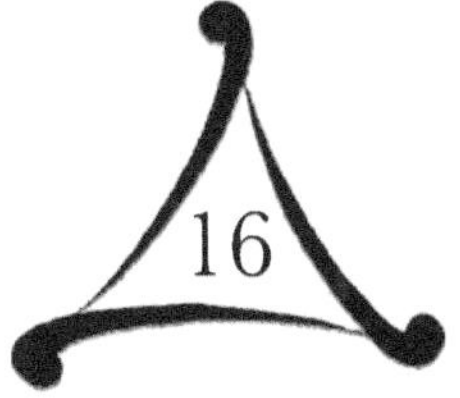

16

No Place is Safe

Devlyn and Ellendren faced each other as he considered his next wield. They were practicing in Gwilnor's main courtyard, its continuous arcade looping around them, interrupted only by the mass forming the library. Now that Devlyn had resumed his studies at Gwilnor, he could wield openly in the safety of the castle—there was no need to practice in the valley anymore. Ellendren had wasted little time upon her return and had insisted that they resume their practice sessions together as fellows.

Now, Devlyn hesitated. He wanted to attempt a wield using a transcendental with the elementals. Wielding an elemental erendinth required him to press outward and into the erendinth, which he could do with easy assurance, but wielding a transcendental erendinth required embracing the erendinth, bringing it into himself. While his confidence with the transcendental erendinth grew daily, wielding them at the same time made Devlyn's stomach twist inside out.

Velaria insisted that he needed to practice wielding the transcendentals. She had also told him that if he didn't learn to wield both simultaneously, he would remain blind to an infinite number of powerful wields forgotten by contemporary ei'ana.

Devlyn had thought that the library might have books that might explain the process of wielding different types of erendinth together and even considered asking Kevn. If such a book existed, Kevn would know. There weren't many books in Gwilnor's library that Kevn didn't know about. Still, could a book teach him how to direct his inner spirit to wield the different erendinth together? Wielding depended on feeling and Devlyn had to place himself in the present whenever he did so. Not in a book or manuscript. So, he hadn't asked Kevn, but he had told Ellendren that he wanted to try during their practice today, and she had insisted that he work with animys first as she didn't trust umbrys.

Do you think we'll be able to manage it? Sometimes, Devlyn wanted the reassurance that Aliel provided.

You're on your own this time—wouldn't be fair to the princess, replied Aliel. *I like her. You should spend more time with her.*

Even with Aliel, Devlyn occasionally felt irritated, and it resulted in grinding teeth. Hiding any of his emotions from the phoenix was impossible. Aliel knew what it meant to become an ei'ceuril and he certainly knew how he felt about Ellendren.

Pushing that aside, and determined to be able to tell Velaria that he'd followed her instructions, Devlyn opened himself to the erendinth, and pulled animys into himself without transforming it into a wield; he had to press into terys and aerys first.

Holding animys, he then focused on pressing into the elemental erendinth without losing his grasp over animys. Reminding himself that this was something he'd done before, he pressed part of his energy into terys and aerys. Performing the two opposite acts made Devlyn unsteady, and his control wobbled when he tried to start a wield. It was an uncomfortable balancing act, but as he concentrated on wielding the three erendinth separately, they seemed to solidify. His grasp over them strengthened with every passing moment.

Feeling comfortable with the separate erendinth, Devlyn wove the three together without a particular wield in mind as he joined them.

He had anticipated that animys would magnify the other erendinth. While he had wielded animys with the elemental erendinth before, it had been without conscious thought—instinct had always driven him. And because of that, he didn't understand how it worked. But now, he had to focus on his wielding and learn from it, he had to understand it. As animys mingled with the other erendinth, it became clear that it was anything but an amplifier.

Wielding the three erendinth together resulted in tiny pellets. He didn't entirely understand how that had happened but took a mental note of how he had woven them.

Ellendren saw the pellets form about him and stood her ground when Devlyn shot them toward her.

While she was not as powerful as Devlyn, she easily held more control than he did, and she was capable of some of the most stunning wields Devlyn had ever seen. Only Velaria was stronger, with a prowess in wielding that was stunning. Devlyn's instinct leaned toward wielding a single erendinth at a time with as much force as possible, but Ellendren naturally intertwined the different erendinth, creating intricate wields. And whenever Devlyn managed to lace the erendinth together, she knew exactly how to undo them, readily dissolving his wield before attacking him with her own.

Unraveling the tiny pellets of aerys, terys, and animys posed more difficulty. Devlyn had grown tired of creating massive wields of incredible strength that Ellendren stripped apart before anything came anywhere near her. Following her lead with this intricate wield, Devlyn smirked as she struggled to unravel the finely compact pellets coming toward her. Her eyes were set and unmoving as she focused, and finally threw her hands up and created a cyclone that sucked Devlyn's attack in at an angle and lifted it to the sky where she rendered the pellets useless.

Ellendren smiled triumphantly, and Devlyn had to admit that what she had done was incredible. Every day, she became stronger in kiara. Distracted and expecting that she would now create a separate wield, he was off guard when a surprise attack caught him. Two strong squalls of air came at him from opposite directions—one from behind buckled his knees as the other crashed against his chest, throwing him backward and lifting him off his feet and slamming him to the ground where he lay, gasping for breath.

Laughter pealed around him. "The big, mighty Phaedryn knocked on his back by a defenseless princess." Ellendren mocked, standing over Devlyn and looking down at him.

"You are anything but defenseless, Elle!" Devlyn wielded the ground beneath her feet, toppling her unexpectedly right on top of him. Devlyn lost all ability to speak as she lay on him, her heart beating just as quickly as his, and not entirely due to their hard work. Nervously, he tried to free himself and stand, but Ellendren caught his eyes in hers. Her sliver-green eyes mesmerized him and Devlyn couldn't access his mental faculties. All he knew was that he did not want her to move.

He looked at her and she looked at him, with the weight of her body pressing into him. It felt as if he dreamed an impossible dream and he did not want to wake up. Devlyn could not count the passing seconds, and their faces drew closer. Just as Ellendren smiled her beautiful shy smile, a whistle came from the near side of the courtyard and Ellendren was off him faster than the cyclone she had wielded just moments ago.

"Is that what happens when boys and girls wield together?" Alex called from beneath the covered arcade, walking into the open courtyard with Kevn and Andrew. "Quite progressive for an ei'ceuril and ei'ana if you ask me. No wonder they caution against men wielding."

Devlyn sat up quickly, heart racing. He wanted nothing more than to punch his cousin as hard as he could; fortunately, Andrew swatted the back of Alex's head. "We were practicing wielding, and…"

"Uh huh, is that what they're calling it now? You could've practiced wielding somewhere more pri…" Alex's words fell away as the ground was pulled from beneath him, and he tipped over, flat on his face. "Oh, real mature, Dev," he called out, as Kevn and Andrew laughed.

Devlyn hadn't so much as touched the erendinth. However, Ellendren wore the most innocent expression he had ever seen, though her eyes sparkled with laughter. Alex pushed himself up, wiped the grass and dirt from his legs and chest, and left them in the courtyard, muttering to Kevn and Andrew as they went back inside the castle.

His cousin was right, of course; they were in a very public courtyard. Not only did windows open onto them from every side, but the most traversed part of the castle formed part of the enclosure. Students and ei'ana regularly walked through the covered arcades along the walls and across the paths crisscrossing the courtyard. While it served as an accepted location to practice wielding, Devlyn was suddenly very aware of all the windows looking down on him. Trethien could easily be on the other side of any of them, keeping an eye on Ellendren. And if Trethien seeing Ellendren fall on top of him was not bad enough, he could only imagine what it would be like if an Albien ei'ana, whose quarters also overlooked the main courtyard, had seen the two.

Devlyn looked at Ellendren, deliberately ignoring all the windows and setting aside his worry.

"Well, you don't think speaking to a princess in such a way is acceptable, do you?" she asked, looking self-righteous with her chin tilted slightly upward, her fingers pulling at her newly gained pin—the sigil of Vyoletryn was now a part of her wardrobe.

Devlyn had to laugh at the situation.

"It's probably best that we quit for the day."

"Yeah, you're probably right," said Devlyn, noting that she took no notice of their lack of privacy. "I've been meaning to ask you, how does it feel to officially belong to the Vyoletryns?"

"Not much has changed, to be honest. It's nice to have my own room again. Not that I minded sharing a room with Fyona, but it is nice to have my own space in the Vyoletryn wing." Ellendren glanced toward the East Tower, the second largest of Gwilnor's towers looming above the main courtyard, its upper levels housing the Vyoletryn wing.

"I didn't know students moved to their own room after the Choosing ceremony. Granted, they never made me share a room in the first place."

"Oh yes, once we choose a School, we move out of the shared dormitories and into the appropriate wing of the castle to begin the second phase of our education. The original intent for this curriculum had student wielders studying solely with ei'ana from their own School, but that was before the Balance was broken and Gwilnor was solely used as a place of study." Ellendren trailed off at the mention of Septyl's past status. "Did you have any private lessons today?"

"I met with Kai this morning, and I'll meet with Julienne before dinner. Have your private lessons resumed?"

Ellendren shook her head. "No, the Vyoletryns have been questioning me constantly."

"What about?"

"Would you like to accompany me to the stables and meet the alicorn who brought me from the Illumined Wood?"

Devlyn tried not to show his bewilderment at the abrupt change of topic, especially since Ellendren never avoided questions.

"Um, sure." Devlyn smiled. He'd been enjoying the quiet moment they were sharing, sitting on the grass in the courtyard, just chatting. They had not had much opportunity to spend time together beyond their practice sessions. Granted, that was an hour each day, but it was a time for working, not relaxing together. When they did come across each other, Ellendren's entourage of friends surrounded her. So, as they moved through the castle toward the stables, Devlyn expected at least three of those friends to find them and join them there. Truth be told, Devlyn really enjoyed their practice afternoons together—alone. Well, as alone as they could be, with Aliel. It felt different with Aliel though, because the phoenix was simply part of him and it would feel odd, even wrong, if Aliel disappeared.

At another time—a safer time—Devlyn and Ellendren could have walked out the large wooden doors at the main entry. It would've been a more direct route to the stables. Instead, they had to travel through the castle's interior, a route that meant crossing the bridge from the White Tower and into the Dragon Tower and going through the school. Two ei'ana stood at each end of the bridge for added protection, each one from a different School, an added precaution against collusion.

As they walked along, passing students gave them side glances, but in many cases, without making eye contact. Devlyn anxiously wondered if someone had seen them lying together in the main courtyard, and then started rumors. *Maybe someone told Trethien?* His body grew damp with nervous sweat, a bead even forming at his temple. *They probably were just looking at Aliel,* he tried to comfort himself, and glanced at Ellendren, to see whether he could tell if she was worried.

She held her head high as always with her shoulders back, quite at ease. Devlyn thought it reflected her composure both as a princess and a future ei'ana, and envied that ease as his robe grew damp from his sweating discomfort.

"Do you think all those students saw us?" He admitted to himself that the eyes were definitely staring at Ellendren and him, not at Aliel. Ellendren shrugged her shoulders, her expression serene. *How does she manage that?* Devlyn thought, pushing his hands into his pockets.

They turned a corner leading into a spacious hall near the only unbarred entrance. Devlyn's heart leapt and raced at seeing Trethien storming toward them. He'd probably heard about it from others who had seen them lying together.

"How could you? The entire castle has witnessed your infidelity toward me!" Trethien aimed each word as a dagger, directly at Ellendren, ignoring Devlyn for the moment. "You disgrace me in front of everyone! Is this how you respect a royal betrothal? A betrothal arranged by the Aryl of Lucillia themselves!"

Devlyn wanted to respond, wanted to punch Trethien square in the face. Just as he took a step forward, Trethien rounded on him before he could utter a single word.

"Don't you dare speak to me, lowborn!" Fire shot from his eyes. It looked like he desperately wanted to slaughter Devlyn.

Devlyn took offense at the epithet, thinking that Trethien might be surprised to learn that as a descendent of Feolyn and the Aryl of Cor'lera, Devlyn was quite possibly higher born than Trethien.

"Is this what you want? A lowborn kien wielder, someone more likely to destroy Eklean rather than preserve it?" Trethien went on.

Ellendren held Trethien in an icy gaze, refusing to dignify his outburst with a response. His face turned deadlier, shifting between rage and disgust, his eyes now red. A tense moment passed as Ellendren just stared at Trethien then he pushed past them, deliberately crashing his shoulder hard enough into Devlyn's to make him stumble before stalking off.

They began to walk away through the gawkers surrounding them. Trethien's outburst had been loud enough for everyone in the next two corridors to hear, possibly even the entire south wing of the castle, let alone those who had been nearby to witness the exchange.

They reached the small entry hall and walked past the Septyl knights standing guard, each in their different colored tunics.

"You are not permitted to leave the castle," said the Septyl knight wearing the purple tunic, looking directly at Devlyn. None of the knights wore their helms; all held them uniformly under their left arm, with their right hand free and ready to pull their sword from their scabbard if necessary. "And we cannot allow you into the city without your escort. You weren't expected to return to the temple until the eleventh bell."

"Are the stables not considered part of the castle?" Ellendren asked, still serene, no sign of their confrontation with Trethien showing.

"Well, technically…"

"Wonderful, so you *will* let us pass as we are not technically leaving the castle." The knights grudgingly parted and allowed them to pass. Even though the knights had to treat every student equally, none of them enjoyed arguing with a princess. Aside from the Temple of Ceur, the quad was the securest location in all Ceurenyl.

Ellendren had a hint of a confident smile as they walked under the large archway to the stables. "I wasn't sure if they would let us pass. We're lucky an ei'ana wasn't on guard duty—the quad is technically considered outside the castle. It feels like we're prisoners in our own home."

They descended a ramp that led to the large stables below an unused wing of the castle. Devlyn had never had reason to visit them and took a good look as they walked along.

Unlike most stables with a single bay of stalls stretching from front to back on either side of a central aisle, Gwilnor's stable had several switchbacks and angles zigzagging throughout. But one thing was the same—regardless of the type of stable, the smell never changed. Memories from Cor'lera surfaced and the countless occasions he had had to clean the abbey school's stables. That felt like an age ago.

They reached a stall set apart from the others where Ellendren's alicorn stood patiently munching from a hay trough. Devlyn smiled at the alicorn then approached to brush her shimmering silver-white coat glistening in the dull light, wings folded against her sides. A silver horn protruded from her head, it too giving off light. The alicorn stirred at Devlyn's touch and acknowledged them, her intelligent eyes assessing them both then shifting to look at Aliel.

"Her name is Laureniel." Ellendren held her hand up to the legendary creature's nose.

"She's incredible, Elle."

"She really is. I still can't believe I flew back to Ceurenyl from the Illumined Wood. We had to be careful and could only fly at night. I thought of flying past Myrium—I had no idea it was under siege—but decided against it. I did see the Protection of the Wood raised around Lucillia though…" Her voice caught in her throat at the thought and her eyes hardened.

"I'm sorry," Devlyn managed. He tried to think of something else to say, but nothing came to mind. He well remembered Vernal saying goodbye just before he'd gone into the Wood, but she'd given no indication that it was final. Was she the one who had raised the shield? Aaron certainly thought so. Should he tell Ellendren about it? "Are you all right, Elle?" Devlyn worried that she had many concerns facing her now, not least that she was grieving. And he still wanted to punch Trethien for what he had said to her.

"How dare he use my parents against me! He knows that one of them died to protect Lucillia. And now there is no aryl. I am not ready to be aryl, and I am certainly not ready to be married." She relaxed her shoulders a hint. It looked like she had finally relieved herself of a heavy burden. "How familiar are you with elven aryls?"

"Not very." Devlyn knew the basics, that some acted as heads of states, while others served as nobles, but that was about it.

"You know how an aryl is composed of a king and queen or lord and lady?"

Devlyn nodded.

"Devlyn, either my mother or my father is dead. There is no Aryl of Lucillia." Ellendren turned away from Devlyn. "As their youngest child, it's my responsibility to fill that role. Before that can happen, I must marry."

"Trethien?" Devlyn held his breath even as his white robe made him want to scratch. Ei'ceuril did not marry. *Could* not marry.

"I've been considering ending the betrothal for a while now. Even before I learned that the Protection of the Wood was raised."

Devlyn desperately wanted to ask who else she would marry but held his tongue. His white robe aside, they were only fourteen years old. No one their age should have to worry themselves over engagements or ruling a kingdom. Devlyn also wanted to hug Ellendren, to provide some sort of comfort.

Ellendren remained silent, her thoughts and doubts held closely to herself. Whether or not she regretted her actions in the courtyard remained a mystery to Devlyn.

"Elle?" Several minutes of excruciating silence had passed, each deep in thought. Devlyn doubted that their thoughts went in the same direction, but he really wanted to ask her a question. He was pleased that Ellendren had wanted to be alone with him, even if he didn't know why, although meeting the alicorn was definitely a pleasure. It could have been the contents of the note she had given him on her return, or it could have been something else entirely. He knew that grooms were somewhere in the stable, so he kept his voice low.

"That note you gave me. I've read it several times yet can't make sense of it. All you said was, 'No place is safe.' I've been meaning to ask you about it, but there's never been an opportunity. Is that why you wanted to talk in private?"

"There's something I couldn't tell you about when we first saw each other, or since then, because we've never been far from prying ears. I wanted to visit you in the temple, but I'm restricted to the castle. I've only seen Aaron briefly a few times in between his lessons here." Ellendren spoke even more quietly than Devlyn had. "Just before I left the Illumined Wood to return to Ceurenyl, I was approached by a woman slightly older than us. She had these amazing blue eyes, yes, the whole eye. She made me wait before going out onto the plain and made sure that I did not make a sound. At first, I was frightened, but there was something familiar about her that I could not place. I'm not certain that she could speak, since she never said anything to me, not even her name."

Leilyn, it had to be Leilyn. "That explains the alicorn. I didn't know she had more than one with her." Devlyn said, although he hadn't intended to say it aloud.

"Well, yes, she did guide Laureniel to me and gestured for me to ride her. But how did you know?"

"Her name is Leilyn; she's my sister." Devlyn smiled just thinking of her. He no longer had to guess about what she looked like any longer, he knew.

"Is she really? No wonder she looked so familiar! Especially the hair—it was hard to tell at night, but even then, it was noticeably unique. But that's not what I wanted to tell you. While we stood there just a little way from the edge of the Wood in the trees, we heard a piercing screech from beyond the Illumined Wood. When I looked beyond the trees, I could see a small figure, a minum, next to a terrifying figure enshrouded in shadow with black wings."

"A minum? A time warden? One was waiting for Aaron and me when we left the Wood too, as well as that man with the black wings. The minum was probably going to bring you back to Ceurenyl." Devlyn paused, wondering if it was the same minum who had brought him and Aaron back to Ceurenyl. "Hold on, are you saying Erynor has a time warden as his prisoner?"

"Yes, and that's not all. I heard whoever was speaking say that they were already in Gwilnor. Devlyn, there are shadow elves in the castle."

"A grim day indeed." Devlyn and Ellendren jumped at the unexpected voice. Neither could see who was speaking. And Aliel hadn't warned him.

Devlyn pressed into terys; the entire stable came to his awareness, every horse in the stalls, the grooms at the far end, and the stone forming the stable with the bulk of the castle above, but Devlyn could not sense the person who spoke and Ellendren had taken a defensive stance, prepared to fight.

"Hmph. You should have done that before you started talking, fool boy!"

Feeling slightly insulted, Devlyn realized that he had never considered wielding as a security measure. However, he did recognize the voice and the insult. It had been a long time since someone had called him a fool boy.

"Oma? Is that you?" Devlyn looked about, trying to locate the dwarf who had journeyed with him, Velaria, and Alex to Ceurenyl from Belin's Watch.

"How many stones have you felt, I wonder? Still blind no doubt, yet not so blind as when we first met." Oma pushed open the gate on one of the stalls and emerged to stand beside him.

Devlyn always had mixed feelings about the dwarf but was surprisingly elated to see Oma after so long. A small part of him wanted to hug her, but a much larger part of him kept him from doing so. Oma wasn't exactly the hugging type.

Still uncertain, Ellendren looked Oma up and down, as if gauging her trustworthiness.

"Hmph, don't bother yourself with worrying over me, child; many others will deserve your worry more than this old dwarf."

Devlyn doubted that Oma's words had put Ellendren at ease, but he had a bigger concern. "Oma, how is it that I couldn't sense you when I wielded terys? That shouldn't be possible."

"Hmph, a dwarf does not become a stone seer just by looking at rocks." Oma didn't seem to think that she needed to explain further and turned her attention to Aliel. "This must be the phoenix. A creature completely other than what we dwarves know. And soon, fool boy, you shall join that otherness unknown to us."

Devlyn had forgotten that sensation of being in a fog of not understanding when it came to Oma and was not at all excited to have it return, so he stayed quiet about the topic of Aliel and their connection.

"I'm sorry, but how did you enter Gwilnor? There have been no reports of dwarves entering the castle, let alone the city!" Ellendren crossed her arms, turning somewhat belligerent about Oma and her unexpected presence.

"Hmph, you chose your School wisely. You will fit in quite well with the Vyoletryns." Oma didn't look at Ellendren, but if she had, she would have seen Ellendren's shock. "You are not aware of any such reports because they were received prior to your Choosing. As well, you're still only a student, and there's much that is kept from students. As it happens, I arrived with Devlyn through a seguian from Everin over a year and a half ago."

Devlyn saw the doubt lingering in Ellendren's expression, her eyes steady and unblinking. "It's true, Elle, we came to Ceurenyl together. But Oma, if you've been here all this time, what have you been doing? The last time I saw you was just after we arrived through the seguian. I assumed you had returned to Belin's Watch."

Oma returned his gaze for a moment or two before replying. "The Seven Chairs requested my service as soon as they became aware of enemies within the city, long before the gates fell. To many, I am not here. To many, I am not searching daily for servants of Shadow. My presence is a secret, even from other ei'ana. They fear their numbers are tainted with Tenebrae ei'ana."

Ellendren shot Oma an insulted look at the mention of such a possibility, but Oma didn't acknowledge Ellendren's affront. Devlyn raised an eyebrow, not clear on why Ellendren should feel insulted. *What's a Tenebrae ei'ana?*

"Shadow elves dwell in this city, yet I cannot sense them. Do you know how such is possible?" Oma pressed. "Only a stone seer can prevent another stone seer from knowing the entirety of the rocks beneath our feet. No one in the schtams would dare prevent my seeing. However, there are those in the Shadow Mountains, who were once considered our kin before the Schtamite severed them from us. Despite their meddling in sinister things, they have not forgotten the stone! And at least one of those dwarves is in this city, preventing me from discovering what I ought, and hiding whatever evil they have wrought from my sight."

No one spoke. There was a lot to think on, and Devlyn had more questions for Oma, but had no idea how to ask them. Not that Oma would answer his questions straightforwardly, if she answered them at all. Thinking of Oma's nature made him recall the first time they met in Belin's Watch, bringing Evellion to mind. "Have the dwarves assisted Evellion?"

"We are unforgivably divided. Those most threatened by the ruin of Evellion have added their own numbers to her armies and strengthened her cities' defenses, but those most removed from the concerns of humans and elves have not. There is concern that if the schtams send too many dwarves, they will be left defenseless if attacked. Hmph! Fools, the lot of them, the Vorn Schtam particularly. The dwarves have might and strength envied by all, but our stubbornness will see our doom if we do not overcome it." Oma halted her rant suddenly and looked to the ground. "I must go. Do not speak openly, eager ears are everywhere."

Quickly, Oma moved further into the stables, disappearing into the gloom beyond. A breath later, footsteps drew near.

"What are you two doing outside the castle? Chancellor Oranna would not be pleased to learn of two of her most gifted students outside the castle." Magister Hannah spoke with concern, not chastisement. Devlyn and Ellendren both released an anxious breath at the appearance of one of their favorite magisters.

"We were just about to return," Ellendren began, relieved to see Hannah. "I wanted to introduce Devlyn to the alicorn who brought me from the Illumined Wood."

"Ah yes, I must admit, I too came here to admire her. Magnificent creature. Tell me, dear, I have not heard how such a creature came to your side." Hannah glanced over at Aliel, perched on one of the alicorn's stall partitions. "Not that it is overly surprising, as the creatures of legends and myth seem to return with every rising sun. Who knows what creature will yet return from what we thought was no more."

CEURENYL STIRRING

A series of knocks came at Devlyn's bedchamber door, jarring him awake. He had just fallen asleep after giving up on a difficult assignment. Reading and writing about history left him exhausted and his essay remained incomplete. Mostly asleep, he didn't stop to wonder how anyone could have entered the apartment past the mirror that was a door, let alone start pounding on his bedchamber door. Rolling out of his bed, he unlatched his door to find Taen and Kaeyth waiting on the other side.

"What are you guys doing here?" Devlyn rubbed the sleep from his eyes.

"They must save these rooms for their favorite students." Kaeyth whistled as he looked around the apartment. "What'd you bribe 'em with? Taen's family couldn't even manage a bribe large enough to get him better rooms. His are just as small as mine! And my parents are farmers."

"Stop it!" Taen laughed.

Since Devlyn had met the two ei'ceuril novices, he had always thought they behaved more like brothers than friends. "Hold on, how'd you find me?"

"The better question is, why haven't you invited us over? This place is incredible. I bet this apartment is nicer than what most stewards have. They must want you to stay or something. Wonder why they don't feel the same about us, right, Taen?" Kaeyth shook Taen by the shoulders.

"Sh-sh-shocking," said Taen. "We were asked to escort you to the Ceurtriarch. We were told where to find you and how to get in."

"Ol' Ealyndol wants to tell you something. Can't imagine what, but I've never known him summon a student for anything good. Actually, I've never heard of him summoning a student."

"You're terrible." Taen turned on his friend, unable to stifle his infectious laugh.

"Well, come on, get your robe on and let's be off. Wouldn't want to keep the Ceurtriarch waiting. Isn't that right, Taen? How long until he nominates you as an archsteward?"

"I'm not even a steward yet."

"I'm sure he'll make an exception for you."

Devlyn turned back into his bedchamber and splashed his face with some water from the bowl on the stand, dragged fingers through his hair, and pulled on his robe, then followed Taen and Kaeyth through the temple corridors, Aliel as always flying above his shoulder. Devlyn had hoped for a quiet undisturbed night without any interruptions from Eagan. Despite what Eagan had said, he never felt fully rested when he awoke after the two spent the entire night in Somnaeniel. Instead, Taen and Kaeyth were keeping him from a good night's sleep. Like many ei'ceuril, they did have the ability to wield and so had been sent to the temple as children before they could cause any harm to themselves or others.

"Will either of you seek permission to learn to wield?" Devlyn hadn't meant to ask them and blamed his lapse on his lack of sleep.

"What, and be able to leave the temple like Aaron?" Kaeyth raised an eyebrow. "Is the rumor about your brother and Jaerol true? Do they really want to become ei'ana?"

"They're not very keen on remaining locked up in the temple," Devlyn replied, while trying to brush the wrinkles out of his robe.

"I think we should," Taen added. "Ei'ceuril aren't meant to be locked away in a temple. Imagine how much good we could do in the world."

"That's what I like to hear! So passionate." Kaeyth again grabbed Taen by the shoulders. "You're gonna try and shake things up, aren't you, little Taen?"

"Oh yeah, let the air in and brush the cobwebs away," Taen replied, waving one hand as though he was getting rid of a few.

Kaeyth rubbed his hands together fiercely with an eager grin.

Devlyn half expected the two ei'ceuril to settle down and walk solemnly through the temple corridors, but instead they joked and laughed the entire way through the temple to the Ceurtriarch's quarters, walking swiftly. And for a good reason—if their raucous laughter woke any of the older ei'ceuril, the trio would be two corridors away before the elders could get out of their beds and reach their doors. Devlyn enjoyed spending time with Kaeyth and Taen; they had an incredibly joyful spirit that was infectiously contagious. They only quieted when they reached the doors to the Chamber of Light.

The temple knights standing guard eyed the three suspiciously. "We heard you ten minutes ago," said the knight nearest the sealed door.

"Just bringing a bit of life to this tomb."

"You certainly brought something. What's that smell?"

Devlyn and Taen both looked to Kaeyth.

"What?"

"Just say the words and get moving."

"I am not worthy to enter into such splendor, but by the will of Anaweh, the Creating Light," they recited in unison.

The doors opened, they entered the Chamber of Light and Devlyn made sure to walk near one side through it toward Ealyndol's quarters. He had that familiar feeling of lightness from within, trying to send him floating, and he resolutely stayed clear of the center of the luminous room. Two temple knights stood at the door to the Ceurtriarch's quarters; Devlyn did not recognize either of them.

The knights gestured them inside and quickly closed the door behind them. It was as if he feared someone uninvited might try to follow them in. *They must be expecting us*, Devlyn conveyed to Aliel. A second set of doors on the opposite side of the room stood ajar, and Devlyn could see Ealyndol sitting at his desk through the opening. He unintentionally made eye contact with the Ceurtriarch, and Ealyndol responded by waving him into the office. Followed by Taen and Kaeyth, Devlyn crossed through the double doors, and found that the room was full of people, including Therril. Taen gazed at Ealyndol as though he looked into the face of Anaweh.

Devlyn looked about and realized that the room held several archstewards, some of the Seven Chairs of Septyl, and wise ones from both orders, none of whom Devlyn had noticed from the entryway to the large office. Feeling slightly intimidated, Devlyn wasn't sure whether he should greet everyone. *What was this about? About his unplanned physical contact with Ellendren? Had Trethien complained to the Chairs? Or worse, had they seen?* His stomach roiled in agitated response to his thoughts.

"Oh, is it good to see you." Therril's jovial tone was there as always. He looked from Devlyn to Taen and Kaeyth. "They trusted you with these two?"

"I don't know what our dear brother is talking about." Kaeyth had the same mischievous glimmer in his eyes as Therril. "After all, much of what we know, we learned from you."

They all laughed; even Ealyndol chuckled, although it was in his usual quiet manner.

"Forgive my intrusion, Ceurtriarch, but we should continue our discussion now that Devlyn has arrived," said Dorien, looking toward Taen and Kaeyth in dismissal.

The two young ei'ceuril bowed and left, closing the door behind them. "Have you ever seen such a gathering? You looked ready to prostrate yourself in front of the Ceurtriarch then and there!" Kaeyth's booming voice traveled through the closed door, Taen's equally loud hushing following swiftly.

Mother Paurel cleared her throat. "As I'm sure you are aware, Ceurenyl's security is jeopardized and has been so since the attack last year. We are quite certain of this following recent revelations. While the city currently remains out of Erynor's clutches, we have strong reason to believe that shadow elves are still in the city and even in Gwilnor. We don't know whether any have breached the temple's defenses." The Chair of Vyoletryn's steady voice commanded authority despite her advancing age.

"For this reason," an archsteward that Devlyn did not recognize went on, "we have agreed that it is in the best interest of all of us here for you to leave the city. Our enemies know you are here, and that you pose a threat to them, but you are far too inexperienced to safeguard the city and will only serve as a target so long as you remain, despite your hard work and practice with wielding."

"And where am I supposed to go?" Devlyn managed to ask even with the shock of his imminent departure. *Please, not back to Cor'lera.*

"You will travel with me to Binton." Velaria made it sound as if she proposed nothing more than a stroll through the park. "We will be accompanied by others who will work with you so that your studies can go on uninterrupted." With that, one of the archstewards pulled out a large book and began jotting notes, adding the finer details of Devlyn's departure as the others discussed them, most of which appeared already determined without any consultation as to his own wishes.

Half an hour later, Devlyn was excused to find his bed again.

The Temple of Ceur was quieter than usual the following morning when he headed to Liam's room. Liam still lived among the temple knights, sharing quarters with Jaerol and a couple of other knights in the lower levels. However, it was a mystery as to how long he would remain in the temple. Ever since he had begun to learn how to wield and with a measure of control gained with practice, the possibility grew that he could study with the ei'ana full time. If Liam chose to abandon his studies without fully learning to control his wielding, he ran the risk of confinement to the temple with the other men capable of wielding. The lay votaries lived in the lowest levels of the temple, furthest from the Chamber of Light, and the temple knights lived on the levels just above them to ensure harmony in those lower levels.

When it had become common knowledge that Devlyn was not the only one in the temple wielding openly, rumors began to spread of a possibility of others in the temple learning control. If they could do that, then they could venture from the temple freely once again. Many of them hadn't seen their families since they were children. Men grown old might have nieces and nephews now, and some of those relatives might have children of their own, and all of these relatives would be strangers to the men who had been confined to the temple for years. Only wealthy families could travel to Ceurenyl to visit, and most had only made the trip once, to see their sons locked away in the temple.

Whether or not these men could learn to control wielding kien was up for debate. Devlyn couldn't imagine that it would come easily at their advanced ages. The ei'ana had good reason for beginning to teach girls to wield at the age of ten. By now, some of the men in the lower levels could have been grandfathers.

More mysterious than the actual rumor was its origin. Devlyn had heard none of the ei'ceuril or ei'ana mention such a thing. While the distrust went both ways, many of the ei'ana's strong distrust for any man capable of wielding was particularly acute toward those in the lower levels of the temple, since the ei'ana were the ones responsible for bringing them to the temple for confinement in the first place.

Winding around another turn in the monolithic temple with its many intersecting corridors, Devlyn came to a series of identical doors. He always had to count them before stopping at the one he knew belonged to Liam and Jaerol. He gave a quick knock and waited longer than he thought usual. The door opened slightly, Liam standing behind it, dressed in a sleeveless shirt and linen pants. His ruffled hair seemed to indicate that he had just woken from a nap.

"Hey, Devlyn, what brings you down here today?" he asked, then opened the door wider so Devlyn and Aliel could enter. He sounded flustered.

"It looks like I'm leaving Ceurenyl again, so I thought I would stop by before I go."

"Again? Come on in. I was on guard duty last night, so I fell asleep while Jaerol was reading up on something. Our other two roommates are off somewhere, doing who knows what."

Jaerol, also casually dressed, his bright red hair equally disheveled, quickly rose from his chair to greet Devlyn. To Devlyn, it looked as though Jaerol had only just taken the seat, and not like he had been sitting there reading for a while.

"Nice to see you, Devlyn. Did I hear you say you're leaving again?"

"That's what I've been told. I thought I would come down and tell you before my lessons begin. It must be nice not having to put that armor of yours on for an entire day."

"You have no idea, I feel practically naked wearing only this." Jaerol gestured toward his loose-fitting clothing. "I'd pay a hundred crowns for armor light as cotton!"

The three joked around for a bit and then their conversation turned a bit more serious when Liam asked, "You weren't planning on visiting the lower levels, were you? The men down there have been growing restless and even hostile toward the wielders who are free to leave the temple. Jaerol and I no longer patrol the corridors there, for our own safety. Just last week Jaerol had a rock thrown at him."

"Only a small one." Jaerol gave Liam a sideways glance.

"I have to admit; I'm curious about what's going on down there. Not to mention the rumor that's been spreading like wildfire about kien wielders learning to wield with control and even potentially leaving the temple." Devlyn paused when his ears caught the far-off sound of a bell tolling. "I guess that will have to wait. It took me longer than expected to walk down here, and I have to get to my lessons. I hope I'll see you later, before I go." Devlyn and Aliel left and followed the corridor upward to the main level.

Today was Thenaen which meant that Devlyn had two private lessons for the day, both with ei'ana in the castle, just as he'd had before his time in the Illumined Wood. His first session was with Oreste, and since it focused on aerys, an erendinth Devlyn was particularly gifted in his ability to wield, he looked forward to it. The next three classes were politics, theoreticals, and language, then an hour-long break before his next private lesson in ignys with Velaria at the twelfth hour. He always enjoyed Kai's politics class; it never ceased to amaze him how intricate and delicate relations could be held in balance. He made sure to sit next to Ellendren, not only because she knew the ins and outs of Eklean, but also because he wanted to try to tell her that he was leaving. But no opportunity presented itself.

He had tried to catch Ellendren between classes, but he was too slow, and her friends had already carried her off.

I guess I'll have to tell her later. I don't want to leave without saying goodbye again, Devlyn conveyed, then blushed at the thought of Ellendren's friends pestering her about their near embrace in the courtyard and the following encounter with Trethien.

You'll see her before we leave. Aliel reassured him from just above his shoulder.

Trethien also attended their politics class, but he had chosen a seat as far from Ellendren and Devlyn as possible, taking great pains to avoid the two since he had accosted them in the corridor. When he was placing his things in his pack prior to leaving the classroom, Devlyn had caught him sneering in their direction. Ellendren paid him no mind, but neither did she speak of or encourage a repeat of their near-kiss in the courtyard. Devlyn knew his feelings for her were growing stronger, but his current status as an ei'ceuril novice precluded any furthering of the relationship. Whatever future they might have was restricted to friendship. *At least she won't end up with Trethien.* Aliel conveyed reassurance in response.

He glumly made his way toward the Dragon Tower, then followed the corridors through the castle and ascended several sets of stairs, noticing how the number of passing students decreased the closer he drew to Velaria's apartment until he saw only ei'ana walking the halls. He and Aliel received a few odd glances from some of them along the way.

He rapped on Velaria's door, and a few moments passed before she opened it to allow Devlyn and Aliel in, then quickly closed it.

"It's only Devlyn," she called out to the empty room.

"Wonderful, just wonderful." Therril's voice boomed from the far side, hidden in a small nook so that someone standing at the outer door would not see him.

"Just because dwarves are capable of hiding quickly does not mean we enjoy it, Azurelle." Oma appeared from beneath a table cloth and took a seat on a low stool. Slightly confused at the presence of not just Therril but Oma as well, Devlyn turned to Velaria.

"Let's just say that not everything was said at our meeting the other night," she said with a gesture that said take a seat. Aliel took his place on the perch that Velaria had set up for his use while she and Devlyn had their private lessons.

"Huh, huh, huh." Therril chuckled in his throaty manner. "To say the least. I had to keep my mouth shut while they needlessly went on about details lest I mention something that lot had no business hearing. The Shadow does indeed walk among us, Devlyn, and that distinguished group is hardly exempt."

"Do you mean to say that you've found shadow elves here in Gwilnor?" Devlyn recalled Ellendren's warning that they were already in the castle.

"Their traces are littered on every stone in this castle. Hmph. I can't tell who exactly it is, the trace disappears as soon as I sense it," Oma said. "But they're here, and their presence also supports our suspicions, Velaria. The Tenebrae are no myth."

Velaria didn't appear unduly worried at Oma's words, at least not externally, but Devlyn still didn't know what Oma referred to, having only heard her mention it once before with no explanation.

"I expect their numbers to be quite significant." Therril seemed to talk to himself rather than anyone there with him. "And, if the Tenebrae School has indeed resurfaced, if ever they went extinct, then it is also likely that there are stewards of Shadow lurking about as well. Fortunately, most of their members won't be found within the temple."

"True, but I can only imagine the sort of lies they are spreading across Eklean." Velaria noticed Devlyn's intent to ask what they were talking about. "I apologize, Devlyn, I forgot that you would not have grown up with this tale. The Tenebrae are an unrecognized eighth School of Septyl supported by Erynor himself. They are bent on power and domination and claim to be the only legitimate School of Septyl and would see the destruction of the others. Erynor supported their movement long before he grew aggressive toward Krysenthiel. There have been rumors and subtle clues hinting that the Tenebrae have returned."

"Yes, and we should have recognized Erynor's intent when he readily embraced the unrecognized School all those years ago, claiming that one School would better benefit Septyl and future generations of ei'ana than seven separate ones would," said Therril.

Devlyn thought about what Therril said. Had he heard the old elf correctly? *Therril had been there? Just how old is he?*

"The Stewards of Shadow are an entity much like the Tenebrae School, but as you might have guessed, they were never ei'ana, but ei'ceuril. They are stewards who once served Anaweh, the Creating Light, then abandoned the Light for Darkness, offering sacrifices to the Evil One by murdering and torturing anyone who worshipped the Light. It's speculated that the Tenebrae School also serves the Evil One." Therril paced beside the fireplace.

Taking everything in, Devlyn's mind immediately went to Abbot Entiel at the abbey school of Cor'lera. "Do you think these stewards of Shadow have reached Cor'lera?"

"I'm certain of it." Velaria had no hesitation. "I can't say how many of the ei'ceuril there serve the Darkness, but Cor'lera was at one time a village of peace, with elves and humans living and working side by side. The village has become a den of thieves, full to the brim with deceit. For a village like Cor'lera, on the edge of society, there would have had to be some external influence."

Oma grew impatient with the discussion. "Enough of this foul talk, tell the boy what you mean to."

A throaty laugh came from Therril. "Well, as it happens, Devlyn, Ceurenyl lacks the proper means for your training. No one capable dwells here. Luckily, as it happens, there remains an unbroken chain of ei'ana, kien and kiara wielders, who withdrew from our arduous wars."

Devlyn remembered what the girl, the Child in the Illumined Wood, had said about elves from before Krysenthiel fell still living in both the Illumined Wood and the Eldin Wood.

"Aside from the city's safety and your own, this is the main reason you're leaving Ceurenyl," Velaria explained. "If it was possible, I would have you remain here for an additional year before we even considered taking this measure, but as it stands, we are left with few options. Binton will be our first stop and our last, as far as anyone else will know. However, our journey will find us reaching the Eldin Wood."

"No one has gone into or, as far as we know, left that forest since before the fall of Krysenthiel. Little is known as to why they chose not to join the forces of Eklean against Erynor, but what is known, is that there is no reason for the Eldinari to have lost their immortality." Therril scratched his beardless chin.

"Not only will they be able to share their insights on wielding, but they know things that have been forgotten over the ages due to our mortal minds," said Velaria with a hint of excitement in her voice. "This expedition will also be a diplomatic one. As a Chair of Septyl, I intend to extend an invitation. Too many centuries have passed since the Eldinari have walked these halls, teaching and studying under this roof."

"You'll have better luck of getting them out of that forest by setting it on fire," said Therril cynically.

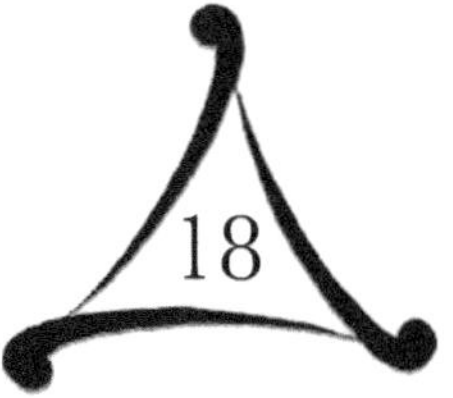

SOJOURNER WAGONS

Devlyn woke with a small start and lifted his head from a thick tome lying open on his desk. Drool from his open mouth fell onto to the page. Wiping his mouth, his heart skipped a beat in horror when he saw the stain on the open page. Pressing into the erendinth, Devlyn tried to delicately remove the moisture without disturbing the ink. Ellendren had loaned him the book and he had no intention of returning it with a drool stain.

Examining the now perfect page with bleary eyes, Devlyn thought back to what he had been reading before he'd fallen asleep so that he could write a few notes, but nothing came to mind. He had spent most of the night searching through this tome for references to the Skyland of Luminare.

Abandoning his research, Devlyn was about to head to his bed when an unexpected knock came at the door. Very few knew about Devlyn's apartment and those who didn't weren't likely to find it unless they knew exactly where it was. Even fewer of those who had been to visit him there would disturb him at such a late hour. Perhaps, word was getting around. Taen and Kaeyth had only just barged in a week ago, albeit at the order of the Ceurtriarch.

A second quiet knock came at the door, so quiet that he wouldn't have heard it if he'd been in his bedchamber and asleep. He looked toward the door hoping that whoever knocked would leave him alone. But the knocking persisted, and he decided to see who it was. Ellendren stood on the other side, in the small antechamber that looked like someone's sleeping quarters.

"Elle? What are you doing here?" While Devlyn always looked forward to seeing her, finding her in his private quarters was unexpected. Not only because he had never told her its whereabouts, but more so because she had broken her curfew to sneak out of the castle.

Ellendren pushed past the entry and into the main living area, then turned to give him a quick hug. "Good, you're unharmed." He was trying to think of a response when she rushed on.

"What essentials do you require? And where is your pack? You should change clothing as well. You can't wear your ei'ceuril robes; put something inconspicuous on."

"It's the middle of the night. Elle, what's going on?" Devlyn found her frantic disposition peculiar and he grew more baffled by the minute. Even Aliel looked over alertly from his perch.

"It's not safe here. I've been telling you that for months now." Ellendren sounded more than anxious; she sounded almost frightened. "We have to leave, and not just us. Now hurry, get what you need, we need to be gone before the sun rises."

Still bewildered, he left her to change and gather a few things.

Devlyn had only just pulled his robe off when she rushed into his bedchamber without knocking. He yelped and covered his all-too-revealing small clothes with his discarded robe.

"There's no time for that, hurry up."

Devlyn grabbed a pair of trousers and quickly pulled them on. He grabbed a tunic just as Ellendren found his pack and started to empty contents from his wardrobe into it.

"Wait, slow down. What's happened?" Devlyn retrieved the purses from his robe pockets and transferred them into his trouser pockets, regretting that while the trousers were far more comfortable, they lacked an inside pocket that was convenient for keeping his extra purse hidden. Hopefully, no one would notice and question why he had two coin purses. The idea of anyone knowing that he carried lumols and a lucilliae made him uncomfortable. The two lumols alone were worth a small fortune, to say nothing of the violet jewel's value.

"Chancellor Oranna is dead. Murdered in her quarters," Ellendren said through clenched teeth. "She had been expected for a meeting earlier this evening, but never arrived. I was sent to her chambers to see if she was there. Her door was ajar; I knocked, but no one answered. When I walked in, I called out again, but she didn't answer. The room looked tidy, but I saw a large pile of blankets on the floor. I went to pick them up and fold them, but when I did, I touched a hand, cold as ice." Ellendren spoke with choked difficulty, pausing a moment before continuing. "When I lifted the rest of the blankets, I found Chancellor Oranna's body. Her skin was charred and cracking. I ran out of there to tell the wise ones who'd sent me. Velaria asked me to remain with them and went to investigate. Several hours passed before she came back to tell me that the Seven Chairs had named Hannah as the new chancellor and that I was to pack what I needed and to find you."

"Light, save us," Devlyn gasped. "Elle, are you all right? I'm sorry, did you know her well?"

"I doubt anyone knew her well. She was very reserved for an Azurelle—you would think she belonged to the Albien School. But she was always kind to me." Obviously upset at retelling the evening's events, Ellendren moved from the wardrobe to his dresser and began opening the different drawers. Appalled at her seeing his small clothes, he pushed her aside and closed the drawer, his face an embarrassed shade of pink.

"Don't be ridiculous, I just saw you wearing nothing but them not a moment ago," she chided, stepping back to let him finish his packing.

He hurriedly shoved his small clothes into the bottom of the pack and out of Ellendren's sight. He packed rapidly, throwing in a few shirts and trousers with no thought to organizing them in his hurry. He was relieved that there was no space for a robe.

"All right, let's leave."

"Who else is coming?" asked Devlyn as he followed Ellendren to the door.

"No one else from the temple," replied Ellendren before scanning the room. "Is there anything else you need?"

Devlyn shook his head as he threw his cloak over his shoulders and picked up his pack. *Are you ready to leave again?* Devlyn asked Aliel.

We are too exposed here. There will be a time when we will not care whether others know of our presence, but not yet, conveyed Aliel.

Taking one last glance at the luxurious apartment, a place where he really enjoyed spending time, a tapestry caught Devlyn's eye. It was the one depicting the Skyland of Luminare that Ealyndol had gazed at when Devlyn first returned to the temple. He joined Ellendren in the hallway and they quickly made their way through the temple corridors toward the Chamber of Light and eventually through the entrance corridor. When they reached the exit, Ellendren had them pause, then passed through the door and into the cold night.

Looking to Aliel, Devlyn was concerned about the light that he gave off. There was no way to diminish it, and even as he thought it, Aliel disappeared from his side. Not at all startled by the disappearance, Devlyn knew that Aliel flew above the city, disguised among the stars.

Taking a hasty but thorough scan of the area, Ellendren pointed to two hooded figures in the distance, just off the plaza in front of the temple, figures that Devlyn couldn't recognize in the dark. Several taps came from their direction and Ellendren responded with similar taps, but at a faster pace. Ellendren led him over to the hooded figures.

"Good, you found him." The shorter hooded figure sounded like Alex.

"What's going on?" asked Devlyn, finally catching a glimpse of his cousin's face beneath his hood.

"No time to explain," said the other person. "Quickly, put these on." From beneath his cloak he pulled two more cloaks similar to the ones he and Alex wore. Ellendren quickly fastened hers tightly, and Devlyn decided to simply throw his over the cloak he already wore.

The stranger guided them across the temple's bridge and through Ceurenyl to the part of the city where Devlyn had lived in the cellar of an inn, not rushing, just keeping to an average pace. With the late hour, only a few windows were lit from within as they passed through several streets until they arrived at a group of covered wagons hitched to horses. A soft glow emanated from inside each of the wagons, shadows moving against the canvas walls.

The hooded figure rapped on the door at the back of one wagon, and an elderly man opened it. Devlyn could just make out the man's tanned, leathery skin in the soft glow of the lamp inside.

"Ah, good to see you have returned safely, Tye," he said. Tye finally lowered his hood to reveal his head and face.

"Thank you, Sojourner Tindol. We had no trouble. Any here?"

"None whatsoever. Now, get everyone in their wagons before it does find us. I don't like us being in a city. It was kind of them to grant entrance to three of our wagons, but we need to regroup with the others camped outside the city walls."

Tye was quick to direct everyone into a wagon, Ellendren into one, and Devlyn and Alex into another. As Devlyn stepped into his assigned wagon, he saw that there were others already inside, and was happy to recognize Oliver and Andrew sitting with their backs against the wooden sides. Andrew had been knighted during Devlyn's novitiate in the Illumined Wood, joining Oliver in the order of the Septyl Knights. Next to Oliver sat another man, someone Devlyn didn't recognize, although in spite of the man's closely drawn hood, Devlyn could tell he was an elf.

Alex and Tye followed him in then Tye pulled the door closed and sealed the canvas flap. A small lantern sat on the table in the middle, both secured in place. Once everyone had a seat, Tye whistled, put out the lantern, and a moment later the wagon shifted and creaked as it moved off. Devlyn heard the horses' hooves clopping against the cobbles.

The wagons moved sluggishly. Devlyn took a breath in to ask Tye where they were going, but Tye put one hand over Devlyn's mouth. Whatever was happening, silence was necessary. It was hard to tell, but Devlyn thought the wagons had reached the ruined gates and now followed the makeshift wooden ramp that still spanned the rubble. Devlyn doubted its stability and held his breath as the wagon's wheels creaked over it.

Soon, hushed voices spoke outside, the wagons slowed, then the pace resumed, but without the clopping; the road now had a different surface, and the ride was rougher. Devlyn assumed they were now outside the city and beyond the bridge. Since he had never entered or left Ceurenyl by road, Devlyn was curious as to how wagons and horses managed to travel the winding road through the mountains to the plains below. He could tell that there was a slight decline, but it was not overly noticeable.

Eventually, when they were well past the city, Tye's voice came out of the dark beside him. "I am Tye, of Tribe Fendur of Dwonia." Tye bent forward and relit the lantern. Devlyn could now see Tye's dark hair, and leathery skin, like the old man's. In the dim light, Devlyn wasn't entirely sure, but he thought that Tye's eyes were also like the old man's dark grey ones.

Devlyn had trouble believing that Tye was from Dwonia. He had never heard of anyone from there traveling east beyond their borders. And did anyone still live in the desert?

"What happened that caused you to cross the Gap?" asked the stranger while Devlyn tried to make sense of Dwonians not just still living, but also leaving their desert home.

Tye's expression was stern, and he took a moment to respond. He looked from one face to another, judging whether to trust them. "My tribe sent me east," he continued, his tone serious. "I was to travel to Lucillia to warn the aryl of trouble stirring in the Purged Desert of Dwonia. I was to inform them that the giants were crossing the mountains into the desert."

"Giants?" interrupted Alex. "Now I'm supposed to believe that giants exist too?"

"When will you begin to understand that the world is bigger than you can conceive?" interjected Oliver. He sounded tired, his voice gruff, although to Devlyn, he didn't look exhausted.

"Yes, that's right, giants," Tye snapped, not at all thrilled at the interruption. "As it happens, I was unable to reach Lucillia due to a magical barrier surrounding the area. Fortunately, I was traveling with the Sojourners who know this eastern land better than I do, and they told me that Ceurenyl was the next best option. I've been here for about a month, and the ei'ana would only meet with me once."

"What are the giants like?" Devlyn found himself asking with a hint of excitement. He'd only heard of the existence of giants once before.

"Depends which ones you come across. Some of them are caring, while others can be extremely brutal. It's the vicious ones, a large group of them, who have crossed the mountains into the desert though." Tye stared intently at Devlyn who wondered what was behind the stare.

"What concerns do the giants have with Dwonia?" asked the stranger.

"Rarely does a giant cross the Frozen Mountains, especially into Dwonia since it became an arid wasteland. And even more rarely in large numbers. My people do not believe that the giants intend us harm, but rather that they march for these eastern lands at the behest of another."

"You're certain that they are heading south for Dwota's Gap, and not the Eldin Wood?" the stranger pressed.

"The giants are a strong and proud race; they might not be the most intelligent one, but they are not overly simple. There are some among them who believe they can overcome the Eldinari in their own lands. I doubt their chieftains would ever permit it; they would either execute the foolish giants or allow them to march into the Eldin Wood to their certain and reckless death." The hooded elf received the news well enough, but to Devlyn, both options seemed terrible.

"You appear more informed than most who travel with the Sojourners." Oliver said, clearly curious about the still-hooded elf, and not a little disturbed by his reluctance to reveal himself.

"You should not underestimate that which you do not know." The elf finally lowered his hood, revealing his Luminari golden-brown hair and silver eyes. *Shouldn't his eyes have a trace of green?* Devlyn thought to himself. "My name is Viren, a simple traveler seeking a land without threat of war."

Alex scoffed, "Let me know when you find this warless land and be sure to invite me to it!" Oliver threw Alex a disapproving look while Andrew just shook his head.

The wagon grew quiet again and only the rhythmic squealing of wheels disturbed the silence. Sunrise was still a way off, so he thought he would take advantage of the quiet and closed his eyes.

Several hours later, hushed voices woke him. Devlyn heard them speaking near him and opened his eyes. The wagon was still moving but he could easily see everyone inside as daylight brightened the canvas from outside. That did not give him any indication as to the time of day, though. Devlyn had expected to dream again about the hunched students in the strange vision of Gwilnor, but hadn't. It was the first night he hadn't had that dream all week.

"Look who's finally stirring," Alex teased. "You slept the entire morning away; did you know that? Even missed breakfast! Nothing fancy mind you, just some fruit."

Devlyn rubbed his eyes to get a clearer image of his surroundings and noticed how sore his back was from sleeping against the hard side of the wagon. Turning his body to straighten it out in hopes of relieving some of the discomfort, he saw Aliel perched next to him, quite alert, eyes bright.

"You should have seen how high Andrew jumped when your phoenix appeared in a quick flash out of thin air; I thought he was going to put a hole in the ceiling or wet himself!"

Andrew punched Alex in the arm. "That was you. Nearly landed on my lap when you came back down too!"

"And I bet you were hoping it was Abbie." Alex rubbed his arm. Laughter filled the wagon, especially when Andrew landed a second punch on Alex's arm.

"How do you manage to hit the same spot every time?"

CHANGE OF SCENERY

A gentle breeze from the open window brushed across Jaerol's body as he lay in his new bed in the North Tower room he shared with Liam. After months of what had been quite heated discussions between the ei'ceuril and ei'ana, not to mention between each of the Seven Schools, they had finally been admitted into Gwilnor Academy as student wielders. Neither had been permitted to attend any of the meetings but had heard from reliable sources that the discussions had tended to escalate quickly. It seemed that the wise ones could not agree on anything.

Following the murder of Chancellor Oranna, who had remained steadfastly opposed to the admittance of kien wielders to Gwilnor, Jaerol had hoped that her successor would take a more lenient stance. He had intended to learn as much as he could about the new chancellor, an ei'ana named Hannah, hoping that with a better idea of her stance on kien wielders, he could figure out an approach that would lead her to granting his greatest desire—openly learning to wield, not as he had done during his time with the shadow elves, but with control.

The temple felt suffocating; he just couldn't understand how the Luminari and humans managed the confinement and being severed from their ability to wield. Did they not realize what they were cutting themselves off from? He knew his control over his wielding had improved since he'd begun practicing with Velaria, but even before that, he had never caused substantial destruction. Not even that one occasion with the cyclone cutting a path through that small village on the outskirts of Broid. He had only accidentally shifted the cyclone's path.

But before Jaerol had had an opportunity to discover Chancellor Hannah's position on kien wielders, the Seven Chairs of Septyl had granted him and Liam admittance. Several ei'ceuril would also begin lessons at the castle, but they would remain ei'ceuril throughout their studies with the ei'ana. However, Liam and he were full-fledged student wielders, set on a path to become ei'ana.

The Arenthylean Bells tolled once, alerting the students that they had three hours until their classes began. He sat up and saw Liam lying on his stomach in his bed across the room, unwilling to wake. Jaerol tossed his pillow and managed to hit Liam's head.

"I'm up." Liam grumbled but didn't move.

Gwilnor's students never had the option of choosing their own roommates so they had been fortunate in their room assignment; that was one of the many items on the chancellor's list of responsibilities. Since Jaerol and Liam were the only two kien wielders studying to become ei'ana, Chancellor Hannah put them together. Not that that disappointed either of them. They had grown quite fond of one another, after Liam forgave Jaerol for his involvement in the Erynien Empire, and for his negligent treatment of Liam's family in the dungeon of Gneal. Jaerol still felt ashamed of his inaction toward Liam's family; unfortunately, he still couldn't think of how he could've changed those events. At least Evellyn, Liam's stepmother and Devlyn's mother, hadn't been there.

Jaerol's feet found the cold stone floor sending shivers through his body, quickly followed by goosebumps. He crossed the room and nudged Liam, hoping he would start moving. "Let's get some breakfast."

Liam rolled onto his back with his blanket twisted about him, then let out a long yawn and stretched before getting out of bed.

Jaerol splashed chilled water from the corner basin onto his face and pulled the grey robe Gwilnor required all students to wear over his head. It was mandatory, whether or not they had lessons. Just as Jaerol pushed his head through the partially buttoned robe, Liam chucked the pillow from across the room at Jaerol's face. When it connected, Liam let out a satisfied grunt.

"Eye for an eye, eh? Are you going to get dressed or do you intend on going to breakfast in nothing but your small clothes?" Jaerol wore a knowing smirk as Liam moved slowly toward his wardrobe.

"I'll get there—it's a shame we can't have it delivered like they used to do for Devlyn," he said, patting at the back of his head in a futile attempt to get the hair to lie flat. Evidently, he'd had a somewhat restless sleep.

Jaerol moved on to brushing his teeth, thinking that Liam had come to know him better than anyone in the past year, perhaps even better than Kiron, his closest and only friend from his time in Broid. Jaerol had had to kill Kiron in the grand tourney, something that had caused him great pain even as it made him accepted by the shadow elves, allowing Jaerol to pass as one of them. Jaerol had lost all hope of ever growing close to someone again after Kiron's death. Liam had also told Jaerol that it had been a long time since he had been able to trust anyone. It was difficult to form friendships in the dungeons of Gneal where the prisoners were watched and could be overheard.

It now seemed odd that they had been so harsh toward one another when they had first met. They had formed a strong bond and he had been incredibly relieved that they had both been admitted into Gwilnor Academy. The thought of being apart and growing distanced from Liam was too difficult to imagine; Liam was the first person he had felt comfortable with since he was young, before the shadow elves.

When they had finally been accepted into Gwilnor, the Seven Chairs had stipulated that to become ei'ana, they would have to experience the same training as all ei'ana, which included the classes that first year students took. Liam grumbled over having to attend classes which he considered below his station. Jaerol didn't disagree, but he still enjoyed the opportunity, despite the considerable age difference between the two of them and their classmates. The temple's curriculum paled in comparison to the rigor of instruction at Gwilnor.

Today's schedule included a full morning block of politics—three whole hours. Magister Kai's lesson revolved around the minums and how they ended up in what became known as Freiton. Liam scowled in disgust as Kai lectured on the abuses the minums had suffered throughout history, due to their mixed background, part human and part goblin. When Kai described their enslavement to the humans of the southern kingdoms, explaining that the goblins had sold the minums to the humans, Jaerol thought that Liam would storm out of the classroom in disgust.

Jaerol had thought that this was common knowledge, since he had learned about the minums' history as a child, but Liam's reaction indicated that it was not so widely known. Perhaps, it had to do with the distance between Cor'lera and the southern kingdoms. But Jaerol's people now inhabited the island that was once the minum's home in the Kinzdol Islands and where the Cyndinari had established Broid. Of course, the minums had been slaves of the Yanileans and Tieli at that point. Liam's limited knowledge shocked Jaerol at first, especially when Jaerol realized that Liam hadn't even known that his pointed ears indicated elven ancestry.

Just as Kai's lesson branched into the rise of the Time Wardens, six bells tolled and signaled the end of the lesson. A rush of chairs scraped against the stone flooring and eager students made for the exit. Jaerol lingered in his seat, even as Liam stood to leave.

"I'll be out in a moment," he said, wanting to ask Kai a question.

At the front of the classroom, Kai was organizing her lesson notes, neat orderly sheets of parchment with a curious swirling script. While Jaerol didn't recognize the script, he hadn't stayed behind to ask about her handwriting. "May I ask you a question, Magister?"

Kai looked up and held Jaerol's eyes in a steady gaze, her narrow icy blue eyes piercing his own. Easily twenty years his elder, she was a formidable woman with white strands forming in her silky black hair. "That was one. What else would you like to know?"

Her abrupt manner added to his nervousness and he wondered whether she had any reservations about admitting kien wielders to Gwilnor. Fortunately, she didn't seem to hold his Cyndinari heritage against him, something he had experienced from many others in both the Temple of Ceur and Gwilnor Academy.

"I apologize if I'm too forward, Magister, but I'm curious to learn where you're from. I've never met anyone with your appearance." Jaerol had spent the past two weeks discreetly trying to discern this mysterious woman's origin. Her thin eyes reminded him of elven eyes, but she was identifiably human. There was something very curious about her, something she didn't have in common with the humans native to Eklean.

Kai paused, her cold look making Jaerol question whether this had been a good idea. "In all my years of teaching here, only one other student has asked me that question." Kai's emotionless tone matched her icy blue eyes.

Jaerol almost excused himself.

"Please, have a seat." Kai sat at her desk, and Jaerol took a front row seat at a student desk. "As it happens, I am not native to this land. You might not be aware of my homeland, but it's far to the west, over the Vespien Mountains, beyond the Purged Desert of Dwonia, and across the Misty Sea. There is a land there named Qien and it has been ruled by a single dynasty since it was unified. Or so they will tell you.

"The Qien were once commonly seen throughout Eklean. But Erynor divided our two continents when he allied with the sea dragons in the Misty Sea, fearing that the Qien Dynasty would aid the Luminari. Those vicious beasts could swallow Mother Velaria's dragon in a single gulp. The sea dragons' only request was to one day gain the Bowl of Theniel, the merpeople's most sacred sea. Legend states that whoever claims the Bowl of Theniel holds all the seas."

The brief explanation only whetted Jaerol's wish to know more, but he was aware that he was holding the magister back. He thanked Kai, excused himself, and joined a patiently waiting but curious Liam in the corridor.

"That took longer than expected. Was there something you missed during the lesson?"

Jaerol had to think back to the lesson's topic. As interesting as it had been, he was much more focused on what he had just heard. *A different continent!*

"I've been wondering about Kai, about her background, so I asked her," he explained, then went on to tell Liam the details about Kai's origins on the way to lunch.

Their afternoon lessons were uneventful and Jaerol looked forward to meeting up with Therril later in the day at the temple. Therril had asked if they would help Aaron train several ei'ceuril with the ability to wield. They had readily agreed.

When they arrived at the plaza just outside the Temple of Ceur at the designated time, Therril and Aaron were waiting for them, accompanied by five young men. Jaerol recognized all but one of them.

"Welcome back to the temple grounds!" Therril greeted them. "These are the kien wielders I told you about." Just as Therril was about to introduce the wielders by name, Kai crossed the temple bridge to join them on the plaza.

"Thank you for agreeing to help, Kai. From what I've heard, you have grown quite proficient with the erendinth, and even more so with Devlyn's influence." Therril's joyful words didn't alter Kai's restrained smile or apparent detachment, but to Jaerol, she was in a good mood.

"Yes, although you had me under the impression that it was I who was to instruct him in private lessons. I should have known that you had something more up your sleeve."

Jaerol hadn't been aware that Therril had asked Kai to assist in training the kien wielders, although he did know that a kiara wielder was essential to training kien wielders. But anyone who knew Therril knew that there was always more to his requests than what he said.

"Now, let's move on to introductions. This is Steward Jacque Nareaux from Myrium," Therril continued, gesturing to the first in line. "Steward Zachary Uradin and Donald Kire from Lankor. It's truly remarkable how they managed to stay out of the hands of Yanilean officials. These two are Taen Taerinior and Kaeyth Illiero."

Jaerol recognized the last two as Devlyn's friends, and except for Zachary, knew the others. He had heard of Zachary, though, because Zachary was the young ei'ceuril steward often mentioned in the temple because he spent all his time studying. Donald was not an ei'ceuril yet, and it would be some time until he would travel to the Illumined Wood for his novitiate, since he was still young, the youngest in the whole temple.

"Now that that's taken care of, let's move away from the temple pla-za. You lot wielding is quite scandalous—wouldn't want some poor refugee to walk up here and comment on how the Ei'ceuril have lost their ways!" Therril turned and walked off a path from the temple and into one of the gardens surrounding the temple, stopping in a clearing shielded by tall cy-press trees.

I thought this was only for ei'ceuril, thought Jaerol. He didn't mind Don-ald tagging along, but he was really very young. Jaerol had spent some time since Therril's request for help in training the kien wielders thinking about ways to do that but was no closer to actually having a definite plan. He hoped someone might have a clearer idea of what was needed.

"Please divide into two groups. Liam, you will lead one group, and Jaerol, you will lead the other. Aaron and I will go between the two," Kai's authoritative tone relieved Jaerol of his worries, especially when everyone followed Kai's directions without question. Politics might have been her specialization, but Kai was an incredible magister, and certainly no for-eigner to teaching wielding. Incredibly, the new students learned quickly, and the lesson proceeded with successful wields from all the young men.

Toward the Plains

It had been several weeks since the caravan had discreetly left Ceure-nyl and every day was the same. Wake up before dawn, eat a quick breakfast, then break camp, and travel through the day until dusk. Velaria ensured their travels would not be a detriment to the students' education. After all, Devlyn, Ellendren, Alex, and Abbie were still students at Gwilnor Academy. She had devised a lesson plan that saw their days devoted to studying the same topics they would have been studying at Gwilnor with the ei'ana, Sara and Reia, who had agreed to accompany Velaria on the journey. For these sessions, all the students rode in the same wagon, limiting the time where they could just walk along beside the wagons, something Devlyn had learned to appreciate after experiencing many bumps when riding inside the wagon on less-than-smooth roads.

Following the more academic topics, the ei'ana then instructed Devlyn and Ellendren in wielding. Alex and Abbie typically excused themselves and either moved to a different wagon or walked outside. Wielding still made Alex anxious. The Sojourners they traveled with had a similar apprehension and requested that their wagons not be used for teaching students how to wield. Instead, Devlyn and Ellendren only sat with the various erendinth, learning to recognize them better.

Reia sat with her eyes closed at the opposite end of the wagon. Devlyn could tell she too connected with the erendinth, but out of respect for their hosts, refrained from fully wielding them. The alluring draw of kien tempted Devlyn to press more fully into the erendinth. He still had little idea of where they were going and wanted to press briefly into terys to scan their surroundings. Aliel was quick to note Devlyn's mind.

They won't appreciate that, he conveyed.

Devlyn grumbled under his breath.

"Is something wrong?" asked Ellendren.

"Oh sorry, didn't mean to say anything." Devlyn glared toward Aliel. "Just tired of being cramped in this wagon."

"Perhaps you'll be able to train with Oliver again tonight. His swordsmanship is truly remarkable," said Ellendren.

"Yeah, he said he wanted to spend every night training Alex, Andrew, and me. Not to mention Abbie—she insists on joining the practice sessions," said Devlyn, now wondering why Viren had never joined the practice bouts. It's not like he was one of the Sojourners who Devlyn had yet to see carry a single weapon. In fact, Viren wore an intricate thin blade at his waist most times, the likes of which Devlyn had never seen. Tye, the only Dwonian in their caravan who was not a Sojourner, kept his spear close and seemed to enjoy the sparring sessions.

"Speaking of the knights, do either of you know how long Abbie has been training with them? I of course heard mention of her spending time with them, but I never anticipated her skill to be at the level it is." Reia's eyes were no longer closed, and she too seemed to have grown bored with just sitting with the erendinth. "I know she's not a wielder; surely if she was she wouldn't waste time using a sword to defend herself. Physical weapons are a very poor substitute for kiara."

"Probably since she first arrived at Gwilnor," said Ellendren. "She's the only girl studying at Gwilnor to do so."

Devlyn had told Abbie that he stopped having that dream after not having it for a full week. Neither of them knew what the dream meant, but its sudden stop worried Abbie; she thought it might be linked to the chancellor's assassination. For Devlyn, it was just one more thing that he preferred not to dwell on.

Dusk fell across the land, and Devlyn heard a commotion outside the wagon. Reia showed little interest and even less concern. She remained unmoved, sitting upright against the wagon wall. The wagon came to a stop and Reia stood and hopped out. Devlyn looked at Ellendren and saw the same questioning expression he wore. They never stopped this early; the sun had only just set.

"We're stopping for the night." Tye peered in through the wagon's flap. "Time to relieve yourselves and set up camp." The flap fell back into place.

Aliel was the first one out, exuberantly flying off to stretch his wings as the others made their way to bushes a discreet way off. Alex, Devlyn, and Aliel regathered by the student wagon at one end of the semi-circle of wagons. When Tindol had said that they needed to join the others that first night, Devlyn hadn't realized that there were seven more wagons in their party, which made it a larger group than he'd initially thought.

Stretching his legs and swinging his arms, Devlyn looked around and saw that someone had already lit a fire in the center of the partial enclosure created by the wagons. Several women surrounded its warm glow, and even from only seeing the back of her hair in the dim firelight, he recognized Ellendren. Devlyn had spent the entire day in a wagon with her, but still felt drawn to her.

He started toward her, but a tap on his shoulder stopped him. Devlyn turned to see a smiling Velaria standing next to him, a shawl wrapped about her shoulders for warmth, leaving most of her curious dress of leaves and flowers exposed. She had only been in the student wagon for an hour today, spending the rest of the day presumably in meetings with the interchanging ei'ana instructors and Sir Oliver, along with writing letters.

"Happy birthday, Devlyn. Have you enjoyed the leisurely journey?"

"Thanks," said Devlyn, acknowledging her good wish but thinking that while the wagon might have been moving along at a leisurely pace, it certainly wasn't a comfortable ride. Those wooden benches had no redeeming qualities.

Alex and the other wagon mates had already wished him a happy fifteenth birthday that morning, before Reia and Sara had all the students read quietly in the student wagon. It was the first of Marenth and unlike almost every other of his birthdays on the first day of spring, this one actually felt like spring. Even after the last couple of years, Devlyn was more accustomed to living in Cor'lera, where the snows only started to melt halfway through the season, a month or more after Marenth.

Reia and Sara left the fire to join them, trailed by Ellendren and Abbie. Before this journey, Devlyn had only known the ei'ana by appearance, since they had not taught any of his classes at Gwilnor.

Both Devlyn and Alex bowed their heads slightly in greeting, Alex smirking as always. What was it about this time? Had he caught Devlyn staring at Ellendren? One thing Devlyn appreciated about Alex being on this journey was that he had been wishing that he could see more of Alex's happy expression after he had returned to Ceurenyl, but they had not had much opportunity to spend time together until now. Alex's appearance had changed now that he was sixteen. He had gained quite a bit of muscle in the past year, maturing into a young man, no longer the boy that Devlyn had grown up with in Cor'lera, even if he still acted the same. Granted, Devlyn had grown and filled out a bit too. He still felt skinny, and his lanky limbs lacked Alex's girth, as they always had and likely always would.

Turning to Velaria, Devlyn had a question begging to be asked over the past weeks. "Velaria, I somewhat understand why we left Ceurenyl, but where are we?" Devlyn had yet to hear anyone mention their destination, or even their current location. Were they actually going to Binton as planned?

"We are near the Plains of Mindale, south of the Shroud and heading toward Binton. I've heard disturbing rumors about the city and intend to uncover the truth behind them," Velaria explained, her voice firm.

Reia waited for Velaria to finish speaking, but her irritation was clear. "Mother Velaria, I understand that you have a wish to achieve a diplomatic relationship with Binton, but what do you think we will accomplish? They will feed us nothing but lies!" Reia's tone held both impatience and resignation. This was clearly not the first time she had expressed her thoughts.

Oliver had joined the small group, and seemed to agree with the Arantiulyn, nodding his head, having his own share of experience with the kingdom of Mindale. "If Torsil has raised her banners against us, you can be assured that so has Mindale."

"War is never the way, sisters and brothers," began Sara. The Auburnis' calm voice had an accent Devlyn had never heard and couldn't place. "If we can encourage the Mindaleans to choose peace, we could avoid much bloodshed."

"Blood will be shed whether they side with us or with our enemy. But I fear they made their choice long before we became aware of it, Ei'ana," responded Oliver.

Considering their course of action, Devlyn was curious about where they thought he and Aliel fell. "Are we to enter the city publicly?" he asked, secretly hoping that Velaria intended no such thing.

"I'm afraid not. Servants of Shadow will be hidden throughout Binton, eager to report your location to their masters, assuming they don't know already. While no one in Binton should recognize us, we still need to remain cautious," said Velaria then turned to Aliel. "I'm sorry, but Devlyn will have to be separated from you for a short while."

Aliel cocked his head, looking toward Devlyn. Unease and understanding passed between them. Aliel would stay with the group for now, but once they neared Binton, he would have to disappear.

While Devlyn wanted to learn their course of action in finer detail, now that it was clear that Aliel would not be part of the initial foray into Binton, he found himself losing interest. The Sojourners had already begun to set up camp, laying out bedrolls inside the partial wagon enclosure, while three of them prepared dinner. Devlyn still didn't know why they had stopped traveling so early. He hoped that the extra time would not be devoted to more lessons, since he really wanted to spend time with Ellendren. He was not the only one who had turned fifteen today. The ei'ana continued their discussion, which resembled bickering more than anything else.

Making eye contact with Ellendren, he gestured with his eyes to the side. She quickly understood and the two excused themselves from the others and walked toward the wagon enclosure's perimeter. Devlyn could feel Alex's eyes watching them. A moment of awkward silence passed between them before Devlyn thought to ask, "Are you enjoying your birthday?"

"It's been nice, not much of a celebration though. And you?" She smiled at him, and Devlyn's heart went aflutter.

"Best one I can remember." Devlyn returned the smile, hoping she caught his reasoning.

"Really? Then the abbey school must have been quite awful."

"That's part of the reason." He blushed a bit at the real reason. *Please don't make me say more.*

"I've been intending to ask how you've been. It's been a confusing time, what with leaving Ceurenyl at a moment's notice, and ending up traveling in a caravan of wagons. Though, we're fortunate that the Sojourners could take us," Ellendren said quietly.

Devlyn searched for the correct words. He didn't want to sound like an idiot. "I guess I'm all right. The wagon isn't all that bad. Although, Oliver and Andrew do snore pretty loudly. I'll be happy to have my own bed again."

Ellendren smiled softly. "I feel the same."

"Was it difficult to leave the alicorn behind?" asked Devlyn sympathetically, imagining how awful abandoning Aliel would be.

"I can't stop worrying about Laureniel. I know she's safe, but so many terrible things have happened."

"She'll be fine," said Devlyn, trying to convince himself as he spoke.

"Honestly, I'm more upset that we left Gwilnor when we did. I was promised a spot on the Vyoletryn's team for the Erendinth Games. I've been waiting since I first came to Gwilnor to compete. The official teams are restricted to student wielders who have completed their novitiate and have chosen a School," said Ellendren.

"Kevn mentioned the Erendinth Games, but I still don't fully understand what they are—never had the chance to see a match in person."

"Oh, they're quite the spectacle. Seven rings encircle the center of the field, each representing a different erendinth, and only by wielding the ball with the erendinth matching the ring can a player score. Naturally, the rings representing the transcendental erendinth haven't been in play for centuries—not since the Balance was broken."

"Sounds fun. Do you think they'll let a kien wielder play?"

"Not on an official team, you have to belong to one of the Schools for that. But there are informal teams that play. I'm surprised you haven't seen the field. It's hard to miss from the south wing. We'll have to play when we get back to Gwilnor."

"Definitely." Devlyn grinned.

"I've been meaning to ask…how is your novitiate with the ei'ceuril going?"

"I guess it's all right," began Devlyn even though he didn't want to talk about it, preferring to talk about anything but becoming an ei'ceuril. The memory of her falling on top of him and the feel of her body on his was still sharp in his mind, even a month after it had happened. "I don't know, Elle. It's just, have you ever felt like you were forced into something even though you know in your heart that it's wrong for you?"

"I do. It comes with the crown," said Ellendren. "I can't tell you how much I've grown to despise Trethien, but it's an arranged courtship, and seeing as either my mother or father is dead, most likely my mother, I can't take the crown of Lucillia unless I marry. Our laws and customs require an aryl—one person cannot rule on their own."

"That sounds awful," Devlyn said, then after a small pause added, "Truthfully, I never liked the guy."

"That much, anyone can see," laughed Ellendren. "My burden is a heavy one, but I cannot imagine what you're going through. Becoming an ei'ceuril is quite different than marrying someone you don't love."

"It's not that much different, I suppose, especially when you are drawn to another." Devlyn bit his lip, trying to force himself to stop talking. "But that prophecy leaves little room to get around it. I still feel like there might be a way. At least, I hope there's a way around it, that way you won't have to marry Tre…" Devlyn stopped himself from finishing, only just realizing what he was saying.

Another quiet moment passed, a terribly more awkward moment. Devlyn thought he should say something, something that would soften his words, but he couldn't think of anything to say. *Better to not say anything than say something like that again,* he thought. *Should I tell her about the jewel her mother had given me? Perhaps, tell her more about Aliel? Anything to change the topic.* Several other options passed through his mind as he cast his eyes in every direction but at Ellendren.

He looked from one wagon to another, then unintentionally made eye contact with her again, and found that he couldn't break away. His heart raced and he could swear that Ellendren's face was getting bigger. *Her head's not getting bigger, it's getting closer*, he thought, leaning closer to her in response.

Ellendren's eyes closed, her head tipped slightly sideways and he had a fleeting notion that he should pull away from her, take several steps back. He was studying with the ei'ceuril—this wasn't allowed. Yet, every fiber of his being pushed him closer until, unable to resist any longer, Devlyn's lips clumsily touched hers. He was no longer aware of anything else, only Elle. He knew they could be seen, they were still within the wagon enclosure, but it no longer mattered. An eternity seemed to pass with his lips touching hers. When she shyly pulled away, he felt as though only a moment had passed. A moment that was far too brief.

Ellendren's cheeks were red and she smiled at him. His shoulders relaxed, and his lips curved into a goofy stupid smile. When she saw his smile, hers widened and it was the most beautiful smile he had ever seen. He knew he was blushing too, but no longer cared.

# Sword Fights

Two months had come and gone since they had left Ceurenyl, and still they had not arrived at Binton. And over a month had passed since Devlyn had kissed Ellendren and those weeks had seemed even longer since they had rarely spoken during that span. Devlyn knew he shouldn't have kissed her, he knew he belonged to the ei'ceuril, but he also knew that something had awoken within him, something that had been there from that first time he had met Ellendren, growing more real and apparent whenever he saw her. After that kiss, it no longer slept, and refused to close its eyes once again.

Does she feel the same? Devlyn asked himself. That thought kept him awake at night as Alex's snoring rivaled Oliver and Andrew together. *Did she have trouble sleeping too?* Devlyn knew that she was not fond of Trethien. He had thought that courtship had ended, but, apparently, there remained a chance that it would actually happen.

Ellendren wasn't the only one who kept communication to a minimum. Devlyn still hadn't learned much about the elf named Viren over those two months, other than that he allowed no one to shorten his name to Vir. Alex had been the recipient of a swift rebuke when he had done so, a month or so ago, as they were unhitching the horses from the wagons after another day of rolling across the grassy plain.

The wagons had just paused for the night and a fire already roared at the center of the semicircular enclosure, and Devlyn saw an opportunity to ask Tindol about the Sojourners, something he had meant to do since Tye and Alex had brought Devlyn and Ellendren to the wagons.

Taking a seat next to the elderly man near the fire, Devlyn asked, "What exactly does it mean, to be a Sojourner?"

The elderly man sat resting his head on one hand, looking into the dancing flames. At first, Devlyn wondered whether Tindol had heard his question since he did not acknowledge Devlyn, nor immediately respond. Devlyn was about to repeat the question when Tindol cleared his throat.

"We are no different from you, if that's what you wonder," Tindol began. "We are anacordel just as every other race is. But we were not always Sojourners." Devlyn had never heard of the Sojourners, and he wondered about their importance, if any, in Eklean. "Neither did we choose the life of a Sojourner. It was a choice made long before the first Sojourners were born that set us on this path.

"When Erynor first started to scheme against Krysenthiel, he sought allies to aid his budding war. The tribes of Dwonia boasted some of the most skilled warriors in all Eklean; our prowess was known both here and beyond the seas. Naturally, Erynor sought us out. He wanted every tribe to join his cause, and although most of the tribes did, two would not.

"Tribe Fendur and Tribe Vadir outright refused Erynor's offer and remained in Dwonia, but the other ten tribes traveled to the Shadow Mountains to pledge themselves to the Cyndinari, setting himself up as an emperor, later founding the Erynien Empire. My ancestors were among that number." Devlyn listened intently; Tindol spoke sincerely and with a touch of remorse for the actions of his ancestors.

"A time came when Erynor ordered our tribes to infiltrate Krysenthiel's cities and kill anyone we encountered. My ancestors did not know that they were to be a diversion for a much larger plot, one that revolved around the Jewel of Life. Battles broke out sporadically across Krysenthiel, and after many years and even more battles, Erynor placed his Shroud over the Jewel of Life, cutting off everyone from its life-giving essence. When the people of my tribe, Tribe Naruno, realized what had happened after the fighting stopped, they did not march for the Shadow Mountains, but for Dwota's Gap. There, they were stopped by the two remaining tribes who did not join Erynor's cause."

Tindol stopped there, and Devlyn wondered whether there would be more to the story but Tindol remained silent. Tye walked into the fire's light and took up the story.

"The Naruno Tribe was given three options. First, return to the Shadow Mountains and kill as many as possible, which they would not because of how much blood they had already spilt. To this day, they refuse to carry weapons. Secondly, if they took a single foot past Dwota's Gap, they would be executed by the two tribes who had refused to join Erynor. Their third option was to spend the rest of their days exiled from Dwonia, which had transformed from a fertile land to a wasteland after the other tribes had left. When they chose the third option, they were stripped of their land and their name. Tribe Naruno died and the Sojourners were born, the tribe without land," explained Tye. Tindol's expression reflected the pain he felt as he listened to Tye.

"My ancestors pleaded to return, but the tribes refused. They told Tribe Naruno that there was only one condition under which they would be permitted past Dwota's Gap; if the Song were found and the seeds returned to the desert to bring it back to its former lushness, they would be allowed to rejoin the tribes of Dwonia. According to legend, there is a song that can bring the seeds back to Dwonia." Tindol looked at no one as he spoke, just into the flames. "When I was younger, we believed that Velaria might hold the answer. That garment of hers was the closest we came to finding the Song."

Devlyn was becoming uncomfortable about Tindol's great sadness and wasn't sure whether it might be better if he left Tindol at the fire to his own musings. He wanted to comfort the elderly man but had no idea as to what he could do to help. Alex approached from the far side of the wagons, pulling Devlyn's attention away from Tindol.

"Come on, you need to practice your swordsmanship," Alex said and immediately returned to the practice area without waiting for Devlyn to respond.

"Well, if there's any way I can help, I'll do my best," Devlyn said then excused himself and made his way to where the others were already practicing. He caught Ellendren staring at him and he tried to smile reassuringly, but it probably looked awkward.

"It's about time. Were you waiting for the sun to rise?" asked Alex.

Having forgotten his practice sword in the wagon, he turned to retrieve it, but Andrew handed him his own. "I'll let you and Alex have a go first," said Andrew. While he had been in Ceurenyl, Devlyn had rarely practiced his swordsmanship, thinking that spending his energy on wielding was the best use of his time. After all, the chances of a sword saving his life where wielding could not, was not likely. But now, Alex and the others insisted that it was important for a man to fight with a sword. Abbie always corrected them, saying that it was important for everyone—a sentiment not shared by the ei'ana.

With that insistence came practice, and he had grown proficient with a sword. He'd also noticed that his body reflected the increased exercise, with firm biceps and more muscular thighs and chest. He and Alex sparred for twenty minutes, Alex's skill far exceeding his own as always, so that he easily blocked Devlyn's attacks and maneuvered around his parries.

Finally calling for a stop so he could catch his breath, Devlyn saw Viren walk toward him carrying an oddly shaped sword. Its golden pommel had a translucent sheen unlike other steel, with scrollwork engraved all along the slender gleaming blade. Catching sight of Viren and his blade, Oliver drew his own sword and stood facing the still-approaching Viren.

When Viren stood immediately facing Oliver, neither spoke, but each bowed to the other. Viren's free hand rose to his heart, as his body flourished into a bow, his right leg in front of his left, a posture Devlyn had never seen. Oliver bowed as any Septyl knight would, his torso simply bent forward.

They lunged toward one another immediately after rising from their respective bows. Devlyn had watched Oliver fight on numerous occasions and expected him to quickly overpower Viren, however Viren pressed his attack masterfully, displaying shocking strength and agility for his age. At first, it appeared that Oliver had the upper hand, but with each passing moment, the scales shifted toward Viren.

The two swords flashed against each other, their forms transforming into blurs of light, until Viren's sword froze an inch from Oliver's neck, causing everyone in the crowd to gasp. The crowd had grown considerably while the two had dueled, and now included everyone, even the ei'ana. Only the Sojourners did not gather to watch the sparring.

Devlyn's jaw had fallen open in awe at how quickly and precisely the sword had stopped. He doubted he could slide a single finger between the blade and Oliver's neck. Even if Devlyn ever managed the unlikely feat of overcoming Oliver in a sword fight, the strength and precision that Viren demonstrated seemed impossible.

Lowering his sword, and taking a step back, a panting Oliver asked, "How is it that you came to such prowess?"

Viren lowered his own sword, one that when seen closely, showed that it was not steel at all. Standing with his shoulders back and his sword relaxed at his side, Viren responded without a hint of exhaustion, "I have dedicated my life to mastering this tool, so that I might better serve justice."

"You speak as a knight would," said Oliver, and Viren responded with a quick sharp nod, then turned to Devlyn.

"I would speak with Devlyn and the phoenix, alone," he said. Devlyn's gut responded with a twist, but from his nearby perch, Aliel assured him that this Viren was trustworthy without providing any reason. Devlyn led Viren off toward Aliel's tree perch, thinking that at least they would be visible in Aliel's light even if they were too far from the others to be heard. Once they were beyond earshot, Viren looked intently at Devlyn, nodded, and spoke.

"One thousand four hundred sixty-one years have passed since I made my oath of fealty to High King Faerndryn and High Queen Ithendryl Lorenthien, Aryl of Arenthyl, and Exalted Aryl of Krysenthiel. Two hundred of those years I served beside my fellow knights before Erynor betrayed us. Once he shrouded Ceurendol, cutting our people off from our shared vitality, Erynor's rise to power was swift.

"Never had our people experienced such brutality. In a desperate measure to preserve a shimmer of hope for the future before the Shroud expanded to cover all Krysenthiel, a hundred Guardian knights, including myself, were tasked in safeguarding the last remaining phoenix egg. We insisted on joining the fight, but were forbidden by Ithendryl herself, one of the last Phaedryn whose phoenix had not yet been consumed by Erynor's dragon.

"Her Exalted Majesty made us vow to preserve what might be preserved and to aid the one the phoenix chose. We did not expect to remain in our fortress for fourteen hundred years, yet our oath bound us, and the phoenix egg granted us prolonged life while our kindred passed to Lumaeniel. Since Aliel's hatching, the eldest of those among us have passed through darkness into the Light beyond. In the name of the Guardians, our service and guidance are yours," Viren finished formally with a flourish.

Shocked by Viren's revelation, Devlyn stuttered his thanks and accepted the knight's offer. Aliel seemed pleased by this development.

Over the rest of the journey to Binton, Devlyn and the others learned more about Viren and the Guardians. The fabled knights still numbered around a hundred. The ei'ana questioned Viren mercilessly about things that had happened long ago, Velaria insisting that Devlyn be present whenever Viren was questioned, deeming it vital that Devlyn learn as much as he could concerning his ancestors. Ellendren also made sure to be involved.

One morning, Velaria reminded Devlyn not to wear anything that might identify him as an ei'ceuril student, which wasn't a problem since he hadn't packed any of his scratchy ei'ceuril robes. None of the others wore anything that would identify them and their ties to Septyl either, not even Oliver, who Devlyn had never seen in anything but his armor or rough jerkins that were common among Septyl knights. The ei'ana still wore colors that represented the School they belonged to, but they looked no different than any other woman wearing traveling clothes of a certain favored hue. However, they had removed the sigil pins depicting their School.

Toward the end of the second day after the reminder to everyone, the city of Binton peeked over the horizon, still far from where they were. "The plains make you think it's closer than it actually is," Sara told Devlyn. She had taken quite an interest in Devlyn and was very curious about his bond with the phoenix. During their walk one day, she had told him that she had almost joined the Albiens at her Choosing, also mentioning that she had always been a curious girl with a great thirst for knowledge, but she had an even greater love for peace, and it was peace that was most needed in Eklean.

The wagons came to a sudden halt in the middle of the day, leaving everyone surprised that they were stopping when the sun was still high over their heads and Binton remained far in the distance.

They shuffled out of their wagon, with Devlyn last, Aliel right behind him. Velaria was speaking alone with Tindol. Not wanting to intrude, Devlyn waited for them to finish their conversation, and as he waited, he noticed others unloading some of the wagons. He was about to join them when Tye approached him.

"It's been an honor traveling with you, Devlyn. I hope our paths cross in the future."

"We're separating?" asked Devlyn, truly shocked.

"Sojourners are not permitted within a day's walk of most cities. Not their rule of course, but the lords of those cities have decreed so. Since I'm traveling with them, I must remain with them."

Oliver, Andrew, and Alex retrieved the heaviest packs from the wagons. Devlyn and Viren insisted on sharing the load, but there were only three heavy packs. After some discussion, they agreed to carry the packs in shifts. Velaria, Sara, Reia, Ellendren, and Abbie found their own packs, and Velaria led the group from the wagons to continue the remainder of their journey on foot. Devlyn thanked Tindol for his hospitality and followed the others heading toward the city. Aliel was with him one moment, then, with an exchange of understanding between the two, just disappeared.

As they drew closer to the city, more travelers appeared on the main road, coming from the many smaller roads to either side, all walking toward the safety of Binton's stone walls. Devlyn guessed many of the people on the road were farmers, since many carried their most prized tools and herded livestock. Devlyn could only imagine how long their journeys had taken, recalling the stubbornness of the few farm animals at Cor'lera's abbey school. The more disturbing thought was that something very awful must be driving the farmers from their lands. It was still late spring and these farmers were abandoning their land well before the harvest.

The number of people increased substantially as they drew near the gates to the city. Devlyn tried to peer around the crowd but the ground was too level, and it was impossible to see beyond his immediate companions.

"What's taking so long?" Alex asked impatiently while standing on his toes to no avail.

"The guards are no doubt closely questioning those who wish to enter the city," Reia said condescendingly. Alex threw her an irritated scowl but said no more.

It took more than an hour until they reached Binton's gate, where several fully armed guards stood watch. Archers peered over the battlements above the gate. A guard barely older than Andrew stood to the side of the gate asking various questions to an elderly couple in front of them. Once he was satisfied, he ushered them through, then eyed the next group and waved them forward. Velaria took the lead and addressed the young guard before he had the chance to.

"Good evening, sir. Would you, by any chance, know if there are any inns with vacancies in the city?"

The young guard blinked, set slightly aback by being asked a question rather than directing one himself. "The cheaper ones are all full last I heard, but if you can spare the coin, there are still rooms available at the pricier ones. They'll probably charge several silver jents a room though."

"I see," Velaria replied, still guiding the conversation. "And in what part of the city might I find these vacant inns?"

"Um, I believe they're all toward the center of the city, the ones closest to the castle that is."

"Wonderful. Is there anything you need of us before we go there?" she asked, surprising the guard yet again.

"Oh yes, of course," said the flustered guard, pausing to order his thoughts before asking what he had asked every traveler entering the city. "By order of his Majesty, King Lawrence of the Royal House Maroven, what business do you have in Mindale's crowned city of Binton?" he recited.

Velaria responded quickly and clearly. "Just passing through. Wars to the east and wars to the north. My sister has invited us to her home, away from all this fighting, across the River Eindol."

The young guard's face lightened at the mention of moving away from the fighting, a wishful desire of his own, perhaps.

Without warning, a vision rushed into Devlyn's mind. A quick series of events spurred through, none of which made sense, but he somehow knew that the young guard would desert the Mindalean army. Devlyn looked behind him at Abbie, who had never looked calmer or more content. *It must be an act*, thought Devlyn. He sighed, remembering that she had insisted that he tell her whenever he experienced a vision. Distracted by the vision and thoughts of telling Abbie, Devlyn did not catch what the guard said in response to Velaria, but they were now walking through the gate.

Velaria continued to lead the way. She was familiar with the city and walked assuredly, followed by the rest of their group through Binton. Devlyn was surprised to see that Binton's builders preferred wood and not stone as a building material, unlike other cities he'd visited. The only exception was the wall surrounding the city, which was constructed of large granite blocks. But even with the distraction of the difference in the construction of the city, something else bothered him, and he approached Velaria.

"I thought you didn't lie," he said, speaking in hushed tones.

"Your uncle, Arlyn, once told me that I do not have to tell my whole truth." Velaria smiled her small smile. "He also asked me to think of where the lie sat. You'll learn soon enough that no deceit crossed my lips."

Devlyn mulled over Velaria's response, and shifted his attention back to his new surroundings. Curious about the layout of the city, Devlyn pressed more fully into Aliel, just enough to share his vision high over their heads.

Instantly, his view shifted, and the world basked in light. Devlyn refocused the phoenix's sight so that he could have a larger perspective of the city beneath. Aliel's vision marveled Devlyn. The phoenix soared far enough above that he might as well be invisible, but he still could see every detail below perfectly. The city was oddly shaped, unlike other cities which favored a rounded character, one radiating from a central hub. Binton had an oblong form and seemed to have grown organically around the roads leading in to and out of the city. It looked like there were originally two villages at either end that had merged following the construction of a castle between them.

A nudge from the side made him return to his own body.

"It would be wise to not do so while in public," Viren said quietly, the reminder meant only for Devlyn.

Panic pierced through Devlyn. *How could I forget about my eyes?* he thought as he remembered that while he and Aliel were bound, his eyes glowed golden. Luckily, it seemed that no one else had noticed.

"I might not fully understand it, but I have lived in an age when such acts were easily identifiable," Viren added. Chastened, Devlyn pulled the hood of his cloak over his head.

With Velaria's determined pace, they soon arrived at a decent looking inn, one with a stone foundation, but the levels above constructed of wood. The castle was nearby but Devlyn could only see part of it above the buildings between them. Nothing about it appeared remarkable.

The inn's common room looked comfortable and there were plenty of patrons. There was no fire lit in the hearth, which was good, since the climate in Binton was much warmer than in Ceurenyl, due to its lack of elevation and more southern location. A jolly looking innkeeper greeted them. Judging by the innkeeper's rounded stomach, rosy cheeks, and the state of his clothing, Devlyn had the impression that he had not experienced many hardships since the wars began. Or ever, for that matter.

A GROWING STENCH

Ellendren felt a gentle nudge. Her eyes refused to open, and she did not think that she had overslept. Her inner thoughts loosely questioned why someone would attempt to wake her just as another nudge came. She reluctantly opened her eyes to find Sara standing next to her bed, one finger held in front of her lips in the universal sign for quiet.

"Get dressed, child, and meet us in the corridor. Mother Velaria is waiting," Sara whispered, then left the room Ellendren shared with Abbie.

Curious as to why Sara had awoken her, Ellendren looked to the darkened window—the sun would not rise for at least another hour. She rose, quietly splashed water on her face and brushed her silvery hair, then found the skirt and blouse she had set aside the night before. Since joining the Vyoletryns, she wore purple garments more often, but her mixed loyalties between Septyl and Lucilla found her in yellow and white for a second day. She was the crowned princess of Lucillia after all.

Ellendren discreetly slipped out of her shared room and quietly closed the door, Abbie still asleep. Velaria, Reia, Sara, and Oliver waited in the corridor outside her room.

"Are we ready?" Oliver wore his sword at his waist. "I don't support this move, Mother Velaria, but I would see it start and finish as soon as possible."

"It is necessary." Velaria led the way to the stairs, through the common room, and out into the predawn air. The city of Binton slept, the streets empty. Curiosity poked at her. Why had they left the inn? Where were they going? Velaria offered no information as she led them past shops and homes—only a few of the buildings showed candlelight behind drawn draperies.

The sun had barely begun to rise, the sky still cast in deep purples and Ellendren wasn't sure of the hour. Unlike elven cities, most human cities did not implement the elven bells to mark the hours of the day. She wondered how humans managed to get anywhere on time without the bells tolling throughout the day.

Ellendren felt a certain fondness for this time of day. She adored that moment just before the sun exploded over the horizon—that moment when the exuberant light cradled the land. It never lasted long. She felt as if she and the sun rose together, both stirring from their stillness over the night. Just now, though, her grogginess insisted on at least another hour of sleep.

Ellendren had studied maps of every major Eklean city, spending a significant amount of time studying the capitals, so when she took note of the names of the two streets they crossed, she knew precisely where they were going. *Surely, Velaria doesn't expect to get into the castle*, Ellendren thought when the castle loomed above them.

But Velaria did not walk toward the castle gates, instead choosing an alley to the left of the gate. They now walked between the wall enclosing the castle grounds and buildings lined against it, a narrow alley barely large enough for a cart. Ellendren's heart skipped a beat when a small gate covered in vines along the castle's curtain wall appeared. Velaria opened the unlatched gate onto the castle gardens, empty at this time in the morning; not even the gardeners had begun their work. Oliver remained in the alley but Ellendren and the ei'ana passed through the gate.

The castle gardens sat along the south side, sprawling along the curtain wall. They offered a delightful escape from the city but were far below Ellendren's standards. Lucillia provided lush vegetation all year round. Flowers bloomed profusely even during the winter months.

There was no one to greet or guide them. *How had Velaria arranged this?* She led them through the gardens to a pergola covered with many vines and flowers. Ellendren couldn't say how long they waited, but she would never have expected the king of Mindale to join them in the pergola without any of his attendants.

"Our friendship is the only reason I agreed to this meeting, Velaria," King Lawrence began pompously.

"Thank you, Lawrence, you have always been a kind man." Velaria responded carefully. Ellendren found the statement odd. She held no ill feelings toward the Mindalean king on a personal level, but his well-known behavior toward women was despicable, particularly toward his many wives. He had cast them aside after they each bore him two daughters. He had finally fathered a son, at an advanced age, but the child's mother had died during childbirth and he had already wed another woman who had borne yet another princess. No one knew exactly how many wives had preceded this one, but Lawrence had more daughters than any other monarch in Eklean.

"Those are surprising words for the King of Mindale these days." King Lawrence took a closer look at Velaria's companions, his eyes falling on Sara and Reia first. "I see that you did not travel alone. If I'm not mistaken by the colors they wear, you brought an Auburnis and an Arantiulyn." Then he noticed Ellendren and her yellow and white attire. None of Septyl's Schools were represented by yellow. "Are you mad? Bringing the daughter of Vernal and Harnyl into Binton!"

"You needed to be reminded who you were siding against," said Velaria. She spoke without threat or challenge, merely putting forth a statement. But Lawrence did not take the reminder well.

"You think I do not know who I've allied Mindale to? That my eyes were blinded when his servants walked through my gates trying to gain my allegiance for their emperor? They had already dined and feasted with my lords, winning them over long before they ventured to Binton. The majority of my own nobility insisted that we side with our southern *friends*. All of them had grown richer and fatter with the assistance of their newfound friendships. This allegiance was unavoidable—I would have faced civil war if I had refused." Lawrence spoke defensively, wanting to make sure that the ei'ana understood that the blame did not belong to him alone.

"Last I heard, Lawrence was the King of Mindale. Not his lords, nor Erynor," said Velaria.

"If I speak my mind about this allegiance, I will lose my crown, and likely my head with it. You do realize that both Everin and Myrium are under siege? How long do you think they will withstand Erynor's might? Their only allies are shielded in Lucillia. I have heard that the dwarves might help Everin, but they stand little chance against Erynor. And from what I also hear, they are far from unified."

Reia had been listening with growing impatience and no small measure of disgust. "Torsil and Tiel both siege Myrium. If the Torsillians had not abandoned the Lucillian Alliance and added their strength to the Sorenth, Myrium would not be so hard pressed, and would have been able to overcome the invading Tieli military and their treacherous queen!" she spat out, tired of the king's cowardice.

"What would you have me do, Ei'ana? Gather all the supporters of Erynor and exile them from the city? Take control of my armies once again and send them north to aid Everin, thereby leaving Binton and my other cities defenseless?" The king's sarcasm was sharp. "New Castle borders Yanil and the moment I move against the emperor, the Yanileans would seize my southernmost city."

A moment passed where no one spoke. Then Ellendren was amazed to hear words flowing from her own lips.

"If slavery and destitution is what you desire for you and your people, by all means, remain loyal to Erynor. However, if you want more for your people, you will have to fight."

<hr>

Abbie Wintyr paced back and forth in the large room shared by the men. Whatever it was that made her so anxious was not obvious to Devlyn, who grew concerned on her behalf. Viren, Alex, and Andrew also waited in the room with them, biding their time since no one knew where Oliver, Ellendren, and the ei'ana had gone, some time before Devlyn and the rest woke.

Andrew had made the mistake earlier of asking whether Abbie's worry was due to the disappearance of the ei'ana, to which she had replied with a snapping "Don't bother me now!" That had been after Abbie had come to their room and she still paced the length of it. "There's a stink about this place," she finally said, making every head in the room turn in surprise toward her.

"What did you expect from a city that's bursting at the seams from all its new visitors? More like refugees if you ask me," said Alex, taking the statement at face value.

She stopped mid-step to glare at him. "Don't be an idiot, I'm not talking about that stink! There is something very wrong with this city, and the sooner we leave, the better."

Something did feel off about Binton. Devlyn didn't know why, but he too felt uneasy inside the city walls, but neither could he sense the stench that Abbie referred to. It was impossible to tell the time without any bells tolling the hours, but Devlyn thought another hour passed with no one talking, the only sound Abbie's pacing feet. Viren maintained a meditative trance and opened his eyes only once.

Why is there such tension down there? Aliel conveyed, feeling it through Devlyn.

Abbie doesn't like this place. She says it has a stench to it, Devlyn replied.

Can you not smell it? It's a foul stench, I can smell it from above the city. I don't like you being there without me; try not to extend your stay. Concern etched through their connection.

"What was that?" Alex jumped from his reclined posture.

"Someone's out there," replied Andrew, picking up his sword as the floorboards creaked outside their room. Viren remained unconcerned and looked to Devlyn to see his reaction. Fortunately, the suspense ended quickly when Oliver pushed through the door. He scanned the room with his piercing eyes before entering completely.

"Where did you get off to?" Alex demanded. Oliver eyed Alex disapprovingly. "Sir," Alex added as an afterthought. Oliver was a Septyl knight after all and Alex still a pupil.

"This place stinks, and I'm not fond of being trapped in places that smell worse than latrines," said Oliver.

Several other voices came from the corridor, drawing nearer, then the ei'ana came in, closing the door behind them. Devlyn felt Reia wield an interwoven lace of aerys and animys, one he recognized as a sound barrier. The second it was in place, Ellendren burst out, "I do not trust this King Lawrence; no king would act so cowardly, not even in the face of a dragon. Forgive me, Mother Velaria, but he is playing us the fool."

"Oh, I like this one." Reia smiled. "I agree, I have no doubt that he's a coward, but he played the part all too well. He wanted to learn something from us; I just hope he didn't get it. It was a mistake to come here."

Velaria concentrated, seeming to consider several options at once. "Oliver, have you secured an exit route for us?"

"That I have, Mother Velaria. There are horses waiting for us in a nearby stable." Oliver had a confident tone that didn't seem to alleviate Velaria's obvious concern.

"We shall leave tomorrow, before the sun rises. I agree, Lawrence tried to deceive us and he has an agenda that we are not aware of. However, we did confirm what we came to learn: Mindale is in Erynor's grasp," Velaria replied, her tone calm and calculated.

Reia allowed the wield to dissolve, and as soon as it did, all could hear dozens of booted feet striding along the corridor outside their room. "I think tomorrow will be too late," said Ellendren, already working on several wields just as a knock came at the door, one that caused all the swords in their room to be unsheathed.

"His Majesty, King Lawrence of the Royal House Maroven, requests your presence," called a loud voice from the other side. Peering outside the window which offered a view of the street below, Devlyn counted no less than twenty guards all clad in armor bearing the sigil of the lion of Mindale.

"We will have to do without the horses; quick, grab what belongings you can," said Velaria, nodding at Ellendren to use the wield of aerys and terys that she had prepared. The knocking on the door became a loud bang as the men outside attempted to break the door down, expecting it to fall inwards. But Ellendren's unleashed wield exploded the door into the hall, hitting the guards on that side.

The guards who had been a little further back in the hallway began to push their way over their fallen comrades into the room. Devlyn pressed into the erendinth and held them. Pressing himself more fully into aerys, he unfurled it outward toward the attackers, forcing them all to lose a step. Everyone capable of wielding did so, including peace-preaching Sara. To Devlyn's shock, she too fought fiercely against the Mindalean soldiers.

The erendinth swirled in the crowded room as more guards forced themselves in, swords flashing. Startled screams came from the corridor, followed by doors slamming shut.

Knowing that they could not fight the entire brigade sent to the inn, they pushed their way toward the ruined door and into the hallway, holding the Mindalean guards at a distance using wields. Velaria led their flight, turning right instead of left in the corridor, away from the main stairway leading to the common room and toward the servant stair to the kitchen instead. When Devlyn reached the corridor just ahead of Viren, he saw why—Oliver and Andrew sparred with guards at the front of a column of guards that wrapped down the main stair. There had to be at least two dozen. Although the hallway was not very wide, Andrew and Oliver could not hold back every soldier and one slipped past to reach the fleeing group headed for the back stair. If that stairway was also blocked, they would have no choice but to fight their way through.

Viren easily overpowered anyone who tried to get near Devlyn, but the constricted corridor made it difficult even for the Guardian knight to maneuver as he subdued two more guards.

Velaria and the larger group reached the end of the hall near the servant stairs, disappearing around the wall down the switchback staircase, relieved that there were no guards there. The first smells of breakfast reached his nose as Devlyn made the last turn on the stair leading to the kitchen right behind Alex and Ellendren. His heart sank when he saw more guards at the bottom, fewer here than at the main stairway but still at least half a dozen. Velaria reached them first, intricately wielding ignys and exploding it just in front of them, causing temporary blindness. Devlyn would not have dared wielding ignys in a wooden structure, afraid he might burn the entire building down. The soldiers hacked blindly with their swords, trying to hit any of their targets, but a blast of aerys easily pushed them aside.

Taking the last stairs two at a time, Devlyn finally reached the kitchen on the ground floor, where hastily abandoned pots boiled over, their overcooked scent reminding Devlyn that they had not eaten breakfast, and likely wouldn't any time soon.

"Now what?" Alex slammed a bar over the door to the common room to prevent any more guards from coming in.

Velaria scanned the unfamiliar kitchen. One door led to soldiers in the common room, and a second led further into the inn. Oliver and Andrew had just reached the kitchen, looked to the unconscious guards piled on the floor and pushed a large kitchen table in front of the stair case then piled assorted loose furniture on top to barricade it. Abbie slipped past the door that led further into the inn, returning a moment later. "There's an exit further down this hallway."

Velaria didn't wait for Oliver and Andrew to finish their barricade. She flew through the door, along the empty corridor, and out into a narrow alleyway. Devlyn was vaguely aware that it was in the opposite direction of the castle, which only meant that they were running for the city walls. They could hear soldiers yelling and forcefully moving, the sound of their metal armor clashing in a nearby street.

The alley opened onto a broader street packed with people, people who were moving aside for the soldiers demanding that they make way.

It became evident that it was impossible for the ten of them to escape as a single unit. Too many soldiers hunted them. Velaria split them into two groups: Devlyn, Ellendren, Viren, Andrew, and Velaria together, while Reia, Sara, Alex, Abbie, and Oliver would try to escape in a different direction.

Viren stayed at the back of the group and Velaria ran at the front, her dress billowing around her. Devlyn risked a concerned glance at Ellendren and found the princess resolute. She wasn't the damsel-in-distress princess portrayed in many children's stories; rather Ellendren wielded the erendinth with a ferocity she hadn't previously shown. Devlyn smiled weakly at her, hoping this was reason enough to move past their awkward encounter, still more concerned about his relationship with Ellendren than being hounded by Mindalean guards. He regretted that their kiss had harmed their friendship.

Five guards plowed through a side street and into the middle of their group. Devlyn pressed into terys, and pulled the guards waist deep into the ground, then solidified the cobblestones around them.

No one else seemed as tired as Devlyn felt, but he was encouraged when they drew near the opened gates just coming into view. Somehow, they managed to run even faster toward the gate, but the portcullis slammed to the ground with a loud thud and soldiers filed out of the guard towers on either side of the gate. With soldiers behind and in front of them, they came to a halt—surrounded.

A single guard stalked to the front of the other soldiers blocking the gate and removed his helmet, revealing diseased, ashen skin. It looked to Devlyn as though it belonged on a corpse, not someone alive and walking.

"You were foolish to come here, Chair of Azurelle," began the shadow elf. "Tell me, did you truly think you could sway Erynor's puppet-king? Are you so conceited that you also thought you could escape this city?" Velaria began a complex wield, and the shadow elf laughed. "Do not try to overpower me, fool girl! You are no match for one such as me! Your weakling grandparents were not even born when I claimed my first life to extend my own!"

Devlyn could feel the dozens of spirits and the strength of their souls trapped within the shadow elf and was both amazed and disgusted by it.

Aliel must have been waiting for the perfect moment to make his appearance, for as the shadow elf began a wield of tenebrys, the phoenix exploded into the street in a flash of light, instantly bonding with Devlyn. Together, they created an incredible wield of vast proportions, melding the four elemental erendinth and adding animys.

Velaria and Ellendren added their strength to Devlyn and Aliel's. Devlyn saw that Velaria once again grasped a small stick—the one that she held when they had fought a shadow elf at Gwilnor. Shocked by the phoenix's sudden appearance, the shadow elf had yet to finalize his own wield when the burst of energy they had wielded exploded toward him and the gate behind.

A cloud of dust obscured Devlyn's sight and when it thinned, he saw that every solider in the immediate vicinity lay unconscious, either wounded or dead. The gate lay in rubble, and yet the shadow elf remained standing. The blast of energy had connected with the shadow elf, pressing into his being, and Devlyn could hear the screams of the many prisoners trapped within, bound to his own wretched soul. He and Devlyn fought each other, Devlyn supported by Velaria, Ellendren, and of course, Aliel. The souls screamed for release, rebelling against their captor, yet with no power to overcome him. Devlyn embraced animys further, knowing it would not be enough to free the trapped souls, but he had to try.

Aliel brought umbrys and its infinite capabilities to Devlyn's mind. Uncomfortable with wielding that erendinth, especially around Ellendren, Devlyn wasn't eager to test it now. However, Aliel's encouragement gave Devlyn enough confidence to seek umbrys, to submit and embrace it to fill his entire being, just as he held animys. Filled with umbrys, Devlyn added it to his wield with the other erendinth.

The shadow elf was aware of the added strength of umbrys in the wield Devlyn and Aliel led and responded with again wielding tenebrys. Aware that his opportunity to act first would soon fade, Devlyn embraced umbrys more fully, and unleashed his wield into the shadow elf's being. The shadow elf fought against it, his power over the darkness he wielded strong, but he soon lost all control.

His body began to disintegrate and the trapped souls were freed. His skin turned from a sickly grey to black, then the erendinth wielded by Devlyn exploded, leaving only dust where the shadow elf had been, and shimmering forms to escape and disappear.

The soldiers who were not severely injured began to stir, pushing their dead or more severely wounded comrades aside. Part of the wall that contained the southern gate lay in rubble. Devlyn took a quick look around, hoping to see the other group, hoping they could all leave together, but there was only Andrew and Viren, swords held defensively in case any of the soldiers had enough strength to attempt once again to stop them.

"We have to leave now!" Velaria urged, aware that the noise of the explosion would only bring more soldiers. Climbing over the rubble, they made their way onto the grassy plain on the other side. As soon as they were together on the other side, Ellendren turned toward the ruined wall and began to wield. The stone shifted under her influence, rising to form a solid wall where the gate had been. It was not as tall as the rest of the wall surrounding the city, but it was high enough to prevent anyone from passing through. "Hurry, it will not be long before they follow us from another gate."

NORTH AND WEST

The sky had grown dark and a chilled breeze came with the setting sun. Still worried that a guard might recognize him, Alex shielded his face beneath his hood. Shortly after their large group had split, Sara and Reia had gone down a street filled with people, then Abbie and Oliver had split off from him, until he was running down an alley alone. He was concerned for the safety of the others, but this wasn't yet the right time to search for them. Too many guards still roamed the streets. A hint of relief washed over him at being able to put off telling Andrew that he had left Abbie to fend for herself—that would never end well, even if she was with Oliver and quite capable of taking care of herself. Alex would never hear the end of it.

Alex rested now, his back against someone's house and mostly hidden by a cluster of barrels from passersby. Arms crossed over his bent knees, he considered the best course of action for the following morning. He knew he had to find the others, but he also wanted to investigate whatever had exploded on the south side of the city, the side where Velaria's group had gone. Whatever had happened had been massive; his ears still rang.

I bet Devlyn had something to do with it, he thought. Alex was very fond of his cousin, but the more Devlyn wielded, especially now that the phoenix had joined Devlyn, the more uncomfortable Alex grew with it. Alex accepted Velaria's reasoning for encouraging Devlyn to wield but that didn't make it natural—no good ever came from men wielding. Alex still had issues with women wielding. Even after spending almost two years at Gwilnor, he still felt uncomfortable whenever an ei'ana or student wielder made the elements move unnaturally. The hair on his arm rose every single time, quickly turning into goose bumps. *At least a kiara wielder wouldn't accidentally flatten a city*, Alex mused.

Shoving his hands into his pockets, Alex felt his coin purse, which was far from empty. Judging the weight of the coins, mostly jents and lewts, it occurred to him that he had no business sitting in an alleyway in the growing cold.

Alex left the narrow alley to look for an inn with a warm common room. He doubted he would be able to sleep tonight, but what he really wanted was a warm fire and a seat close to the exit.

The wooden sign above the doorway of the first inn he came to had a lion's paw. When he went in, he quickly noted that it was nowhere near as nice as the one they'd slept in the night before, but he also wasn't going to hand over a single silver jent to sleep in a bed. *Last night's bed* was *comfortable though*. Dozens of people crowded the common room, most in farmer's clothing, rough looking trousers, and simple tunics and cloaks. A tall man, presumably the innkeeper, was giving instructions to several people simultaneously as they hurried through the inn. Approaching the man, Alex cleared his throat in hopes to get his attention.

"Yes? What do you want? A room?" the man responded, giving Alex a quick glance.

"Well, yeah, if you have any," Alex said. He doubted falling asleep in the common room would be acceptable.

"You're just looking for a room now! What, were you drinking your angots away while the sun was up?" The man sniffed at Alex, hoping to catch a whiff of alcohol. "No, I guess not."

"Um, no, but where I was staying tried to charge me an arm and a leg to stay another night," Alex improvised.

"I see. Well, I have no rooms and even if I did, I'd charge just as much for you—asking at such a late hour. But there might be space in the stables; mind you, half of the men here are sleeping out there. I won't let any women stay in the stables; I don't need those problems here. I will expect coin in payment, of course, two lewts. Now, find a seat at one of the tables and we'll bring you some food and drink. You'll find the place is abuzz with gossip about today's events!" The inn keeper directed Alex to one of the few vacant chairs at a nearly full table.

A mix of patrons sat around the large wooden table, a few around his own age, most decades older. Alex sat down mid-sentence. "...with my own eyes! A kien wielder! Can you believe it! And the southern gate obliterated! And once past the rubble, before they ran, one of them wielded again and made a wall come up to block our soldiers from chasing after them," said a man in his thirties. The odor emanating from the man, especially as he waved his hands about to emphasize his words, clearly indicated that bathing was a rare occurrence. Happy and relieved to hear Devlyn and the others had escaped, he did his best not to show it.

"That lot got away then?" asked a woman. Her short grey hair stuck out in all directions and was desperately in need of a wash.

"Each and every one of them! They can't have gone far though, afoot. The soldiers will catch those witches and that abomination soon enough," said the same man.

Curious about how much was generally known, or guessed at, Alex asked, "Does anyone know who these people are?"

"Have you been under a rock the past months? Septyl assassins of course," said one of the younger men at the farther end of the table. "The king said so himself, said the ei'ana have finally shown their true foulness, just as the Yanileans have been preaching all along. They're just like the Lucillians, the Sorenth, and the Evellions. Thirsting for nothing but dominion over everything. I've never trusted them. Mark my words, there's something rotten about Ceurenyl. Those ei'ana have probably corrupted Anaweh's blessed temple as well!" His eyes gleamed dangerously, as if he wanted to pick up a sword that very instant and charge on Ceurenyl tonight. "And this proves it, they're even training men to wield again. They'll shred Eklean to pieces, leaving nothing but ash and everybody dead."

"All right, enough talk," a young woman said, "are we going to play cards or not? I intend to sleep soundly tonight with all your coin in my purse. Now deal our new friend in, Dan."

Dan dealt everyone in, including Alex, who now had a stew of mostly potatoes in front of him. Almost an hour later, Alex had handed some angots over to the girl—she seemed to be quite an able card player—but Alex's own angot count had grown from the others at the table who lost to him. He was thinking that it might be time to find the stable and get some sleep when he felt a cool breeze against the back of his neck as the door opened behind him. A few minutes passed, then a cold hand gripped his shoulder, nearly causing him to leap from his chair.

"You are a fidgety one, aren't you? Come on, we've been looking for you," said Abbie. Her red frizzy hair formed a fuzzy cloud around her head, and her bright green eyes gleamed in the lamplight.

He said good bye to the group of people at the table and followed Abbie out the door and into the cold night, rather pleased that he hadn't given the inn keeper a single angot to sleep in a stable and had added a few to the coins in his purse.

He followed Abbie through the streets and toward the western edge of town, neither of them talking to avoid drawing attention. They arrived at a small wooden house with a thatch roof that rustled slightly in the breezy night. Abbie gave a quick knock then opened the door and walked straight in and through the front hall toward the rear of the house. Alex followed her into a small kitchen, where Oliver, Reia, and Sara crowded around the table with three others Alex didn't know.

Oliver, his back to the far wall, was the first to notice them, but just gave a small wave. Sara looked happy to see him and stood to hug him. "We were so worried; we thought they caught you after we separated," confessed Sara, still holding onto Alex.

"Ha!" Abbie laughed. "Found this one playing cards with the locals."

Oliver glared at him, but Alex shrugged and grinned. He saw no harm in playing cards and taking his winnings from the locals, especially those who spoke ill toward Devlyn. *Should've stayed longer and won everything I could from that scoundrel.*

"Now that he's here, we need to discuss our next plan of action." Reia had little patience. "We can't chase after the others in case we too are followed. Luckily, Velaria never intended for us to remain together throughout the entire journey."

This was the first Alex heard any such thing. There was no room left at the small table, so he slumped against the doorframe, his eyes lingering on the three strangers.

"Don't pay them any mind," said Oliver, following Alex's stare. "They're Vyoletryn observants and we're in their safe house. Velaria asked them to keep a watch on the city months ago. Confirmed her suspicion too—there's a spy at Gwilnor."

"Word about a kien wielder heading to Binton reached our spy network three weeks ago," said the oldest of the three observants.

Alex was tired and resigned to Velaria concealing most if not all her plans. He waited to hear what else Velaria had not mentioned. "So, do we stay here, hiding, hoping that the Binton guard don't recognize us?"

Reia appreciated Alex's bluntness. "No, we leave tomorrow as planned. But we do not head west; we go north."

"North? Have you forgotten that there is an army invading Evellion? And besides, what can you possibly hope to gain by going north?" asked Alex.

"Who said anything about Evellion?" added Oliver, finally speaking. "It's Parendior that we're headed to. We need allies, and since we didn't find any here, we need to look for them somewhere else. You better still have friends there, boy."

"And how do expect to get past the Cyrillean Pass, not to mention all of Perrien?" Alex raised a doubtful eyebrow.

———

Devlyn was happy to be sitting against the back wall of the abandoned farmhouse they hid behind. He was out of breath and doubted he could continue running from their pursuers much longer. It was night, and the stars and moon were visible behind thin clouds. Now that they finally stopped to rest, Devlyn noticed how much the temperature had dropped as a cold wind washed over the open plains.

Velaria sat beside him and rummaged through her pack, checking her belongings.

"Do you mind if I ask what that stick is?" asked Devlyn. "The one you use while wielding sometimes. It's the second time I've seen you use it."

Velaria continued searching through her pack, without turning to Devlyn. "It's called a verathn. They were incredibly common during Krysenthiel's height, but were largely corrupted or destroyed by the Erynien Empire. I don't know what type this one was once called, but I've grown fond of calling it a wand. It can't replace the erendinth, but it can supplement a wielders strength." Velaria now held the verathn and offered it to Devlyn. "They came in all shapes and sizes. Some looked like weapons, others like statuettes—small and large.

He readily took it and felt a power inside the faintly glowing stick. It hummed in his fingers and he sensed the additional strength the wand offered—though it paled in comparison to his bond with Aliel.

"Do you still carry those two coins?" Velaria asked quietly, even though the others were foraging for something edible. They had managed to escape with most of their belongings, but only had enough provisions to travel on horseback. They now had to make their supplies last an extended journey on foot.

"What coins?" Devlyn replied, knowing exactly which coins she meant. Of course, he still carried them. He had never seen finer coins, not that he had seen many golden coins, but there was something unique about the pair found in the Cor Inn on his thirteenth birthday. They had also felt heavier after Chancellor Oranna had revealed that he carried a small fortune in those two coins. Devlyn still couldn't believe she had been assassinated.

"You did not hide them well at the Cor Inn, and I caught you looking at them when you thought no one was looking while we traveled with the Sojourners," replied Velaria with her small smile. "There is magic tied to those coins, and others like them. I meant to tell you sooner, but I had so much else to share with you, that I pushed it aside. Those coins show the Exalted Aryl of Krysenthiel. For over fourteen hundred years, those coins bore no profile."

"What about the Aryl of Lucillia?" asked Devlyn, confused over the significance of the coins.

"Might I see one of them?" asked Velaria, not responding to Devlyn's question. He dug through the coin purse where he kept the lumols and the violet jewel from Lucillia. He'd wrapped the jewel in a rag to prevent its purple light from emanating. Retrieving one of the coins, Devlyn noticed the shimmering profile of a feminine elf as he handed it to Velaria. The subtle light given off by these unusual coins still baffled Devlyn.

"She looks familiar, does she not? But as you can see, she wears no crown, nor will the figure on the other coin. That will not come to pass until the Exalted Aryl sits on the Crystal Throne, in Arenthyl, the City of Light." Velaria handed the coin back to Devlyn.

Devlyn knew that Velaria referred to Ellendren and her husband, but he did not want to think about who she might choose as her king, brushing such thoughts aside. "I think it's possible to disperse the Shroud," he said quietly, his eyes focused on replacing the lumol in the purse.

Looking toward him curiously, Velaria raised an eyebrow. "And how would you manage such a feat?"

"We've pierced a hole into it—Aliel and I."

Before Velaria could respond, Andrew approached and knelt beside them. "We need to make for the river, now. I don't know how you intend on crossing, but if we're going to try, it must be now. The Mindalean soldiers will catch up to us by morning if we don't lose them," said Andrew in a serious tone. "And I have doubts that we'll lose them even after crossing the river."

The three stood, and joined by Ellendren and Viren who had not been too far off, gathered their few belongings. With a quick wield, Velaria erased their presence around and behind the farmhouse. Within minutes, they were heading toward the river at a swift pace.

How far to the river? Devlyn asked Aliel, hundreds of feet above their heads. To everyone else, he appeared as a single star among many, but Devlyn knew which particular light above was Aliel. Grudgingly, Aliel had agreed to remain in the sky since his incredible light was a beacon for the soldiers.

If you leave now and move with haste, the sun will not reach his peak before you reach her banks, Aliel conveyed. Devlyn still found it odd that Aliel referred to everything as a he or she, reminding him of Brother Bernard, who did the same thing. Bernard had been one of the few ei'ceuril who had treated him kindly at the abbey school in Cor'lera. Since he and Alex had left, he had heard nothing about the state of his home village. The last he'd heard was what Velaria had told them, that those in the original village walls continued to resist Perrien's forces.

But it was not the time to dwell on Cor'lera; Devlyn needed to remain focused on his current situation, and the small group hurried on toward the river. Several hours after they had left the farmhouse, the sun had risen, Devlyn's legs ached, and he longed to sleep. An odd noise filled his ears, but he couldn't distinguish exactly what it was, too tired to figure it out.

Viren had also noticed the sound, and called to the others, "Those are horses; we need to move faster!"

No one needed a second warning and they all pushed themselves to their limits. Knowing that they could not outrun horses, Devlyn pressed himself against the erendinth, gently touching several elemental erendinth at once, but not yet fully. Velaria and Ellendren must have had the same idea, for Devlyn sensed them also preparing to wield.

The sound of galloping horses increased and Devlyn turned to see how close the Mindalean cavalry was, glimpsing the approaching riders. Still running, he pressed himself into terys and lifted boulders from beneath the grassy plains to suddenly dot the ground. Within his wield, he felt horses crash fiercely into the boulders they could not avoid at gallop. Men yelled and horses screamed. Loud orders carried across the plain as the soldiers reorganized themselves, spreading out across the plain. Again, he wielded stones from the ground, but the riders were wary now, and it was nowhere near as effective.

Devlyn sensed Ellendren wielding aquaeys and terys beneath the horses. She'd had a similar idea, but rather than throwing impediments in the horses' path, she made them sink into a newly created muddy mire, preventing them from galloping.

The mire's effectiveness was incredible, but it did not bind all the soldiers. Devlyn joined Ellendren in wielding aquaeys and terys to expand the mire, and Velaria wielded ignys and hurled fireballs toward those who had bypassed the muddy trap. The soldiers meeting Velaria's fire were either scorched or their horses were so frightened that they bucked and fought the reins to gallop to safety, many without a rider.

"Keep running, we're almost there," yelled Velaria. "Devlyn, call down Aliel."

He did not question Velaria, but summoned Aliel, who quickly dove from high above and within seconds flew next to Devlyn. "You don't intend on making him carry us over the river, do you?" asked Devlyn, still wielding against the soldiers, wishing that Yelaris was with them to help.

"Don't be absurd," said Velaria between quick gasps. The horses were close enough for the archers to unloose their arrows. "I need your combined strength to accomplish what I intend."

There was no time to ask what that was. He and Ellendren abandoned the muddy mire and started attacking the soldiers directly. *How did they get so close?* Pressing himself into aerys, Devlyn wielded a strong gale then brought the stronger winds from above to intensify the wind a hundredfold. The horses could no longer gallop and a few soldiers were thrown from their saddles, while others were brought to a complete stop in the forceful wind.

The sound of rushing water finally came to Devlyn's ears and he felt Velaria's wielding prod his own, inviting him to join forces with her, requiring him to stop wielding aerys.

Still bound with Aliel, Devlyn ran over to Velaria, who held her wand. She nodded. They had reached the riverbank and it was time to wield together. Devlyn felt Velaria's wielding rub against his own again, seeking control over his, seeking his submittal to the other. It was an odd sensation, and if he and Velaria had not previously worked this type of wielding, he would be more cautious now, especially since he was bound with Aliel. It felt wrong to allow another to intrude on their unique connection.

But Velaria wasted no time, wielding aquaeys as soon as Delyn submitted. Devlyn felt the incredible force of the River Eindol push against her wielding; if it were not for his and Aliel's added strength, the river's might would have consumed Velaria. A small pathway appeared in the middle of the water and everyone understood Velaria's intention. The soldiers were nearly upon them as they stepped on the soft river bed, their feet sinking into the now exposed sand and mud.

Velaria only kept the open space large enough for them to walk safely forward, allowing it to close behind and over them even as it opened in front of them. As they progressed across the river bed, the water rushing behind them cut off the following soldiers. Ellendren gasped when arrows pierced the water next to her, but the current swept them downriver before they could strike.

The river wanted nothing more than to collapse their air bubble and wash away the force that pushed against it. Warily, they trudged deeper through the wide river and its rushing waters, the early sun a distant shimmer high above. The mighty Eindol flowed deeply below its banks, fed by both the Vespien and Laudien Mountains, with water coming from as far north as Perrien. Only the River Meyien rivaled the Eindol.

Eventually, their trek through the soft slippery riverbed finally began to slope upward. Their ascent to the opposite river bank took twice as long as their descent, as they slowed their pace to carefully climb through the sludgy riverbed, knowing that if they slipped out of the air bubble, the current would wash them away.

When they drew closer to the surface, the light from the sun grew stronger and the water above their heads thinned to a few splashes. Fresh air filled their lungs again. Moving up the last part of the slope, Devlyn wondered about their pursuers. He turned to look back and could just make out tiny dots on the far side of the Eindol. The soldiers could not follow them through the river. They would have to make their way north for the closest crossing.

"We can rest for a moment," Velaria said, facing west, "and regain some strength. It will not be long until our crossing of the Eindol is discovered."

THE POOR LADY

Five days after crossing the Eindol River, the Ashton Wood crested the horizon late in the afternoon, still several miles off. They had kept a steady pace, taking brief rests, and even managing to sleep for a few hours. They were still pursued and had barely avoided a group of soldiers two days past, scouts no doubt searching for them. Aliel had warned them long before the soldiers drew near, allowing them to hide in some of the thick brush. Fortunately, the scouts had not dismounted to search the area; if they had, they would have easily discovered four elves and one human.

Another group of soldiers had passed them just a few hours ago. Like the previous ones, they stayed in their saddles and did not search the land carefully. Devlyn had a hunch that the Mindalean soldiers knew their destination and thought that it wasn't necessary to locate them now when it would be easier to cut them off later. Despite that possibility, Velaria urged them onward.

Devlyn doubted they would reach the Ashton Wood by nightfall, especially if they had to hide in a stand of bushes again. Against all expectations, they didn't come across any more soldiers the rest of the afternoon and they drew close to the forest when the sun had just begun to set, but night wouldn't blanket the land for another hour. Devlyn was the first to notice movement at the edge of the forest. He focused his eyes yet was careful not to bond with Aliel; the golden glow given by his bond with Aliel would have easily given them away. The stirring on the forest's edge was due to a group of men, soldiers most likely.

"Soldiers on the edge of the forest," Devlyn whispered carefully.

Velaria peered toward the trees then nodded in agreement. "We'll have to wait until nightfall, then take them by surprise." They made their plans as the last shades of the purple dusk finally faded to night, then Velaria and Andrew approached the Ashton Wood first, just south of the soldiers, Ellendren and Viren from the north, leaving Devlyn to stalk from the east, their original position. Velaria didn't want the soldiers to have proof of their destination and hoped to catch the soldiers off guard, and prevent them from sending word that the fugitives had indeed gone into the forest. Devlyn watched aghast as Velaria and Andrew advanced on the idle soldiers, but then stopped and just stood there.

Devlyn immediately assumed that a nearby shadow elf had stunned them both. Ellendren and Viren must have thought the same for they sprinted softly toward the soldiers, while Devlyn pressed forward sooner than they'd planned, fearing the worst.

Three Mindalean soldiers sat on the ground, eyes closed, breathing heavily. Devlyn looked to Velaria who just shrugged her shoulders.

"Do you plan to wait for them to wake?" asked a voice from further into the trees.

"Who's there?" Ellendren was nearest to where the voice had come from, but still spoke in a loud whisper.

Immediately, an elf of incredible beauty came out from behind a tree, her slender face and fair skin noticeable even in the subtle moonlight. She had the elven silver eyes, but it was difficult to tell the color of her hair, covered by a white veil. Her cream and brown clothing reminded Devlyn of the clothing worn by the poorer folk in Ceurenyl; he thought that the lady should be dressed in the finest silks and living in a manor or even a palace.

"I am known as the Poor Lady, a name that came long ago. But, as a child, I was named Clara, and those who know me call me Abbess Clara."

Velaria must have known this woman, for she inclined her head and then reached forward to embrace her. "Oh, it's so good to see you again! I never expected we would cross paths a second time," she said, still wrapped in Clara's arms.

"The pleasure is mine," Clara responded with a warm inviting smile. "We cannot remain in the open though. I put these soldiers to sleep but would prefer not having to do so again." Clara looked up at the pale moon, then turned and walked further into the forest. She did not move quickly, but it couldn't be said that she moved slowly either. To Devlyn, it felt odd to not be rushing after running and hiding from the Mindalean soldiers for so long, but Abbess Clara just moved along serenely.

Curious about their destination, Devlyn meant to ask Clara as they walked, but whenever the question came to the front of his mind, the need to ask dissipated.

The Poor Lady exuded a peacefulness that Devlyn was unfamiliar with, but that had an unexplainable contagious nature. Later, he would not be able to say how long nor how far they walked into the Ashton Wood, and to his own surprise, it did not matter. The trees in this forest were not particularly tall, especially when compared to those in the Illumined Wood. Most of these trees were ash trees, and both the forest and the Mindalean House which oversaw these lands took their name from them.

A stone structure soon appeared, hidden among the trees, its protective wall constructed of river rock and nearly concealed by many ivy vines. Devlyn could easily see several thatched roof lines beyond the wall, some taller than others, but could not see the gateway into the enclosed area. He was taken aback when Clara walked directly toward the solid stone wall. She stopped just in front of it, waved a hand, and Devlyn felt the air shimmer.

She wielded.

"Oh," gasped Ellendren quietly from beside him as an archway opened in the stone, just wide enough for a single person to enter at a time. One by one, they followed Abbess Clara through and even Aliel appeared and flew through. Devlyn and Andrew both looked back to see that the arch had already closed.

"Welcome to the Monastery of the Poor Ladies," said Clara when they stood around her in the courtyard of an expansive, low-standing building. It was the only building within the wall, but it sprawled throughout the entire enclosure, and varied in height. The same stone as the outer wall formed the building, but unlike the outer wall, the building featured windows and doors. A portion of the building resembled a chapel with a pitched roof, and from it came a beautiful chant, all women's voices. "Come, let us praise the Light for your safe arrival." Everyone followed Clara to the chapel.

When Clara opened the chapel's simple wooden door, the volume of the chanting rose and poured out over them. Inside, a brilliant light pulsed from thirty women, all clad similarly to Clara in creams and browns, but their veils were brown, not white like Abbess Clara's.

The women sat in two groups on opposite sides of the small chapel facing one another, the chanting alternating from one side to the other creating a sense of motion, pulsing between the two, two lungs breathing life into the small chapel. Clara invited them to sit in the available seats near the entrance then chose a seat among the women.

The newcomers remained silent, listening to the beautiful sound produced by the women, one voice from many. As they chanted, a wondrous light emanated from the women's bodies, pulsing from either side of the chapel. Time ceased and all that mattered was the chant.

Devlyn woke in a simple bed in a very small room. The sun had not yet made himself known, but Devlyn felt as if he had had a full night's sleep, even though he knew that it was not likely. The hour had been quite late by the time they had been shown to their chambers in one wing of the building. Aliel perched at the end of the bed near his feet, his head nuzzled beneath his wing. With Devlyn's waking, Aliel stirred and looked at him.

What happened last night? I mean, what were those women doing? Devlyn asked, wondering how the chanting led to the light emanating from the women.

What you experienced last night was believed to have been lost for over a thousand years. It is a prayer, one that only a female steward is capable of leading. The female stewards were all believed to have perished, killed by Erynor and his shadow elves, taking their secrets with them. But Clara seems to have outlived that catastrophe, Aliel conveyed.

I thought only men could be stewards?

Just because only men are stewards now, does not mean it was always so. Much like their male counterparts, they bring the Light into the world, but in a different expression. It seems that Clara has been busy bringing women into her monastery to share her gift.

Trying to wrap his mind around the added intricacies of the ei'ceuril, Devlyn splashed water on his face from the wash basin on the little dresser and pulled a clean shirt from his pack to put on. He only had two pairs of trousers, so he put on the pair he had worn yesterday. Fully dressed, Devlyn left the small bedchamber and walked through the monastery, his stomach grumbling with hunger. He was to meet Ellendren and the others in the refectory for breakfast and to decide their next steps. Unfamiliar with the building's layout, and not coming across any of the monastery's women who might provide some guidance, he wandered for a time before coming to a door leading outside into the open courtyard. A light fog covered the monastery grounds, and Devlyn heard chanting from the chapel again. This time, he did not enter, but remained outside to listen to the lovely tune.

As he strolled around the courtyard, he noticed a young woman sitting on a bench near a rose bush, and thought to approach her to ask for directions to the refectory. The woman was chanting softly to herself, participating in the prayer, and Devlyn stepped quietly, hoping that she would notice him.

"Good morning," she greeted him. "You were one of the visitors in the chapel last night, were you not?"

"Um, yes, Steward," Devlyn guessed at an appropriate title. She chuckled at his formality.

"You can call me Sister Katherine. And yes, I am a steward. Abbess Clara came to me in a dream when I was very young. I don't know how she knew, but I always had a desire to live such a life. I almost went to Ceurenyl, before she found me," said Katherine, blushing as she spoke.

Diverting his gaze, Devlyn noticed that the rose bush she sat next to had no thorns. Katherine noticed his surprise and disbelief. "It can be said that this is Abbess Clara's only true prized possession. When she left her original monastery on the outskirts of Quellion, she cut off a sprig from one of the rose bushes there. Legend says that the bushes had belonged to a man of peace and goodness, and it was only after he fell into the bushes that the thorns disappeared. The legend says that not even the thorns could bear harming this man of peace and goodness," Sister Katherine explained.

"Possessions we have not, sister," said Clara, approaching the two without either noticing. "That being said, the rose bush this one came from is very special. A zealous young human, Francesco, fell into it a long time ago. He called himself a lesser brother and inspired a movement the world had never seen. He even influenced Mainor Auburnis, a Founder of Septyl. It was from his example that no one here has personal possessions. His life was short, even among human standards, but his impression is seen even today."

Devlyn had had no idea that a human had made such an impact on the elves, especially on a Founder of Septyl. A few moments passed where no one spoke, Clara seemingly lost in her own memories.

"Did you know him?" asked Devlyn.

"Oh yes, he taught me many things. I was a young elf when we first met, and truth be told, I was quite eager to make his acquaintance. His reputation compelled me to leave Aldinare before even joining one of the eight aldarchs. Since I chose to become an ei'ceuril, it is assumed that I pledged myself to Aldarch Theseryn. While we elves lived prosperously in our Skylands, the humans below wrought terrible war among themselves before Thellion united all Eklean and even more war after that kingdom dissolved and segmented. Francesco preached peace and goodness, wearing nothing but tatty rags. He was never without a song on his lips. He died when I was still young but before he died, he helped me to establish a monastery with his values. He called me his first flower taking root in the world. You'll have to excuse me, I could speak of him for a very long time, but we must speak of something else at the moment. Sister Katherine, would you excuse us?"

Katherine inclined her head then excused herself and left.

"This place has been my home for many years, Devlyn. I have remained hidden while the world fell into chaos. If things out there continue on their current projection, the chaos will only worsen. I have the ability to help, to bring Balance back. Like yourself, I too was born an elya, but I chose a life of peace and solidarity in a monastery. However, my talents are greatly needed if those of the Light hope to remain out of Darkness. I have decided that I will instruct men to learn control of their wielding, and I will begin with Arlyn, your uncle, who remains in Cor'lera. From there, I will make my way to Ceurenyl and offer my help to the Ceurtriarch. Too many years have passed since I last entered the Chamber of Light and basked within the Empyrean Sphere. You too must return to the temple and enter the Empyrean Sphere if you desire to wield lumenys," explained Clara.

Devlyn shifted uneasily. He had been in the Chamber of Light many times but had never heard any ei'ceuril mention anything about an Empyrean Sphere. "I thought I had already wielded lumenys," replied Devlyn as he recalled his experience in the Illumined Wood.

"I can feel its mark on you, but it was not you who wielded that erendinth. It flowed through you and Aliel, yes, but you do not yet have the ability to wield it. And in fact, neither of you wielded lumenys; what you experienced was Verakryl, the Tree of Life, connecting with you as you called out for it. Only those who present themselves within the Empyrean Sphere and are found worthy by the six winged anadel will receive the gift of the ability to wield lumenys. I fear this is one of the many things that has been forgotten by the ei'ceuril in the Temple of Ceur," shared Clara.

"Is that why Erynor could not conquer Ceurenyl when he first tried, and how he so easily besieged the city this time?" asked Devlyn beginning to understand.

"Partly. There is a much more sinister reason for his recent success," said Clara, then she changed the subject. "You will have to leave here today, and you cannot take the path you came from. The enemy knows that you are here, and there is a powerful ally among them. You have met him and are no match for him at present, so you will have to flee further west. If you take any other path, they will surely enslave you. The sooner you leave, the less likely they will reach you. Let no one know what you carry until the time is ripe."

"How do you know?" Devlyn's fingers went to his pocket. The mention of a powerful enemy made Devlyn think of Aren, and he frowned even as he tried to convince himself that he was safe with Aliel at his side.

"No cloth can subdue that which lies in your pocket. It's been many years indeed since I have felt the faith of the Luminari. I had begun to fear it had been extinguished. Keep it safe, child. Now, join your friends. I believe they are in the refectory, taking the time to get a nourishing meal in before you leave. It's just down the hall to your left when you enter."

"Thank you for your guidance and hospitality, Abbess Clara; I'll do everything I can." Devlyn left Clara in the courtyard. As he made his way to the refectory, he thought about Clara's last comment, trying to figure out how she could possibly know what he carried. Not even Velaria knew. *Does it really give off an aura?*

Those who remember its touch will know what you carry, Aliel conveyed from above his shoulder.

Once Devlyn found the others, they ate quickly, gathered their packs and said goodbye to the ei'ceuril. Velaria led them out and took them south through the forest. The peace which had emanated in the monastery and around Clara remained with them for a time, but eventually faded the further they went. Fear and anxiety soon resurfaced.

As they traveled through the Ashton Wood, Devlyn had noticed that Andrew looked troubled.

"What's bothering you?" Devlyn asked, concerned for his friend, thinking he was worried about Abbie. Andrew seemed to be considering something, clearly experiencing an interior struggle.

"I don't know, Dev; it's just those women back there."

"What about them?"

"Look, I say my prayers to the Light like anyone else when they're troubled, but those women made this Anaweh the ei'ceuril preach about seem alive. As if it wasn't some figment of their imagination, but an actual being—a real person. Sure, I believe such a thing exists, but something about those women scared me; not one of them talked about the Light, but never have I been so compelled to believe," confessed Andrew.

"I can't say that they're the scariest group of women I've ever come across—you should meet Alex's mother, but don't tell him I said that," said Devlyn with a quick nervous laugh, not sure how to counsel his friend.

Shaking his head, Andrew said, "Don't joke, I'm not talking about that kind of scary; Abbie scares me more than anyone else, and not for the same reason either! But I don't know, I've never lived the best of lives, nor do I make the best choices, and seeing those women live such pure lives scares me. Why would anyone choose to live such a life if this Creating Light being wasn't real?"

"I don't know. I can't imagine anyone choosing that life if they didn't believe Anaweh was real. I guess I believe in the Light; I've never put too much thought into it, much less than other ei'ceuril novices, that's for certain." Devlyn grew troubled by their conversation. The reason those women and every other ei'ceuril chose such a life was not because some prophecy demanded it of them, but because of a special connection they felt they had with Anaweh. Devlyn still hadn't spoken with Ellendren about their kiss and he felt much more strongly about her than he did about becoming an ei'ceuril.

Andrew's face contorted slightly. "I'm not saying that the Light doesn't exist, but if it's true, then tell me why is there so much pain and chaos in the world? It shouldn't be possible with this so-called benevolent Light!"

Andrew had a point that Devlyn could not see past, bringing his own doubts to the fore.

Devlyn felt Aliel enter his mind. *When a child rebels against a parent, and commits horrible crimes, is the parent held responsible?* Aliel asked, not waiting for a reply before continuing. *Just so, should that parent prevent their child from committing those heinous acts? Lock them in a cage, like a slave? If the parent did, the child would grow to despise the parent who deprived them of freedom. Every parent wants their children to grow in happiness and goodness; the same is true for Anaweh.*

Devlyn conveyed his gratitude to Aliel, and walked beside Andrew for a time, neither speaking, each considering what it all meant.

BENEATH THE ASH TREES

A simple path stretched beneath their feet, weaving through the ash trees further west into the forest. There were no signs of anyone following them, putting everyone a little more at ease as they walked leisurely along the shaded pathway. Once they had left the Poor Lady's monastery, Ellendren had reminded Devlyn that the forest was watched over by Lord and Lady Ashton, and peculiarly enough, they were of a Mindalean noble house that shared little in common with other Mindalean nobles. Ellendren's knowledge of politics and persons of interest in Eklean never ceased to amaze Devlyn, and he didn't care that Ellendren's only comments to him were about political affairs in Eklean—they were talking again. A sense of normalcy had returned to their friendship, although neither mentioned their kiss, as though avoiding the topic would make the memory disappear.

While the Ashtons had never held the throne of Mindale, they were nonetheless an influential and powerful house. Unlike in the past, when the Royal House Maroven eagerly sought their counsel, it was widely known now that House Ashton strongly disapproved of their king's support of Erynor. This had led to their withdrawal into their lands, taking with them all their famed archers, thus depriving Mindale of the best archers of the human kingdoms.

Velaria confidently led the small band westward through the thickening forest, the leafy trees soon completely concealing the sun above. Her acute familiarity with different lands always baffled Devlyn, making him wonder if they would ever come across a path or a road she didn't know.

Taking in the scenery the Ashton Wood offered, Devlyn appreciated the odd sounds and various scents of different creatures he noted. Suddenly the sounds stopped. Not a single bird chirped and the forest seemed to be holding its breath.

"No one move," Viren warned, just as several archers appeared, not just on the path ahead, but above and behind them. They wore brown leather and hues of green, blending into the colors of the forest, making them all but invisible.

"Who enters the Ashton Wood? Identify yourselves." demanded one of the archers, an arrow nocked and ready to fly.

"Velaria Treyven, Chair of Azurelle."

Simultaneously, the bows eased and the archers lowered them. "Our apologies, Mother, we were not expecting your arrival," the lead archer said, bowing slightly. "I am Captain Markel."

"I gave no notice, Captain, since I hoped that no one would discover our entrance into your lands," said Velaria.

"Please, allow me to escort you to Lady Ashton; his lordship is away scouting our southern borders. Our informants received disturbing rumors of giants heading for the Gap. The manor is still a day's walk west." Velaria accepted Markel's offer with thanks. The other archers vanished back to their hidden posts and the small party moved on through the forest.

The following day, toward mid-afternoon, just as Devlyn noticed that the walkway was growing wider and the trees sparser, they followed Captain Markel to a large grassy area giving on to a large manor house where its surrounding trees had a groomed and manicured appearance. The captain led them toward the front entrance and spoke briefly with the household guards in hushed tones, too low for Devlyn to overhear. One of the guards took a second glance at the guests, and a longer one at Aliel, then vanished into the inner part of the manor while Captain Markel led them toward a parlor off the entryway and left them there. It was comfortably furnished with plush seating arranged around an unlit fireplace.

They had barely settled into their chosen seats when a woman entered the room. Devlyn presumed that this was the Lady Ashton and noted that Ellendren was admiring the intricate green embroidery on Lady Ashton's silver dress.

"It is good to see you again, sister," Lady Ashton said with a smile, embracing Velaria as old friends. Then Velaria stood back, and introduced everyone.

Glancing from Velaria to Lady Ashton, Devlyn could not see any resemblance between the two women. Lady Ashton was clearly human. *Maybe she's an ei'ana,* offered Aliel.

Velaria did tell that guard in Binton that they were traveling to see her sister, Devlyn responded, surprised that Velaria had spoken truthfully to the guard in Binton. On second glance, Devlyn noticed that Lady Ashton's eyes shared the same vibrant silver usually seen in elven eyes, but her ears were rounded, not pointed. *Definitely human. But how had she come by those silver eyes?*

Perhaps there's a trace of elven ancestry? Aliel offered.

Lady Ashton was pleased to meet everyone, but could not remove her eyes from Aliel, a usual response when someone saw a phoenix for the first time. "You are all welcome here as long as you wish," she said. "I'm surprised that your group is not larger. The roads have not been safe for quite some time."

"Our group was larger when we started out, but events in Binton led to some of us taking a different path. I do not believe it was ill fated," said Velaria, making Devlyn wonder whether she had intended so all along.

"I see," Lady Ashton replied. Devlyn had a hunch she was all too familiar with her friend's usual closely kept intentions when she let the matter drop. "Since you are here, would you be interested in seeing our gardens? They have been described as most vitalizing; we have the best gardeners tending them."

Everyone followed Lady Ashton through the manor toward the rear, where several large glass-paned doors opened out onto an expansive garden surrounded by a high vine-covered stone wall. A small stream flowed through the garden, entering and exiting through a low grated archway at the base of the wall on either side. Devlyn scanned the grounds, then blinked a few times when it seemed that some of the shrubs moved.

Your eyes are not deceiving you, conveyed Aliel, reassuring Devlyn.

"Why are your shrubs moving?" asked Devlyn, bringing notice to the activity that neither Ellendren nor Andrew had noticed, although Viren seemed relieved and Velaria smiled knowingly. Before either could respond, someone else spoke.

"Shrubbery doesn't move, you silly elf," said a familiar squeaky voice. "Settlings, on the other hand; you can't keep them still until they finally decide to settle!"

"Arbol?" Devlyn asked after a pause while he searched his memory for the name of the faun he had met in Perrien so long ago.

"It seems you elves are beginning to get your memory back," Arbol said wryly. "Come, I'll introduce you to some of the brave ones."

Devlyn glanced over at Velaria. "There are details that Lady Ashton, Viren, and I must discuss. Enjoy the gardens," she said kindly. Devlyn, Ellendren, and Andrew followed the faun into the garden, Devlyn introducing Arbol to the other two.

"How did you make acquaintance with a faun?" Ellendren's right eyebrow rose in question.

"Oh, it was after Alex and I fled Gneal with a Vyoletryn observant—Karl, I think." Devlyn leapt at the chance for a normal conversation with Ellendren again. "That was before meeting up with Velaria again and meeting my brother."

"I don't believe I've heard the whole story. You'll have to tell me all of it when we have a chance to rest again," said Ellendren.

Devlyn's heart leapt at the chance as a goofy smile replaced his melancholy.

The lush gardens brimmed with flowering but stationary bushes, scattered about among the curious and moving settlings. Elegant ash trees claimed much of the garden, but without the density of the forest beyond the estate's walls, letting sunlight spill into the area.

Something about the garden made Devlyn's body feel light, even rejuvenated. It reminded him of the Chamber of Light in the Temple of Ceur, and he was about to ask Arbol about the phenomenon when they approached a small creature covered with leaves, vines, and flowers. Between the greenery, and just below a particularly large but still closed flower bud, Devlyn saw an odd green face.

Devlyn drew nearer to the settling, who remained planted in place staring at him then sprinted away into a large manicured bush just when Devlyn was only a few paces away. Ellendren and Andrew broke out in laughter behind him. Despite their amusement, Devlyn's heart skipped a beat at hearing Ellendren laugh again. To him, it was beautiful; not even Aliel's song compared to hearing her laugh.

"I've heard of these before," Ellendren managed through her laughter. "They are incredibly skittish, and rarely allow anyone to draw near."

"They used to live in the lush meadows of kryseniels that surrounded Lake Saeryndol. They were very fond of your ancestors, especially since the Luminari managed to bring their own fauna from Luminare to this land below, which the settlings adored," explained Arbol. "Yet, when your people fell from their high places, there was no one to protect them. And mortals began to hunt them for their rejuvenating powers."

"That's terrible," interjected Ellendren.

"Well o'course, it is," said Arbol, acknowledging the interruption, then went on. "Since then, we fauns took it upon ourselves to search the lands for them. Unfortunately, the rulers of Yanil and Tiel still manage to snatch them. They farm them, leading the settlings to an unnaturally young death. That Tieli queen deserves a swift execution for the number of settlings she's murdered to make her elixirs over the centuries."

Reaching out to Aliel, Devlyn felt him soaring just above the trees, high enough to enjoy the beams of the sun uninterrupted, yet low enough that no one would notice him in the distance. *Do you think these settlings would remember a phoenix if they saw one?*

Aliel descended to the garden below, singing his marvelous tune as he flew just above the ash trees, transforming the garden into a near utopia when every plant began to flower. He flew through the entire garden, singing all the while, before finally coming to Devlyn's side.

Dozens of settlings followed the phoenix toward Devlyn, none taller than his knees, but all with various plants covering their bodies and the closed flower bud on the top of their heads. Several of the settlings grabbed their hands, pulling Devlyn, Ellendren, and Andrew further into the garden. They had a surprisingly strong grip for creatures so small, ushering their taller companions along a graveled path where soft pink and yellow flowers bloomed on every side.

As the settlings pulled them around a corner, Devlyn saw a large squat tree with blooms of various colors. It was certainly beautiful, but Devlyn thought it an odd tree compared to most. Unlike the more typical brownish color of most tree trunks, this trunk was green and wider than it was tall. Impelled to draw near the peculiar tree, Devlyn placed his palm on the bark and was startled that it was warm to the touch and oddly soft. Aghast, he quickly pulled his hand back and turned toward the others who had kept their distance.

"What's wrong?" asked Ellendren, noticing Devlyn's abrupt movement.

"It's warm!"

"What? Did you expect her to be cold?" Arbol's tone was almost scornful.

"What do you mean by *her*?" asked Andrew, turning on Arbol.

Arbol glanced at Andrew, shaking his head before replying. "*She*," he repeated, "was the first to find comfort among the Ashtons. She was among those who fled from Krysenthiel when the fighting began."

"She's a settling, isn't she? A mature one, that is." Ellendren drew close too, placing her hand on the warm green trunk. Several of the settlings made an odd sound, making Devlyn think Ellendren's comment had insulted them.

"I don't think they liked what you said about them," said Devlyn playfully as he lowered his hand to the smaller settlings. "It's all right, I don't think you're immature."

Rolling her eyes, Ellendren turned her back on Devlyn and began running her hand across the green trunk, as several more settlings pushed against Devlyn's legs.

"After they settle, they're more commonly known as miervae, but not until they're a few millennia old. This one won't be a true miervae for quite some time," Arbol explained.

"Careful, she can be quite ticklish," said Lady Ashton, appearing with Velaria and Viren. Her warning was too late—the large settling seemed to shiver, then made a noise curiously like a sneeze, immediately followed by a showering of petals and pollen.

Devlyn watched a whole flower fall to the ground near his feet. Without thinking, he picked up the yellow flower and was about to hand it to Ellendren when he realized what he was doing. Pausing as if frozen, he stumbled when someone shoved from behind, causing him to nearly collide with Ellendren in the process. From the corner of his eye, he caught a glimpse of a closed flower bud shuffling away. *Did a settling jut push me?* The vague irritation at being pushed faded before it fully formed when Ellendren turned, brushing petals from her clothing, and noticed Devlyn standing uneasily in front of her with the yellow flower. She blushed at seeing the flower, then took it from the awkwardly smiling Devlyn and tucked it behind her pointed ear, her own embarrassment easily noticeable despite her responding smile.

Neither said anything throughout the exchange. Devlyn wanted to, but his tongue was glued to the roof of his mouth and his lips refused to part. He hoped that the awkward interchange wouldn't strain their friendship again.

"Ah, to be young." said Arbol, reminding Devlyn that they were not alone. "I forgot to mention that settlings have this curious effect of stirring certain, shall we say, passions."

"That's quite enough, Arbol," admonished Lady Ashton. "If you will, please follow me. There's a gazebo nearby where we can speak in comfort," she said and then led the group away from the settling that had first made its home in the Ashton's garden.

As they walked along, Viren bent toward Arbol. To Devlyn, it looked as if Viren wanted to hug the faun. "I can't begin to say how grateful I am for what you and the other fauns have done. I feared that all the settlings had perished during the Ceurendol War."

"Not to worry," Arbol replied, his face bright with the acknowledgement. "We could not bear the loss of such creatures. But it would be kind of you to help your younger kindred to remember who the settlings are. Their forgetfulness is quite an inconvenience and there simply isn't any time for it." Viren patted Arbol on the shoulder and followed the others to the gazebo. Arbol waved farewell and went deeper into the garden, leaving them to their discussion.

"What did he mean by that?" Devlyn asked Viren, having overheard the exchange.

"Exactly what you think he means," Viren replied unhelpfully just as they arrived at the intricately carved gazebo of light wood. There, everyone took a seat around a table in the center.

"Velaria has told me that you wish to go to the Eldin Wood to continue your training. I wish I could give you encouraging news, but only those with Eldinari blood can enter their wooded domain," Lady Ashton explained.

"Are we to turn around and return to Ceurenyl after traveling this far?" asked Devlyn, frustrated by the news. How was he supposed to further his training if not in the Eldin Wood?

Velaria replied before Lady Ashton could. "Not necessarily. The Eldinari have remained secluded within their lands for over fourteen hundred years. While isolated, they would not have left the fate of their security only to an enchantment."

"What are you saying, Mother Velaria?" asked Ellendren.

"Devlyn must learn the ways of kien from a wielder who has fully reached his or her potential. I propose that we go to their borders, because I believe that they will not ignore us."

"But how do you anticipate getting to the Eldin Wood?" From the looks on the faces of the others at the table, Andrew was voicing everyone else's concern. "The borders of the Ashton Wood were surrounded by soldiers when we came into it. I doubt they will let us stroll out unmolested as we make our way for Dwota's Gap. And even if we do manage to outrun the soldiers, we'll have to travel through a desert to reach the Eldin Wood. That requires special provisions," said Andrew. Velaria glanced at Lady Ashton, who took up the reply.

"As it happens, there is no need to travel through Dwonia. House Ashton has long maintained a special relationship with the Eldinari; as a token of our friendship, a passage was crafted between our two forests long ago, a passage beneath the Vespien Mountains."

"That's fantastic," said Devlyn, yet even as he spoke, he felt an uneasiness pass through his bond from Aliel.

Aren't you pleased that there's a way to the Eldin Wood? Devlyn conveyed, his elation fading.

Sariel and Mundi are not the anadel watching over us. We are of Uriel, Lord of the Stars. Phaedryn do not belong hidden under mountains. When you and I bond completely, there will be no need to crawl beneath Teraeniel's crust, for we will soar on Lereniel's winds, where we belong.

Suddenly, traveling through the tunnel had a foul quality. Discouragement filled him with the reminder that he and Aliel were not yet a full Phaedryn. The conversation continued without Devlyn paying attention, lost in thoughts of dark tunnels and elves and phoenix and what felt right for bonded pairs. He was surprised when the others stood to leave the gazebo a short while later.

"Are you coming?" asked Ellendren, her voice soft and gentle. Rising to his feet, Devlyn followed the others toward the manor.

"Where're we going?" he whispered to Ellendren, hoping only she would hear. He smiled as he noticed the yellow flower still placed in her hair, secretly hoping it meant she did have special feelings toward him and not Trethien.

"Weren't you paying attention? We have to leave. Lady Ashton fears that if we remain here for even a single night, soldiers might arrive without warning. Her scouts have informed her that the soldiers believe us to be somewhere in the wood. She fears retaliation should they learn that House Ashton gave us shelter," replied Ellendren. "She can't keep the settlings safe if House Ashton starts to openly oppose the Crown of Mindale."

Devlyn wished that they did not have to leave Lady Ashton so quickly. Even though their time at the Ashton Manor had been brief, he somehow felt revitalized, as if his exhaustion from the past months of traveling had washed away. The only explanation was the supposed rejuvenating effect of the settlings, but that seemed impossible. Even as he thought it, a sense of amusement passed from Aliel through their bond, validating the possibility.

A butler waited at the manor's entrance for Devlyn and Ellendren. Their short conversation had caused them to fall far enough behind the group that when they entered the manor, there was no telling where the others had gone. The butler led them along a wood-paneled corridor, passing through the kitchens, and into a large storeroom where Lady Ashton was instructing an attendant to retrieve dried meats and fruit preserves. Velaria turned down more than half of the supplies that Lady Ashton had tried to give them, knowing it would be impossible to carry them all. Lady Ashton grudgingly sent back the unwanted supplies then escorted them to the entrance hall.

"Is this goodbye, then?"

Velaria nodded and embraced Lady Ashton. "The Emradiels still ask about you, Daphne."

"I might be an Emradiel but inviting even one of my sisters here would have dire consequences for the settlings. My gardens would endlessly overflow with ei'ana and sooner or later, Queen Alesei of Tiel would hear about a sequestered settling colony and march on the Ashton Wood—burning every tree that obstructed her path."

"Until next time?" Velaria smiled.

"Try to pull Lara away from Everin when you come next. I haven't seen her since our days at Gwilnor." Lady Ashton looked from Velaria to the others in the group, graciously accepting their thanks even as she still held one of Velaria's hands. "Well, you best be off," she said and let go. "There's no telling when Mindale's soldiers will arrive to ask prying questions. They still consider my husband and me, and everyone who lives in this forest, as traitors."

Velaria led them across the grassy area to a narrow path going northward. Devlyn appreciated that his connection to Aliel provided an incredible sense of direction, and he no longer had to look for the moss growing on trees to know where north was. Better still, the phoenix didn't have to fly high over Teraeniel either—Aliel just knew precisely where they were.

The path they now followed looked much the same as the one that had taken them to the manor house but was noticeably less traveled. The farther they went from Ashton Manor, the steeper the path became as it neared the foothills of the Vespien Mountains. The path disappeared entirely as they continued their ascent at the edge of the mountainside. Lady Ashton must have told Velaria the tunnel's exact location, for she continued to confidently lead the others, never hesitating.

Without warning, Velaria halted and looked to the mountainous slope to the west. Devlyn had a feeling that they were near the tunnel's entrance. Expecting that Velaria would draw closer to the mountain, he was surprised when she turned and walked away from the slope, instead making her way toward a sizable moss-covered tree, many of its large roots protruding above ground. Devlyn examined the tree with curiosity as Velaria circled it.

"This is it."

Devlyn couldn't see what made Velaria sure that this particular tree was it, and thought it was more likely a marker for the tunnel's location. But Velaria lightly touched the tree while speaking softly under her breath, and almost immediately, they saw the roots of the tree stir. Two particularly large ones spread apart from each other, and as they did, an opening appeared, starting at the ground but also seemingly splitting the bark of the tree, forming a portal of sorts. They stood looking at it, mouths agape. Seeing everyone's amazement, Velaria commented, "Well, you can't expect that elves would have the same sort of tunnels as the dwarves, can you?"

UNDER AND OVER

Water dripped from the ceiling of the tunnel and moss clung to the walls and much of the ground, which occasionally meant they had to walk carefully. The tunnel did not stand tall, especially when compared to those excavated by the dwarves but was rather the height of a normal corridor at Gwilnor, and easily lit by Aliel's luminous form. Also, unlike dwarven tunnels, this one noticeably curved and shifted in elevation, making it far more comfortable for Devlyn than the dwarven tunnels. Still, Aliel's concern rang true the longer they traveled through the mountain; elves were not meant to traverse underground—after all, the Skylands were once their domain. Aliel's reminder of Uriel and Lereniel echoed through Devlyn's mind.

Everyone commented on the tunnel's musty smell, and while no one liked being in one, Andrew seemed the most uncomfortable. Andrew was Sudernese and before beginning his studies at Gwilnor to become a Septyl knight, he had spent his entire life in the coastal city. No Sudernese would dare spend a single day inside a mountain breathing stale air—let alone several consecutive days. Viren displayed the least annoyance; he had spent the last fourteen hundred years secluded in the Guardians' Keep, somewhere up in the mountains surrounding Lake Saeryndol but outside the Shroud's confines. Still, the Guardian had lived above the mountain, not in it.

A sense of urgency and impatience overcame Devlyn. His mind nagged at their pace, insisting that he needed to progress faster. He grew weary of waiting to bond fully with Aliel, aware that if they had, they could have flown over the mountain rather than scurry beneath it. The more impatient he grew, the more he wanted to arrive at the exit of the tunnel. Growing irritable, Devlyn had to stop himself from insisting that the others move faster.

They slept in the tunnel five times during their passage, resting when they assumed it was night. Devlyn thought he had slept through the whole night each time, but never woke feeling fully refreshed. Fortunately, Eagan's temporal visits had ceased, but it still was not restful sleep. At least, everyone took full advantage of the tunnel's width and had spread out while they slept.

On the sixth day, they saw a faint shimmer of daylight in the distance. At first, the light grew more distinct and brighter as they walked toward it, and Devlyn hoped that they would not have to spend yet another night sleeping in the tunnel. All of them walked a little faster in anticipation of leaving the tunnel, but the light seemed to be fading the closer they drew, and Devlyn assumed that dusk had fallen.

By the time they reached the end of the tunnel, Aliel was providing the only light. Devlyn ran excitedly toward the tunnel's mouth, relieved to breathe fresh air again, air not thick with moisture and the smell of damp moss. But one step into the open air and his breath caught in his throat as his lungs tightened in complete fear. He stood at the very edge of a precipice, a gap the width of the tunnel they had come through forming a sheer drop and separating him from a solid canopy of trees at the same height. His heart pounded as he tried to determine how tall these trees grew since thick foliage hid the ground beneath.

Did you not notice the cliff? Aliel inquired, noticing Devlyn's quickened heartbeat.

No, I assumed it would open onto level ground. You could have warned me.

You can sense our surroundings just as well as I can.

Clearly not that well. Next time I'm unknowingly running toward the edge of a cliff, please tell me.

I intend for you to fly the next time you fall.

Devlyn ignored Aliel's provoking comment and peered over the precipice trying to get a sense of how high they were but could only see thirty feet down as branches and leaves obscured his view. Still alone at the tunnel opening with the sun setting far in the west, Devlyn thought it odd how slowly the others had followed. None of them wanted to remain in the cave any longer than necessary, and as he turned, Devlyn's initial panic at nearly plunging into the chasm escalated when he saw them all slumped on the ground, breathing heavily in a deep sleep. Appalled at the turn of events, Devlyn bonded with Aliel and pressed into the erendinth. His awareness heightened, yet he could not tell whether the wielder who had cast his friends into their unnatural sleep was near, or whether this was a more permanent enchantment.

It suddenly occurred to Devlyn that a plausible reason for the Eldinari withdrawal from the rest of Eklean had nothing to do with maintaining neutrality. Instead, these seclusive elves might have in fact allied themselves with Erynor long before the Ceurendol War began, allowing the Erynien Empire to succeed in their aggressive overtaking of Eklean. Devlyn's heart raced. *How else could they have survived unmolested?* Devlyn asked Aliel. The possibility of being in enemy territory while his support group was incapacitated left him terrified.

Aliel didn't respond, but Devlyn felt his disagreement, even as the phoenix soared up, then into the thick canopy to seek answers that Devlyn couldn't find from the cliff. Seeing through the phoenix's eyes amazed Devlyn. The forest reminded him of the Illumined Wood, with trees towering above their expected height.

As they soared further into the forest, they felt another's presence. Devlyn's alarm heightened. Scanning the trees, they saw an elf sprinting along thick branches and leaping through the trees toward the cliff, his jet black hair flowing behind as he leapt from tree limb to tree limb. His simple dark-brown tunic melded with the trees, and only the green and silver decorative threadwork stood out from the scenery.

The elf wasn't looking at Devlyn, but at the phoenix soaring through the canopy. He had to know that what he saw was an extraordinary thing. Even in their seclusion, the Eldinari had to know of the Ceurendol War's results, including the demise of the phoenix. Devlyn returned to his own body, disconnecting from Aliel, and the world dimmed as it always did but now, he looked at the elf through his own eyes. The elf appeared to be his own age, still young, no older than sixteen at most. Devlyn's skin itched. Did the elf intend him harm?

"Welcome, Child of Luminare. I am surprised that you do not slumber with your companions." The elf leapt from the nearest tree branch to the cliff, nimble as a cat. "Perhaps there is more to you than your connection with the phoenix."

"What did you do to them?" Devlyn demanded, standing defensively between the elf and his friends.

"Long ago, my kindred enchanted our borders so that anyone who is not of our blood would fall asleep before having the opportunity to cause us harm," the elf explained while inspecting the others who lay slumbering. "You travel with a Cyndinari; were you aware?" asked the elf in a tone that Devlyn didn't care for.

"Few could measure next to Velaria Treyven, Chair of Azurelle."

The elf acknowledged Devlyn's defense with a peculiar smile, then poked gently at Viren.

"I take it he was one of the last Guardians tasked with the protection of the phoenix egg. Interesting company for one so young as yourself to travel among."

"Young? You look no older than me," said Devlyn, slightly insulted.

"You and I are nowhere near the same age, Child of Luminare. I might remain a youth among my people, but I've seen two hundred eighty-three winters pass."

With those words, Devlyn recalled the girl he had met in the Illumined Wood and how she had spoken of elves still possessing immortal life. The realization struck home and his eyes lit up. "But how is it possible? I thought all the elves lost their immortality when the Jewel of Life was encased in the Shroud."

"Only those responsible for the crime against Life and those who placed their Life into Ceurendol were affected. The Children of Eldinare and Aldinare never did so; we did not place our Life into the jewel, nor did we commit the crime against it, as did the Children of Cyndinare. Hence, we were not bound to its fate." The elf spoke with sadness, then with a quick scan, added, "We must leave now. There are those who will be most eager to meet with you." He beckoned Devlyn to follow him. "My name is Wyn, Child of Eldinare of House Lierafen."

"I'm Devlyn."

Wyn didn't seem to appreciate the informal, and by most elven standards curt, introduction, yet extended his hand in greeting, nonetheless. Then crouching low, Wyn took a few swift steps and leapt from the cliff to the nearest branch, landing with perfect balance. Standing confidently on the branch, he looked back to Devlyn.

"What about my friends?" asked Devlyn.

"They'll be safe. There are other star wardens nearby who will tend to them."

Taking one last longing look at his friends, especially at Ellendren, Devlyn turned from them and focused his attention on the gap between the cliff and the large sinuous branch. He took a few steps back and, stomach in knots, took a running leap from the cliff's edge. Before he knew it, there was nothing beneath his feet except air for what felt like an eternity, then his feet landed next to Wyn, who grabbed him as he wobbled on the branch. He crouched low, grasping it with both hands.

"Don't be ridiculous. These limbs are wide enough to sprint across blindfolded," chided Wyn with a smirk as he moved off, jogging across the branches, deeper into the forest canopy.

You'll catch me if I fall, right? Devlyn asked Aliel and caught the phoenix's returning amusement. Devlyn stood slowly and followed Wyn through the canopy. Unsure of his every step at first, Devlyn yelled to Wyn to slow down so he could catch up to the Eldinari. The further they jogged across the branches, the more confident Devlyn grew and soon found himself moving faster with every stride.

They had been moving through the forest's canopy for several hours when weariness began to overtake Devlyn. Unfortunately, Wyn showed no sign of slowing, and another hour passed before Wyn finally came to a stop at a large tree.

"Where are we?" asked Devlyn, curious about why they had stopped here, but glad that they had, given how exhausted he felt. They had passed many large trees in their travels, so what was special about this one? Or, perhaps, Wyn too was finally getting tired?

"This is the dwelling of House Lierafen. I suppose you would know such places as cities where you're from," Wyn said, and placed one hand on the trunk of the large tree. Devlyn had grown quite accustomed to cities and, well, this was not a city. There were only trees with thick and tall trunks in the area, and bird songs and the ruffling of leaves and branches filled his ears. Clearly, this elf needed a lesson regarding the definition of a city.

As he looked about, Wyn chanted an odd tune, then Devlyn saw a knot in the tree begin to expand, soon forming an opening large enough for a person to walk through.

"Welcome to Lierthyl," said Wyn, gesturing for Devlyn to go through the opening, where Devlyn stepped onto a platform in the middle of a stairway that than spun upward and downward. Aliel slipped in behind him.

Once the three of them were inside the tree trunk, the opening sealed behind them. With the entryway closed, Devlyn was surprised to see that Aliel was not producing the only light. Hundreds of small green lights shimmered along the tree's interior, shining more brightly the higher they climbed.

"What are they?" Devlyn asked, awed by the phenomenon.

"Seeds of the stellendae trees," Wyn replied, without stopping, climbing the spiral stair two steps at a time.

"I thought the trees here were called stellendi." Devlyn grazed his hand across the smooth wood of the tree's interior, noting that Wyn used a different suffix for the tree's type.

"It's been a long time since an outsider has seen a stellendae tree up close. I'm surprised the name wasn't butchered more."

They came across another opening at the top of the stair, although Wyn didn't have to wield this one open. They walked through, Devlyn noticing that the wooden floor they now walked on was the same wood as the stairs, seamlessly changing its purpose to suit the need. The chamber they walked into was a hollowed-out part of the tree with smooth polished surfaces. Here, the stellendae seeds he'd seen along the stair formed intricate patterns throughout the entire room. Glowing glass sculptures filled alcoves along the room, and when he saw them, Devlyn thought of the Arenthylean Bells back in Ceurenyl. Drawing near one, a sculpture of a proud woman, Devlyn touched it, noticing that the translucent material felt more like stone than glass. "I thought it was odd to have glass bells," Devlyn said, not realizing that he spoke out loud.

"What do you mean?" asked Wyn, not understanding Devlyn's reference.

"Ceurenyl has a set of Arenthylean Bells in a tower. The bells toll through the night and they sound like glass chiming," explained Devlyn. "I was told they symbolize the Eldinari."

"Eldaryl is unique to Eldinare. Unlike the other elven folk, we never used the unique substance of our Skyland to form buildings. Instead, we reserved it for artistic purposes. We use the stellendae seeds similarly. While their greatest function is the growth of the stellendae trees, we also use them for art and adornment as well," said Wyn, leading Devlyn and Aliel to another opening. "I must take you to the Aryl of Lierafen. It is not lawful for anyone but the Eldinari to walk beneath these boughs. And how it is that you are not in a deep slumber is beyond me."

Devlyn followed Wyn through the opening and stepped onto a large flat branch, sheltered on all sides by interweaving vines, covered with not just stellendae seeds, but with luminous flowers of varied colors and aromas as well, some resembling the glasslike nature of the eldaryl.

A whimsical music that made Devlyn think of stars filled his ears as he followed Wyn along the passageway. It came from somewhere off in the distance, but its source and direction were unidentifiable. They passed several elves who also had hair like Wyn's, black and velvety. Devlyn heard them whisper among themselves, especially when they saw Aliel. The further they walked through Lierthyl, the more black-haired elves they came across.

The passageway that wound through the treetop city along the branches widened into a plaza of sorts with an intricately arcaded facade at its far end. Devlyn couldn't tell whether the facade was part of a tree or whether it stood separately in front of it. The facade's design reminded Devlyn of the architecture of Lucillia, but unlike in the Pilgrim City of the Luminari, this building rose with the height of the stellendae. They crossed the broad plaza and went through one of the archways of the facade, into yet another tree, this one much wider than the first one with the staircase and the room with the sculptures.

Devlyn followed Wyn across the room toward a staircase nestled in the smooth walls of the tree. The stair curved gently, following the tree's natural circumference and opened onto many landings, but Wyn continued to climb the stair until it ended in a large room with nothing but the branches and leaves above their heads. Intertwining branches and vines woven in a wondrous delicate pattern formed the floor. Several elves sat at leisure on couches toward the center of the room. Everyone turned toward the stair when Devlyn and Aliel entered the room.

"Ei'terel Dalenya and Ei'denai Fendryl," said Wyn, bowing. "I present Devlyn, and his phoenix. I fear our protective enchantment needs tending. As you can see, this Child of Luminare and his phoenix walk through our realm unhindered. They arrived with four others who could not pass through and who remain in slumber at the entrance of the tunnel to Ashton Wood."

One of the women rose from her seat and closed the distance between them. She looked warmly toward Wyn and then turned her gaze toward Devlyn, looking with great interest into his eyes. It felt as though she looked through them and into his very soul.

"Wyn, do you not recognize our great-great-grandson as your cousin?" said Dalenya, leaning forward slightly to run her hand through Devlyn's hair, teasing the strands of red, blond, and black intermingled with the light golden brown.

Devlyn's mind went blank.

"I am Dalenya, one of your ancestors. And this is Fendryl," she added, when the man who had been sitting next to her approached. "Tell me, child, do you know the reason for our granddaughter's deeply troubled state and her seclusion for over a decade? What has come to pass of her son, Dolan, your father?"

"I'm sorry? My father was born of the Telvin family," Devlyn managed, barely able to comprehend what the Eldinari woman was saying.

"Dearest child, Dolan, your father, was no human; he was born to our granddaughter, Leienya," said Fendryl. "Regrettably, his conception came through malice and hatred. His father is Cyndinari, and so our immortal life did not pass to our great-grandson. Shortly after his birth, the child was taken to a young noble family in Cor'lera, a family named Telvin. It was thought that if he lived among us, he would learn that he would age and die long before Eldinari children are even considered youths. It would have been a tortuous life for any mortal. The young Telvin couple promised to conceal his origin and raise him as their own," said Fendryl.

"I barely knew him," Devlyn confessed as he tried to remember his father's face from the few images he had seen of him. "He died when I was very young, murdered by a man he thought was his brother."

"That is saddening news. Leienya must have felt his passing," said Dalenya somberly. "It would greatly lighten her heart were she to learn that Dolan's son lives and is bound to a phoenix. But such glad tidings must wait until she returns from her seclusion."

"Your companions slumbering at the tunnel's mouth, do you trust them?" inquired Fendryl.

"With my life," said Devlyn as their faces came to his mind.

"Including the Cyndinari?"

"Unquestionably," replied Devlyn, trying to mask his annoyance.

"Very well. They shall be seen to. Tynelle, prepare a tea of stellendae flowers for our guests. Now, Devlyn, if you would, follow us," said Fendryl.

"Where are we going?"

"Did you and the phoenix not travel to the Eldin Wood so that you could further your training? We make for Stellantis. Wyn, I would ask you to accompany us," said Fendryl, and Wyn inclined his head in acknowledgement. Devlyn, still puzzling over how the elven lord had even known his intentions, was concerned for his companions left behind at the tunnel entrance.

"What about the others?" asked Devlyn.

"They will, of course, follow us when they are able. Their journey will be a longer one than our own," replied Fendryl, as he made his way toward an obscure archway. This doorway was different than the others Devlyn had seen so far in Lierthyl, all woven from the wood of the trees. This one was made from a semi-opaque stone that Devlyn had only seen once before, at Gwilnor. Even the form of this doorway replicated the odd pointed arches surrounding the school's main entrance in a semicircular plaza. The stone had a shimmery texture and a pale golden light seemed to hum from within, gently pulsing, barely noticeable. The stone made Devlyn think of lumols, the coins he had found at the Cor Inn.

"Do you not recognize lumaryl?" Fendryl asked, noting Devlyn's pause to examine the door.

Devlyn shook his head rather than respond. He had never heard that name before and had never inquired about the stone arches at Gwilnor. Who there might have known what it was?

"What sort of age do we live in when a Child of Luminare knows not of lumaryl?" said Dalenya in a melancholic tone. "Have the lucilliae also vanished from memory?"

Devlyn's stomach twisted, and he asked, "Are you talking about the city named after Lucillia?"

"No, child. While the city was named after Lucillia, she in turn, was named after the lucilliae, jewels created from the lumaryl, the very substance of the Skyland of Luminare; light taking on the form of a jewel—it's said that Kien was involved in their creation; he was quite inventive. No substance could compare to their radiance, nor did anyone imagine that anything could outshine them," Dalenya explained. "Until seven lucilliae were chosen to create Ceurendol, the Jewel of Life. Their brilliance was magnified by the pouring forth of the Life of the Luminari, aided by Verakryl, the Tree of Life."

Dalenya grew quiet after speaking of Ceurendol. The absence of it visibly caused her great pain. She did not resume speaking, but walked toward the archway of lumaryl, resting her palm against its post, then through it, the color of her body shifting slightly as she entered the room on the other side. Devlyn followed her to the lumaryl arch, and the closer he drew to the opening, the more he could see of the other room. It stood impossibly larger than this one, and rather than a leafy canopy forming the walls of that space, instead, wood lined the entire perimeter. *That's not possible*, Devlyn thought, stepping across the threshold. Aliel followed, then Fendryl and Wyn. Devlyn's body felt odd; he felt misplaced, yet he recognized the sensation.

"Welcome, Child of Luminare, to Stellantis," said Fendryl.

This isn't possible, Devlyn thought again. A moment before, he had been standing in a room at the highest reaches of a tree where the leafy canopy formed every wall. Now, a shocked Devlyn stood within a much larger tree trunk.

"Surely, the minums have taken you through a seguian before," Wyn said.

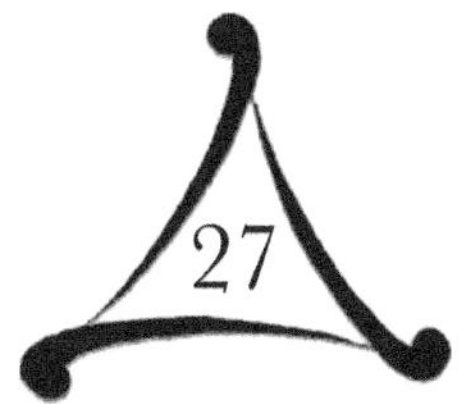

What Once Was

Devlyn still found it difficult to believe that he had walked through an ordinary doorway in Lierthyl, and directly into the heart of the Eldin Wood, leagues to the north. Only a few nights had passed since he had come to Stellantis, but he already had dozens of questions.

Fortunately, he did have the answer to one, after Wyn had explained how there could be a seguian without a minum, otherwise, he doubted he would have slept at all. It seemed that before the Exalted Aryl of Krysenthiel bestowed the minums with the Time Wardenship, seguians were readily produced by any wielder powerful enough. The Eldinari were thus able to keep their separate dwellings unified by tying the seguian wields in place, using lumaryl arches as anchors.

Devlyn waited in one of the interior rooms of the massive trees of Stellantis, trees so large that they dwarfed those of Lierthyl. While these did not reach the heights of the trees in the Illumined Wood, their girth shamed the eastern wood.

He sat on the floor of the bare room, pondering everything that had occurred over the past few days. Aliel rested in an elliptical opening in the wall, an opening that allowed a quiet breeze to flow through the hollowed-out room. He didn't know why Wyn had brought him here so early in the morning, just to sit and wait. He had thought that he would meet his new wielding instructor, but an entire hour must have passed since he had come into this small room.

Perhaps, there was something useful he could do while he waited? He tried to recall the last time that he had meditated. Thinking about recent events and how quickly they had all come to pass, he simply couldn't remember when he had last had a chance to quiet his mind and enter his heart.

Devlyn crossed his legs, closed his eyes, and became very aware of all his anxieties and passions. A plethora of distractions waited to pull him away from the solitude of his inner self. He felt a turning inside, as if his disposition reoriented itself, then the familiar sensation of his heart beating. He listened to its rhythmic pumps, focusing solely on it, allowing it to pull him further within himself. With his loosened grip on the exterior world, a steady peaceful aura filled his consciousness, leaving him unaware of time passing in the process.

"I wondered how long it would take for you to begin," came a voice Devlyn did not recognize. His eyes flashed opened to see a wizened elf with silky white hair falling over her shoulders standing before him. "I've been waiting over an hour. It's been a while, hasn't it? It doesn't come as naturally as it once did; that is, when it was part of your daily routine."

Puzzled, Devlyn wanted to ask her who she was, but the elf sat on the floor facing him, uncomfortably close, with her legs crossed, then grasped both his wrists and closed her eyes. With their knees inches from touching, Devlyn could smell and hear the older elf's breath. Devlyn reluctantly closed his eyes once more to listen to his heart beat and slip from the exterior to the interior life. A steady rhythm returned to his breathing when he focused on the quiet, but he simply could not enter within himself. The sound of the other elf breathing distracted him; she sat far too closely. Then, to top it off, he began to think about Ellendren.

Giving up on the meditation, he opened his eyes to look at the elf, and in frustration, asked, "I'm sorry, but who are you?"

A demanding question for one so young, came the elf's voice in Devlyn's mind. She did not open her eyes, nor did she move a single muscle. *I am old, very old. I am also an elf of Eldinare. For one so old, there are many aspects to my identity; you will learn some of them in time, but for now, you must be patient.*

"What's your name?"

Ah, a name says much of a person. Mine is Alethea Lenwyn; I was once Aryl of House Lenwyn. Now, close your eyes, quiet your mind, and let's enter that heart of yours.

Not at all eager to allow old Alethea within his heart, Devlyn closed his eyes. His mind remained uneasy, making it difficult to focus, yet Alethea did not push him to hurry. She waited quietly for him to reach his interior. It was impossible to say how much time passed, but to his surprise, he eventually found himself within the quiet of his heart once more. Just beyond that threshold, he felt another's presence. An ancient yet youthful spirit patiently observed from there, awaiting invitation within.

Much is forgotten, came Alethea's voice. It was not the same as when he and Aliel communicated. Theirs was a deeper, more innate form of communication. No words passed between each other; rather, it was that which came before words. Alethea, on the other hand, managed to transfer her own thoughts to Devlyn, just as Leilyn had done in the Illumined Wood.

I'm sorry? thought Devlyn, hoping that the ancient elf might hear him as he thought the words and ignored his ongoing discomfort with others hearing his thoughts, especially when it was someone sitting right in front of him.

That which once was common knowledge among the Luminari dwells hidden within your heart and you remember none of it.

Devlyn felt himself grow defensive. He had had nothing to do with his upbringing. How was he supposed to know of Luminari traditions if he hadn't even known he was an elf before meeting Velaria? How was he supposed to know everything that his ancestors once knew? In fact, he doubted that even Ellendren knew the full extent of their ancestors, despite her knowledge of many historical events.

The path of self-knowledge lies in our past, our future, and most importantly, our present. The past and future are often hidden from our sight, but not all those mysteries need to remain locked away.

Devlyn felt a hand touch his temple. His eyes remained closed, but he knew Alethea's fingers gently caressed his head. Even if there had been someone else in the room with them, somehow, he would recognize that it was the Eldinari's touch; it matched her spirit as it interacted with his own.

Opening his eyes, Devlyn saw gold flowers spanning an open field with mountains beyond and streams reflecting golden light trickling by. A city of domes and arched spires stood in the distance, a city made of a stone that glowed a wondrous golden hue, reminding him of his curious lumols. "Where are we?" Devlyn asked, using his voice as he gazed across the unfamiliar surroundings.

"This is the Skyland of Luminare, not the first dwelling of the Luminari, but the dwelling that distinguished them," said Alethea, also speaking aloud. The surroundings slowly faded and then Devlyn found himself standing inside the city he had just seen in the distance. Devlyn touched one of the stone walls as Alethea continued to speak. "Ah, lumaryl. Truly a wonder of Teraeniel. Every rock of this Skyland is lumaryl. Neither granite, nor marble will you find here. Not even the precious metals and gems of the lands below belong to this place."

Again, the location shifted. This time they stood atop a high mountain on the northern edge of the Skyland. To the north, Luminare's mountain streams cascaded into the clouds. He spun around to see the entirety of Luminare to the south. Lush golden forests dotted the landscape. Seven cities built of lumaryl lay strewn across the land, yet one stood out. Nearly double in size and with a brilliance that Devlyn could barely look at, it outshone the others. "Mar'anathyl, first and greatest of the cities of Luminare, center of art, philosophy, academics, wielding, political power, and much more. The Lorenthiens hailed from Mar'anathyl as did the Seven Founders of Septyl."

"I know that name." Devlyn tried to think back to where he had heard it.

"The notion of a king and queen were foreign concepts among our kindred when we dwelt in our Skylands, the Cyndinari being the only exception. Not even the aldarchs of Aldinare fashioned themselves as monarchs. Several families had risen in influence and came to govern the Skylands; they were named aryls. The Lorenthien aryls prospered in the city of their governance, Mar'anathyl. It once paled in comparison to the greater Luminari cities and it was much later in Luminare's history that Mar'anathyl flourished.

"When we elves left our Skylands and came to Eklean, we found the land scarred by an ancient war. The remnants of the once great kingdom of Thellion were divided and each new kingdom fought with the other, constantly tearing territory from their neighbor. Numerous states rose and fell before our only choice was to settle within the strife grasping Eklean. When the warring kingdoms saw that our civilizations thrived in peace, they pleaded with the Lorenthiens to accept a crown as high king. The Lorenthiens resisted at first, wary of wearing a crown as the High King of Eklean, but eventually accepted with the caveat that they maintain the Luminari custom that a monarch must never be unwed. No single elf would reign alone. Only an aryl could rule, and thus a high king and high queen would reign together as the Exalted Aryl," said Alethea. She paused, seeming to be thinking about what to say next.

Waiting for Alethea to continue, Devlyn took the opportunity to look across Luminare. He could see the entire Skyland in fine detail, down to the ornamentation on building facades.

He was about to pose a question when Alethea cleared her throat. "You are a Lorenthien. *You* are heir to the Crystal Throne, which has not been filled since Krysenthiel fell."

The mention frightened Devlyn. "How do you know that?" he asked, slowly stepping away from Alethea in an unsuccessful attempt to ignore the possibility of becoming a king. "What about Ellendren and her family? Roendryn was chosen to lead his people, not Feolyn."

"A much nobler lineage than Lucillia runs through your family. Do you not recognize your own memories within your heart?"

"What are you talking about? I know when I walk in the World-in-Between," said Devlyn, insistent on avoiding any talk of him being an heir to an empty throne.

Alethea chuckled, then abandoning talk of his ancestry, went on. "Clearly, you do not. To enter this place in Somnaeniel is not possible. Darkness has claimed those lands. These are your memories. Imprinted on your soul from parent to child since before your kindred left Luminare. These are part of you."

"How's that possible? I've never seen any of this before," said Devlyn, nervousness thick in his throat. He looked around again, his eyes falling on the largest of the cities to the south, the one he knew as Mar'anathyl. Not because of Alethea; she had not indicated which of the cities out there was Mar'anathyl. He somehow knew from within; his body and soul recognized it. It *was* Mar'anathyl. Calming his tempestuous thoughts with effort, Devlyn asked, "Why is it that the Luminari left this place? Surely no other place could rival it."

Alethea's grin faded at the mention of the elves leaving the Skylands. "The Skylands and their wonders are lost to us. There, the stone and ground were as the trees we know here below. We could sing to them and they would interact with us, crafting beautiful dwellings as do the stellendae trees. Elven wielding did not make Stellantis nor Lucillia. The trees themselves wrought such cities at our need. The trees above in that blessed land were more akin to us; they joined our song and danced fluidly about, not unlike the tree spirits in the Illumined Wood. They were fully awake and rarely remained in a single place; never did their roots grow deep. The trees native to Eklean sleep unless stirred by song, and the stones and dirt died long ago; not even our song can reach their deaf ears. The beasts face us with hostility; they are difficult to calm and easy to rouse. They see us as adversaries rather than stewards," lamented Alethea in a voice heavy with loss.

Since she had not answered his question, Devlyn was about to ask yet again. But Alethea continued, "In the Fourth Era, also known as the First Age among the humans of Eklean, a menacing storm gathered about the four Skylands. We thought the clouds would pass, but they only grew in intensity, for centuries. Our lives were not short, so we paid little heed to their lingering and intensifying. When we finally realized that the thunderous clouds threatened our homes and were slowly engulfing the air around the Skylands, elves went to investigate. From our Skylands, we watched in horror as the storm consumed our kin, ending their very existence. In all our wisdom and power, we knew nothing of these clouds, nor how to subvert them. We sought guidance from the enthiel, but neither Vespiel, Boriel, Meridiel, who betrayed Anaweh, nor even Auriel, knew how to circumvent the menacing clouds. They sought Uriel's guidance, first of the irythil.

"Uriel feared Ramiel's influence. Also known as the Evil One, Ramiel had been imprisoned long before the Great Blessing. We elves could not agree on what to do; some wanted to leave, others demanded we stay and fight. The Eldinari abandoned our Skyland first; as aryl, I was part of that decision. We feared our beloved Eldinare's fate, so we took with us as much as we could and settled in this very place. At the time, there were few trees in this forest, and only beasts lived here. We brought with us our trees and fauna, beasts great and small, fruits and plants, all native to the Skyland of Eldinare. We named this forest the Eldin Wood, in memory of our beloved Skyland.

"The Luminari were the next to leave their Skyland. It is said that Jaequlyn Lorenthien had a dream of a crystal tree inside a mountain resting at the center of an expansive lake. She told her dream to her husband, Aren Lorenthien, and the two presented the dream to Auriel, who entered Jaequlyn's heart to discover the dream's source. To Auriel's wonder, it came from Anaweh, the Creating Light, beseeching the Luminari to leave their Skyland and claim for themselves Mount Verinien, Lake Saeryndol, and the surrounding land, which became known as Krysenthiel, realm of the Luminari. With their divine initiative, the Luminari also gathered everything of their Skyland and settled on the land given them by Anaweh. From their own trees, they grew a forest and named it the Delmira Wood. And from the lumaryl, they created many cities, grander than anything these lands below have ever known or dreamed. Not even Mar'anathyl could compare to the city which became known as Arenthyl.

"Knowing that their Skylands were lost, the Luminari sent Phaedryn first to Cyndinare to coerce the Cyndinari to abandon their Skyland. To their horror, they discovered the Cyndinari studying the storm and trying to replicate the negative energy. The Luminari forbade such study and effort and deemed it dark magic. I personally doubt that the Cyndinari caused the destruction of the Skylands; however, they certainly were not ignorant about whatever the cause was or is. They eventually left their Skyland and settled in the Kinzdol Islands with the goblins and named their new city Broid, claiming the central island as their realm.

"Lastly, the Phaedryn went to Aldinare, which was completely consumed at this time by the menacing clouds. Aren and forty Phaedryn fought through the storm of black lightning before reaching the Skyland. The aldarchs and their sanctums were unreachable, and the Aldinari were in a panic. Anyone who tried to leave was pierced by the dark lightning from the sky. Whatever those black clouds were, they prevented the opening of seguians. The Phaedryn's diplomatic mission became a rescue mission. They saved as many as they could, redirecting the negating energy away from those trying to flee Aldinare. Each Phaedryn was able to escort four Aldinari on two of their alicorns. But, to do so, one of the Phaedryn had to remain on the Skyland to safely see his brethren and Aldinari to safety.

"Aren Lorenthien remained as he ushered the others to safety. All forty of the Phaedryn escaped, along with one hundred and sixty Aldinari and eighty alicorns. Of Aren, nothing is known of him since his sacrifice."

The mention of Aren stirred a sour feeling in the pit of Devlyn's stomach, a feeling that worsened when he realized that Alethea's tale meant that he was distantly related to him. "He's not dead, and he's nothing of what he once was," he said, thinking of the miervae murdered at Aren's hand. Without knowing how, he knew that Alethea saw his thoughts of Aren and what he had become.

"I see," said Alethea as Luminare faded and they returned to the uncomfortably small room, still sitting with their legs crossed, practically touching. "That is disheartening to hear. For one so great to fall so low is a major loss for us."

PATIENCE

Over a week had passed since Devlyn and Aliel came to Stellantis, yet his friends still had not arrived. Whenever he saw Wyn or the Aryl of Lierafen, he inquired about their whereabouts and why it was taking them so long to reach Stellantis. Fendryl finally explained that those not of Eldinari blood must never learn of the seguians connecting the dwellings of the Eldin Wood, lest someone unfriendly to the Eldinari abuse them, thereby jeopardizing the security of Stellantis and the other dwellings. Unfortunately, Fendryl did not explain how the others were traveling or why it was taking so long.

Devlyn had spent several hours each day with Alethea being, in her words, properly trained to wield. Shortly after his training began, it became evident that she was not particularly fond of how Gwilnor functioned and never had been. She often commented that a wielder required a single mentor to reach his or her potential and should not be passed around from one ei'ana to the next like a water skin in the desert.

Wyn often joined them for his own lessons in wielding, and today, he accompanied Devlyn to the edge of Stellantis where Alethea had asked to meet them. They took one of the many paths through the canopy, covered by thick foliage on every side.

Devlyn's mind swirled with questions about the Eldinari. He still found it difficult to accept that Wyn had been alive for nearly three centuries.

"Is everything all right?" asked Wyn. "You seem particularly puzzled; your face is all scrunched up." Devlyn hadn't noticed and instantly relaxed his face.

"So, I know you're considered young by Eldinari standards and Alethea is considered old. But, just how much of an age difference is there between you, really?"

Wyn seemed amused by the comment. "We're actually related, through my father who was born in House Lenwyn. There are many generations between them though. Alethea's children were born on Eldinare, before she and her husband became Aryl of Lenwyn. I'm considered a youth among my people, as I assume you are by yours. Where I haven't seen three hundred winters yet, Alethea has easily surpassed ten thousand winters. She hasn't been an aryl for at least five thousand of those winters."

"That's mind-boggling! I never even knew my grandparents. I can't imagine having a ten-thousand-year-old ancestor around."

"Well, she's your ancestor too and is considered one of the oldest of the Eldinari. Most pass to Lumaeniel near their eight thousandth winter."

"You mean they died? I thought the Eldinari were immortal," said Devlyn, confused about how those who called themselves immortal could die.

Not slowing his pace, Wyn replied, "Well, of course we're immortal, but being immortal does not mean living all our days on Teraeniel."

"So where do they go? Those who no longer live here," asked Devlyn, convinced that Wyn spoke in riddles.

"Simply put, they pass to Lumaeniel, the World-Beyond, the dwelling of Anaweh and the anadel," answered Wyn.

"But only those who die go there. Surely no one living can enter such a place, especially if they still have a body. A person with a body could not get there even if they wanted to," said Devlyn, his voice rising in argument.

"It is possible, although not many choose it before they are called. When one of my people leave this World-Below, while it is of their own choosing, it is not of their own timing. Anaweh, the Creating Light, calls them to that blessed realm and if they heed that call, their entire being enters Lumaeniel; body, soul, and spirit," said Wyn, his voice as calm as when they started speaking.

"But, that's death."

"If that's the word you choose to describe the great transition. But you are wrong in choosing such a word. Death is a painful, lonely absence of what should be. The great transition to Lumaeniel is neither painful nor lonely for those who are immortal. When we are called to leave Teraeniel, we do so with light hearts, and enter the all-consuming Light of that realm," continued Wyn waving to Alethea who waited for them in a park of sorts.

"Death has no hold over elves, nor should it for any anacordel. Death is an absence of life. There are those among us who lose their lives in despair and heinous acts, however that is not the sort of death that the mortal races speak of. They die so young and spend so brief a time with their loved ones that when they transition to Lumaeniel, it is a sad and lonely venture for those left behind as the corpse of their loved one turns to dust. Few understand the true nature of the death they speak of, but it is not what they believe," explained Alethea. Devlyn was surprised that she was aware of the conversation he and Wyn had been having. Was her hearing so good that she had been able to make out the discussion as they walked the pathway to the meeting?

Pausing to take in what Alethea and Wyn had said, Devlyn gathered his thoughts before speaking again. "If that's the case, if Anaweh does call certain elves at certain times, what prevents them from not leaving this world?" asked Devlyn, thinking he had finally asked the right question.

Wyn looked to Alethea. Clearly, he wanted to answer, but was deferring to his elder.

"Nothing," said Alethea. "If one with immortal life wishes to remain on Teraeniel, they may. Never underestimate free will. However, those who have chosen to do so have been known to live wretched lives. Some among the Cyndinari began to refuse the call before we left our Skylands. They said it originated in fear of the true reality of Lumaeniel. There is truth in saying that the corruption and eventual downfall of the Cyndinari began with a lie about the true nature of Lumaeniel and fear of that which was not."

"Where would such a lie originate?" asked Devlyn, thoroughly confused and deeply concerned.

"The guardian anadel of the Cyndinari, the enthiel named Meridiel, was believed to have turned from Anaweh to Ramiel, the Evil One. In his pride, he turned from Anaweh's will and set himself at odds with the Creating Light. Ramiel dwells in a prison of his making far beneath the crust of Teraeniel. It is believed that some of the Cyndinari, and Meridiel, located Ramiel and listened to his accursed tongue. For all we know, this occurred before the Skylands were lost to us. But what was only speculation in the past is now certain, made clear to us by the deeds of the Deurghol and shadow elves."

Surprised that their discussion of death had led to talk of the Deathless and shadow elves, Devlyn asked, "Those are the ones you spoke of, those who are truly dead, that is."

"Yes, they have forsaken Life," answered Alethea. "Now come, there is much we must accomplish before your friends arrive this evening."

Instantly, Devlyn's mood improved after all the talk about death. Ellendren and the others would finally reach Stellantis. It felt like an eternity since he had last seen them asleep in the tunnel. Not a single night had passed since then without him thinking of them before falling asleep; they had even appeared in his dreams on occasion.

"How are they getting here if not through the seguian?" he asked, following Wyn into a round room in one of the slenderer trees.

"Griffins," said Wyn, as though nothing was more obvious.

"Open your awareness to the erendinth," instructed Alethea, interrupting Devlyn's thoughts on griffins and what they had to do with his friends' arrival. He obediently closed his eyes and opened his awareness.

Alethea had Devlyn and Wyn spend the entire day sitting in silence while pressed into the erendinth, but also forbade them to wield. They were to simply remain within the erendinth, learn them, experience what the erendinth experienced, but refrain from wielding them. The urge to press more fully into them remained unceasingly present. To rest within the erendinth brought his restlessness to the surface, a restlessness that begged for action of any sort. The longer he sat, the more fervently he desired to wield.

The erendinth danced before him. Through his being, he felt them move through the world. There was nothing they did not interact with. Thinking about Velaria's instruction during one of his sessions in the hidden valley outside Ceurenyl, Devlyn joined his will with Aliel's. He didn't know if Alethea knew about their current connection, but she said nothing to prevent their binding. Whenever they bonded, Devlyn saw the world more fully, as if his own eyes couldn't see properly what they ought to. With his enhanced feeling, his desire to press into the different erendinth increased; they even seemed to invite it.

Devlyn's patience was reaching its limit when Alethea asked, "What have you learned?"

Startled by the suddenness of the question, Devlyn didn't know how to answer, but found himself saying. "That was torture; all I wanted was to wield the erendinth. I could barely pay attention."

"Both of you, press into aquaeys," instructed Alethea, without giving a reason. Eager to wield after the torture of just sitting with it, Devlyn pressed himself fully into the watery erendinth, just as Wyn did the same. Devlyn's sense of the moisture in the air heightened; he felt the branches and the foliage surrounding him thick with it.

"Pull the water from that leaf there," Alethea instructed. Curious, Devlyn felt the liquid held within the leaf and pulled it away. A growing droplet of water floated just beyond the leaf. The larger the globule grew, the drier the leaf became until it turned a shade of brown and Devlyn could feel no more liquid within it.

"What have you learned?"

"Leaves require water," answered Devlyn.

"Wrong," said Alethea then looked to Wyn, who shook his head. "Water holds life. If a wielder has ill intent toward you, he could do the same to you as you did to the leaf. The erendinth hold life within them: the light of lumenys, the spirit of animys, and the shadow of umbrys; the stone of terys, the air of aerys, the water of aquaeys, and even the fire of ignys. Just as they all hold life, they can also cause the destruction of life. The erendinth rest in a balance among themselves, each independent, yet also connected to the others."

"How can lumenys, or rather the deprivation of it, cause destruction?"

The old elf wore a slight smile; she knew something that Devlyn did not, increasing his desire to know more. "You will learn in time. Some things words cannot teach."

Dissatisfied with Alethea's explanation, Devlyn did not bother to ask further; he knew he wouldn't learn more today on that subject. Looking out the odd window formed from the tree itself, Devlyn noticed that the city was not as bright as when he had come into the room with Alethea. Every lesson he had with the ancient elf lasted longer than seemed possible. It felt as if time simply disappeared during their lessons.

Alethea noticed that Devlyn's mind had turned toward the time of day. "If I'm not mistaken, your friends will arrive soon."

Devlyn couldn't hide his excitement, nor did he intend to. He couldn't even be frustrated at having only recently learned of their imminent arrival, no longer caring that no one had said anything sooner. It did not matter; they would be here soon.

He wanted to rush from the small room to where they would meet, but it dawned on him as quickly as he desired it that he had no idea where they would come into the city in the trees. Stellantis was anything but a small area, and unlike most cities where one could watch something fly in from the sky, foliage completely enshrouded Stellantis.

"You will find them at House Lierafen," said Alethea before Devlyn darted from the small room with Wyn on his heels.

Anticipation rose with every footfall. They didn't run, but Devlyn walked much faster than he had on the way to today's lesson with Alethea. When they arrived at House Lierafen, Devlyn looked eagerly about.

"They'll arrive upstairs," said Wyn, and then led the way up the winding stairs. When they reached the third landing—not the top, Devlyn noticed—they walked toward one end of the room to the largest balcony Devlyn had ever seen. The Aryl of Lierafen, Dalenya and Fendryl, stood waiting to welcome their guests on the otherwise empty balcony. A small entourage stood nearby. Aliel hovered at Devlyn's side, sharing in his excitement. Just as Devlyn greeted Dalenya and Fendryl, he heard ruffling wings in the distance, then caught sight of seven griffins, each carrying a rider.

The large creatures landed one after the other on the balcony in a rush of wind and feathers, their orange and yellow talons making scratching sounds as they stepped carefully aside to allow the others to land. Looking past the three unknown Eldinari riders who had landed first, Devlyn also happily ignored the griffins' unusual appearance—eagle-like heads with black, grey, brown, and white feathers, with a transition to darker fur over the rest of their bodies—and took in his friends' expressions. They varied from Velaria's usual serenity, Ellendren's excitement, Viren's normal stoic calm, and Andrew's wide-eyed discomfort, all four of them quite wind-blown. Andrew clearly preferred mounts with four legs that stayed on the ground.

They slid off their griffins and began adjusting their clothing and hair, their disarray an indication of the griffins' speed. While they did so, the Eldinari riders led the exit of all seven griffins, making the balcony appear quite spacious once again.

"Welcome to Stellantis, friends from distant times," Dalenya said, moving forward to greet the newcomers. "I am Ei'terel Dalenya, and this is my husband, Ei'denai Fendryl. We are the Aryl of Lierafen."

"Thank you, Aryl," said Viren, placing his left hand over his heart and moving his right leg in front of the left in an elegant bow as he spoke. Andrew did the same, mimicking the knight carefully, while Velaria and Ellendren performed a slight curtsy. Devlyn smiled at Ellendren, but beyond a quick flashing smile in return, her gaze remained on her hosts. Had their reconciliation vanished during their separation?

"Thank you for your gracious hospitality," said Velaria.

"It's Mother, is it not; Chair of Azurelle?" inquired Fendryl.

"That is my title," Velaria replied with a small smile.

"Welcome to the Eldin Wood, Mother Velaria," Fendryl said, then held a hand out to the man standing next to him. "This is Father Phendien, Chair of Emradiel," said Fendryl. While both Devlyn and Ellendren could not disguise their shock, the news didn't seem to startle Velaria who graciously extended her hand in greeting.

"I hope the necessary deceit concerning my absence is forgivable by the other Chairs. The entirety of the Eldinari had instructions to withdraw. I cannot begin to recount the great desire that I and the other ei'ana here have had to return, especially when we learned of Septyl's demise and again when we discovered that the Ei'ana beyond our woods only held kiara wielders. Perhaps if I had never left, the Balance would still be in place," said Phendien.

"Or, you might have perished with the other kien wielders. May I be the first to welcome your return, Father," said Velaria. "I must ask, is Tiera aware that she is not the Chair of Emradiel?"

"A secret that they have carefully guarded since my untimely withdrawal. Only the one who sits in my place is aware."

"I see. We will have much to discuss during this visit," said Velaria. "The Ei'ana of Septyl have many secrets, but yours is undoubtedly the best guarded; I confess that I am somewhat shocked that it has been maintained for such a long time. May I introduce Ellendren of the Royal House Roendryn, crowned princess of Lucillia. She's a student wielder at Gwilnor Academy and has chosen the Vyoletryn School." Ellendren curtsied as Velaria provided her name, title, and station. "And this is Sir Andrew of Sudern, a knight of Septyl." Andrew did not attempt to repeat the intricate bow that he'd copied from Viren moments before, but simply bent from the waist this time.

"You are all very welcome to Stellantis," repeated Dalenya, smiling. "Especially you, Sir Viren Dekenurel. Many winters have passed since a Guardian knight last graced our home."

How do they know him? Devlyn thought, noting the lack of introduction.

"High Queen Ithendryl's will to safeguard Aliel's egg is the only reason I still breathe while my brother and sister knights have perished."

"Your sacrifice and theirs will not be for nothing," said Dalenya. "Now come, dinner will be served shortly. Until then, you'll all be shown to your accommodations."

Several elves appeared from the stairway, as though Dalenya's concluding remarks had summoned them to escort the newcomers to their quarters. Before a younger elf led Ellendren away, Devlyn rushed up to her and grinned encouragingly. "It's good to see you've made it here. I've missed you."

"Thank you, Devlyn. Honestly, I feel disoriented after that unexpected slumber—I have no recollection of any time passing. We were told that we only slept for a few hours, but the unnaturalness of that sleep has left me unsettled, to say nothing of our travel here. Velaria was very concerned that you were not with us."

An attendant waiting to show Ellendren to her quarters coughed politely.

"I'll see you later, Devlyn." Ellendren followed the elf into an arched doorway further into the tree.

They spent the remainder of the day at leisure. The newcomers were exhausted following their journey and took the opportunity to rest, except for Velaria. She wasted no time in asking Dalenya and Fendryl to introduce her to the other aryls in Stellantis and arrange meetings with them. Devlyn doubted that the leadership would have changed much since the last time the Eldinari had interacted with people beyond their realm.

Devlyn desperately wanted to spend time with Ellendren. Ever since she had returned from the Illumined Wood, they had rarely gone a few days without seeing each other. It felt odd that over a week had passed since they were last together. It just added to the unsettled feelings he'd had now that Alex was hundreds of leagues from him yet again.

With the others resting and Velaria meeting the Eldinari aryls, Devlyn and Wyn walked through the city with Aliel flying just above in the passages created by the branches and leaves. Devlyn was grateful that lessons were finished for the day because he doubted that he could pay attention to his own breathing for another moment.

"So, what's the status between you and the princess?" asked Wyn with a knowing smirk.

"Sorry?" replied Devlyn.

"Don't play coy," said Wyn. "You couldn't take your eyes away from her. She knows you like her, right? Is it reciprocal?"

"I don't know, it's complicated." Devlyn felt his cheeks redden. "I'm still with the ei'ceuril. In other words, entering into such a relationship isn't possible."

"It always amazes me how people who pass at such a younger age manage to find love in so short a time," said Wyn.

"We're not in love. I've only known her for a little over two years," said Devlyn. "And besides, we *can't* be, well, you know."

"Your cheeks say otherwise, cousin," chided Wyn. "But, that's not what I wanted to comment on. I'm two hundred eighty-three years old, and my heart belongs to no one but myself. And not for lack of searching, take my word."

"I'd imagine it would be difficult to fall in love when you're living alone in the woods guarding your borders."

"We're not always on our own," said Wyn looking down at the great branch they walked across. "Besides, Alethea has hinted that it's time I move on from my post as a star warden and devote more of myself as an ei'ana."

"I didn't know you were an ei'ana," said Devlyn.

"Many of the Eldinari are. Wielding is part of our culture; not everyone becomes an ei'ana, but a good enough number do. It's good that we've had a Chair among us, or else no one would have become an ei'ana after our withdrawal. Granted, we weren't given much of a choice when it came to choosing which School to join; the whole lot of us, except those who were ei'ana before our withdrawal, are Emradiels."

DARK WINGS

Holding his wife's hand in his own, Ferinn looked into Karina's blue eyes as they looked back into his. She was tired, as always these past months, spending most of her days in meetings with her lords and generals concerning the armies camped outside the city. And when she wasn't in meetings, she wrote letters to the armies sieging her city. She wrote directly to those leading the siege from the field, and she wrote to their monarchs safely ensconced in their own capitals of Trest and Josque.

Ferinn thought sending peace messages to Josque was a waste of her time. Everyone knew that Queen Alesei belonged to the Erynien Empire. She had submitted her allegiance to Erynor as a pet monarch once he had regained his power. While she had never made a public proclamation, everyone knew it, had known from the beginning. Rumors of endearment between Alesei and Erynor had also spread.

Such thoughts made Ferinn sick. *All they know is hate*, he thought as he looked into Karina's eyes. He did hope that she would have better luck with King Gordon. At least a history of friendship existed between Sorenthil and Torsil. Ferinn had once admired the Torsillian king. He had appeared to be a respectable man, prideful like most kings, but he seemed to balance that pride reasonably well. Not with humility of course; kings rarely knew that humility was a virtue worthy of praise. Yet his cowardice in joining Erynor and betraying long standing alliances had revealed his true nature, and that warranted neither respect nor honor.

Pushing his dark thoughts aside, Ferinn asked, "Have you prepared your address? Sorenth refugees have come from every corner of the kingdom. I have heard whispers on the streets of their love for you."

"That is kind of you to say," Karina said, her voice conveying the depth of her fatigue more than her eyes had indicated. "Despite the doubt clouding my mind, I have managed to prepare something. Their trust in me is admirable, but I wonder if it's appropriate. Sorenthil has had her fair share of wars, but never have the Myrish remained hidden behind our walls. It's confirmed that Daerinth has abandoned us. It appalls me that a Sorenth province now belongs to the Erynien Empire. How long before they raise their swords against their brothers and sisters?

"Ferinn, I do not know how this war will end. Erynor gathers more strength by the day; his shadow elves openly wander about in public and, still, people support him. Whether from admiration or fear I cannot say, but the more who turn to him, the fewer who remain to resist his tyranny as our allies. With every message of peace, I receive threats in return. My love, I am afraid." Karina confided with the fatigue in her eyes changing to something else entirely.

"Do not let your mind be troubled, my love. Take what strength and courage you need from your people, your daughter, and your husband. We all love you and are here to support you," comforted Ferinn, massaging her hand in his own. "Perhaps, you should rest until it is time for your address."

Ferinn knew that his words did not soothe his wife, but he also knew that she appreciated them. She was right, they were in desperate need of allies. Their most obvious option was Evellion, but they had their own battles, trapped within their mountain cities with enemies banging at every gate. Even the Lucillians were of no use. Whether it was from cowardice or not, they had activated the Protection of the Wood, and none could enter or leave. Ferinn wondered just how long they intended to bide their time. And if the dwarves did not help the Evellions, neither would they come to the aid of the Sorenth.

Their options diminished with every kingdom that chose to close itself and its people off from the war. *Perhaps, I could travel to my own people and beseech them for aid*, Ferinn thought, not for the first time. It would require a Meridean Conclave to bring the merpeople into the war; a meeting of all the heads of families to overthrow their previous decision to remove themselves from the wars of the land dwellers. The merpeople had enough troubles beneath the waves.

They didn't have enough time. Even if Ferinn decided to implore the merpeople to involve themselves, that would mean leaving Karina.

Preparations went on for Karina's address to the Sorenth gathered in front of her palace. The gates to the palace grounds stood open and people flooded into the square, which, despite its name, was more of an ellipse than a square. The Myrish Guard lined the palace square to prevent anyone from trespassing past the designated gathering space and onto the rest of the palace grounds.

Karina's advisors objected to her very public and exposed address-es, but she insisted that they were a necessity. Ferinn stood behind and slightly to Karina's left side. As usual, he wore one of his many blue robes, but now he also wore a crown of sorts. It was not the crown of a Sorenth king, though, for Ferinn asked only for Karina's love, not her crown. When Ferinn had married Karina, he had become the royal consort. His background had never been made public, since few believed that merpeople still existed and even fewer knew that he was one, but everyone did know that he was not Sorenth.

Queen Karina sat in a large chair meant to replicate her throne, waiting for the crowd to settle in the square and the volume to quiet. Ferinn knew that the crown that rested on her head was heavy, despite its deceptive appearance of lightness. Only the wearer knew its true weight.

Karina's daughter, Princess Myranda, sat on her mother's right side. Her safe arrival had brought incredible relief to his wife. The princess shared both her parents' determination, and her expression showed it— Myranda looked ready to bring the fight to Myrium's besiegers. Behind the three, nobles, attendants, and ei'ana filled the rest of the balcony and the room beyond it.

Trumpets blared that it was time for the address. They blew a few long bursts then transitioned to the Sorenth anthem. Sunlight gleamed off the trumpets, blinding Ferinn momentarily. The crowd accompanied the trumpets in song, mighty and beautiful, the tune flowing smoothly, yet powerfully, much like the River Meyien, which rushed on either side of the island city of Myrium. As the anthem came to its end, Karina stood and walked to the edge of the balcony.

"Sorenth," she began in a commanding voice, "I remember fondly when our city gates stood open and our bridges flowed with travelers and merchants to and from this Jewel of the River. I would see those days returned…" Her voice quivered, bereft of its previous strength; she no longer looked to her people gathered below, but above, her face no longer showing the confident zeal she always presented to her people. Ferinn searched the sky, seeking the cause.

"Guards" Ferinn yelled, pulling Karina back from her exposed position at the balcony railing. His entire being shriveled in horror at the sight of the creature above, its wings darker than the deepest depths of the ocean, surrounded by a shadowy cloud. The arrows unleashed by the queen's archers flew toward their mark, turning to ash as they passed through the shadow, useless against the creature. A second volley of arrows flew into the sky with the same effect.

Ferinn looked to the princess. He knew she had become a powerful wielder and he saw that the ei'ana now stood beside her, but only Myranda waved her arms rhythmically. Ferinn could not see what she did, but the princess seemed strained.

Then an ear-piercing scream filled the air when Karina was lifted from the balcony. Ferinn raced to grab her legs amidst the confusion as arrows flew into the air, no longer in unison but as fast as individually possible, each archer trying to save their queen. Even the people gathered in the square tossed their belongings toward the sky in vain attempts to strike the creature above. Ferinn managed to grasp one of Karina's feet, shocked when it burned hotter than a flaming coal, agonizing pain searing through his hands. He desperately held on, knowing that she had to be experiencing far worse, as they rose high above the balcony. Tears rolled down his face as he screamed her name.

The pain in his hands and arms increased, followed by a force throwing him down onto the balcony with a crack. A horrified servant rushed to his side, shrieking at the sight of the ruined flesh of his hands and forearms. Ferinn did not care; his eyes remained glued on Karina as she screamed above.

Karina's screeches intensified, louder than the wails from every direction of the plaza. Shouted orders to soldiers still trying to rescue their queen were useless. Ferinn guessed that the ei'ana were fighting against the creature in ways that no one could see. He tried to get up to try to reach Karina again, but his legs had broken when he had fallen, and all he could manage was to reach out for her as her screams continued. No one could do anything for their queen.

Then the creature aloft grew even darker. His arms waved menacingly, and Darkness shot from them, dark bolts of lightning that was not lighting, directly at Karina's chest, piercing through her. Ferinn felt his ears begin to bleed from Karina's endless agonized shrieks.

The sinister wield disappeared suddenly and Queen Karina Lariviere fell to the balcony, her midsection landing on the balustrade, her legs on one side, and her limp torso on the other, facing her people. Her crown fell from her head and clanged onto the square below then clattered as it rolled away amidst the stupefied and silent crowd, too horrified to draw breath. In extreme pain, Ferinn watched the shadowy creature fly south into the distance.

Devlyn woke from a brief nap, drenched in sweat, his throat parched and raw as if he had been screaming.

"He's coming out of it," he heard someone say, a voice he didn't recognize. Wyn, Velaria, and another elf stood at his bedside. Aliel perched on his other side, brushing his warm feathered head against Devlyn's face. Once Devlyn noticed the warm caress, Aliel's presence flooded into his own, overwhelmed with concern.

"Devlyn. Devlyn!" Velaria was unable to disguise her worry. "Devlyn, speak to us. Say something, anything."

Shaking with fright, cold from drying sweat, Devlyn tried opening his eyes, but the light seemed to pierce them, so he clenched them tight. "The queen…" he stuttered as he tried to speak, "is d-dead. Aren m-murdered Queen Karina."

"It's all right. Karina is safe in Myrium, surrounded by knights and ei'ana. She's safe," said Velaria soothingly. She sounded confident, but what Devlyn had said frightened her.

"No, she's not," he cried out, struggling to sit up in his bed, tears flowing. "I saw it. Aren, he…he killed her in front of her own people. Tortured her before he exploded tenebrys through her."

Rubbing his back to calm him down, Velaria said, "You never met or saw the Sorenth queen. How is it that you had a nightmare about her?"

"He's a Dreamer," Wyn said calmly, but there was concern in his voice as well. "Aren't you?"

Devlyn hugged himself and nodded; there was nothing else to say. The atrocious act of violence he had seen tormented his mind and heart.

Velaria looked to Wyn, her expression demanding an explanation.

"Dreamers are able to enter Somnaeniel. The gift has long since diminished among us, but we still know of it. The aldarchs first mastered the Dream, shortly followed by the druids of Kweil Aitch, capable of entering and leaving at will. Devlyn has just experienced a vision of reality. Whether it happened as he saw it, I cannot say. It is possible that the event has already occurred; it is also possible that it will occur soon. I don't know, but judging by his state, I think he saw it as it occurred. Events in the future are not so definite to cause such a reaction."

"Devlyn, how long have you known that you are a Dreamer?" asked Velaria. "When we first met, Alexander mentioned your dreams. Did you know then?"

"Not then." Devlyn shifted under the blanket, drenched by his sweat.

"I just thought they were odd dreams that sometimes came to pass. Then Abbie Wintyr hinted that my dreams were something more and when I resumed my studies at Gwilnor, she took me into Somnaeniel."

"Abbie's not a wielder; how did she manage that?" asked Velaria.

"She's from Kweil Aitch, isn't she? She's a druid," Wyn replied. Devlyn nodded. "Entering Somnaeniel doesn't require the erendinth, just as those who pass from this world do not wield to enter Lumaeniel."

"Has Abbie been instructing you as a Dreamer?" asked Velaria.

"Yes, and her brother, Eagan, as well," Devlyn replied.

Devlyn felt Aliel soothe his mind as he listened to people talk around him. Several others had come into his room, but he barely noticed them. He felt someone place a hand on his leg, the touch stirring an emotion which only intensified when he realized that the hand belonged to Ellendren. Her smile comforted him—dispelling some of his anxiety. Had she been in the room the whole time? Had she heard the details of his dream, heard what had happened in Myrium?

The rest of the day was a blur, while various people came and went. All of them probed. Different elves asked him specific questions about his vision, while others asked about Somnaeniel in general. Throughout it all, Velaria never left his side. He knew she was concerned for him, but all he wanted was rest; rest, not sleep. He feared slipping back into Somnaeniel if he slept. All he had done before was lie down to rest his eyes and have a brief nap.

The probing didn't stop at questions. Ei'ana and ei'ceuril—it seemed that there were many of each among the Eldinari—pressed into his being. They wielded in ways beyond his own training. At any other time, their strength and prowess in the erendinth would have impressed him, but today, he did not care. When the time for the evening meal approached, everyone except Aliel, Velaria, and Ellendren finally left. Someone brought dishes of fruits and grains to the room, and Devlyn realized just how hungry he was. The food Ellendren set out before him disappeared in moments, leaving him to watch Ellendren and Velaria eat their own meals at a much slower pace.

He sat at the table, eyes downcast, quietly thinking. Ellendren made a couple of attempts at small talk and then just stopped talking, letting a restful silence take root. Velaria kept a careful watch on him, even as she immersed herself in the erendinth. She did not wield, just maintained a vigilance. The likelihood of harm reaching them in Stellantis was inconceivable, but she remained watchful from within the erendinth, nevertheless.

Without looking up from his empty plate, Devlyn said, "We have to go to Myrium."

"Why do you say this?" Velaria gazed steadily at him.

"They're going to attack, both armies at once. The city won't stand a chance if we're not there," said Devlyn, a steady determination in his tone.

"How do you know this? Another vision?" inquired Ellendren.

"No, and it wasn't part of the earlier one. All I know is that their queen is dead, they're mourning, and they're immersed in confusion as to next steps. What better time to attack?" asked Devlyn, his voice gathering strength and surety with every word. He rose, and turned to walk from the room, but Velaria stopped him with a gentle hand on his arm.

"Do not be rash, Devlyn. Think this through. Our added strength cannot overcome two armies supported by shadow elves. There's also a significant risk of confronting Aren," she said, but Devlyn gently removed Velaria's hand and left the room.

He needed time to think. He couldn't remain in his room any longer with others making sure he was well. He wanted to be alone.

Aliel of course followed him, but that was normal. Their connection meant that the entirety of Eklean could lie between them and their minds still would not be separated.

Devlyn followed a path on the far side of the treetop quarters assigned to him, knowing that although it was nowhere near the central tree, if he kept walking in this direction through the canopy, he would reach the center.

Just ahead, an elf of incredible beauty walked at a slow pace. She was taller than most and had the ebony hair of the Eldinari, but her gown was truly remarkable. To Devlyn, it looked like a master seamstress had spun starlight into the fabric. Just as Devlyn came abreast, she spoke. "Listen." The elf paused and looked up through the trees. Until then, he had not heard anything, but now, a subtle chanting reached his ears. It was beautiful, sad yet wondrous at once.

"My children lament the human queen of Sorenthil. To be torn from Teraeniel in such a manner is sorrowful indeed. Her memory will live among her people as she transitions to Lumaeniel."

"I have to help them. The same will happen to everyone in Myrium if I don't go there and help." Devlyn turned to look at the elf and noticed that she had silver eyes—he had never seen eyes so bright. It looked as if an inner light tried to escape through them.

"Perhaps. Perhaps not. Even one who can see cannot say what will be. But those with such vision must not be careless and lose sight of prudence," replied the elf. "To receive it, you must recognize it within yourself."

"How is not helping those doomed to death and enslavement not prudent?" Devlyn spoke more harshly than he'd intended.

"Such prudence was asked of the Eldinari, long ago. My children could not see past the present, but the one who asked could. He asked them to wait, to remain uninvolved, until the time came when my children's aid would be of greatest assistance. Their enduring restraint is reaching its conclusion."

"I can't not help," Devlyn replied weakly even as he wondered what the elf referred to.

"I agree. But prudence does not entail doing nothing. You shall act, but you must do so prudently. Haste will bring only failure," she said as she slid her hand into a fold of her dress. Withdrawing her hand, she opened it to reveal an indigo-colored jewel of amazing brilliance, a jewel that reminded Devlyn of another. "This was given to my children long ago that we might act rightly during those dark days. Reclaim this gift from your people. May the gift it brings reach those from whence it came."

Devlyn accepted the jewel from the elf's extended hand, and felt a surge through his being, filling his mind with thought and care. The prudence of his ancestors coursed through the lucilliae into him. Looking up from the jewel's depths to thank the elf, he found that she had vanished.

Do you know who she is? Devlyn asked Aliel.

Yes. Her children will tell you her name.

Prudent Counsel

Sitting on the floor in the center tree's hollowed-out chamber, Devlyn gazed at the slender translucent tree, the verathel, at its core. It looked very much like the one he and Aliel had called forth from the ground in the Illumined Wood. This one was not a twig though, nor did it stand particularly tall. The verathel's girth paled in comparison to most of the stellendae tree's branches. This sprout of the Tree of Life stood at what Devlyn considered an average tree's height.

After having called forth a verathel himself, there was no mistaking what stood before him, even in its mature state. He recognized its aura; it felt unlike anything he had ever encountered. The tree's semi-opaqueness made it impossible to see completely through. Its trunk obscured his view of the other side of the room. Transparent flowers and fruits dangled from its branches among leaves of the same crystalline hue. The tree gave off its own subtle light and it hummed faintly, as if a heart thumped within, the sound rising from the base and ending in the leaves, fruits, and flowers.

Clutching the jewel of prudence, Devlyn allowed its power and influence to wash over him as he gazed into its depths, clarifying his mind. It possessed an odd quality that he had not recognized in the jewel of faith he had received in Lucillia. With this one, he felt an external presence from the jewel wash through him, noticing that it interacted with something already inside of him. The result of the interaction lay still inside him, stirred by the jewels influence.

Someone came into the central chamber. Devlyn couldn't tell who it was, but he heard the newcomer's feet pad softly on the bare wood.

"So, this is where you've been hiding," said Wyn teasingly, with an uncertain note about whether he'd be welcomed.

"Sitting, not hiding," Devlyn insisted. Wyn squatted next to him on the floor.

"I see." Then Wyn caught sight of the lucilliae Devlyn still held, having foolishly forgotten to conceal it. "How did you get a hold of that?" Wyn's voice rose accusingly.

Just as he regretted not concealing the lucilliae, Devlyn also didn't feel like explaining. "It was given to me," he said simply, hoping not to have to go into further detail.

"By whom?"

"I don't know her name. She didn't tell me. But she was beautiful; her eyes looked like stars and she was the tallest elf I've ever met. She kept talking about her children." Devlyn tried to remember the elf's other features, now curiously forgotten.

Wyn raised an eyebrow at Devlyn's description. "That's not possible."

Confused by Wyn's determined reaction, Devlyn asked, "How is it not possible?"

"You describe the North Star, holder of the North Wind, Boriel, the enthiel who guides the Eldinari," said Wyn in disbelief.

"She looked like an elf to me, just a tall one." Devlyn found it difficult to believe that he had spoken with an anadel, let alone one that was an enthiel.

"Of her own choosing! Rarely does she reveal herself," Wyn exclaimed before changing the subject. "We'll have to talk about this later. Your presence is requested at a conference. Velaria agrees that aid must be sent to the Sorenth. The aryls are discussing the matter as we speak."

Devlyn's mood lifted at the possibility of helping Myrium. Without hesitating, he followed Wyn to where the others waited, taking care to place the lucilliae into his coin purse with the other one, and felt Aliel's approval of his caution.

They went up the stairs through the central tree to a level that felt closed off from the rest of the spaces, and nowhere near as open as the verathel chamber below. This area had a honeycomb feeling as they went from one room to another, eventually coming to a round chamber.

Velaria, Ellendren, Viren, and Andrew sat at a wooden table that seemed to be an extension of the tree itself. Fendryl, Dalenya, Alethea, and six other elves he had not yet met also sat at the table. Fendryl welcomed Devlyn, and the other Eldinari stood to incline their heads slightly as a greeting.

"Devlyn, let me introduce you to Ei'denai Vanoreh and Ei'terel Eli-alen, Aryl of Illia; Ei'terel Nyrah and Ei'denai Eohire, Aryl of Shendielle; Ei'denai Indryn and Ei'terel Diera, Aryl of Allandis." Fendryl gestured first to the aryl standing next to him, then around the table to the rest of the group as he mentioned their names.

"Pleased to meet you." Devlyn smiled at the gathered aryls.

Wyn had taken on the responsibility of teaching him their culture. Since politics and culture always fascinated her, Ellendren had made sure to find herself included in these lessons. They had learned that there were four major Houses and eight minor Houses, Alethea belonging to one of the minor Houses.

"We have been informed, Lord Phaedryn, that you wish to leave our dwelling after your brief visit. Is there anything we might do to encourage an extended stay among us?" asked Elialen.

Inclining his head out of respect, Devlyn replied, "If I could continue to enjoy your hospitality, I would, but Eklean burns under Erynor's grasp and I wish, no, I *need*, to help." An image of Queen Karina flashed in his mind—silently screaming in agony. Surprising himself with the strength of his reply, Devlyn wondered whether Aliel, resting nearby, had provided some extra confidence.

"Your training with Alethea has only just begun," said Nyrah. "Surely, you have not yet benefited from all her wisdom."

Before Devlyn could reply, Alethea cleared her throat to speak. "Far from it, Nyrah. However, the bond to the phoenix is something our people have never fully comprehended. While he most certainly requires more training as a wielder, he is not defenseless when he and the phoenix are bound. Instinct drives them both."

"Is it your intent to leave the Eldin Wood with the Phaedryn and his companions?" asked Diera.

"No disrespect to the ei'ana," began Alethea, turning toward Velaria and Ellendren as she spoke, "but much has been forgotten since the massacre at Septyl and the breaking of the Balance."

Fire brimmed in Ellendren's eyes at the slight to the ei'ana outside the Eldin Wood. Devlyn looked to see whether the same inferno stirred in Velaria, but she maintained a neutral expression, not even a twitch of her facial muscles indicating a reaction.

"Also," continued Alethea, "I do not intend on being the only Eldinari to go beyond our borders. To start, Wyn will accompany me." At the look of shock on Wyn's face, it was quite clear that Alethea had not mentioned her intentions to him before informing the others.

"Do you intend to borrow griffins to reach Myrium?" asked Indryn.

"Only to the edge the Eldin Wood, if that's acceptable, of course," Velaria replied, her more usual small smile replacing the earlier neutrality. "Before I became an ei'ana, one of the free blue dragons living in hiding among the easternmost peaks of the Laudien Mountains, deep in the Illumined Wood, befriended me. Her name is Yelaris and I have already reached out to her. She and her kin fly from the Illumined Wood at this very moment, to a location of your choosing."

Several stunned voices arose at once at the mention of the dragons, some astonished, others promoting caution, but all loudly providing comment. The aryls argued among themselves about the wisdom of using dragons. Then, a quiet tune began to resonate in the room, one that Devlyn immediately recognized. Slowly the others took note of the melody and as the arguing lessened, the lovely sounds grew louder.

Devlyn felt Aliel press himself into the minds of those in the room. *The blue dragons are allies. Many of their flight died when Erynor gained power and they tried to prevent other dragon flights from supporting the Erynien Emperor against their will. They have remained alive, far from Erynor's influence, for nearly fifteen hundred years. They have chosen to reveal themselves now, risking extinction to rise against their former masters.*

No one spoke, stunned to silence. Direct communication from a phoenix had not occurred since Erynor's vicious dragon had consumed them all during the fall of Krysenthiel. Devlyn had grown familiar and comfortable with Aliel's form of communication, and the whimsical character within the phoenix's consciousness, something wholly other than the music he was accustomed to, but he could understand the others' amazement.

Alethea was the first to break the silence, looking carefully at each of the aryls in turn. "I ask you, does the Blue Dragon Flight remind you of anyone? A civilization cut off from their world to rejoin once again in its greatest hour," she said calmly and calculatingly.

Again, no one spoke. It seemed that they weighed her words, the words of an elder.

"I know what you seek, and it cannot be granted. We must remain in our forest. That is the direction from the lucilliae and that must be our status," said Eohire.

Ellendren wasted no time in responding. "You would leave us and all Eklean to battle Erynor and his forces alone? His might will overwhelm the free people of Eklean and the Luminari will be enslaved once again. Giants make their way across the Purged Desert of Dwonia as we speak. Myrium has been under siege for over a year now, while Everin is pushing two years. Out of fear, once-neutral kingdoms have sided with the Erynien Empire. Minums are being captured and enslaved. Who can say how long they will last before breaking under Erynor's ruthless torture?" cried Ellendren.

"Princess, your own people urged us to remain out of the conflict. Auriel advised Boriel to stay the hand of her children even as heinous crimes were committed against the Luminari. We wanted to fight, but were gifted with prudence to not do so," said Nyrah.

"That was fifteen hundred years ago," said Ellendren, not as fierce as before but more bewildered than anything.

Fendryl had said little throughout the proceedings, but once the discussion turned to the involvement of the Eldinari in the war, he said, "A thousand years might seem like an eternity to the mortal races, yet we in this room remember the counsel given us by High King Faerndryn and High Queen Ithendryl Lorenthien, the last Exalted Aryl to sit on the Crystal Throne of Krysenthiel. To help us maintain our decision to withdraw, they gave us one of their prized lucilliae, the jewel of prudence, to safeguard, knowing that their demise drew near. I cannot say if it is at last the hour when we Eldinari pick up our arms to join our brethren, but such an important and complex decision will not be made at this meeting."

Ellendren's anger was not appeased. She stood, excused herself from the meeting, and walked out. Devlyn wanted to follow, but Andrew caught his eye, gave him a slight headshake, and rose to follow Ellendren out of the room.

Eohire did not look pleased about Fendryl's words but did not argue. He maintained his scowl, letting his expression tell the others where he stood on the matter. The room grew quiet once more, no one commenting on Ellendren's departure.

Just as Devlyn began to wonder what would come next, he caught a burgeoning light out of the corner of his eye. Aliel had not moved from his other side, so he turned to see the source of the expanding light and recognized the elf who had given him the lucilliae. No, not an elf, but an anadel, one of the enthiel.

Boriel.

Her brilliant light surpassed even Aliel's beautiful glow, but she still managed to walk around the circumference of the room without anyone else noting her presence. Devlyn wondered whether any of them could even see her. Then she spoke.

"My children, do not hold grudges against one another." Her voice seemed to be the key to the others being able to see her, and several gasped in shock and awe. "You must unite yourselves to face a common foe. Alliances will be wrought, and others will crumble as anacordel choose their own fate. Too long have the races been divided. The Luminari fashioned Ceurendol so that equality might exist among all. The elves would no longer stand privileged among the mortal races. But Erynor would see such a gift wiped from the memories of all anacordel. He would direct the elves to crush the mortal races. He would have Deurghol and shadow elves kill any elf that resists what he considers to be their proper, subservient station."

None of the Eldinari spoke, but all raised their hands to their hearts simultaneously, eyes closed in reverence.

"The lucilliae no longer belongs to its caretakers. It has been returned to its rightful owners. Ei'ethil Devlyn Lorenthien, if you would, please retrieve the lucilliae from your pouch for my children to look on once more before it leaves Stellantis."

Devlyn reached into his bag for the jewel. He brushed against both lucilliae but was careful to take only the indigo one, then held it out on his open palm for the others to see. They looked at the lucilliae with the same wonder and respect as Devlyn had felt earlier that day. Its indigo light washed across the round room, dimming slightly in the light cast by Aliel and Boriel.

"Recall that it was said that you shall withhold your might for a time, until it was needed once again." Boriel smiled at Devlyn, then vanished taking her light with her.

In unison, the Eldinari aryls chanted, "Boriel, guide us in the Light of Anaweh."

While everyone looked to the lucilliae, Viren could not remove his eyes from Devlyn. Even Velaria's mouth hung agape at the name remembered only in legends.

Dalenya stood. "No more need be discussed today. Return to your households and spread word of Boriel's appearance."

The chamber emptied, leaving only Devlyn and Viren who approached Devlyn, bowed, then fell to his left knee, his head lowered. Then he extended his semi-opaque sword, held crosswise with one hand on the hilt and the other at the tip, and said, "Ei'ethil Devlyn of House Lorenthien, my sword I give to you; I vow that not a day shall pass that it will not guard and protect, serve, and uplift, ever ensure justice. I, Sir Viren Dekenurel, pledge my life to you and the Crystal Throne of Krysenthiel as a knight—a Guardian knight."

Unsure as to what the proper response might be, Devlyn took a guess, placed his hands on the knight's shoulders and asked him to rise. It felt odd to receive an oath from a knight, and certainly had never been part of his training, since he was supposed to be an orphan from an inn-keeping family. He suspected that Ellendren had probably spent her entire life practicing for events like this. She would know the right words.

With Viren standing ever more vigilant—if such a thing was possible—Devlyn followed Fendryl and Dalenya through Stellantis. They traveled northeast toward the Lierafen household, where they would notify the minor Houses bound to them of Boriel's surprising appearance and what her words meant to the Eldinari.

They found the entrance of the Lierafen household crowded with elves, expecting news of some sort. Speaking quietly, Devlyn asked Viren, "How did they know to come, that Dalenya and Fendryl had news for them?"

How do you think they managed it? came Viren's voice, startling Devlyn. He had grown accustomed to Alethea speaking to his mind, but even that was unnerving most of the time, let alone it now coming from someone unexpected. *The Eldinari are not incorrect in saying that much has been forgotten.*

Unsettled by what felt like an invasion, but also thinking it was a rather useful ability, Devlyn asked, "Will you be able to teach me that?"

The Guardian knight chuckled softly. "I am no teacher of such arts. You will have to rely on Alethea to help with that and depend on my knowledge with the sword instead."

Devlyn was lost in thoughts about the difference between the telepathic communication and how he and Aliel communicated when Dalenya's raised voice brought him back to his surroundings. She spoke to the gathered elves, representatives of the minor Houses, as well as her own household. She did not mention the lucilliae, but she did tell them of Boriel's appearance while in council.

The announcement did not take long and those not of House Lierafen soon went back to their other pursuits, although there was a lot of chatter between them all. Devlyn saw Wyn sitting against the wall formed by the house's tree and made his way over to him. Head against the wall, he slid down the side of it until he too sat with his back against it.

"Everything all right?" asked Devlyn.

"I'm fine," said Wyn. "It's just, I've never left the Eldin Wood. Few of us born after our borders were closed have, and those who have were gone only briefly. It's not that I'm afraid of what will happen out there, but rather, that everything will change once we leave. Eldinari will die in battle—we *are* affected by mortal wounds—and our immortal life will be tainted as we watch our brethren pass untimely from Teraeniel to Lumaeniel. This is one of the last sanctuaries where violent death has not come to pass."

Devlyn didn't know what to say. He was intimately connected with the death of others, having first experienced it as a toddler, even though he couldn't remember any of it outside of his dreams. But that his father, Dolan, had been murdered by Lex, the man he'd known as his brother remained present to Devlyn and weighed heavily on his heart. Thankfully, since encountering his Eldinari relatives in the Eldin Wood, Devlyn had learned that Lex was no relative of his. That revelation also meant that he was not Alex's cousin, but he was Wyn's. That would be difficult to adjust to, especially since he was close to Alex. And while Devlyn knew that his father was dead, his mother's whereabouts—or even if she still lived—remained a mystery.

Still trying to think of what to say, Devlyn was relieved when Fendryl came before them. "Grim thoughts, indeed. Come, sit with me, and we'll talk of this." Fendryl turned and walked to a small chamber off the larger room. Devlyn and Wyn stood to follow and found Fendryl already sitting in one of the chairs, leaving the couch available for them.

"The enemy wants death to be feared," Fendryl began. "The word is of Ramiel's choosing and has been translated into every language of this world. Before the spread of that word throughout every land, we knew it as the Calling, when Anaweh would call us to Lumaeniel to live in splendid Light. But through Ramiel's influence, and simultaneously, although few know it, also Meridiel's, the enthiel designated to guide the Cyndinari, the significance of the Calling took on a grim nature. His most abominable achievement is that he stirred a fear of the Calling, using another name—death.

"With that fear, the Cyndinari began to refuse the Calling, choosing to remain 'living.' However, what they feared most, they wrought, eventually becoming shadow elves, who feed off others to extend their lives. But they are nothing compared to the ones who wrought the shroud. Those known as the Deathless, the Deurghol. But, in truth, it is not those who pass from this world to the next who die. It is the shadow elves and the Deurghol who are truly dead. Life has no place in their corrupted hearts."

Both Devlyn and Wyn listened attentively. Devlyn had never heard such a thing before; to him, death was a negative thing. But his understanding of death was not actually death at all, but something the elves experienced as a Calling. Some sort of divine invitation. It was difficult to wrap his mind around the concept and Devlyn found himself asking, "If death, understood as the Calling, is not an evil, then why did my ancestors create the Jewel of Life?"

A proud smile filled Fendryl's face. "Such a question was asked by nearly every elf who did not come from Luminare. The act still baffles many Eldinari, and my explanation will pale in comparison once you discover it for yourself," said Fendryl, pausing for a moment to consider how to best define the desire of the Luminari to create Ceurendol. "The way it was described to me by one of your Lorenthien ancestors was that, since elves are immortal, we have the freedom to accept or deny the Calling to Lumaeniel. None of the other races could share in that freedom; their bodies would decay, no longer capable of supporting life, meaning the person would leave this world whether they wanted to or not. Your ancestors wanted the freedom of choice to be available to the other races. They did not believe it belonged only to elves."

Devlyn was not completely satisfied with the explanation, just as Fendryl had said he would not be, yet he was grateful all the same.

"One more thing," said Devlyn before Fendryl could go. "Will the Eldinari travel to Myrium and defend the city?"

"No," replied Fendryl, his smile fading. "We cannot travel such a distance with enemies so near. We will wait until the giants make their destination clear before we decide our path. Once we leave our forest, our enchantment will fade, as it depends on our presence here. But, Everin will be our priority. There are tunnels there that expose not only us, but every dwarven schtam connected by the Great Dwarven Tunnel. If Everin falls to the hands of the Erynien Empire, the damage wrought would be insurmountable. However, I can send a hundred of my House's star wardens to Myrium's defense. Please excuse me now, as I must join Dalenya."

His spirits lifted by the thought of help going to both Everin and Myrium, Devlyn thanked Fendryl. He then sat for a few minutes with Aliel and Wyn in the small chamber, doubting his decision to go to Myrium since it meant that he still would not be able to help Everin. Queen Lara had been an incredible host during his short visit and not helping her and her kingdom in their time of need troubled Devlyn. That Fendryl and the Eldinari would also help Everin was comforting.

GROWING AWARENESS

In his small hollowed-out room in one of the trees of Stellantis, Devlyn sat on the floor, eyes closed and legs crossed. His back was straight and both his mind and heart felt clear. Through Aliel's lighted vision, he saw the Eldin Wood in a wondrous array. The entire forest pulsed with its own heartbeat, a subtle green light highlighting the beauty of the canopies of the monstrous stellendae trees stretching for the sky as Aliel wove around the massive trunks, larger than most houses. The trees glowed through Aliel's vision, a glow that reminded Devlyn of the stellendae seeds and their starlit resonance. He couldn't see the glow of the trees through his own eyesight; this enhanced vision only came through Aliel.

A knock on the door brought him back to his own vision to see Alethea entering his room. "Forgive my intrusion, but there is a lesson I have in mind before we leave." Alethea paused, and then added, "Your eyes are glowing, by the way. It won't be long until they change completely."

Perked by the mention of the change in his eyes, Devlyn asked, "Do you know how much longer? It seems that I've been waiting an eternity to become a full Phaedryn."

"Impatient, again," said Alethea, chuckling. "Neither I nor any Eldinari have ever seen or shared in the gift of becoming a Phaedryn. While some blood of the Eldinari flows in your veins, you are without a doubt a Child of Luminare. That being the case, our knowledge is limited to what was common knowledge to us. I dare say, your own understanding has already surpassed what we know of the Phaedryn. Now come with me, we're going to the forest floor for our next lesson."

Disappointed that his question remained unanswered, Devlyn followed the older elf out of the room and through the large stellendae tree. Devlyn wished that his impatience didn't show. It wasn't something that he displayed often, at least, he thought he didn't, and he hoped that only Alethea had noticed. Few matched her intuition.

As they descended, they came to a winding stair that spun in a continuous downward swirl, and which seemed to go on for what felt like a lifetime. The steps had a roughhewn quality that Devlyn doubted had anything to do with someone carving the steps. Like everything in the Eldin Wood, someone had to sing them from the stellendae trees. All Stellantis had come about in this way, the trees bending to the needs of the Eldinari. They cherished their trees; none would use knives or axes, or any tools on them. He often wondered how the elves felt about the other races felling the mighty forests of Eklean for construction materials.

We do not approve, said Alethea.

"Then why is nothing done?" Devlyn asked before registering that he had not spoken his thoughts on felling trees aloud and neither had Alethea when she responded. "Wait, how did you do that? And isn't there some rule about not reading another's mind?"

"What most do not understand, is that their thoughts are often expressed physically by their bodies without their intention. Our entire being communicates. Also, when the mind is very active, especially in a young one, it often shouts so that others cannot help but hear. For those who remember how to communicate telepathically, there are no such rules, for we do not see it any differently from speaking through our mouths. Our minds are always receptive to others. It's not considered an intrusion of privacy, but neither do we consider seeing another's body without clothing an intrusion of privacy. The naked body reveals a person as they are, and the mind does so to an even greater extent, but the two can never be separated, they are one," explained Alethea causing Devlyn to blush at the thought of others seeing his naked flesh.

"That's an awful habit you've developed; I also sense it in other elves who have forgotten themselves and allowed humans to influence them. I sense shame in your fear of exposure, both physically and even more so emotionally, deeming it indecency. Why is this?"

Still blushing, Devlyn searched for an answer. "I guess it has something to do with not wanting others to see us as we are, as if by seeing us completely, they will reject us," answered Devlyn, surprised that he had found the words. He also felt Aliel's amusement, since they were still connected even while the phoenix continued to stretch his wings through the forest above.

"How times have changed. I do hope the Luminari discard that habit once they regain their Life. Such belittling sentiments have no place among the elves, let alone any anacordel. When we left our Skylands, we were to influence those below, not succumb to their failings."

They at last reached the bottom step where Alethea pressed her hand on the wood before her and sang softly. The wood slowly parted, the tree creaking and groaning, wood scraping against wood. It was only when Devlyn was out on the forest floor that he realized the tree roots had moved. As soon as he and Alethea stood far enough away from the tree, the sinuous roots returned to their original positions, concealing the winding stair.

The forest floor shared few similarities with the canopy city of Stellantis. While foliage blossomed in every direction above, the forest floor had a sparse quality below. The stellendae trees stood far from one another and could easily contain a small village between each. Their massive roots covered much of the ground, forming sinuous patterns, many taller than himself. Looking skyward, Devlyn searched for signs of the city he knew was above his head. There were no signs of the walkways and certainly no signs that the trees were home to a large city.

"Stellantis' design does not alter the stellendae trees, making it all but invisible to anyone below," said Alethea, readily responding to Devlyn's still-exposed thoughts. "It is possible to conceal your thoughts from others. But such effort is taxing. The worst deceivers create false thoughts to replace their true ones, making everyone believe that their intentions are pure. Erynor and many other Cyndinari did so. I doubt the shadow elves bother with it today, but Erynor enjoys deception far too much to not."

"Are you going to teach me how to know others' thoughts?" asked

Devlyn.

"You have forgotten too much. It has nothing to do with entering another's mind, and it is quite different from what you and Aliel experience. It can be best related to an awareness of others. And not to offend you, but you are numb to such sensitivity, as I would assume are the majority of the Luminari these days. The more sensitive you are to your surroundings, the more will your awareness grow; do not forget, sensitivity is a muscle worth developing, not a weakness to be ignored," said Alethea.

Her words seemed ridiculous to Devlyn. Women were the sensitive ones, not men. Men usually mocked other men for their sensitivity, for acting like girls.

"The mystery keeps unraveling," said Alethea, making Devlyn feel uncomfortable and ashamed for even thinking that. "I will tell you only once: abandon such thoughts of what either gender is intended to be, they do not belong to you. An individual is their own person and all of who they are is a unique gift. Now, close your eyes and open your awareness to your surroundings."

Alethea's words stung. Obediently, he sat on the ground and crossed his legs. To him, beginning with a posture and position that was best for quiet and calm was an effective way to start. He was instantly aware of Aliel soaring through the forest a league to the southeast. Tempted to connect more fully with Aliel and experience the phoenix's awareness, he refrained, recognizing that it would not strengthen his own sensitivity. The very word made his skin crawl. His biased thought replayed through his mind and every word now pierced him. Is that what he really thought? At the abbey school in Cor'lera, he had often been mocked by his peers, mostly human, for his already heightened sensitivity. Ever since, he had made a conscious effort to suppress his emotions. Or at least, to conceal them from others—to protect himself. The thought of allowing himself to embrace his emotions to become more sensitive irked him.

"If you had embraced your emotions earlier and cared less for misguided prejudice, perhaps I would not have to instruct you in today's lesson," Alethea gently admonished.

Pushing thoughts of his childhood aside, Devlyn considered the ground beneath him. It felt soft, yet tough at the same time. He knew that the roots of a stellendae tree surrounded him, but his interior awareness didn't tell him that. Rather it was a memory of the last thing he'd glimpsed before closing his eyes.

Do not block your emotions. If you ignore your interior, you will not experience what it experiences, Alethea guided.

Great, Devlyn thought to himself, aware that Alethea would know that thought as well as all his conflicting emotions. With that thought came an emotion akin to unwillingness. He simply didn't want to delve into his emotions. How could a link between them and the world make any difference? He delved into his heart. It felt like diving into a thick pool of sludge, like an awful invisible grime encased it; it was burdensome to navigate through after he had let it build up by not giving it attention.

His feelings for Ellendren lay closest to the surface. He tried to hide the affection from Alethea, especially how he had felt when they had kissed. But Alethea had more to say.

Trying to hide such a thing would be criminal. Besides, even those without eyes can see the connection between you two.

Devlyn felt blood rush to his face in a fiery blush. But he allowed the emotions surrounding his feelings for Ellendren to wash over him. It felt as though something fluttered in his stomach and his heart felt light. Forgetting that Alethea was aware of his emotions, he wanted to remain within this particular pleasant and warm feeling that made everything seem right in the world.

But then, the thought of the world brought forth a series of unrelated and unpleasant feelings involving Teraeniel's actual state. Fear, anxiety, and despair clenched his heart. The emotions were his, not from an outside force, and though he didn't want to admit that this was what he felt, most of all to Alethea, he somehow found the courage to delve into them. Navigating through them proved difficult. These emotions contained nothing pleasant or warm. Devlyn longed to return to his sentiment for Ellendren. Instead, as he pushed through these dark feelings, he felt them weigh his spirit down.

He tried to ignore the increasing depression they caused, hoping that if he pretended that they did not exist, they would not affect him. *They only grow stronger with ignorance*, Devlyn heard Alethea say. Uncertain about how to confront them, he turned on them and looked directly at them. They were ugly and voracious in their ability to cause despair. Devlyn remembered the first time he had looked into the jewel of faith. The beautiful violet lucilliae held the belief and vigor of the ancient Luminari, all dead now. He remembered how it had affected his heart, and how it still somehow touched him, even though he had not gazed on it in quite some time, afraid that an enemy might see him holding it and discover that he possessed it.

The light within his heart produced from the small virtue held in that lucilliae smoothly diminished the fear, the anxiety, and even the despair. They simply disappeared. It was odd that just thinking of the faith of the Luminari could dispel the emotions that tormented his mind.

"You've learned a valuable lesson today," said Alethea quietly. "Never ignore negative emotions, for if you do, they will only grow and fester. Before you know it, they will overpower you. Pretending that they do not exist is only a lie to yourself. Your emotions do not define you, but they are part of you, and must be processed."

"Why did the fear diminish at the thought of the jewel of faith?"

"Never underestimate that smallest virtue, for truly it holds within it the largest," said Alethea, piquing Devlyn's curiosity. "Those troublesome emotions will return. But the reason they could not remain in you is that they did not belong; they are not proper to your being, nor to any of us. And I speak not only of the elves, but of every anacordel. Emotions are irrational; they tell you much about yourself, of your current state of being and much more. But there is much they cannot tell us on their own. To discover whether such emotions belong, you must process them and discern their true meaning. And not just the bad ones, the good ones too."

"I thought you were going to teach me how to increase my awareness of my surroundings without seeing them."

"Did you not? Close your eyes if you need to."

With his eyes again closed, Devlyn opened his awareness. It was a peculiar sensation, akin to when he wielded or bonded with Aliel, although nowhere near as vivid, but he felt his surroundings as though through a haze. Sitting on the ground, he felt his senses reaching out, and he pushed his reach beyond what he had seen with his eyes, beyond the edge of the forest, and knew that he could stretch it out to the ocean if he chose to. In his immediate vicinity, he could feel the large tree he and Alethea had come out of, its large roots intertwining through the dirt below. He delved into the root structure which burrowed deep under the dirt into Teraeniel, supporting the immense tree even as its roots intertwined with the roots of the neighboring trees. Experiencing the stellendae tree in a whole new manner, he now felt the life force within it, a consciousness he had not expected. Surprised, he withdrew from it, his heart racing.

"It's alive!"

"Of course, she's alive. All trees are alive," said Alethea.

"Well yes, but I felt her consciousness—like a person's."

A slight smile crossed Alethea's face. "The Eldinari are not the only ones who escaped the ruin of the Skyland of Eldinare. We could not abandon the stellendae trees to their doom, so our exodus included bringing the stellendae trees to this place below. They have become a forest."

"You transported whole trees?" Devlyn imagined trees soaring through the air like birds.

"I think we are done with today's lessons," said Alethea, standing. "Time passes swiftly when broadening our awareness."

Thinking that they had only spent a short time together on the floor of the Eldin Wood, Devlyn found it strange that Alethea mentioned the time passing. "We weren't here that long, no more than an hour," he said as he too stood.

"Five hours have passed. It would have been three, but you chose to test your increased awareness." Alethea moved unconcernedly toward the tree they'd come from.

Startled by her revelation, Devlyn sought Aliel to validate the length of time. He bonded and immediately noticed that the sun had passed its peak, going completely from one side of the sky to the other. Alethea spoke truly. Five hours had passed.

Devlyn joined Alethea at the roots of the stellendae tree concealing the hidden stair. Again, she pressed her hand against it and hummed softly. The roots shifted and opened.

When they reached the top of the very long climb, Ellendren waited by the stair.

"Oh good, you're done. Velaria has been waiting for you."

"Is everything all right, Elle?"

"Couldn't be better. Yelaris and the other blue dragons will reach the Vespien Mountains in three days. Everything is taken care of, we leave Stellantis to meet the dragons within the hour," said Ellendren glancing toward Alethea as though seeking acknowledgement.

Alethea simply nodded her head and left to prepare for her own departure, leaving Devlyn confused about the lack of interaction between the older and younger elf. "That was, uh, odd," he said, hoping Ellendren would clarify.

With a disheartened expression, she said, "Velaria and I had an interesting conversation with her last night. Velaria asked her if she would be willing to teach at Gwilnor."

"I bet that went well," said Devlyn, knowing Alethea's thoughts on Gwilnor Academy.

Ellendren shot him a stern look. "As it happens, she has never been a supporter of the standardization of the education in wielding. She says it must be fluid and natural, that the classroom setting is the reason ei'ana have grown so weak! She knows very well that the only reason the Ei'ana of Septyl have grown weak is because the continuous chain of wielders was shattered by Erynor and the Balance broken!"

"Well, there is something to say about one student learning from one teacher," Devlyn replied, causing Ellendren to erupt.

"You agree with her!"

"I'm just pointing out that I've learned a great deal in the past couple months in Stellantis."

"Nothing you could not have learned in a classroom! Besides, imagine how much could be gained by having her teach at Gwilnor. Who could better instruct kien wielders than she could? We might increase our chances to successfully engage Erynor and his shadow elves. Oh, and you know what else? Guess who Velaria and I met with this morning."

Devlyn shrugged his shoulders. Stellantis was full of elves that he had never met. Several seconds passed before Ellendren said, "Phendien, the Chair of Emradiel. He told us that only a third of the ei'ana are willing to come to Gwilnor. A third!"

Devlyn was truly surprised by the news. He had expected that with Boriel's blessing to return to the lands beyond the Eldin Wood, a greater number of the Eldinari would choose to take up residence at Gwilnor. No one had ever mentioned exactly how many Eldinari were ei'ana, but what was clear was that the vast majority were wielders. Whether or not they pledged themselves to Septyl was also not clear. While the revelation was indeed shocking, he did not understand why it had caused Ellendren to become so worked up. He would have liked to ask, but worried that if he did, they would just argue. He was suddenly grateful for the jewel of prudence in his hidden pocket. *I could say she looks very nice today, and she would still lash out at me*, Devlyn mused, not daring to share that particular thought, and even more grateful that she could not know his thoughts in the same way as Alethea could.

SURROUNDED

The navy protecting Josque, the capital of Tiel, welcomed the familiar ships of the Jahronese seafarers—or as most believed, pirates—letting them approach the city's main harbor. Every inhabitant of Josque recognized the Jahronese ships. They docked at the Tieli capital frequently, to trade many marvelous wonders to the residents before setting sail once again. The inhabitants must have thought that the great volume of ships arriving today meant that they brought a large supply of goods, most likely plundered from unsuspecting coastal towns. Every Jahronese ship served as both a war vessel and merchant ship. But the Jahronese had never had reason to show aggression against the seductive city of Josque.

So the cannons exploding above the surface of the sea as debris floated on its roiled waters was a shock. The Tieli naval ships lost precious time in reversing their initial welcome to organize themselves for an aggressive response to the Jahronese cannons firing against them. Among the roar of commands and screams of panic, a single word drowned the rest, "Pirates!" The derogatory accusations at the mysterious seafarers had previously been reserved for occasions where none of the so-called pirates were in earshot.

No one would ever have expected the pirates to attack their most profitable port in all Eklean. Not even Lankor served them as well as Josque. However, what Ferinn knew that the Tieli didn't was that the Jahronese seafarers had a history and maintained a strong friendship with Sorenthil. The enduring siege on Myrium made tensions thick between the seafarers and those they sold their wares to while in port along the southern cities, Josque in particular. Following Queen Karina's death, the seafarers had swiftly agreed to join the fight against the Erynien Empire. Many in Eklean believed that the so-called pirates were a nomadic people with no allegiance, drifting along the ocean in their individual ships. No one had ever considered them a unified force, and least of all, a threat.

Ferinn also well knew that the Jahronese seafarers were not nomads. In fact, they had called the same archipelago home for nearly two thousand years. The Jahro Islands were not illustrated on any Eklean map; in fact, not even the Sorenth possessed such a map. The seafarers kept their islands secret from the entirety of Eklean, for the Jahronese were all too familiar with how quickly the Eklean kingdoms picked up their swords.

The Jahronese also possessed the most advanced ship building technology in the world. No other nation could surpass the workmanship of their superior ships, nor brave the seas that the seafarers crossed daily. The southern seas were not the still waters of those cradled by the Kinzdol Islands and Dagger's Point. Hurricanes commonly tore through the Tempestien and Unarian Seas, sinking any unseaworthy ship. Only Jahronese ships could endure such storms, and they sold their ships to no one. Jahronese captains built their own ships with their own crews, bonding them for life.

Beneath the warring ships, Ferinn and his fellow merpeople used their spears to pierce the hulls of the Tieli ships, causing them to take on water without anyone onboard knowing why.

Ferinn knew that he would have to face repercussions for his actions. He hadn't had the time to swim to the Bowl of Theniel and call for a Meridean Conclave, so he was now acting against the long-standing edict made by his people. Retribution would come swiftly, but not now. Despite going against the edict made at the last Meridean Conclave, to withdraw from the affairs of the land dwellers, others had agreed with his thinking that it was time for the merpeople to return to the surface. Karina's shocking death struck likeminded merpeople hard, for the Sorenth held a special place within their hearts.

The water dulled the sound of the cannons exploding above, yet Ferinn knew their mission was successful. The Tieli navy lay shattered behind them, and the Jahronese seafarers and merpeople made their way upstream toward Myrium. He hoped that Myranda was handling the siege and her mother's passing well. He had revealed his intentions to her and had told her that he would not return without a force to repel the invaders. Eventually, messages would reach the Tieli generals sieging Myrium about the pirates who had attacked Josque as they sailed north on the Meyien. However, no message would include word of the force concealed beneath the water. They would pay dearly for their act of aggression against Myrium. With any luck, both the Jahronese seafarers and the hidden merpeople would reach Myrium before the messages.

Wings beat against the air as the dragons soared with ease through the sky, amidst the much smaller griffins carrying Fendryl's promised star wardens to bolster Myrium's defenses. Devlyn sat on Rusyl's back, a male dragon of the Blue Flight, Aliel flying to his side. Rusyl was the youngest and smallest of the dragons who had come out of hiding, but he was easily one of the fastest. The female dragons were even larger than the male dragons, and by no means were the male dragons tiny.

Devlyn was still in awe at the sight of the dragons descending toward the Vespien Mountains just hours ago to carry Velaria, Viren, Ellendren, Andrew, and himself to Myrium's defense. Both Alethea and Wyn chose to remain with their griffin companions, even though two dragons flew without any riders. At a distance, the dragons had looked like sparkling sapphires soaring in the air. In descent, their wings were steadily elevated, with the occasional powerful flutter. The astonishing sight had not been seen in over fifteen hundred years, except in children's dreams, where they rode the magnificent beasts in a world they knew not.

The arrival of the dragons had stirred Devlyn deeply. On Rusyl, Devlyn felt more powerful than he ever had before. There was something about flying on a dragon that encouraged valor. Unlike when he had ridden Yelaris, fleeing Ceurenyl from Erynor's attack on the city, this time, he flew toward a city in distress, hoping to bring help to the beleaguered citizens.

But Devlyn sensed Aliel's uneasiness. Every day that passed where they did not become a full Phaedryn, the more uneasy they both grew. They wondered if they had done something wrong, stirring insecurities in them both. Devlyn's feelings of strength from flying on the dragon only increased the phoenix's distaste for the necessity of it.

They were a Phaedryn, yet Devlyn had to depend on a dragon to fly. Devlyn felt Aliel's displeasure pass between their bond. *We'll get there*, Devlyn shared with Aliel in their special form of communication.

A feigned sense of relief passed between them, but it was forced. Neither wanted to dwell on their current inaptitude to bond more fully. Aliel flew in front of Devlyn, making Devlyn long to bond and become a full Phaedryn.

The journey to Myrium took six days. The second night, the large party had rested north of the Plains of Mindale, still in Everin. The Delmira Wood was near, but it lay concealed within the Shroud. When Devlyn asked Rusyl whether they were going to fly over the Shroud, Rusyl told him that they would not. Images poured into Devlyn's mind, their intention clear as he translated them into words. *It pulls anything and everything within, feeding off them.*

Devlyn knew he could dissolve the Shroud, and he desperately wanted to, but he also knew that he didn't have enough strength to do so. At least not yet. It had taken all his and Aliel's energy to dispel a small circle within it from Gwilnor's highest tower that night so long ago. Who knew what it would consume of himself and Aliel if they were to attempt to free the entirety of Krysenthiel?

The fourth night of the journey was spent on the eastern edge of the plains. Verenthyl, a Krysenthien city within the Shroud, lay to the north, presumably in ruins. Devlyn would have liked to visit the ruins of the once great kingdom of Krysenthiel, home of the Luminari, but the Shroud prevented him from even glimpsing his heritage. An icy grip extended past the Shroud to the lands beyond and Devlyn found himself using an extra blanket when they camped for the night. The next day, the group flew along the southern edge of the Shroud for that entire leg of their journey, remaining hidden from any vengeful eyes. Few traveled so close to the Shroud; even shadow elves avoided it when they could.

Finally, on the sixth day, their course diverted away from the Shroud, carrying them south. When the sun passed its peak, the River Meyien and its jewel, Myrium, like a diamond on a golden ring, came into view. Even so, it was another two hours before they began the descent toward the island city.

White stone walls extended from the riverbank, guarding the city built of matching stone. Four large semicircular alcoves pushed into the city from its cardinal points. The east and west alcoves had oblong shapes forming the city docks, while the smaller north and south ones had a similar shape, forming parks with manicured trees. Rising on a hill at the center of the island stood what had to be the royal palace, with spires piercing the sky and a vast dome sheltering the central mass. From Devlyn's vantage, the city's footprint looked like a stretched-out oval with four bridges arching over the Meyien to either side of the island.

It suddenly occurred to Devlyn that a flight of dragons and over a hundred griffins descending on a sieged city would appear to be an aerial attack. Not yet knowing how to communicate telepathically with others beyond Aliel, despite Alethea's continued efforts each evening while they rested, he worried about the reaction of the city guard to the dragons' arrival.

Quickly, go to Myrium and let them see you so they don't try to attack us, Devlyn asked Aliel who flew off at a speed Devlyn had not seen before, making him wonder whether the phoenix was showing off to the dragons. *I'd much rather fly with you,* Devlyn added, and was rewarded with a flow of pride.

While Devlyn was relieved that he didn't have to discover how the city intended to defend itself against dragons just yet, it was an important question. As the large aerial group drew closer to the city, it struck him that a defensive strategy against Erynor's dragons would need to be devised for Eklean's cities. The Cyndinari still had dragons but had not yet unleashed them. They easily could destroy Myrium.

Corrupted under the tutelage of the shadow elves, the enemy dragons were said to have scales of every color imaginable; beauty difficult to compare. The flight of blue dragons displayed more shades of blue than Devlyn thought existed—not a single scale the same tone as another and each dragon entirely unique. Some were overall darker, others lighter, and some brighter. The differences were endless.

Devlyn's wandering thoughts came to a halt when they all landed with a thud in a grassy park at the city's northern point where the River Meyien diverted onto either side of the island city.

Mounted knights rushed into the park, spears extended. Their armor reflected the beaming sun above, but they paled in brilliance next to the dragons' scales. Among the knights was a slender figure, visor drawn. Dismounting, the armored person lifted the visor revealing Princess Myranda's bright blue eyes.

The aerial force dismounted, the Eldinari star wardens almost simultaneously and uniformly while those who rode the dragons slipped off the larger beasts and slid down their sides. Andrew's rushed descent resulted with him twisting his leg and recovering quickly to stand straight, making it seem as though nothing had gone wrong. The Eldinari star wardens were a threatening force, even when unarmed, but each gave a uniform slight bow, their arms never leaving their sides. None of the Myrish Guard dismounted, remaining watchful, clasping their sheathed swords in one hand, while gripping their spears with the other. Viren had taken a position by Devlyn, slightly behind and to his side, honoring his station as a Guardian knight to personally protect Ei'ethil Devlyn Lorenthien—a prince and heir to the Crystal Throne of Krysenthiel.

"Myranda, it's good to find you well," Velaria greeted the young woman. Devlyn and Andrew bowed their heads in respect, Devlyn thinking how grown up Myranda appeared.

Before Myranda could respond, a knight to her side said, "Her Majesty, Queen Myranda of the Royal House Lariviere, welcomes you to Myrium and is grateful for your presence, Mother Velaria."

"It's true then, about your mother," said Velaria, responding to the news of Myranda's new position.

"I will not pretend to guess how you have come across such news, but yes. Nearly a month has passed since she was assassinated. We have not been able to send any news or messages beyond our walls since then. Enemy archers shoot down every bird we send. Not even our hawks have managed to successfully escape the city."

Devlyn was about to offer his sympathies when Ellendren rushed over to her friend, embracing her in a warm hug, tears forming in her eyes.

"It's all right, Elle," Myranda spoke steadily. "I miss her dearly, but Sorenthil's protection must come first. Are the dragons willing to fight on Myrium's behalf? I'm not sure how much longer we can hold them off. They press against both sides daily. Our archers loose volley after volley, but our supply of arrows dwindles with every passing day. It's as if they're trying to make us run out."

Coming forward from the back of the group, Alethea approached the young queen and said, "If you would permit, I could solve your arrow shortage." She then brushed a hand against the bark of the nearest tree.

"These trees have stood since before this city was founded," said Myranda. "Myrium's parks have been maintained by her inhabitants for thousands of years. I could not permit their felling. Although we have considered it as our desperation increases."

"They are old," Alethea agreed, her palm still resting on the tree, "but you misunderstand me. I have no intention of hewing anything from them. I am an elf of Eldinare, with descendants older than these trees. They are beautiful trees; felling them would be a punishable crime among my people. An art exists among my kin, a song of sorts. I imagine these sleepy trees would delight in stirring once again to defend the people who have cared and nurtured them for so many years."

Bewildered, Myranda turned to Ellendren, then turned back to Alethea at Ellendren's nod. "The Eldinari have not been seen since the fall of Krysenthiel. No living Eklean monarch has ever met an Eldinari, let alone received any sort of correspondence. Why come out of hiding now?" Myranda's eyes lingered on the many elves beside their griffins.

"We never hid, and it was only by the last Exalted Aryl's insistence that we withdrew into our forest home," said Wyn. "We came to usher in a new era of long-awaited harmony."

Devlyn thought he noticed the queen's cheeks flush when Wyn spoke, revealing himself from behind one of the dragons. It had never crossed his mind that Wyn was an attractive young elf, and that even a mourning queen amidst a siege might notice.

"Your aid is welcome." Myranda's gaze shifted from Wyn to the dragons then to the griffins. "The city is filled with refugees due to the siege, leaving the inns filled to capacity, and the palace barracks already have soldiers alternating between beds and the floor. And while our stables are large, I don't know if they would properly accommodate your…"

"Griffins," Alethea filled in. "And they've never been fond of stables. With your leave, the star wardens can set up camp in this park with their griffins."

"That's quite agreeable. There are some unoccupied rooms still in the palace." Myranda turned to Velaria. "After settling in, I believe my generals would be most interested in arranging a war council meeting. We've stayed behind these walls long enough; I think it's time we take the offensive."

33

SUPPORT ROLE

Horns blew through the city, reverberating off the stone walls and waking anyone still slumbering, although Devlyn doubted that anyone still slept. He and Aliel had spent most of the first day in Myrium exploring the palace with Wyn and Andrew. Myranda had called her war council shortly following their arrival the previous day, and while Velaria, Ellendren, Viren, and Alethea received invitations, Devlyn, Wyn, and Andrew had not. Before retiring that evening, Viren rapped on his door to inform him that Sorenthil's generals had agreed it was time to march out of the city. They had decided that at the third hour of the day, Sorenth soldiers would confront the Tieli forces to the east, while Myrium's archers would occupy the Torsillian army to the west. The star wardens on their griffins would be split between the two to provide additional support to both.

Viren had also told Devlyn that he was to join four other wielders to support the southern battalion. After the Guardian knight left, Devlyn had slumped in his bed and had stared at the ceiling for at least an hour before falling asleep. He had slept somewhat restlessly but felt refreshed regardless. Despite the rest, his nerves prickled and anxiety threatened to overwhelm his mind. He felt sick.

He'd never marched into a battle before, and while he was not going to fight with a sword unless absolutely necessary, he would be standing among the rearguard, wielding against the shadow elves hiding in the Tieli army.

A young squire arrived to help Devlyn don his armor. At first, Devlyn refused his assistance but when he found it nearly impossible to fasten the various straps across his body, he was relieved that the squire had stayed to help despite Devlyn's initial refusal. The squire must have fastened armor on dozens of knights since he finished with Devlyn in mere minutes before hurrying off to find the next person in need of assistance.

Viren stood at the open door, waiting for Devlyn. "Remember, kien is your weapon. I will defend you as needed in my capacity. Your strength in the erendinth far exceeds your skill with the sword or any other forged weapon."

Devlyn agreed, not eager to fight with a sword, although he still remembered hearing stories as a child, stories that spoke of the valor exhibited by lords and knights as they fought against evil threats. None of the stories involved wielding, though; all were about men with swords.

"Viren, how is it that you're a Guardian knight and not a knight of Krysenthiel? Wasn't most of the order Luminari?" asked Devlyn, surprised that he'd asked the question, unsure of why it had come to mind.

"Eklean has only known one kingdom fighting against another, or rebellion within," replied Viren. "With the establishment of the Guardian Senate, our knightly order was founded as a military extension. The Guardians—senators and knights—swear to uphold peace and justice for all Eklean, not only Krysenthiel. By the time I was knighted, our influence and protection had extended beyond this continent to all Teraeniel, with the Guardian Senate directing our lead. If we had identified ourselves as the knights of Krysenthiel, we would have never left our borders to protect and serve Teraeniel. We would have represented only Krysenthiel. As Guardian knights, we belong to all. It's true, most of our order were Luminari, but not all. Humans, elves from other Skylands, dwarves, merpeople, and even a few giants, served among our ranks. Today, I will show you what it means to be a Luminari. The Erynien Empire targeted our people because of who we are and what we believe in. We serve everyone. None is greater, and none lesser; only those who choose to do so, diminish themselves in vice."

Devlyn listened attentively, absorbing every word. The honor and valor Viren spoke of was beyond his comprehension. "But don't be mistaken, just like the Eldinari, each Luminari aryl had star wardens at their command, loyal only to their aryl," said Viren.

Devlyn had more questions, but the horn blasted a second time. The time had come to march across the eastern bridges and confront the Tieli army.

"Before we leave, it would be prudent to leave a certain purse in your quarters. War holds no certainties."

Devlyn felt his stomach turn. He had never considered leaving the lumols and lucilliae behind, and now that he carried two lucilliae, his sense of responsibility toward them had only magnified. The thought of someone stealing them from his quarters plagued his mind as he considered whether to heed Viren.

"You're in Sorenthil's royal palace, not some backwater inn; they'll be safe here."

"Ok, close the door though, just in case someone walks by."

Viren stepped into the room and closed the door behind him. Devlyn felt his eyes on him as he scanned the room for an acceptable hiding place. The writing desk and bedside table felt too obvious as choices. Those would be the first places he would look for valuables. He went to the bed and lifted a pillow.

"The palace servants will tidy your room and fluff the bed, pillows included."

"Then, where am I supposed to hide it?" asked Devlyn.

"Anywhere, but keep it secure by wielding."

Devlyn decided to place the coin purse in the bedside table drawer. Then, he pressed into the erendinth and wielded terys, aerys, and ignys, the elements weaving around the drawer to seal it. Devlyn doubted a giant could pull the drawer open. And just in case someone managed to overcome the wield, he wielded ignys to spring as a trap if the drawer did open.

"Do you think anyone would try to remove the entire table?" Devlyn studied his wield.

"While there might be shadow elves or servants of Shadow disguised in the palace, none know what you carry," said Viren, turning to the door.

"Ready?"

Devlyn nodded, appreciating the reassurance Aliel conveyed when the two followed Viren into the palace corridor, the knight's sword smacking against his thigh as it hung from his waist. Viren walked naturally, without effort, wearing his armor as though it was linen clothing. Devlyn had not seen Viren's armor before and noted that it was distinctly different than Devlyn's or any other armor he'd ever seen. The metallic material had a woven pattern and looked to be more flexible. Devlyn caught himself gazing at the material, intrigued by some undefinable quality that he had never seen before.

The horns continued to sound at regular intervals as they made their way out of the palace and through the city's curving streets, to reach a crowded elliptical plaza filled with Sorenth soldiers ready to march through the southeastern city gate. Viren led the way through the orderly squadrons, evidently knowing who they were to report to, and stopping before a middle aged Sorenth captain.

"Ah, Sir Viren, I presume? I'm Captain Corvin; I didn't receive notice that you and the kien wielder would be joining our squadron until early this morning. I'm told your experience is rather exceptional." Corvin looked from Viren to Devlyn. "You'll find the ei'ana in this squadron in the rearguard, and you'll answer to them. Your role is purely supportive; I don't want anything unnatural happening on that battlefield. Understood?"

"What about the shadow elves?" asked Devlyn. He kept his voice level but grew angrier with every word this captain spoke. Corvin obviously had no love for wielders.

"You'll have to deal with them from the rearguard. I'll not be responsible for a kien wielder wreaking havoc among my troops."

"Thank you, Captain," said Viren, sensing Devlyn's unease, and turned away to accompany Devlyn to the rearguard.

"Your experience would be better served next me, knight," Corvin spoke to Viren's back.

"My sword belongs with the Phaedryn." Viren continued toward the back of the squadron where four ei'ana awaited them.

Devlyn didn't recognize any of these women but noted that they were all Crimsyns by both their pins and red clothing. *He expects us to be healers and nothing more,* Devlyn conveyed to Aliel. *How does he expect to fight shadow elves with healers?*

I don't think they've fought against shadow elves yet, Aliel conveyed.

The four ei'ana clustered together, their eyes never leaving Devlyn. "You're the Phaedryn we've heard so much about then. I'm Linette, head of this group. I've never bonded with a kien wielder, and I'm not particularly looking forward to it, so we will avoid doing so unless absolutely necessary." Linette turned from Devlyn and looked to the sky just as seven low flying dragons swooped over the white walls and gate tower. Devlyn could only see their blue underbellies, making it impossible to tell if anyone rode the dragons into battle, but imagined he would be much more effective fighting from one of those dragons than healing from the rearguard.

Another series of horns trumpeted through the city, the southeastern gate creaked open, and the portcullis lifted. Devlyn stood at the back of the column of soldiers marching across the southeastern bridge over the Meyien, sweating in his metal armor under the hot Meridenth summer sun. He heard dragons roaring across the water. *Were the dragons forcing the Tieli forces back?*

He stood on his tiptoes to see past the spears, shields, and helmets blocking his direct view across the bridge, but had to glance left to see the blue dragons sweeping down to hold the Tieli forces back, allowing the Sorenth battalions to cross the bridge safely.

When they had flown into the city, the bridges had appeared low to the river, but he now discovered their true height; they arched high enough over the river for the tallest ships to sail beneath with ease. Aliel flew close to Devlyn, bound just as Devlyn had reached the exposed bridge beyond Myrium's walls. Neither wished to hide their identity any longer.

Tieli horns answered the Sorenth horns. The Tieli favored a high pitch and deep sound, menacing by its very nature. A second horn, foul and demanding dominance, came from the Tieli ranks. Whoever that horn belonged to made the Tieli invaders seem innocent and almost lovable by comparison.

Devlyn was only half way across the bridge, now at its highest point above the river, and could easily see his own column of soldiers engaging the enemy. Even with the dragons pushing the sieging armies back, the Sorenth were forced to instantly engage the enemy once they spilled off the bridge and onto the muddied field. The ring of metal on metal filled Devlyn's ears as he reached the field trampled by thousands of feet over the past year, and he tried not to flinch as arrows flew over his head, traveling much further than he thought possible. Griffins soared above, carrying the Eldinari star wardens.

Holding his breath as he searched for the rendezvous point for the ei'ana, he eventually made his way to a slight crest in the field which provided a better view of the fighting. Captain Corvin already stood on the crest, but toward the rear of his battalion, shouting orders to them. Corvin immediately dismissed the wielders with a quick nod, preferring to direct his soldiers. Despite his evident distrust for wielders of any kind, it was clear that Corvin, as well as every Sorenth soldier and knight, had been waiting for the chance to confront the invaders in open combat. Their desire to fight had only grown with the assassination of the late queen.

Devlyn's awareness of the field and his strength in the erendinth were substantially increased by the bond with Aliel and when he pressed himself into the erendinth, he felt the world around him in a very different way. The erendinth coursed through the field, and he could feel others wielding. He easily recognized some wields, but not all. Devlyn focused on the erendinth wielded further within the field, presumably by shadow elves. Those wields had a dark quality laced through, as though they were subjugated by another force, uncommon to a wielder's influence over the erendinth. Rather than guiding the erendinth, these held a corrupted, horrible element that Devlyn could feel, aware of their inherent destructive chaos.

Linette cleared her throat, disrupting Devlyn's concentration. "Our role is to heal and support the soldiers. The captains can scan the field just fine."

"They're wielding tenebrys out there!" Devlyn rounded on the ei'ana. He knew Crimsyns were talented healers, but they couldn't just stand by and not fight.

"Don't be ridiculous—that's a fake erendinth meant to frighten student wielders and nothing else. Now, you will disengage." Linette crossed her arms.

"Were you not at Ceurenyl when Erynor attacked? His forces obliterated the city gate and portions of the wall and they did not use one of the seven erendinth to do so!" Devlyn didn't know where Velaria was, but someone with more authority than this Crimsyn had to talk some sense into her.

"That sounds unlikely and as a matter of fact, my place was here in Myrium, and as this is *still* my place, you will listen to me as your commanding officer and disengage."

Corvin heard their dispute and turned. "There isn't time for this, the Tieli are much stronger than we anticipated. Your role, boy, is to heal when needed; now follow your orders."

Devlyn couldn't believe it. Shadow elves were wielding tenebrys against Sorenth soldiers and they were keeping him from fighting them! It wasn't long until the first wounded soldiers reached the ei'ana, and then it was a continuous rotation of new injuries. Devlyn felt more useless than he did when Yelaris had flown him away from Ceurenyl.

As Devlyn soothed and healed a nasty gash in a soldier's side, he sensed tenebrys striking out wildly across the battlefield. The dragons flying above had to keep their distance; not even their hides could protect them against the corruptive erendinth, and the griffins had to maintain an even greater distance. None of the soldiers engaging the shadow elves would reach the healers. If the shadow elves didn't kill them instantly, they would claim their soul for their own to elongate their unnatural life. Devlyn's stomach turned in disgust that he was restricted to healing when he knew he and Aliel could prevent those atrocities from wielding tenebrys.

The soldier Devlyn was currently healing had lost a significant amount of blood, and while Devlyn managed to heal the wound, he could not replace the soldier's spilled blood. This soldier should not return to the battle, but he was determined to do just that. As he walked from the hill crest, a wield of hazardous lightning struck across the field, exploding against the soldier's chest. He didn't even have a chance to scream before he crumpled to the ground.

Devlyn locked eyes with the shadow elf responsible for the wield; he'd somehow managed to bypass the bulk of the Sorenth troops and was fighting his way toward the healers. Devlyn had no idea if the ei'ana were even aware of the shadow elf, but he also did not care to ask their permission to fight him either.

Pressing himself further into the erendinth, Devlyn wielded ignys, terys, and animys against the tenebrys wield now launching toward him. He delved further into it and set himself to unraveling the wield. It was intricate, difficult to maneuver through, resembling lightning without light, tearing a hole of Darkness through the air. Seconds turned into minutes as Devlyn worked to disengage the shadow elf from the erendinth. It was difficult to concentrate with swords clanging against swords and shields, and soldiers yelling and cursing at one another around him. The noise rose, both in volume and intensity.

Just as he thought he nearly had the corrupted wield dissolved, Devlyn felt a stir in the air and heard a menacing crackle. He *knew* that something threatened to tear everything and everyone apart. Relying on his instincts and with Aliel's lead, they wove a wield of the four elemental erendinth laced with animys toward the sinister, tenebrys-laden wield, nothing but pure Darkness.

The two wields met in an explosion, drowning the noise of the battlefield in a death-defying thunder before fading to let the familiar sound of metal clashing on metal return.

Quickly pressing himself into another wield, Devlyn delved into terys and exploded it beneath the feet of the shadow elf who had thrown that wield, causing him to fly backward before hitting the ground.

The shadow elf quickly recovered and Devlyn felt the very air condense into the wretched wield once again. Forming the same complex wield as before, Devlyn blasted it from his stance toward the shadow elf.

In all the action, the shadow elf had advanced so that he was now only twenty paces away. Every soldier who had stood between them was either dead or had fled to avoid the explosion. The ei'ana could only watch in terror, offering no assistance in battling the shadow elf. Devlyn had tried to reach out to them, to add their strength to his own, but they weren't even wielding anymore, focused on getting the injured away from the confrontation. Devlyn's disgust for these ei'ana grew tenfold with their refusal to help. The new wields met in a second blast, but Devlyn managed to hold the wield and push it against the other as the shadow elf did the same. Even with his increased ability while bound to Aliel, the shadow elf was still stronger. His evil wield crackled and forked toward Devlyn. This shadow elf was much stronger than the one he had defeated in Binton, but even then, the defeat had only been possible because Velaria had added her own strength, enhanced by her verathn, to his own.

Panic surged through him as he raced to find a way to overcome the wield of tenebrys. Then, with a death-defying screech, it faded; the streak of negating darkness simply vanished.

A scream more horrendous than anything Devlyn had ever heard filled his ears. The shadowy form convulsed as the dark shadow surrounding him grew even darker, just before tiny lights rushed from the shadow. The multitude of liberated spirits caged within the shadow elf were released, and simply disappeared. Sprawled on the ground with darkness oozing from his body lay the corpse of the shadow elf, his decapitated head slowly spinning to a halt next to it. Then, without the captured spirits to sustain it, the corrupted body disintegrated to dust.

Viren stood over the dust, his sword still at the ready. Devlyn thanked the Guardian knight, grateful for the timely intercession. The strength of the shadow elf had been beyond what he had expected, and Devlyn had scarcely held his own against the monster.

Without Viren's help, he would now be dead.

34

Rising Waters

Exhausted, Devlyn scanned the battlefield to find the Sorenth lines shrinking. Linette and the other ei'ana had given up on Devlyn to resume their healing duties. The four women infuriated Devlyn. If he hadn't engaged the shadow elf, they would have died. Rather than thanking him, they simply glared at him, as if he shouldn't be capable of doing what he did. What world were these ei'ana living in? Could they not know the threat that the Erynien Empire posed? Alethea was right, much had been forgotten.

Devlyn pressed again into the erendinth and felt tenebrys lash across the battlefield. Dozens of shadow elves wielded beyond the enemy lines, some focused on defusing the dragons' effectiveness and keeping the griffins and Eldinari star wardens at a distance, while others struck down Sorenth soldiers. Barely able to locate the enemy wielders, Devlyn knew he couldn't remove any of them from the battle—they were too far away.

Fixated on the tenebrys wields, Devlyn almost didn't feel someone grip his shoulders. Devlyn withdrew from the erendinth and gave a questioning look to Viren behind him. Only then did Devlyn recognize the Sorenth horns calling for retreat, accompanied by captains shouting the same order. Devlyn's disgust rose at seeing the ei'ana healers reach the bridge first.

"Their priorities need to change." Viren also watched the women.

"Were the ei'ana always like that?"

"They were never warriors, but neither did they hide behind walls and only heal when Erynor began his war."

Devlyn nodded and joined the flow of soldiers retreating in defeat across the bridge back to Myrium. Without any instruction to the contrary, Devlyn returned to his room in Myrium's palace, and found the same squire waiting to help remove his armor. He sent Viren to find his own bed, thankful for the Guardian knight's protection that day. Exhausted, the thought of refusing the squire's help didn't even cross his mind and the boy unlatched and untied the different pieces. After wearing the suffocating armor all day in the hot sun, he sighed in relief when fresh air brushed against his bare skin. Devlyn thanked the young squire before he left, then threw himself on his bed. After a few moments of lying there utterly spent, he remembered his hidden cache, and tugged at the bedside drawer, which didn't budge. Reassured, he lay back and promptly fell asleep.

He woke some time later when a knock came at the door. It seemed he might have taken some time to hear and respond, since it seemed to be growing louder. Sleepily, he looked toward the window, and saw that the sun had long since fallen. How long had he been asleep?

"Come in," Devlyn managed through a gaping yawn.

A small globe of light hovered through the door, just ahead of Wyn's smiling face illumined by the small light. "How are you feeling?"

Devlyn hadn't given a thought to how he felt beyond his initial exhaustion and now took notice. "Sore," he admitted. "Those shadow elves are strong. I've never been so depleted by wielding before."

"I had similar difficulties, and the ei'ana I was with insisted that healing was more important. We can't confront the shadow elves individually; we need to work together. In fact, one of the reasons I came to find you is that Velaria asked me to accompany you in future bouts." Relieved, yet not wanting to admit that the shadow elves were beyond his abilities, he thanked Wyn.

"The other reason I'm here is to ask if you'd like to join me. Put some clothes on, we'll get something to eat in the dining hall."

After a quick wash and getting dressed, Devlyn accompanied Wyn through the palace corridors. Aliel insisted on following, and his light flooded the corridor. The sound of the dining hall reached their ears just as Ellendren turned a corner in front of them. Freshly bathed and wearing a clean dress of Sorenth blue, she offered a weak smile, sending shivers through Devlyn.

"Hi, Elle." Devlyn waved as she drew near.

"There you are," Ellendren replied. "Myranda is holding a war council meeting, and both your presences are requested."

"How many ei'ana will be there?" Devlyn asked. He was too tired to restrain himself if they insisted on their role as healers.

"I can't say, but we should hurry, the meeting has already begun."

Devlyn's stomach groaned when the scents from the dining hall lingered in his nose as he followed Ellendren down the corridor she had come from.

The war council was meeting in a large windowless chamber with only a single door. It was in stark contrast to the rest of the palace, which readily featured large windows with a multitude of balconies. This room made Devlyn think he was in a fortified keep and not a luxurious palace. Over a dozen people stood around a central table where a detailed map of the city and surrounding country lay before them. Devlyn instantly recognized where his battalion had fought at the southeastern bridge, now littered with wooden figurines depicting Tieli forces. The same figurines sat at the other eastern bridge, while Torsillian figures occupied the two western bridges.

"Our scouts have confirmed the siege towers' movements. Why they waited until now to use them is beyond me," said a general, moving more figurines across the map. "They won't let us stew in our walls this time. They're also tired of this siege."

"How long do we have, Percy?" asked Myranda.

"If they don't rest tonight, your Majesty, those siege towers can reach our bridges by morning, and you can be certain they'll continue their push to our walls the same day. And we won't be defending only one side of the city either—the Torsillian forces have started their move as well."

"I see." Myranda surveyed the map. "Why weren't the blue dragons more effective?"

"As expected, shadow elves are among the enemy ranks; their wielding dissipated the dragons' fire before it could reach the enemy. Landing amidst the battle would have been suicide—they have no defense against tenebrys," said Velaria.

"With all due respect, Mother Velaria," a plump ei'ana broke in. "You don't honestly believe tenebrys is real, do you?"

Devlyn glared at the ei'ana, holding back his strong desire to yell at her. Fortunately, Alethea cleared her throat. "Tenebrys has long been favored by Erynor and his pawns. The Deurghol and shadow elves did not come to be until we lost the Ceurendol War, but the enemy's wielders have long known of the forsaken erendinth, possibly since the Skylands were lost to us."

"And how would you know this?" remarked the same ei'ana.

Had no one briefed this ei'ana? Devlyn felt uncomfortable with her disrespect toward Alethea.

"Much has been forgotten among your people," Alethea said calmly.

"You didn't answer my question." The ei'ana crossed her arms.

"Karen," snapped Velaria, "Alethea Lenwyn is a former aryl and one of the last remaining elves who once lived on the Skyland of Eldinare. Your disrespect warrants an apology."

Karen was much older than Velaria and a Crimsyn wise one. If Velaria had not been a Chair, Karen would have outranked her. She scowled then grudgingly uttered an apology. A look of horror flashed across her. Devlyn smiled, recognizing the startled expression he too had given when Alethea spoke inside his mind that first time.

"Now, we have to rethink our tactics as wielders," said Velaria. "I understand that as Crimsyns, you're dedicated and talented healers, but if you continue as only healers, the entire Sorenth army will perish from tenebrys before you have a chance to heal them. If all seven Schools of Septyl were present, we could divide our wielders to include support roles, but we do not have that luxury. We have to find a way to negate their wields before they can harm the soldiers."

"Will the Eldinari—these star wardens—fly above the battle on their griffins again?" asked Myranda.

"They will do as asked," said Alethea.

"Good—I would like them to resume that post." Myranda turned to her generals. "I want wielders concentrated above every city gate and small groups dispersed between each gate. Whatever these shadow elves are capable of, arrows won't be enough to keep them from marching into our city. Anyone who can pull a bowstring should be defending our walls, with our more skilled archers and swordsman near the gates."

"Your Majesty," said Percy, staring at the map, then looking to Devlyn and Wyn. "Most Sorenth soldiers are uncomfortable with wielding, especially men wielding. After all, we've been carting away our boys capable of wielding to the Temple of Ceur for as long as anyone in this kingdom can remember."

"It's new for all of us, general," Velaria replied, "but the Balance is returning and in our own lifetimes there won't be a single kien wielder restricted to the Temple of Ceur."

Devlyn had grown accustomed to people's unease around him; it was there even at Gwilnor where every wielder knew he was not a danger. Still, Eklean required much more time before kien wielders would be accepted.

"Is there an issue, general?" asked Myranda.

"No, your Majesty, we'll do as commanded."

"In the case of a breach, do we have enough battalions to meet the enemy at the gates?" asked Myranda.

"They'll be spread thin, but they can be supplemented by the forces on the walls," Percy replied.

"What if the giants arrive?" asked Devlyn.

"Velaria has told us about the giants. Their pace is markedly slow, and unless this siege lasts another year, they most likely won't reach us in time," Myranda replied. Suddenly, exhaustion lined her face, and when she continued, it was in a slower yet still determined tone. "Tomorrow will decide Sorenthil's fate. Let's get some sleep so that we can better defend our freedom." Myranda signaled everyone but her generals to leave and remained staring at the map of Myrium. Devlyn had no idea where Myranda and the generals found strength to continue their work into the night.

Although Myranda had said that their fate would be decided the next day, two days passed with the gates of Myrium barred. Archers, soldiers, and ei'ana alike took defensive positions atop the city walls. Devlyn occasionally found himself patrolling the walls, looking over to see both armies on either side of the river. The Torsillian army made feeble attempts to cross the western bridges, but Sorenth archers prevented any advancement. It was somewhat surprising, since everyone had anticipated that the Tieli and Torsillian armies would attack the city following the defeat of the Sorenth on the battlefield. Instead, they seemed to be waiting for Sorenth horns to call her soldiers to arms.

Myranda and the generals hoped to avoid open battle with Torsil. The Sorenth simply didn't have the strength to mount two attacks, and there was no way to send messages to call the Sorenth forces spread throughout the kingdom to come to the defense of their capital. Ever since Queen Karina's assassination, the Sorenth had not been able to send any messages. Sorenth nobility beyond the Myrish court had no idea that Karina was dead and that Myranda had taken her mother's place. Even should the city's defenders manage to prevail against the Tieli, it would only mark the beginning of this war. Unlike the Erynien Empire, Sorenthil did not have an infinite number of resources to call on.

Fortunately, there were still no signs of giants east of Dwota's Gap. Devlyn dreaded the day they would march into battle with Erynor. He well remembered Tye's explanation for his decision to travel past Dwota's Gap to warn of the giants crossing the Frozen Mountains and through the desert.

Suddenly, horns reverberated throughout the city. Frantic soldiers rushed through the streets to their positions, a few to the gates and the majority taking posts along the top of Myrium's walls. Devlyn fell in with a squadron hurrying to the eastern section, Viren and Wyn at his side, and Aliel bound with him. Four ei'ana waited at the southeastern gate tower's base—Linette among them with her arms aggressively crossed. Devlyn groaned inwardly for he had hoped he would be placed with a different group of ei'ana.

"I received direct orders from our wise one that we are to engage the enemy directly. When we spoke our Counsels as Crimsyn ei'ana, we promised to heal, not hurt," said Linette.

"My people understand this burden," started Wyn. "We do not enter into battle light-hearted, and while we were asked to stay our hands during the Ceurendol War, our absence can never return the hundreds of thousands of Luminari who died in the Erynien Empire's clutches."

"You speak wisely for one so young," said Linette.

"You confuse my youthful appearance with my age." Wyn smiled.

"Right, well, let's get to the top of that wall and defend this city," said Linette as a drift of griffins soared above. Devlyn watched them for a few seconds before entering the gate tower.

His spirit sank when he reached the top of the crowded gate tower; across the rutted field toward each of Myrium's four bridges on both sides of the Meyien, tall wooden monstrosities crawled.

The slender contraptions could easily cross the bridges to carry the invaders over Myrium's walls. They lurched toward the bridges crossing the River Meyien, followed by lines of soldiers on both banks of the river, carrying shields to protect their heads and sides.

Devlyn watched in horror as arrows from archers on both the city walls and flying on griffins pinpricked the wooden contraptions, doing little to slow them down. Devlyn felt one of the ei'ana wield ignys, and shortly after, saw a ball of fire hurl from her hands toward the closest construction on the bridges. Watching with anticipation as the fire neared the siege tower, Devlyn's heart stopped as the fire simply went out harmlessly several paces before reaching its target. A dragon flew from inside the city and over the gate tower toward the same siege engine and breathed fire down on it and the column of soldiers behind, only to have it dissipate just as the ei'ana's wield had done.

Pressing into terys, Devlyn exerted his will down through the gate tower, over the bridge, and up the wooden construction to sense dozens of soldiers concealed inside—shadow elves among their numbers. "There're shadow elves inside those things," Devlyn yelled.

Once they reached the walls, not only would the invading soldiers have entrance into the city, but so would shadow elves. The thought struck Devlyn to the core. He scoured his mind for a solution—any solution to prevent those things from breaching the city.

"We have to form a bond," Devlyn said to the ei'ana, knowing that they had never formed one with kien wielders before.

Devlyn pressed himself into the erendinth, more forcefully in aquaeys and aerys. He felt the ei'ana, Wyn among them, and linked himself to them, supplementing his already heightened ability from Aliel.

The bridges rose too high over the river to flood, which was Devlyn's first thought. Aquaeys and aerys pulsed through his surroundings; he was not the only one wielding them. Starting in the river, Devlyn pressed himself into it, guiding it, allowing the natural force of the river's current to supplement his own strength. With a burst of energy, Devlyn brought a torrent of water from the Meyien to crash against the siege tower nearest him. The water's force seemed enough, but Devlyn was unwilling to risk failure. Pressing deeply into aerys, Devlyn brought a gust of wind from above to intensify the water. His wield crashed into the siege machine and he felt the wooden construction stagger and moan as he pushed it against the edge of the bridge. Devlyn felt resistance from within the siege tower, not from wielders who were busy preventing it from catching fire, but from the soldiers inside trying to keep it from toppling, attempting to steady the shoddy contraption.

With a final groan, the siege tower creaked against the side of the bridge and toppled over completely, crashing to its watery grave. Removing himself from aerys and aquaeys, and breaking off from the ei'ana, Devlyn heard a last scream from within the siege tower before the sound was drowned by the rushing waters of the Meyien, swallowing those trapped within the wooden contraption. Shouted commands from atop the city walls brought arrows raining down on the column of soldiers which had been tailing the siege tower, and they fled toward the opposite side of the river, their formation broken. Those who had been closest behind the tower fell to the arrows while those toward the rear narrowly managed to retreat out of range.

The ei'ana at the other gate towers had taken note of Devlyn's accomplishment and followed his lead, although none matched his strength, especially when he and Aliel were bound together. Only Alethea and Wyn rivaled Devlyn. Their immortality had allowed them to hone their abilities far longer than any other present. Even so, the shadow elves remained exceptionally strong and few could overpower their wielding. Unfortunately, they caught on to the new tactic and were directing their energies against the forces of water and air.

Devlyn could not tell if any of the other siege towers were forced over the bridges, but his victory was short lived when one reached the wall.

Devlyn was not near the siege tower, nor could he see the soldiers rush over the walls, yet he heard commands yelled through the city, supported by assorted horns and bells, signaling that the walls had been breached. The same alarms sounded again, but from the other side of the city. Devlyn waited in dread for the third to sound, signaling a third breach, but it never came. *Well at least that's one less we have to worry about,* Devlyn shared with Aliel.

An explosion came from a breach on the west side of the city, the next closest gate, and Devlyn, Aliel, Wyn, and Viren raced to see whether they could help, leaving the four Crimsyn ei'ana behind at the southeastern gate. The shortest route had them rushing down the gate tower and across the city's width to the southwestern tower, and Devlyn feared the worst as they hurried up the gate tower. He could hear the sharp sound of metal ringing against metal accompanied by the agonizing sound of injured soldiers, and an occasional blast.

Invaders filed on and over the gate tower parapets, and pushed through Myrium's defenses, leaving a trail of mortally wounded and dead soldiers behind, trampling across them as if they were nothing more than a cobblestone road. Amidst the carnage were seven ei'ana, none dressed for a battle, the wise one named Karen among them. Surrounded on two sides by Tieli soldiers were three shadowy figures. Devlyn could see the hate in their eyes from where he stood. The shadow elf in the center was older than the two at her sides, their bodies nowhere near as corrupted and diseased as her own. Devlyn had managed to best a single shadow elf on the field, but that had been because Viren had decapitated him. Now, he and Wyn stood shoulder to shoulder, both pressed into the erendinth. Yet even with their combined strength, Devlyn felt his confidence waver—they could not overcome three at once, and Viren was busy fighting off the Tieli soldiers.

A maniacal laugh escaped the old shadow elf. "So, the treetop elves have finally decided to come out of hiding and fight again," she cackled, stepping over the fallen ei'ana. "Tell me, little elf, do you value your immortality so little that you are willing to throw it away now as I suck your spirit from your young body? Perhaps your pretty immortal skin will return me to my own youthful appearance."

Ignoring her taunt, Devlyn and Wyn formed a wield using all four elemental erendinth, mingled with animys and umbrys, then launched it at the shadow elves just as a volley of arrows came from a group of Eldinari flying above on their griffins, directed at the soldiers climbing over the wall.

The shadow elves were ready with their own unified wield. Devlyn felt the familiar sensation of tenebrys fill the air. Bracing themselves, Devlyn and Wyn embraced animys and umbrys more fully, trying to form a barrier of sorts. Devlyn desperately wished that he could wield lumenys as the tendrils of lashing chaotic energy launched at them. The Poor Lady had made it clear that only those who had entered the Empyrean Sphere could wield lumenys.

The wield exploded against their barrier, draining their strength with every second it tried to break through. Then two ei'ana appeared behind the shadow elves, one of them Velaria holding her verathn in her right hand. Now, the shadow elves had two targets, the younger ones focused against the two ei'ana, while the older continued her attack on Devlyn, Wyn, and Aliel, her high-pitched evil laugh continuously taunting them. Trying to keep breathing as he wielded, Devlyn didn't know how much longer he could stand. Then he caught sight of dozens of ships sailing swiftly upstream from the south. The shadow elf saw them too.

"So those pirates have finally come to their senses!" she said, cackling gleefully.

35

QUIET LIGHTS

Refusing to allow the ships to distract him, Devlyn pressed himself into the erendinth and lashed recklessly and furiously against the shadow elf. Several quick bursts flew from his grasp followed by a strong wield, nearly knocking the shadow elf from her feet. The sounds of the exploding cannons firing from the ships filled his ears as he attacked and he braced himself for the imminent impact.

The shadow elf snarled as she held Devlyn in her eyes, waiting for the scales to tip further in her favor with the pirates' arrival. The destructive sounds lingered in the air, followed by a resounding thump, a thump that didn't shake the walls. He had heard the cannons explode. *Did they all miss the city?*

Devlyn risked a glance over his shoulder past the city walls to see where the cannons directed their fire. They continued to blast and Devlyn was shocked to see the cannonballs explode against the invading armies gathered along the shores opposite the island city.

"How dare they!" screamed the shadow elf, her attention also divided between her wield and the ships.

Devlyn couldn't risk another look over his shoulder since the shadow elf had intensified her wield, evidently enraged by the cannon fire against the Tieli troops. No longer able to look at the mysterious ships, Devlyn tried to maintain his focus on the shadow elf, but from the corner of his eye, he thought he saw the water level rising. And was it going in the opposite direction?

Devlyn couldn't resist turning to look at the river, and saw the ships coming toward Myrium riding on a large wave, the water supporting them rising higher than usual in the River Meyien, as it rushed north. The river had turned, flowing against its natural direction, and it continued to rise the closer it drew to Myrium. Devlyn thought he saw something jump out of the wave and dive back in the water. *Was that a fish?*

Another leapt from the water and Devlyn saw people with fish-like tails swimming abreast the ships. Who were they, and who was sailing the ships? *Definitely not pirates.* His attention divided, Devlyn's grasp of the erendinth slipped. Forcing himself to ignore the astounding events in the river below, he returned his focus fully to the erendinth and redirected the shadow elf's wield, hurling the black lighting skyward.

The shadow elf cursed, her eyes flashed in fury at something behind Devlyn.

Devlyn heard the water roiling behind him just as a monstrous wave crashed into the bridge nearest him, reaching and spraying water over the walls, soaking him and everyone nearby. When he had wiped his eyes free of the water, he saw that the siege tower and the dense column of enemy soldiers no longer stood on the bridge, swept away by the colossal wave. Only the white stone bridge remained, dripping with water.

"Who dug them from their watery depths?" spat the shadow elf. Without understanding what she meant, Devlyn returned his focus to her. But as he did, Rusyl swooped from the sky and lifted the stunned shadow elf off her feet to throw her into the river.

With only the two younger shadow elves remaining, the odds became much more favorable. Still, they fought on, undeterred by the soaking and still throwing bolts of tenebrys-laden black lighting in every direction. Pressing himself into the erendinth, Devlyn hurled a blast of air at them, slamming them against the edge of the parapet, where Viren was finally able to move in to use his sword in a magnificent swipe that caught both shadow elves. A terrible sound escaped them when they drew their last breaths and several captured spirits escaped. Relieved by the minor victory, Devlyn exhaled and joined the other defenders with him in leaning against the wall to regain his strength, his head hanging in exhaustion.

"Look, flames!" Wyn called out.

Standing again to look over the wall, Devlyn's heart sank as black flames fell from the sky on one of the ships that had come to Myrium's defense. The flames licked at the sides of the slick vessel, and horrendous screams came from inside the ship. Looking up for the source of the destruction, Devlyn's breath caught in his throat, horrified at the sight of the winged figure completely enveloped in darkness hovering in the sky.

Aren hung motionless, observing the destruction he'd caused, and a form appeared before him as he prepared a second attack. When Aren unleashed it, black flames exploded on the city. Rubble flew and people screamed in agony as the flames reached their target.

Devlyn's heart ached and his mind raced for ways to help even as he despaired at the turn of events. Then Rusyl landed on the wall and bent his forelegs, looking determinedly at Devlyn, insisting he climb on. Devlyn moved swiftly to take his place on Rusyl, who immediately bounded up, evading Viren's frantic attempt to pull him back down.

In the sky on Rusyl and bound to Aliel, Devlyn now sought Aren who had disappeared in a dense cloud pulsing with thunder and lightning wielded from tenebrys. His heart pounded with the blood rushing through his veins. Hundreds of innocent civilians had just died because of Aren's tenebrys wield. Devlyn could not believe that this creature—this Dark Phaedryn—had once been heralded as a savior.

Soaring high in the sky on Rusyl, Devlyn soon found Aren near the southwest bridge. Cloaked in Darkness as always, Aren hovered and waved his arms menacingly, negative energy forking around him. Devlyn felt the air ripple around the terrible wield that was forming. Rusyl bolted toward Aren as Devlyn and Aliel pressed into aquaeys, aerys, and animys. Calling on the River Meyien, they brought a torrent from its watery bed, blasting it upward, catching Aren and launching him away from the city.

The air no longer rippled, but Aren didn't appear much affected. Devlyn had hoped that he would have at least disoriented him. Aren's expression remained blank, emotionless, as he prepared another attack. Again, the air rippled and Rusyl flew toward Aren and added his own blast of fire to the ignys and animys that Devlyn wielded. The force met Aren in an explosion in the sky, the impact nearly throwing Devlyn off Rusyl.

In a rush of his dark wings, Aren lifted himself higher above the river, Rusyl chasing behind the Dark Phaedryn. The battle—now far below—raged on, and with the help of the strangers swimming in the river and on board the ships, in Myrium's favor, but that mattered little given Aren's dark strength. Devlyn knew that Aren could easily destroy the city and everyone there. Devlyn and Aliel formed yet another powerful wield—composed of all the elemental erendinth, mixed with the two transcendental erendinth he could wield—Rusyl eager to charge again, but without warning, tenebrys exploded against Rusyl's chest. Devlyn had not noticed the lashes barreling toward them before they struck the dragon, throwing him clear off Rusyl and knocking him into near-unconsciousness.

Darkness took Devlyn's vision. He couldn't see but knew he fell, his groggy mind unable to process coherent thought. Even as he struggled to think, he caught sight of the dark figure above, oozing shadow as it floated aloft on wings darker than death.

His body ached, but the rushing wind was stronger than any of his pains. The grogginess cleared, replaced by panic as Devlyn searched for Rusyl who was nowhere to be found. Was the dragon dead? And would he die too? Even if he managed to fall into the River Meyien, he fell from too great a height, and the water would not soften the landing.

Aliel flew beside him, diving just as fast as Devlyn fell. An insistent thought pushed to remind him of something, something critical, but it was easier to let everything go, and he closed his eyes. Then, Aliel's whimsical consciousness swirled within Devlyn's. Urgency and concern screamed through their bond and Devlyn opened his eyes once more and felt the air pound against his body, his heart racing at the thought of the fast approaching ground.

But he was a Phaedryn!

Yes, we are a Phaedryn! Aliel conveyed, and pressed himself more fully into Devlyn's heart, where a quiet light, a single dim star in the night, stood vigilant. An immeasurable darkness surrounded that quiet light.

Devlyn heard a familiar whimsical song, one he well remembered from his mother cradling him while humming that very tune. Had he died and was he now in the World-Beyond? Was this Lumaeniel? But the tune felt real, alive, and as always, within his heart. Aliel sang it.

Thinking that the phoenix flew somewhere above, his eyes searched heavenward. The song in his heart grew and he noticed a small light shining from his chest, but he couldn't see Aliel.

From below came the phoenix's harmonious call. He looked to the sound, wind stinging his eyes as he looked down. *It's so close. Aliel!* To Devlyn's astonishment the phoenix was not high above in the heavens, but below, between Devlyn and the ground. Devlyn relaxed, embracing the coming impact.

But it did not come. Tapping that small flickering light within, Aliel ignited it with his own quiet light, enflamed with dignity, purpose, and awareness. During his time in the Illumined Wood, Devlyn had become aware of the quiet light hidden within himself, one that was wholly himself yet also wholly other, but he had never managed to tap it. It had been frightening to delve within and even more frightening when he had met the light within Aliel.

An eternity passed as their most interior existences mingled, time frozen. Devlyn was no longer aware of falling.

It was not their souls that mingled but something more intimate; it was that which animated the soul. As the soul animates the body, so did this most interior entity animate the soul. His spirit coalesced with Aliel's and his world transformed in a barrage of brilliant light.

The darkness surrounding the quiet light was gone and he now saw as Aliel saw, both within and without, yet from his own eyes. Or did he look from the phoenix's?

He felt different; he *was* different, and he saw differently.

But not just Devlyn, Aliel as well. They had become one. They were Phaedryn. No longer elf, no longer phoenix. Aliel's consciousness intermingled with his own, reminding him of that first time they had managed to communicate.

How's this possible? asked Devlyn, the thought instant, without words, just there.

Only because it is.

Still falling at a rapidly increasing speed, Devlyn thought to stop his fall and as the idea formed in his mind, he felt powerful wings, his wings, fight to pull him upward. His back and shoulder blades ached, the new unfamiliar muscles connected to the wings working against the air and slowing his descent!

No longer falling, but aloft, Devlyn hung in the air, a chill wind brushing against his naked skin. He no longer wore his armor, and had even lost his small clothes, his entire luminous body hanging naked in the sky for all to see. There was no time to think or be embarrassed about his nakedness though; others died below.

Devlyn scanned the skies. He could not see Aren anywhere, but noticed a dark figure far off, flying south. Devlyn wanted to chase Aren, but fighting continued to pulse through the city below, while the enemy beyond the bridges fought in small bands against people wearing blue armor. As he approached the city, Devlyn felt a tenebrys wield forming, and saw a shadow elf wielding it chaotically outward toward anything that moved. Embracing animys, Devlyn overwhelmed the shadow elf holding it so that Sorenth soldiers were able to strike and destroy the crazed shadow elf, freeing the souls he had consumed.

But he could still feel tenebrys, and a streak of black lightning bolted toward him. Devlyn sought the interior presence in his heart, calling forth strength he had never before experienced in himself, submitted to the transcendental erendinth, then allowed animys to fill him before directing it toward the corrupted tumultuous wield, completely engulfing the shadow elf who wielded it from the ground.

The battle continued for several hours as shadow elves fought on, refusing to submit, only eliminated from the battle when wielders and soldiers combined forces, the wielders to contain the shadow elves in their wields, and the soldiers to then destroy them with calculated sword blows. The Tieli and Torsillians were less inclined to fight to the bitter end, laying down their weapons as more and more of the shadow elves perished.

From his vantage point above the city, Devlyn saw two separate groups on either side of the river. Each group faced a larger mounted force clad in Sorenth blue, and Devlyn understood that the Tieli and Torsillian generals had finally conceded defeat. Rather than joining the Sorenth generals to accept the enemies' surrender, Devlyn turned to fly over the city, searching for Velaria.

On the western edge of the palace walls, Devlyn noticed a large column of prisoners being led to the dungeons while other soldiers fled east and west and eventually south. Velaria stood at the front of that column, her verathn still clasped in her hand, overseeing the enemy soldiers who had made it into the city being led to their cells, inspecting each one prior to their incarceration in the palace dungeons. Devlyn landed next to an exhausted Velaria who smiled happily at Devlyn, pleased at his transformation. He attempted to cover as much of his nakedness as he could with his wings, embarrassed by his lack of clothing.

"How did you manage it?" she asked, aware of the struggle he and Aliel had gone through.

"It's hard to say." Devlyn thought back on that incredible moment. "It's as if our spirits became one, yet they're still separate."

Velaria's smile grew wider when a soldier came up, holding a blanket for Devlyn to cover himself, a look of near-reverence on his face. Devlyn quickly wrapped it about his waist, then looked on horrified as it burned to ash. The soldier was equally shocked, and promptly backed away.

"I can't go around naked all the time," Devlyn said, appalled and even more embarrassed.

Remember what Alethea told you? But we can separate, if it bothers you so, Aliel conveyed.

Will we be able to do this again? asked Devlyn. He would allow every anacordel in Eklean to see him naked if it meant remaining a fully realized Phaedryn.

Aliel did not answer, but pressed against his innermost presence, his spirit against Devlyn's, assuring Devlyn that it was possible, then pulled away. Devlyn felt Aliel go, and the world, and his enhanced vision, dimmed. The wings disappeared, leaving him with only his hands to inadequately cover himself—the wings had provided better cover. Velaria unfastened her cloak and handed it to Devlyn, her leafy dress in full view.

Devlyn quickly swung the cloak over himself, relieved that it remained whole.

"Perhaps, in the future you should start wearing clothing proper to a Phaedryn," said Velaria. "From what's been preserved in the scrolls and books concerning them, none were known to fly through the clouds naked. I believe the Luminari had a special fabric that didn't turn to ash."

"A shame you were not wearing such clothing today," chided Wyn, appearing suddenly next to Devlyn, staring into his eyes.

"What's wrong?" asked Devlyn, uncomfortable with Wyn's stare.

"They're still gold," said Wyn.

"I wonder if the color is now permanent." Velaria looked into his eyes as well. "Anyone familiar with tales of the Phaedryn will now know you as one, even if Aliel is not with you. You should know, Devlyn, that this victory today is in no small part due to you. Even with the merpeople and Jahronese assisting, we would not have been able to withstand a Dark Phaedryn."

Devlyn offered a weak smile, aware that he hadn't done anything to Aren, who had simply flown away. For all Devlyn knew, Aren could return later that night.

"There are still some soldiers on the field refusing to surrender, but they can't resist much longer," said Wyn.

"Do either of you know what happened to Rusyl?" asked Devlyn who had not seen the dragon since he had fallen from the dragon during Aren's attack.

Velaria's smile disappeared. "He's alive, but barely. The merpeople caught him in a wield as he fell and brought him to the river bank to see to his injuries. I'm told that they can do marvelous things with aquaeys. Some of the other dragons are watching over him as he recovers, Yelaris among them."

Relief instantly washed over Devlyn. While he was not bound to Rusyl as Velaria was to Yelaris, he still felt a kinship with the dragon who had flown him into battle to confront Aren.

"It's uncertain whether or not he will heal completely though," said

Velaria. "Aren struck him square in the chest with tenebrys. It's a miracle that he still breathes. We are very fortunate that there weren't any dragons with the enemy today; if there had been, Rusyl would surely have been destroyed as he fell from the sky."

"Can we visit him?"

Velaria nodded, then looked at Wyn to make sure that he would accompany Devlyn, since she had the defeated prisoners to see to.

"Let's find Viren first. He was furious when you leapt on Rusyl," Wyn said. "He really doesn't like it when you're not in his immediate vicinity. He says he can't fulfill his duty as your guardian if you choose to place yourself in danger that he can't do anything about."

They found Viren almost immediately just past the dungeon area, and he acknowledged Devlyn and Aliel's new status with a reverent bow, but not until after he too stared into Devlyn's eyes longer than usual. Viren also handed over a pair of trousers, a tunic, and a pair of boots, apparently having taken the time to seek out replacement clothing. Devlyn still found himself uncomfortable with the Guardian's loyalty and initiative but was also incredibly grateful for the ancient knight's sword and shield.

While Devlyn dressed, Wyn left to quickly return Velaria's cloak to her, then led the way through the rubble on the streets, many of the once magnificent buildings of Myrium charred or destroyed by the enemy. It was hard to believe that just yesterday, the city had been untouched after the year-long siege.

Here and there, Sorenth soldiers rested against the sides of buildings, many of them wounded, some dead. Those still able rushed through the streets with medical supplies, working with the ci'ana to locate the injured and heal where they could.

Devlyn's heart ached that he could not be of more help in the healing since he was not particularly talented at it. He knew Ellendren was quite likely somewhere in the city healing the wounded with the Crimsyn ei'ana; even though she had chosen to become a Vyoletryn, the Crimsyn gift of healing was still very much a part of her.

Sitting alone against a building in a large pool of his own blood was a man with a shattered leg. A gash in his armor revealed a deep wound already beginning to turn foul. The sight held Devlyn, and Wyn tugged his arm so that they could move on; Devlyn resisted Wyn's pull and took a step toward the wounded soldier.

"You can't help him," Viren said, and put out a hand to stop Devlyn. "He was impaled by a corrupted verathn; wretched things. It infects the wound with a painful disease, quickly spreading to corrupt the entire body, and it is impossible to remove. Not even the best healers were able to cure wounds infected by a corrupted verathn when Krysenthiel fell."

Devlyn shuddered involuntarily, feeling the disease within the dying soldier; it seemed as though it could spread beyond the doomed man to consume another. They left the doomed man to live his last hours; his body would have to be burned after he died.

The southwest gate tower loomed before them and they passed beneath the opened portcullis and across the bridge. Finding Rusyl was easy since he was surrounded by three other blue dragons and a dozen merpeople at the river's edge. Alethea was among those gathered to watch over the wounded dragon. Rusyl slumbered, his breathing heavy and pained.

"He will survive, although I do wish more of the Crimsyn ei'ana had survived this battle. They should have been better trained to defend themselves; their healing abilities would have been appreciated," said Alethea. She walked up the river bank, expecting Devlyn to follow.

Walking up the bank behind her, Devlyn felt a lamenting hymn before the sound reached his ears. His heart rose and fell with the tender lull of the Eldinari who had come to Myrium's aid. The battle for the Jewel of the River had ended, at least for now. Thousands lay still on the Meyien's banks, their last breath taken hours before.

The song harkened Devlyn to the blood-stained grass. Still bound with Aliel, he felt the ground wail in anguish as the dead piled upon her.

"Is the song to soothe the land or a prayer for the fallen?" asked Devlyn.

Alethea answered indirectly. "Later, the young queen will hold a feast, celebrating Sorenthil's victory over those who wished her ill. But we do not celebrate the death and murder of others, even in war. This is the true crime of Erynor; pitting anacordel against anacordel. The Eldinari came to Sorenthil's aid, but at great cost to ourselves, not for our own safety, but for the sin which now stains our souls."

Devlyn looked to the elderly elf, his brow furrowed. "Isn't the greater sin leaving Erynor to enslave and pillage all Eklean?"

Alethea turned from Devlyn to the north, where Boriel shone softly in the form of a star. She hung in the sky, exuding the same sadness that Devlyn heard in Alethea's voice. "It is. Our lament is for the fallen and for ourselves."

A Queen's Feast

Devlyn sat near Queen Myranda at the high table in the palace's banquet hall. Unlike Gwilnor's rectangular dining hall, this one had an elliptical shape. The room's many tables surrounded an open center where people had already begun to dance. It was a welcoming room this evening, its light blue walls and deeper blue marble columns lining the perimeter washed in light from sconces all around the room. Large sculptural molding of the same hue rested on the columns with an elliptical dome rising above. Statues seemed to leap from the walls, and the paintings hanging there appeared as if they would dance away to join the folks in the center of the room. Devlyn couldn't tell where the room's architecture ended and the art began. Floor to ceiling windows lined the curved wall behind the high table, the only windows in the banquet hall, and they drew the guests' attention forward, not just beyond the room to the exterior, but to the high table itself.

Earlier, when he'd met Velaria in the hallway outside their bedchambers in the palace, she had mentioned that he should dress like a Phaedryn for the evening's feast. Delyn had no idea how a Phaedryn was supposed to dress, but luckily, Myranda had had a page bring him a black robe with mesmerizing gold threadwork that highlighted his new eye color. When he had thanked her for it as he took his seat at the table, she claimed it had belonged to her father, the late King of Sorenthil. Devlyn thought that it really wasn't necessary to dress so magnificently, since between his golden eyes and Aliel resting on a perch behind his chair, every eye in the hall repeatedly turned to look at the Phaedryn.

Devlyn didn't know whether he looked like a Phaedryn. He had stared at himself in the large, free-standing gilded mirror that stood in the corner of his bedchamber, trying to figure it out when he'd first donned the robe. *Does anyone know what a Phaedryn looks like anymore?* But he was certain that in this robe, he no longer looked like an ei'ceuril novice. Devlyn had often chafed at having to wear the ei'ceuril robes; they never had fit properly and they were incredibly itchy, leading him to constantly wonder whether they were the robes he was truly meant to wear. Over the past two years, Devlyn had appreciated the occasions when he had had to blend into crowds and not draw attention to himself and could wear the customary trousers and tunics of his pre-Gwilnor student years.

Today was another exception and clearly, Myranda did not intend for him to blend in; it wasn't just the black robe, it was also his placement at the high table. Devlyn sat there not as an ei'ceuril, but as a Phaedryn and a hero of Sorenthil. Myranda had directed the high table's seating personally and his part in defending the city had placed him as close to the queen as a non-royal could be, not immediately next to the queen, but one seat over, Ellendren having the chair beside her friend and fellow royal. Devlyn wondered how his role would change. He wasn't just a Phaedryn, he was a Lorenthien and heir to the Crystal Throne of Krysenthiel.

Devlyn thought that Ellendren's place at the table made it difficult for the guests to identify which of the two young women was their queen. Ellendren's dignified posture demanded respect, and her composure could only belong to a queen. It was only Ellendren's pointy ears that told the Sorenth that they should be bowing to Myranda.

The festivities didn't look to be ending any time soon, so Devlyn gave thought to how he might get out of the ei'ceuril without setting aside the prophecy that required his death or Erynor's success. As he mused on a way, he looked across the banquet hall filled with people he never would have thought existed. For instance, there were the supposed-pirates who were actually Jahronese seafarers, now harbored at Myrium's crescent shaped docks. During the pre-dinner mingling, Devlyn had learned that they were fully aware of their reputation as pirates and had deliberately tolerated it—perhaps even encouraged it—so that their more vicious neighbors would not interfere in their affairs. And apparently, selling an object to a merchant who thought you were a pirate was far more profitable.

More remarkable than the seafarers were the people dressed in aquatic blues and blue-greens, reminiscent of the ocean. Even the cut of their clothing made Devlyn imagine rolling waves. He remembered watching them swimming up the River Meyien alongside the Jahronese ships, taking the Tieli and Torsillian soldiers by surprise. He wondered whether the surprise lay in the additional aid to Myrium or was due to the merpeople joining the battle.

A merperson named Ferinn sat at the high table near Myranda. Devlyn had been introduced to Ferinn, royal consort to the late Queen Karina, but they had not had a chance to speak at length. Ellendren had explained that in his grief, Ferinn had been the one to persuade both the merpeople and the Jahronese to come to Sorenthil's aid. While hundreds of merpeople had answered his call, only some now feasted in the banquet hall due to its size. The rest of them were celebrating with the Sorenth soldiers at a feast set up in a nearby plaza. Devlyn was just accepting a wedge of cheese from the server, when Ferinn spoke behind him.

"Lord Phaedryn." The title still made Devlyn uncomfortable, despite its accuracy. He stood so that he and Ferinn could speak comfortably. "I wish to echo Queen Myranda's appreciation and recognition, and express my deepest gratitude, to both you and Aliel. Your assistance played a large part in saving the city. It has been my beloved home for many years now, and I cannot tell you how greatly I appreciate your intervention." He bowed to Aliel, then reached out to tightly clasp Devlyn's shoulder and pull him away from the table where the others sat. Somewhat perplexed, Devlyn waited for Ferinn to continue.

"Would I be incorrect in saying that you search for the seven lucilliae that form Ceurendol?" Devlyn felt his heart pound, uneasy about anyone else knowing of their existence, but unable to tear his eyes away from Ferinn's. "It is only an assumption and you do not have to say anything if you do not wish to. But know that my people and yours share a common goal and that the merpeople have known the location of one of the jewels since Krysenthiel fell."

"Do you have it?" Devlyn managed to ask.

"No. It lies forgotten in the ruins of a once great city, a city swallowed by Nauto's Wrath. If you ask, we will help you retrieve it." With that, Ferinn nodded and left Devlyn to return to his seat at the high table.

Devlyn couldn't believe it. A third lucilliae! If he could manage to find it, he would have almost half the jewels in his possession. *How does a city get swallowed? And what's Nauto's Wrath? Who is Nauto?* Devlyn thought as he too returned to his seat. Ellendren turned to him.

"Why the distress?" she asked, her smile warming Devlyn's insides. "Did you not enjoy speaking with Ferinn? I had never suspected that he could be a merperson. Honestly, I don't think Myranda knew either. Imagine, a merperson right under our noses all these years."

"Weird, isn't it?"

"I suppose it is. But, imagine what else might be right before us without our knowing."

Not entirely certain about what Ellendren meant, Devlyn found himself blushing regardless. "Would you like…" Devlyn stuttered without intending to speak before trailing off, and then pushed on. "I mean, would you like to dance with me, Elle?" He felt his cheeks turn even redder when he realized that she had noticed his discomfort.

He waited for her to respond, but she merely sat quietly smiling at him. It felt like an eternity passed before she held out her hand to him.

Devlyn happily took it in his and led Ellendren to the dance area where it suddenly struck him that he had never danced before and didn't really know what to do. He had only asked because it had felt like the right thing to do. His heart pounded and he felt his entire body flush in embarrassment. Ellendren didn't seem to notice his panicky state and began to move her feet while they held on to one another. As they moved across the floor, he grew more comfortable, and found himself taking the lead.

"You dance well." Ellendren glided across the floor. Goosebumps rushed down his arms as she spoke so near, he felt her breath on his neck. Devlyn could count the occasions they had been this close to one another on a single hand.

"How come it took you so long?" asked Devlyn, then realized that he had not specified what had taken so long.

"It wasn't that long, only a minute," Ellendren replied with a knowing smile. Devlyn wanted to tell her how much he liked her smile but he heard Alex in his head, telling him that he should never tell a girl how much he liked her. "And also, technically, you are still with the ei'ceuril despite your golden eyes and newly-acquired Phaedryn status."

The reminder made the pit of his stomach queasy. "What if I were to tell you," said Devlyn, searching for the correct words, "that I don't think I should be an ei'ceuril."

"Why would you say that?" Ellendren asked, still smiling.

"It doesn't feel right. It's like I'm pretending at the whole thing; like I'm being forced into it because of someone's interpretation of a prophecy."

"Well, if it's any consolation, I don't think you should be an ei'ceuril either." Ellendren's cheeks blushed a rosy pink.

"Really!" Devlyn froze before taking a step back in excitement, mostly to see her more fully, but bumping into another dancer, then having to wait to continue their discussion while he apologized to the couple. He eagerly returned to face Ellendren, still holding her hands in his.

"I think the prophecy has been misinterpreted. You are a Phaedryn, not an ei'ceuril, nor should you be an ei'ana. To make a Phaedryn become either is ridiculous. Think about it! One of the ei'ceuril vows is to not cause harm to anyone, including to those who harm them. How are you, as a Phaedryn, to be of any use in this war if you can't fight?"

"I guess that makes sense."

"Of course, it does." Ellendren beamed and swayed to a new dance as the song changed tempo, forcing Devlyn to keep up. "We'll have to speak with Velaria and figure some way to have you released from that commitment. I'm certain it's been on her mind as well. She was the main Chair to oppose your entrance into the ei'ceuril; she must have her own theories as to why it should not have occurred in the first place."

Devlyn was elated that Ellendren thought so, as if her approval validated his own thinking. He wanted to tell her how much it meant to him to hear her say it, but just as he was about to say so, she went on.

"Secondly, this is the first time that our affection toward each other is on public display." At hearing her words, Devlyn took a quick glance around to see if they were being watched and noted that many of the couples dancing nearby were indeed sneaking quick glances at the two of them. No wonder it had taken her so long to agree to dance with him. Ellendren was far more astute than he was about how others might view, or construe, actions and events.

"What's that matter?" he replied. "It's not like any of them saw us kiss. Besides, it was only once," Devlyn went on more quietly, his voice hushed so that only Ellendren would hear. Her responding blush made him smile. Thinking about that kiss brought on another worry. They had only recently reconciled and Devlyn didn't want another kiss harming their friendship again.

"It matters a great deal. Think of it, the crowned princess of Lucillia and the first Phaedryn born since the fall of Arenthyl enjoying a dance together. Not a single person in this room will overlook it, and before long every city in Eklean will proclaim that we are already wed, or at a minimum, betrothed. A nasty way for Trethien to discover there's no longer a future between us."

"Why would they jump to those conclusions? We're just dancing and talking. We're only fifteen years old." A nervous bead of sweat dripped down Devlyn's temple. The room was hot with all the bodies, and he was rather excited to hear that she had decided to officially end her betrothal to Trethien.

The dance ended, and as the musicians announced that they would take a break, Ellendren seized the opportunity. "Would you like to get some air?" She must have taken notice of his beaded brow.

Devlyn agreed and they walked to the glass doors opened to the balcony. They stood at the balustrade and looked over the city and the river beyond to the north. The water rushed against both sides of the island, but the festive sound of everyone in Myrium celebrating their victory drowned out the sound.

"You will have to grow accustomed to your every move being

watched and not just commented on but criticized."

"I know, it's just weird, Elle; why do people care so much about what I do?"

"Because your decisions have an impact on their fate. They expect you to make the right choices and live prudently and justly. If we make mistakes it could cost them their freedom, or even their very lives."

She said we, Devlyn thought, his heart racing once more.

"Share with me what you know of prudence." Devlyn felt the weight of the two lucilliae concealed in the coin purse hidden in a pocket of the fancy robe near his breast. When Devlyn had finally returned to his bedchamber after the battle, and as soon as he had dressed in the black robe, he had returned the coin purse to its proper place, on his person. Fortunately, the attire Myranda lent him did have a secret pocket lining the robes' interior.

"Making careful and deliberate decisions with right knowledge, of course."

"You don't think there's more?" asked Devlyn, the gift received from the lucilliae still fresh in his mind and heart.

"I suppose there could be," said Ellendren as she looked down. "Every virtue is more than a simple definition. Whole books are devoted to each. It's said that the library at Septyl, the actual city now engulfed by the Shroud, has the largest library in the world; Gwilnor holds only a fraction of the books and scrolls lost there. And then there's the lost library of Quellion."

What Devlyn wanted to share was not written in a book lost in a library. He took a quick look over his shoulder to see if anyone else stood on the balcony, hidden in the shadows near the doors where he might not see them, but there did not seem to be any others taking in the night air.

"I want to show you something, but you can't tell anyone," he said. Ellendren nodded uneasily at his serious tone, unsure about what she was agreeing to keep secret. Her eyes were on his hand as she watched him reach into the secret chest pocket.

"Remember the jewel of faith that was in Lucillia?"

"What do you mean *was*?" said Ellendren somewhat aggressively, frowning at him.

"Oh, right, I never had a chance to tell you. Your mother gave it to me."

"You've had it since before you went into the Illumined Wood! What were you thinking, taking it there? And imagine what could happen now, if it fell from your pocket or if someone tried to pick your pocket!" said Ellendren in a hissing whisper, throwing quick looks around to see if anyone might overhear. Devlyn carried Lucillia's most prized possession.

Feeling abashed at her accusations for his recklessness, Devlyn withdrew the jewel of faith from the coin purse to reassure Ellendren that the lucilliae was secure in his keeping. Her chastising gaze softened slightly at its violet brilliance.

"This actually isn't what I wanted to show you," said Devlyn as he returned the violet lucilliae to the pouch secured in his robe and took out the jewel of prudence.

The brilliant indigo light of the lucilliae resembled the violet one's light, yet the jewel was distinctly different—it even felt different. The two lucilliae had the same size and oval shape, and similar colors. Both gave off a brilliant soft light, but they had different effects. The jewel of prudence glistened as he put it in her hand. It was reflected in Ellendren's eyes where a deepened understanding brimmed over.

"How did you come by this?"

"It was given to me; Wyn said her name was Boriel."

"One of the enthiel came to you, personally?" Ellendren gasped and covered her mouth in shock.

"Wyn didn't believe me either, but she truly did."

"It's not that I don't believe you," Ellendren hurried to reassure Devlyn. "It's just that, there haven't been any recorded modern encounters between anacordel and the enthiel. It's as though they deserted us."

"I can't say why she came to me; perhaps, things are changing."

"I wonder whether Auriel will reveal himself again," Ellendren said, more to herself than to Devlyn, and gave the lucilliae back to Devlyn with a motion that indicated she thought he should hide it away again. She turned toward the glass doors and the banquet room beyond. "I suppose we should return; the longer we're away, the more rumors will we have to deal with."

Devlyn would have much preferred to stay longer on the balcony alone with Ellendren, despite the rumors she promised. It seemed odd that others took such an interest in him now; he was still only Devlyn, an elf—who had not even known he was an elf—from the small village of Cor'lera. But now, he was a full Phaedryn, golden eyes and hidden wings and all, and he guessed that the number of people who paid him attention would increase. His bigger concern though was where Aren had gone, and better yet, why he had fled. Aren was much more powerful than Devlyn, even with his final transformation to a full Phaedryn. Devlyn took one last look over the River Meyien to the south before following Ellendren inside.

It was impossible to overlook the multitude of eyes staring at them as soon as they returned to the banquet hall. That was also the moment when Devlyn realized that he had missed his chance to kiss Ellendren again. When would another such moment of seclusion happen? No one could have seen them, it had been so dark out there, even with the light spilling out from the banquet hall; no one would have seen them kiss. He gave a small cynical huff when he realized that everyone probably assumed that that was precisely why they had gone outside in the first place.

He slowed his pace so that Ellendren reached the high table to retake her seat next to Myranda, both giggling in their usual way. Devlyn really would have liked to know what they talked about—him, maybe?—and why it was so funny. While he was inclined to return to the high table as well, just as he drew near, he made a sudden turn, catching Ellendren's eye as he did so and smiling at her. She smiled in return, and it sent goose bumps across his entire body.

Devlyn found Wyn, Alethea, and Viren sitting at a nearby table with three ei'ana who were burdening them with countless questions. He took an empty chair next to Viren.

"So, it's true then that the stone of Arenthyl and the other Krysenthien cities is actually from Luminare. How did they get it here?" an Albien ei'ana was asking as Devlyn shifted to accommodate the long robe he wore.

"Wielded it," Viren replied. "Enough lumaryl was brought down to construct the cities. In fact, those cities should still be standing beneath that cold Shroud; not even Erynor can harm lumaryl."

"Fascinating," said a Crimsyn ei'ana, and then she turned to Devlyn. "Oh, Devlyn now that you're here, would you mind if I picked your brain? What you accomplished has not occurred in well over a thousand years."

"I would like to know as well," Viren immediately followed up. "Please, tell us, Devlyn, how does it feel to win your first victory over an invading army? I remember my first battle, but our victories were short lived, as you all know," Viren deflected, knowing full well that the ei'ana had not been referring to the battle.

Devlyn had not really had the time to digest the earlier events and gauge how he felt about it all. He certainly felt exhilarated, but he also was apprehensive about what would come next. "It's exciting, I guess." He really would rather still be on the balcony with Ellendren.

"You'll have to do better than that," interjected Alethea, bringing a pleased smirk to Wyn's face. He well knew Alethea's insistence on delving into one's feelings. "Tell me, how did it *feel* to tap that secret place within your heart? Do you still consider my lessons useless?"

The Albien ei'ana raised an eyebrow, as if Alethea had said something beyond her comprehension, which was startling for an Albien since they always gave the impression that they knew everything. "What do you mean by secret places in the heart? There is nothing further within the heart. Anacordel are comprised of body and soul, yet you speak as though you believe there is an additional component."

"I speak such because such is," said the ancient elf wryly, a slight smile. "Comical the day an Emradiel has to lecture an Albien. If Septyl has truly forgotten what lies within the heart, then Septyl should look to the Auburnis."

"The Auburnis? Their scholarship has never been remarkable; what could they possibly instruct the entirety of Septyl on?" the Albien ei'ana scoffed.

"Their wisdom originates not in the mind, but from that spark within the heart which I mentioned. The next time you come across an Auburnis, it would benefit you greatly to ask the right questions."

"We shall see," said the Albien.

Devlyn could not tell whether she spoke sincerely or whether she was dismissing Alethea as an old fool in the same way that many ei'ana dismissed Therril for his ways. Simply thinking about Therril made Devlyn recall the lessons he'd had with the old elf, lessons which seemed to pass in an instant yet required hours of concentrated attention. The teaching style of the two elves was incredibly similar, so similar in fact that Devlyn could not believe he had not made the connection earlier. It had been Alethea's mention of the Auburnis that had sparked Devlyn's memory.

"Do you by any chance know a peculiar old elf by the name of Therril?" asked Devlyn, not expecting that Alethea would.

"So, you've met the Auburnis ei'ana I so readily think of as representing the spirit of the Auburnis. Except, of course, Mainor Auburnis, himself," said Alethea as Devlyn nodded. "Good, I expect he has managed to supervise your training quite well."

"That can't be the same Therril. He's an ei'ceuril."

"Ei'ceuril? Odd, I have always envisioned him as having a family and remaining an ei'ana. Truth be told, I wasn't sure whether he still lived."

"If it is the same Therril, how old is he exactly?"

"You'll have to ask him that yourself. I never did manage to discover how many winters he's seen—autumns in his case. But he's certainly older than Viren here, although still a babe compared to me."

Baffled by Alethea's age comparisons, Devlyn tried putting the pieces together. "But, that would make him thousands of years old! How could he manage that following the loss of access to the Jewel of Life? Every Luminari placed their life immortal in Ceurendol."

"And that they did," said Alethea. "However, whoever said Therril is Luminari? He's one of the few Aldinari not trapped in Arenthyl. I'm not entirely sure how he managed to get out, but I intend on asking him exactly that when next we meet. Now, come with me, there is somewhere that we must visit. You have not been there in quite some time."

Alethea provided no further information, but simply rose and headed out of the banquet hall with Devlyn trailing behind wondering where they were going. They strode through the palace past celebrants of every sort, including the palace's servants. How they managed to carry the many dishes in and out of the banquet hall without dropping anything on the rich blue carpets lining the halls was a mystery to Devlyn, considering their current jovial disposition. Soon, Alethea stopped at a nondescript door in one of the inner hallways. Devlyn had never been in this area of the palace before, or in most of the palace's interior for that matter, so he remained confused about Alethea's insistence on him returning there for a visit.

He followed her into a small plain room with a sofa and a few simple chairs set around a low table. As soon as the door closed behind them, Alethea pressed her hand to Devlyn's temple and his vision shifted. They no longer stood in the palace and surprisingly, his body no longer ached from the day's earlier activities. But it didn't feel rejuvenated either, it simply *was*, or at least that's what he thought. He had only felt this way in one place.

"Why did we come here?" he asked.

"Because you refused to come of your own accord!" replied a familiar accusatory voice.

"Abbie," began Devlyn, startled yet pleased to see her. "Is everyone all right? Are you still with Alex? Where are you?"

The questions poured out of Devlyn's mouth in an uncontrollable torrent. He had not seen Abbie nor Alex for several months, not since they had split up in Binton.

"We're fine, all of us. We've been trekking across Perrien," said Abbie as she looked to the atypical dark sky, swirling with black and grey clouds. Every time Devlyn came to Somnaeniel, the sky had a brightness akin to seeing through Aliel's vision, yet this time, the bright light was hidden by ominous clouds. "The Evil One is growing stronger. It won't be long until he claims this as his realm again."

"I remember when the elves dared not venture into this place," said Alethea as she looked toward the clouds. "It was poisoned from his touch. The ability of the aldarchs and druids to navigate safely here has always amazed me, an ability I'm sure you hold dear, as did the Aldinari aldarchs."

"When did the sky change?" asked Devlyn. He was unable to move his gaze away from the threatening clouds.

"Within the past week," came a second voice. Devlyn turned to find Eagan standing just behind him. "His prison grows weaker by the hour. We have no explanation for it."

"Where is his prison?" asked Devlyn, even as he wondered how anything could confine this so-called Evil One. Was it truly the same creature mentioned in children's stories to make them behave? And if they didn't behave, the Evil One would steal the naughty ones away.

"It should not be possible for his prison to weaken," said Alethea a little distractedly as she pondered how such an event could occur. "It lies beneath Lake Saeryndol, which is currently inaccessible and frozen solid due to the Shroud. Even if Erynor wished to unleash the Evil One on Teraeniel, not even he could destroy that which prevents him from escaping."

"And what, exactly, is that?" asked Devlyn.

"Roots of Verakryl, the Tree of Life," Alethea replied. "As you should know, they encompass the entire world; all of Teraeniel is laced with those roots. However, they originate where the tree stands, in the center of Lake Saeryndol, within Mount Verinien. There is a portal of sorts on the bottom of the lake, a portal completely covered with the only exposed roots in the known world, locking the Evil One within his prison."

"It's not only the sky that has changed," said Eagan and walked away, leaving the rest to follow at their own pace.

Devlyn wondered why they did not just shift between where they were and where they were going. Surely, they could save precious time if they did. Both Eagan and Abbie halted after a short distance, not daring to venture further, but not preventing Devlyn and Alethea to do so.

The sky was the same here, with dark forbidding clouds, but nothing else had changed. The grass remained green, water flowed in the distance, and the breeze rustled the leaves. They walked along a dirt path heading south, side by side. Devlyn still had many questions for Alethea and was about to ask them when she extended her arm out to prevent Devlyn from walking into something he had not noticed as he looked about.

Lying in the center of the path was a still pool of black ooze, so thickly black that it was impossible to see its depth. It could easily be only a few inches deep, or it could be hundreds of feet deep. There was no way to tell. Devlyn leaned forward to get a better look into the dark pool.

"Do not gaze into it," warned Alethea. "Don't go near it. Don't even think on it!"

Concerned by the fear lacing Alethea's tone, Devlyn asked, "What is it?"

"It is Death. Not the blessed Transition to Lumaeniel filled with Anaweh's Light, but the death that closes one's eyes to such light forever. Step away, and never draw near to such abomination."

Here ends the Second Part of
The Jewel of Life:

HIDDEN WITHIN

Look for the Third part of

The Jewel of Life:

Fading Lights

Appendix A

Glossary of Terms

ABBEY SCHOOL

The preferred system of education for children throughout Eklean. Those deemed capable are sent to higher studies, preferably at Gwilnor Academy.

AELISH

Native language of the elves. Largely forgotten, only used in academic circles.

AERYS

An elemental erendinth. The essence of air.

ALBIEN

One of the seven Schools of Septyl. Albiens focus on truth and care for many of Eklean's libraries. Motto: Truth is discoverable. Emblem: A naked male and female elf holding unraveled scrolls with an owl perched behind, cast in gold on a white field. The chair of Albien is known as the Seeker.

ALDARCH

Deific rulers of Aldinare who reigned from their sanctums.

ALDINARE

Western Skyland of the Aldinari, one of the four elven kindreds. Lost to the Darkness. Only a hundred Aldinari escaped the Skyland with their lives.

ALICORN

A legendary beast native to the Skyland of Aldinare. A winged unicorn.

ANADEL

Spiritual creatures that predate Teraeniel and Somnaeniel. Their native home is Lumaeniel. There are four known classifications of anadel: irythil, enthiel, lorendil, and naril.

ANACORDEL

Creatures of both body and spirit.

Anaweh

The Creating Light.

Animys

A transcendental erendinth. The essence of spirit.

Aquaeys

An elemental erendinth. The essence of water.

Arantiulyn

One of the seven Schools of Septyl. Arantiulyns focus on strength and protection and oversee the Knights of Septyl. Motto: With fortitude, we will protect. Emblem: A naked male and female elf in a fighting stance with swords in hand with a lion prowling cast in gold on an orange field. The Chair of Arantiulyn is known as the General.

Archsteward

Part of the Ei'ceuril hierarchy, they are elevated wise ones. Before kien wielders were restricted to the Temple of Ceur, archstewards lived in every major city of Eklean tending to those faithful to Anaweh, the Creating Light.

Arenthylean Bells

Twenty-four bells composed of four materials that ring every hour.

Aryl

The united head of an elven house composed of a king and queen or lord and lady.

Auburnis

One of the seven Schools of Septyl. Auburnises focus on inner peace. Motto: To love is our gift. Emblem: A naked male and female elf offering a garland with larks flying above, cast in gold on a brown field. The Chair of Auburnis is known as the Pilgrim.

Aurephaen

Feast day of the Luminari, commemorating Auriel and the dawning sun. Celebrated on the 15th of Aurenth, the spring equinox.

Azurelle

One of the seven Schools of Septyl. Azurelles focus on the advancement and training of the erendinth. Motto: The zealous soul must be temperate. Emblem: A naked male and female elf wielding the powers with a dragon behind, cast in gold on a blue field. The Chair of Azurelle is known as the Blue Dragon.

Belin's Watch

An Evellion city in the Vespien Mountains comprised of humans and dwarves. Named for Belin, the dwarf who sheltered Thellion refugees in their greatest hour of need.

Borephaen

Feast day of the Eldinari, commemorating Boriel and the sleeping sun. Celebrated on the 15th of Borenth, the winter solstice.

Bowl of Theniel

Sea set apart by the merpeople as sacred. The place where Theniel brought the waters to Teraeniel.

Centaur

Anacordel dedicated to protecting the forests of Eklean, particularly the Illumined Wood. The upper body is like an elf's but broader and more rugged while the lower body looks much like a four-legged horse.

Ceurendol

The Jewel of Life. Created by the Luminari by placing their life essence within seven jewels of incredible brilliance which allowed them to share their immortality with every race in 1.3a (7085.3E). Also known as the Light Diamond, the Lieben Stone, and the Heart of Hearts.

Ceurendol War, the

A cataclysmic war instigated by the Erynien Empire which began over a philosophical difference over the Jewel of Life and whether immortal life was proper for the 'lesser races.' The war divided Eklean in two factions, those faithful to the Luminari and those subjugated by the Erynien Empire. As the fate of the war grew clear, emissaries and merchants from other continents withdrew from Eklean, fearing the Erynien Empire. 322-500.3a (7407-7585.3E).

CEURENYL

City founded by the ei'ceuril. Home of the Temple of Ceur and Gwilnor Academy. The only city not to fall into Erynor's control when Krysenthiel was lost to the Shroud.

CEURTRIARCH

Leader of the ei'ceuril, known as High Archsteward and Arbiter of the Light.

CHANCELLOR

The head of Gwilnor Academy under the authority of and appointed by the Seven Chairs.

CHILDREN

When capitalized, refers to the proto-race.

COR'LERA

A small village in eastern Parendior and in disputed territory claimed by both Lucillia and Perrien. The vineyards of Cor'lera produce the coveted ice wine, the Cor'leran Blue.

CRIMSYN

One of the seven Schools of Septyl. Crimsyns focus on healing and run many hospitals and infirmaries throughout Eklean. Motto: Through healing, hope is given. Emblem: A naked male and female elf dancing with a dog, cast in gold on a red field. The chair of Crimsyn is known as the Physician.

CYNDINARE

Southern Skyland of the Cyndinari, one of the four elven kindreds. Lost to the Darkness.

DAERENETH

Continent south of Ogren and west of Ja'Horan. Tropical continent.

DEURGHOL

The Cyndinari directly responsible for the Shroud. They are neither living nor dead. Also known as the Deathless.

Dragon

Legendary creatures bound to the erendinth.

Druids of Kweil Aitch, the

Secluded faction of humans who learned to walk Somnaeniel, the World-in-Between, early on.

Dwarf

Anacordel who sought the deep roots of the mountains.

Ei'ana

An organized group of wielders. Since the Balance was lost during the Ceurendol War, there are only kiara wielders among the ei'ana. There has not been a kien wielder among the ei'ana for over a thousand years.

Ei'ana Counsels

A series of norms ei'ana are to follow in regards to wielding. The counsels prohibit men from becoming ei'ana due to their inability to wield safely after the Balance was lost. The counsels also require ei'ana to bring kien wielders to the Temple of Ceur for their own protection and the protection of their communities.

Ei'ceuril

A religious order, currently a majority of men, focused on serving Anaweh, the Creating Light. Because a kien wielder is not capable of wielding with control, every male ei'ceuril capable of wielding is confined to the Temple of Ceur.

Ei'denai

Elven lord serving as aryl with his spouse. Head of House.

Ei'ethil

Elven lord.

Ei'lythel

Elven lady.

EI'TEREL

Elven lady serving as aryl with her spouse. Head of House.

EKLEAN

Continent where the anacordel first stirred as Children.

ELDIN WOOD, THE

Home of the Eldinari.

ELDINARE

Northern Skyland of the Eldinari, one of the four elven kindreds. Lost to the Darkness. The Eldinari were the first to evacuate their Skyland for the lands below.

ELEMENTAL ERENDINTH, THE

Forces wielded to influence the elements. *See Erendinth.*

ELF

Anacordel who changed little when the different races were created. Because they wished to retain their original form, their immortality remained, and they were gifted the Skylands. There are four elven kindreds, the Luminari, Cyndinari, Aldinari, and Eldinari.

ELYA

Powerful wielders born of any race who learn to wield instinctively and are not limited to the restrictions common to normal kien and kiara wielders.

EMRADIEL

One of the seven Schools of Septyl. Emradiels focus on beauty and life. Motto: Only the prudent thrive. Emblem: A naked male and female elf gesturing with open palms toward the beauty around them with a stag behind, cast in gold on a green field. The chair of Emradiel is known as the Tender.

ENTHIEL

Anadel dedicated to one of the seven irythil. The enthiel are very involved with the anacordel. A single enthiel guides an entire people.

ERENDINTH, THE

The erendinth are the wielded powers believed to have created Teraeniel. Tradition says that there are seven powers, three transcendental: lumenys, animys, and umbrys; and four elemental: aquaeys, aerys, terys, and ignys. Much is forgotten or unknown about the full extent of the erendinth which are dependent on inner spiritual and emotional workings.

ERENDINTH GAMES, THE

A game of wielding created at Gwilnor Academy, involving the wielding of all seven erendinth.

FAUN

Short nocturnal anacordel with the hind legs of a goat from the navel down. Some fauns have horns.

GIANT

Anacordel that were drawn to the frozen north. During the Great Blessing, their physical features became capable of withstanding the harsh tundra of Glacien.

GLACIEN

Northern frozen continent spanning the northern pole. Connects Eklean and Ogren.

GOBLIN

Anacordel native to the Kinzdol Islands. Known for their monetary shrewdness.

GOBLIN GUILD

Infamous bank and guild of Eklean. Regulates the majority of Eklean's currency. The Goblin Guild is based in the Kinzdol Islands with branches in every city and most villages.

GREAT BLESSING, THE

Event recorded in the Theseryn where Anaweh blessed the growing differences among the anacordel and solidified their choices by making each their own distinct race.

Guardian Knights

Order of knights once based in Krysenthiel that served and protected all the land from injustice. The Guardian Knights were largely composed of Luminari and were defeated during the Ceurendol War.

Guardian Senate, the

An international body, crossing countries and continents to ensure the wellbeing of Teraeniel. Disbanded toward the end of the Ceurendol War.

Gwilnor Academy

The foremost school dedicated to the education of wielders, located in Ceurenyl.

Holy Tomes

Volumes recorded by various ei'ceuril, some being prophets, and from which the ei'ceuril base their beliefs and practices.

Human

Anacordel that differ among themselves more than any other race. They traveled the furthest from the Valley of Saeryndol, migrating across the entirety of Teraeniel.

Ignys

An elemental erendinth. The essence of fire.

Illumined Wood, the

A vast forest with mysterious qualities and inhabitants.

Irythil

The seven anadel who, under Anaweh's guidance, introduced the erendinth, thereby creating Teraeniel.

Ja'horan

Continent south of Eklean. Inhabited largely by nomadic peoples.

Jahro Islands

Island chain in the Unarian Sea. Believed to be the home of pirates.

Keeper

Head of the time wardens and possessor of the time key.

Kiara Wielder

A female wielder. Kiara wielders learn to control the erendinth easily but require a kien wielder to reach their potential strength. Because the Balance was lost, kiara wielders are not able to reach their potential strength.

Kien Wielder

A male wielder. Kien wielders reach their potential strength easily but require a kiara wielder to learn control of the erendinth. Because the Balance was lost, kien wielders are not able to wield safely, and if any male begins to show an aptitude to wield, he is sent to the Temple of Ceur where wielding is impossible.

Kinzdol Islands

An archipelago in southern Eklean, homeland to the goblins and Cyndinari.

Kweil Aitch

Island east of the Illumined Wood. The place where the veil is thin between Teraeniel and Somnaeniel.

Lay Votary

A non-clerical class of ei'ceuril.

Lorendil

Anadel that guard and protect individual anacordel. Some anacordel are known to communicate with their lorendil.

Lucillian Alliance, the

An alliance of the Eklean kingdoms established to return peace and order to Eklean following Emperor Erynor's disappearance.

Lumaeniel

The World-Beyond. Dwelling of Anaweh, the anadel, and those anacordel who have passed beyond.

Lumenys

A transcendental erendinth. The essence of light.

Luminare

Eastern Skyland of the Luminari, one of the four elven kindreds. Lost to the Darkness. The Luminari evacuated their Skyland for the lands below where they established Krysenthiel.

Mar'anathyl

City on the Skyland of Luminare. Governed by the Lorenthien aryls.

Masters, the (Seven Masters, the)

Vigyl Vyoletryn, Cyrelle Azurelle, Lanielle Emradiel, Lyon Arantiulyn, Mainor Auburnis, Caelyn Crimsyn, and Saeyrn Albien are the founders of the Seven Schools of Septyl and Gwilnor Academy.

Meridean Conclave

Governing council of the merpeople.

Meridephaen

Feast day of the Cyndinari, commemorating Meridiel and the noon sun. Celebrated on the 15th of Meridenth, the summer solstice.

Merpeople

Anacordel who longed for the depths of Teraeniel's oceans.

Miervae

Anacordel who longed to nurture Teraeniel's forests. Miervae are also referred to as Great Trees and begin their life as Settlings.

Minum

The least of Eklean's races. A short half-bred creature of goblin and human origins. Before the elves migrated to Eklean, they were enslaved, sold by goblins to humans.

Naril

Anadel reminiscent of the seven erendinth. There are seven types of narils and they are commonly known as nymphs.

Nymphs

See Naril.

Observant

Non-wielders who have dedicated themselves to one of the Seven Schools of Septyl.

Ogre

Brutish anacordel covering the vast majority of Ogren. Half-bred creature of giant and human origins.

Ogren

Continent east of Eklean and west of Qien. Mountainous land with a mixture of forests and deserts. Inhabited by giants, humans, and ogres.

Phaedryn

Those bound with a phoenix.

Purged Desert of Dwonia, the

A vast wasteland in western Eklean that was rumored to have at one point been fertile. Home of the Twelve Tribes of Dwonia.

Return

The final stage of formation of an ei'ceuril toward becoming a steward. Often occurring in the Illumined Wood.

Sanctum

Expansive complexes housing the aldarchs and their courts on Aldinare.

Schtach

Language of the dwarves.

Schtam

(1) A dwarven people. (2) The dwellings of the dwarves.

Schtamite

The eight dwarven Schtams.

Seguian

A portal created to traverse space and time. Traversing time is restricted and only the keeper can use the time key to traverse time.

Septyl

(1) The Order of Ei'ana composing the Seven Schools of Septyl. (2) The city of the ei'ana in Krysenthiel and now lost in the Shroud.

Septyl Knights

Order of knights dedicated to Septyl. The knights receive their training at Gwilnor Academy and vow to serve one of the Seven Schools of Septyl.

Servants of Shadow

Secret organization carrying out the orders of shadow elves and, in some instances, the orders of the Deurghol.

Settling

Tree-like creatures that wander about in their youth until finding an appropriate place to settle their roots and grow into a Miervae, also known as a Great Tree. Settlings have unique vitality qualities.

Seven Chairs of Septyl, the

The leaders of the Ei'ana. Each of the Seven Schools elects its own Chair who leads his or her particular School and participates in the leadership of Septyl. Responsible for admitting student wielders into Gwilnor Academy and selecting a chancellor.

Seven Schools of Septyl, the

The order of Ei'ana, composed of Albien, Arantiulyn, Auburnis, Azurelle, Crimsyn, Emradiel, and Vyoletryn Schools.

Shadow Elves

Cyndinari who consume the spirit of others to prolong their own life.

Shroud, the

A diseased-looking fog placed by the Cyndinari over the entirety of Krysenthiel. It severed the Luminari from the Jewel of Life, cutting them off from their life essence and making them mortal, as well as any others who had benefited from it. An unanticipated result was that the Cyndinari also lost their immortality with that placement of the Shroud over the Jewel of Life. The Shroud's mysterious origin is one reason no one has been able to remove it.

Skylands, the

Four island countries, Aldinare, Cyndinare, Eldinare, and Luminare, floating in the clouds thousands of feet above the ground. The dwelling places of the elves before they were forced to evacuate to the land below.

Sojourners

The exiled of Dwonia who sought reentrance after forming an allegiance with the Erynien Empire.

Somnaeniel

The World-in-Between. A realm visited by dreamers. Gateway between Lumaeniel and Teraeniel.

Star Warden

An elven military unit, typically ensuring the protection of their lands.

Steward

A clerical class of ei'ceuril with the ability to wield.

Temple of Ceur, the

Home to the ei'ceuril and pilgrimage site for the faithful. It is impossible to wield within the temple walls. All kien wielders are confined to the Temple of Ceur.

Temple Knights

Order of knights dedicated to protecting the Temple of Ceur and the city of Ceurenyl. Some of the temple knights are men who were brought to the temple when it was discovered that they could wield. These temple knights are prohibited from leaving the temple.

Tenebrae

An unrecognized School of Septyl intended to replace the other seven Schools. Its adherents focus on power and dominance. Motto: Might conquers. Emblem: A naked male and female elf standing triumphantly on seven broken emblems, cast in gold on a black field. The chair of Tenebrae is known as the Conqueror.

Tenebrys

A corrupted form of the erendinth, unrecognized by the Ei'ana of

Septyl as one of the erendinth and absolutely forbidden to wield. The essence of Darkness.

Teraeniel

The World-Below. Composed of the continents Daereneth, Eklean, Glacien, Ja'Horan, Ogren, and Qien.

Terys

An elemental erendinth. The essence of stone.

Theseryn

Holy tome recording the creation of Teraeniel and the anacordel, written by the first Ceurtriarch of the Ei'ceuril. The Theseryn states that seven irythil, under Anaweh's guidance, introduced the erendinth thereby creating Teraeniel.

Time Key

An artifact created by the Luminari to restrict the ability to traverse space and time. It was entrusted to the minums, the least of Eklean's races.

Time Wardens

A select group of minums entrusted by the Luminari with the ability to create seguians, allowing them to travel to any place and any time.

Transcendental Erendinth, the

Wielded forces to influence the ethereal realities of lumenys, animys, and umbrys. The ability to wield the transcendental erendinth is forgotten.

Tree Spirits

Narils who agreed to bond with the trees under Sariel's guidance.

Umbrys

A transcendental erendinth. The essence of shadow.

Vaer

Fruit native to the Illumined Wood.

Valley of Saeryndol

Birthplace of the Children, the first anacordel.

VERAKRYL

A crystalline tree within Mount Verinien which brought life to the world and is connected to Anaweh. Also known as the Tree of Life.

VERATHEL

Sprouts of Verakryl, the Tree of Life.

VERATHN

Weapons of power.

VESPEPHAEN

Feast day of the Aldinari, commemorating Vespiel and the setting sun. Celebrated on the 15th of Vespenth, the autumn equinox.

VYOLETRYN

One of the seven Schools of Septyl. Vyoletryns focus on justice and diplomacy. Motto: With justice, peace. Emblem: A naked male and female elf holding a staff with an eagle soaring above, cast in gold on a violet field. The chair of Vyoletryn is known as the Watcher.

WIELDERS

Anacordel capable of wielding the erendinth.

WISE ONES

(1) Part of the Ei'ceuril hierarchy. There is no certainty how many are among the ei'ceuril. (2) Part of the Ei'ana hierarchy. There are seven wise ones for every School of Septyl.

YANILEAN, THE

The undisputed monarch of Yanil, always male. Used both as the monarch's title and as his name during his reign.

DAYS OF THE WEEK

(Based on the seven anadel involved in the creation of Teraeniel)

Gwynthaen–Thenaen–Uraen–Ramaen–Lerenaen–Saraen–Karaen

Months/Moons

(Based on the anadel attached to the elves)

Spring – Marenth, Aurenth, Delenth

Summer – Dynenth, Meridenth, Reventh

Autumn – Kyrenth, Vespenth, Orenth

Winter – Estlenth, Borenth, Lierenth

Currency

Goblin Guild currency – 16 iron angots for a copper lewt. 9 copper lewts for a silver jent. 13 silver jents for a gold crown. 3 golden crowns for a lumol.

Luminari currency – 8 kenols for a narol. 4 narols for a lumol.

APPENDIX B

DRAMATIS PERSONAE

AARON ROENDRYN

Luminari. Prince of Lucillia, brother of Ellendren. Ei'ceuril.

ABBIE WINTYR

Human with emerald eyes. Student at Gwilnor Academy. Druid of Kweil Aitch.

AGNELLE PHANSTIENNE

Luminari. Ei'ana and Chair of Auburnis.

ALESEI

Queen of Tiel. Of the Royal House Ziera.

ALETHEA LENWYN

Eldinari. Emradiel ei'ana and former Lenwyn aryl.

ALEXANDER (ALEX) VAERIN

Human from Perrien, whose family migrated to Cor'lera. Devlyn's cousin on his father's side.

ALIEL

The first phoenix born since the fall of Krysenthiel, bound to Devlyn.

AMRY THELLION

King of Evellion. Married to Queen Lara.

ANDREW

Human from Sudern. Student knight at Gwilnor Academy.

ARBOL

A faun searching for settlings.

AREN LORENTHIEN

Luminari. Led a rescue party to Aldinare and did not return. Now a Dark Phaedryn in service to Erynor.

ARLYN

Ei'ceuril steward from Cor'lera. Devlyn's uncle on his mother's side.

Bernard

Human from Perrien. Ei'ceuril, librarian, and magister at the abbey school of Cor'lera.

Clara

Aldinari. Ei'ceuril, steward and abbess of the Monastery of the Poor Ladies in the Ashton Wood.

Danielle Aequin

Luminari of House Aerquin. Student wielder at Gwilnor Academy.

Daphne Ashton

Human from Mindale. Lady of Ashton Wood. Emradiel Ei'ana.

Devlyn Telvin

Ward of Cor'lera's abbey school. Physical features indicate Lucillian ancestry.

Dolan Telvin

Father of Devlyn, Leilyn, and Liam. Husband of Evellyn. *Deceased.*

Eagan Wintyr

Human. Druid of Kweil Aitch, and Abbie's brother.

Ealyndol Roendryn

Luminari. Ceurtriarch.

Ellendren Roendryn

Luminari. Princess of Lucillia. Student wielder at Gwilnor Academy.

Emdian

Human from Sudern. Ei'ceuril steward.

Entiel Telvin

Human from Perrien. Ei'ceuril, steward, and abbot of the abbey school of Cor'lera. Devlyn's uncle on his father's side.

Erynor Meriden

Emperor of the Erynien Empire. Disappeared after Lucillia gave birth to the twins, Roendryn and Feolyn in 7857.3E. First Cyndinari born on Eklean.

Evellyn Telvin

Luminari from Cor'lera. Mother of Leilyn and Devlyn. Wife of Dolan.

Ferinn

Merperson. Currently resides in Myrium.

Fyona Orendi

Luminari. Student wielder at Gwilnor Academy.

Gordon Carvil

King of Torsil. Of the Royal House Carvil. Supporter of Erynor.

Hannah Torin

Human from Mindale. Azurelle ei'ana and magister of the Art of Wielding at Gwilnor Academy.

Harnyl Roendryn

Luminari. Aryl of Lucillia. Married to Queen Vernal. Father of Prince Aaron, Princess Kaela, and Princess Ellendren.

Jaerol Solaris

Cyndinari. Former Erynien emissary.

Kaeyth Illiero

Luminari. Ei'ceuril novice.

Kai

Human with physical features that suggest an origin other than Eklean. Azurelle ei'ana and magister of politics at Gwilnor Academy.

Karina Lariviere

Queen of Sorenthil. Widow of the late King Dorian. Mother of Myranda.

Karl Olney

Human from Perrien. Observant of Vyoletryn.

Kevn Weyvien

Luminari. Student at Gwilnor Academy. Previously studied to become an ei'ceuril.

KIARA

A mythical woman believed to be the first female wielder.

KIEN

A mythical man believed to be the first male wielder.

LACUS

Human from Torsil. Ei'ceuril steward.

LARA THELLION

Queen of Evellion. Married to King Amry. Azurelle ei'ana.

LAWRENCE MAROVEN

King of Mindale. Of the Royal House Maroven. Supporter of Erynor.

LEILYN TELVIN

Sister of Devlyn, believed to be living in the Illumined Wood. Daughter of Evellyn and Dolan.

LENORA HANARYLD

Human from Ceurenyl. Ei'ana and Chair of Arantiulyn. *Deceased.*

LEX TELVIN

General from Perrien, key player in events surrounding Devlyn's family. Devlyn's uncle on his father's side.

LIAM TELVIN

Son of Dolan. Half-brother to Devlyn and Leilyn.

LILLIANNA

Human from Mindale. Ei'ceuril and formerly an Emradiel ei'ana.

LORETTA JAVIE

Human of Sorenthil. Ei'ana and Chair of Crimsyn.

LUCILLIA

The woman who gave birth to the twins, Roendryn and Feolyn.

Myranda Lariviere

Princess of Sorenthil. Student wielder at Gwilnor Academy.

Oliver Penault

Human from Perrien. Septyl knight of Vyoletryn.

Oma

Dwarf of the Oern Schtam. Stone seer.

Oranna

Luminari. Azurelle ei'ana and chancellor of Gwilnor Academy.

Oreniel

Centaur of the Illumined Wood.

Paurel Roendryn

Luminari. Ei'ana and Chair of Azurelle.

Phendien

Eldinari. Ei'ana and true Chair of Emradiel.

Reia

Luminari. Arantiulyn ei'ana.

Rusyl

A free dragon of the Blue Flight.

Saendre

Luminari. Student wielder at Gwilnor Academy.

Sara

Human from Briel. Auburnis ei'ana.

Selenya Waeyn

Luminari. Ei'ana and Chair of Albien.

Skimp

Minum and time warden.

Taen Taerinior

Luminari. Ei'ceuril novice.

Therril

Ei'ceuril magister of theoreticals at Gwilnor Academy.

Tiera Weldon

Luminari. Ei'ana and Chair of Emradiel.

Tindol

Human from Dwonia. Member of the Sojourners.

Trethien Narielle

Luminari of House Narielle. Student knight at Gwilnor Academy.

Tye

Human from Dwonia. Member of Tribe Fendur.

Velaria Treyven

Cyndinari born in Lucillia. Ei'ana and Chair of Azurelle.

Vernal Roendryn

Luminari. Aryl of Lucillia. Married to King Harnyl. Mother of Prince Aaron, Princess Kaela, and Princess Ellendren. Direct descendant of Lucillia.

Vine Vaerin

Human from Perrien. Mother of Alex. Devlyn's aunt on his father's side.

Viren Dekenurel

Luminari. Guardian Knight.

Waleisius

Merchant in Cor'lera, more commonly known as Walei.

Wyn Lierafen

Eldinari. Grandson of Dalenya and Fendryl. Star Warden. Emradiel ei'ana.

Yelaris

A free dragon of the Blue Flight bound to Velaria.

The Seven Irythil and their Associated Enthiel

Uriel – Lord of the Stars, whose name means Anaweh is my Light. Irythil who brought Anaweh's Light to Teraeniel.

Auriel – The Dawn Star. Guardian of the elves of Luminare.

Meridiel – The Noon Star. Guardian of the elves of Cyndinare.

Vespiel – The Evening Star. Guardian of the elves of Aldinare.

Boriel – The Night Star. Guardian of the elves of Eldinare.

Gwynthiel – Lady of the Lorendil, whose name means Strength of Anaweh. Irythil who brought Anaweh's spirit to Teraeniel.

Ramiel – Lord of Death, whose name means Arrogant toward Anaweh. Betrayed Anaweh and all creation. Irythil who brought shadow to Teraeniel.

Theniel – Lady of the Seas, whose name means Anaweh Heals. Irythil who brought water to Teraeniel.

Nauto – Guardian of all humans living along the coasts.

Aquae – Guardian of the merpeople.

Sariel – Lord of the Land, whose name means Command of Anaweh. Irythil who brought substance to Teraeniel.

Tera – Patroness of harvest and nourishment. Often referred to as Mother Tera.

Mundi – Guardian of the dwarves.

Lereniel – Lady of the Winds, whose name means Friend of Anaweh. Irythil who brought air to Teraeniel.

Kariel – Lord of Peace, whose name means Who is Like Anaweh. Irythil who brought fire to Teraeniel.

Appendix C

Civilizations of Teraeniel

Aldinare

Remnant of Aldinari rescued from the Skyland Aldinare by Aren and accompanying Phaedryn. They are considered part of Krysenthiel.

Race: Elf

House/Aryl: Avign, Eraen, Kenoril, Threilen

Audun

One of the eight Schtams composing the Schtamite. Situated at the westernmost edge of the Laudien Mountains.

Head of State: Patriarch Dridn IV, son of Dridn III

Race: Dwarf

Briel

River valley kingdom situated between two rivers forming the River Reifen and the slopes of the Dead Wood.

Capital: Briel

Head of State: King Irvienne of the Royal House Haert

Motto: Seek the message

Sigil: Black raven on a yellow field

Race: Human

Brunst

One of the eight Schtams composing the Schtamite. Situated within the Vespien Mountains. Close friends with the Eldinari.

Head of State: Patriarch Thraen, son of Anuun

Race: Dwarf

Charren

A kingdom spanning across two continents, Ogren and Daereneth.

Capital: Karithel

Head of State: King Sanhir of the Royal House Irithru

Race: Human

DAER EMPIRE

Oldest continuous human empire in Teraeniel and advocate of slavery and colonialism. Situated on the continent of Daereneth.

Capital: Daer

Head of State: Body of the Daer Senate

Race: Human

DWONIA

Desert country once controlled by the Twelve Tribes of Dwonia. Only two tribes refused to ally with Erynor and remained in the desert.

Heads of State: Chief Kodin of Tribe Fendur and Chief Genin of Tribe Vadir

Capital: Nynev

Sigil: Red lion on a yellow field

Race: Human

ELDINARE

Eldinari society secreted away in the Eldin Wood.

Head of State: Aryl Fendryl and Dalenya of House Lierafen

Capital: Stellantis

Houses/Aryls: Aeris, Allandis, Glaeda, Illia, Jamsyl, Lenwyn, Lierafen, Nyen, Oreleste, Shendielle, Rudyn, Taureh

Sigil: White tree on a green field

Race: Elf

ERYNIEN

Cyndinari empire founded by Erynor Meriden, its sole emperor. Responsible for the Ceurendol War and enslavement of the Luminari.

Capital: Broid

Head of State: Emperor Erynor Meriden

Sigil: Bronze sun on a red field

Race: Elf

EVELLION

The mountain kingdom where the Laudien and Vespien mountain ranges meet. Original inhabitants were the refugees of Thellion.

Capital: Everin

Head of State: King Amry and Queen Lara of the Royal House Thellion

Motto: The pure will soar

Sigil: White eagle on a blue field

Race: Human

FRIETON

The free city-state of Frieton. Given to the minums on their release from slavery.

Capital: Frieton

Head of State: The Keeper (identity unknown)

Race: Minum

GESTORIA

Fallen kingdom situated on the Plains of Orithil. Once great allies to Thellion and Krysenthiel. Obliterated during the Ceurendol War.

Capital: Quellion

Motto: Will triumphs pride

Sigil: White gold winged lion on a blue field

Race: Human

GLYOL

One of the eight Schtams composing the Schtamite. Easternmost and only schtam in the Illumined Wood.

Head of State: Matriarch Vylma, daughter of Toreldn

Race: Dwarf

Harol

One of the eight Schtams composing the Schtamite. Situated in the Laudien Mountains.

Head of State: Matriarch Loewn, daughter of Brenola

Race: Dwarf

Ja'horan, Tribes of

Nomadic civilization on the continent of Ja'horan.

Race: Human

Ja'nalihn

Short lived kingdom covering all of Ja'horan.

Race: Human

Jopht Schtam

One of the eight Schtams composing the Schtamite. Southernmost Schtam in the Vespien Mountains and staunch defenders against the Shadow Schtams from northern infiltration.

Head of State: Patriarch Oerth III, son of Oerth II

Race: Dwarf

Krysenthiel

The kingdom of the Luminari. Currently lost within the Shroud. Translates to land of the golden flowers, named by a human trying to speak Aelish, the language of the elves, to describe the countryside.

Capital: Arenthyl

Head of State: Exalted Lorenthien Aryl

Houses/Aryls: Aerquin, Clarion, Ginielle, Lauriel, Lorenthien, Narielle, Reyndien, Taerinior

Sigil: Seven golden kryseniels blossoming from a larger central kryseniel on a white field.

Race: Elf

Lucillia

Kingdom of the Luminari after gaining their freedom from the Erynien Empire. Named after Lucillia, the woman who gave birth to the twins, Roendryn and Feolyn.

Capital: Lucillia

Head of State: Aryl Vernal and Harnyl of House Roendryn

Race: Elf

Mindale

A kingdom east of the southern Vespien Mountains.

Capital: Binton

Head of State: King Lawrence of the Royal House Maroven

Motto: Mind over body

Sigil: Brown ox on a green field

Race: Human

Nunstol

Shadow Schtam that was cast off by the Schtamite for their actions in Mount Cyngol.

Head of State: Patriarch Uriden, son of Urodrn

Race: Dwarf

Oern

One of the eight Schtams composing the Schtamite. Belin belonged to Oern Schtam and sheltered Evellion and his people as they fled Eloth-kar.

Head of State: Patriarch Forvl VIII, son of Forvl VII

Race: Dwarf

Parendior

A hilly country north of the Laudien Mountains and west of the Il-lumined Wood. Most Parendians are farming folk, and when Perrien invaded, they had no means of defending their land.

Capital: Gneal

Head of State: Perrien Council

Motto: Protect the harmony

Sigil: Purple doe on a beige field

Race: Human

PERRIEN

A kingdom north of the Laudien Mountains where the citizens overthrew their monarchy and replaced it with a council and doubled their territory by invading Parendior.

Capital: Gneal

Head of State: Perrien Council

Motto: Swift to action

Sigil: Grey rider and horse on a white field

Race: Human

QIEN EMPIRE, THE

Empire of the Hundred Kingdoms on the continent of Qien, west of Eklean.

Capital: Zhongshi

Auxiliary Capitals: Beishi, Dongshi, Nanshi, and Xishi

Head of State: Empress Qien Wei

Race: Human

SORENTHIL

A kingdom along the River Meyien.

Capital: Myrium

Head of State: Queen Karina of the Royal House Lariviere

Motto: Flow with the waters

Sigil: Blue dolphin on a light blue field

Race: Human

SUDERN

A city state on the Dagger's Point peninsula. After a bloody civil war with Josque, the inhabitants declared themselves independent.

Capital: Sudern

Motto: Hidden daggers

Sigil: Red ship and dagger on a white field

Race: Human

Thellion

The fallen Eklean kingdom covering all the lands east of the Vespien Mountains. Met its downfall through a civil war relating to succession.

Capital: Elothkar

Motto: Eternal wisdom

Sigil: Silver winged horse on a white field

Tiel

A southern kingdom bordering the Erynien Bay and the Unarian Sea.

Capital: Josque

Head of State: Queen Alesei of the Royal House Ziera

Motto: Eternal wisdom

Sigil: Orange serpent on a blue field

Race: Human

Torsil

A weak kingdom with little influence on its neighbors.

Capital: Trest

Head of State: King Gordon of the Royal House Carvil

Motto: Stronger together

Sigil: Grey wolf on a red field

Race: Human

Undol Schtam

One of the eight Schtams composing the Schtamite. Deeply religious and situated in the Laudien Mountains surrounding Lake Saeryndol. They have strong ties to the Luminari.

Head of State: Matriarch Miurel IV, daughter of Miurel III

Race: Dwarf

VORN SCHTAM

One of the eight Schtams composing the Schtamite. Situated at the northernmost edge of the Vespien Mountains.

Head of State: Matriarch Tiltha, daughter of Tilma

Race: Dwarf

YANIL

Southern kingdom along Erynien Bay. Yanil was once jointly ruled by the Yanilean and the Judges of Yanil.

Capital: Lankor

Head of State: The Yanilean

Motto: Deep as justice

Sigil: Black castle on a blue field

Race: Human

ZORIK

Shadow Schtam that was cast off by the Schtamite for their actions in Mount Cyngol.

Head of State: Matriarch Jiora, daughter of Jiorza

Race: Dwarf

About the Author

Ryan D Gebhart first started writing the Jewel of Life series in 2012 in Philadelphia, PA, shortly after concluding his undergraduate studies in philosophy. This unexpected passion evolved over the years and has remained a constant companion through his career changes, from a Capuchin Friar, to a Claims Processor, and finally in his current endeavor as an Architectural Graduate Student in Washington, DC. Ryan D Gebhart is originally from Wilmington, DE.

Keep up with Ryan D Gebhart at www.RyanDGebhart.com

www.ingramcontent.com/pod-product-compliance
Lightning Source LLC
Chambersburg PA
CBHW020235110726
47898CB00004B/1276